HELEN
BIANCHIN
Seduction Assignment

HELEN
BIANCHIN
COLLECTION

February 2016

March 2016

April 2016

May 2016

June 2016

July 2016

HELEN
BIANCHIN
Seduction Assignment

MILLS & BOON

First Published in Great Britain 2016
By Mills & Boon, an imprint of HarperCollins*Publishers*
1 London Bridge Street, London, SE1 9GF

SEDUCTION ASSIGNMENT © 2016 Harlequin Books S.A.

The Seduction Season © 1998 Helen Bianchin
The Marriage Deal © 1999 Helen Bianchin
The Husband Assignment © 2000 Helen Bianchin

ISBN: 978-0-263-92151-9

09-0716

Harlequin (UK) Limited's policy is to use papers that are natural, renewable and recyclable products and made from wood grown in sustainable forests. The logging and manufacturing processes conform to the legal environmental regulations of the country of origin.

Printed and bound in Spain
by CPI, Barcelona

THE SEDUCTION SEASON
HELEN BIANCHIN

Helen Bianchin was born in New Zealand and travelled to Australia before marrying her Italian-born husband. After three years they moved, returned to New Zealand with their daughter, had two sons and then resettled in Australia.

Encouraged by friends to recount anecdotes of her years as a tobacco sharefarmer's wife living in an Italian community, Helen began setting words on paper and her first novel was published in 1975.

Currently Helen resides in Queensland, the three children now married with children of their own. An animal lover, Helen says her two beautiful Birman cats regard her study as much theirs as hers, choosing to leap onto her desk every afternoon to sit upright between the computer monitor and keyboard as a reminder they need to be fed...like right now!

CHAPTER ONE

IT WAS neither wise nor sensible to drive for hours through the night without taking a break, but Anneke didn't feel inclined to covet wisdom.

And 'sensible' wasn't a suitable word to apply to someone who, only that morning, had told her boss precisely what she thought of him, then walked out of his office and out of his life.

Men. Anneke swore viciously beneath her breath. Words at which her sweet Aunt Vivienne would have blenched in dismay had she heard them uttered from her favourite niece's lips.

'Oh, darling, *no*,' Aunt Vivienne had responded in genuine empathy to Anneke's call. 'Come and stay with me for a while. The weather is beautiful, and you can relax.'

Family. How wonderfully they rose to the occasion in times of need, Anneke reflected fondly. Especially this particular member, who was surrogate mother, aunt, *friend*.

The small seaside cottage situated on a relatively isolated stretch of beach in northern New South Wales was idyllic, and it had taken Anneke only an hour to make a few essential phone calls before tossing some clothes into a bag. Then she locked her elegant small flat in Sydney's suburban Lane Cove, slid behind the wheel of her car, and headed for the main highway leading north.

'I won't arrive until late,' she'd warned her aunt, who had blithely responded it didn't matter in the least; the front door key would be left in the usual place.

Anneke glanced at the illuminated digital clock on the dashboard. Three minutes past midnight. It would take another hour to reach the outskirts of Byron Bay, a few more minutes to traverse the road leading down to her Aunt's beachside cottage.

It was a dark night, with no moon to cast an opalescent glow over the countryside, and she leaned forward to switch on the air-conditioning in an attempt to sharpen a brain dulled by more than nine hours of driving with only two minimum breaks along the way.

The car's headlights probed the ribbon of asphalt and its grassy fringes, and she held back from increasing speed. A semi-trailer barrelled past her, its rig brightly lit, followed a few minutes later by another. Drivers on a tight schedule hauling freight overnight.

Anneke stifled a yawn, rolled her shoulders, then turned on the radio, scrolling through the stations until she found one providing upbeat music.

It was one o'clock when she reached the familiar turn-off and only minutes before she drew the car to a halt on the grassy verge adjacent her aunt's garage.

The outside light was on in welcome, and Anneke switched off the engine, withdrew her bag from the boot, then trod the path quietly to the front porch, retrieved the key and let herself in.

It was an old brick cottage, renovated over the years to incorporate modern conveniences, and immaculately maintained. Its design was basic, with rooms leading off a wide central hall that ran the length of the cottage. Lounge, dining room and kitchen on the right; three bedrooms, bathroom and laundry on the left.

Anneke shut the front door and locked it, then moved quietly to the rear of the house. She'd deposit her bag in the guest bedroom, then make a much needed cup of tea.

There would, she knew, be a cup and saucer set out on the buffet in readiness, and a small plate of sandwiches beneath film-wrap waiting for her in the refrigerator.

A thoughtful gesture by a very kind lady.

The guest bedroom looked endearingly familiar. A double brass bed occupied centre space, with its old-fashioned white lace bedspread heaped with lace-covered cushions. Above the headboard was a snowy white canopy holding a billowing mosquito net. Superfluous, considering the screened windows, but Aunt Vivienne had wanted to retain the old-fashioned ambience, so the canopy remained.

White lace frilled curtains at the window, old-fashioned wooden furniture, and highly polished wooden floors.

It would be so easy to slip off her shoes, shed her clothes, and sink into bed. For a moment she almost considered it. Her shoulders ached, her head ached, and she was so tired, not to mention emotionally exhausted.

She was inclined to add 'devastated'. Although that wasn't quite the description she wanted. Angry, certainly. With Adam, her boss. And herself. Especially herself, for believing in him. She'd been a fool to think she was different from the steady stream of women who inhabited his life.

The type of man, she reflected viciously, who constantly sought challenges on a professional and personal level,

Adam knew all the right moves, which buttons to press. He was very, very good at setting the seduction scene.

But not quite good enough. She retained a clear image of his surprise when she'd announced her intention of walking out. The practised hurt when she'd refused to accept his assurance *she* was very important to him. The slightly wry smile and the spread of his hands in silent acceptance of her vilification that he'd never change.

The only satisfaction she had…and it was very minor…was the knowledge she'd been the one to end the affair. Something she was sure had never happened to him before.

The bravery had lasted as she'd walked out of his office, and all through the long hours of driving.

Now that she was here, reaction began to set in, and she could feel the prick of angry tears.

A quick shower first, she determined wearily, then she would go into the kitchen.

Five minutes later she emerged from the bathroom wearing an oversize tee-shirt. Her face was scrubbed clean of make-up, and her hair hung loose halfway down her back.

In the bedroom she reached into her bag and extracted a few necessities, then she made her way towards the kitchen.

If she didn't know differently, she would almost swear she could sense the subtle aroma of freshly brewed tea.

A faint frown creased her forehead, and she suffered a pang of guilt. Surely she hadn't disturbed Aunt Vivienne, and the dear woman hadn't risen from her bed to offer tea and comfort at this late hour?

It was typical of her caring aunt, and she summoned a warm smile in welcome as she entered the kitchen.

Only to have the smile freeze on her face as a tall, dark-haired stranger shifted his lengthy frame from a leaning position against the servery.

A very tall man with broad, sculpted features, dark grey eyes, and black hair that fell thickly almost to his shoulders.

Anneke swept him from head to foot in a swift encompassing appraisal, and didn't like what she saw.

He was in need of a shave, and bore what looked like a full day's growth of beard that, combined with his dark eyes and long loose hair, gave him a decidedly devilish look. Add well-washed tight-fitting jeans, a black sweatshirt, and he resembled a man who was the antithesis of 'friend'.

'Who the hell are you?'

Uncertainty, defensiveness, fear. He glimpsed each of them in the fleeting emotions chasing across her expressive features.

He should, he reflected with mild exasperation, have taken the time to shave. And, if he'd had a mind to, he could have bound his hair into its customary ponytail at his nape. Could, perhaps should have changed into casual trousers and a polo shirt.

Except the story had been running hot, and he'd lost track of time as he transposed the images in his head into words on the computer screen.

And he'd promised Vivienne that he'd pop over the minute her niece arrived and explain in person why the cottage was empty.

'I've made some tea,' he indicated in a faintly accented drawl. 'Vivienne said you favour Earl Grey.'

Anneke's eyes narrowed. Vivienne. So he knew her aunt. That meant he wasn't an escapee, a felon, or someone of ill repute. Although, looking at him, she wasn't too sure about amending the last description.

'I locked the front door.' Eyes flashed a fiery emerald, then deepened in wariness. 'How did you get in?'

She was attractive, if you had a penchant for tall, slender, long-haired blondes, he mused. Natural, although these days it was hard to tell without getting intimate. Lovely green eyes, beautiful mouth. He felt something stir, then banked it down. Women could complicate a man's life, and he didn't need the aggravation.

Anneke. Pronounced Ann-eek. Scandinavian mother, English father, no siblings. Twenty-seven, para-legal secretary. Just walked out on a louse.

He took one long look at her, and just knew she'd hate it that Vivienne had confided in him.

'Sebastian.' He leant one hip against the servery, and attempted to keep the amusement out of his voice. He partly lowered his eyelids to diminish the gleaming depths. 'And Vivienne gave me a key.'

For tonight? Or had he possessed a key for a while? Aunt Vivienne and a toyboy? The latter aroused an improbable scenario which she instantly dismissed.

Anneke drew herself up to her full height, unaware that the hem of her tee-shirt rose two inches up her thighs. Her voice rose a fraction. 'Sebastian *who*? And you'd better explain real quick why Aunt Vivienne asked you to come into her house at this ungodly hour.'

Dammit, was she wearing anything beneath that thing? Definitely not a bra. Briefs? If she lifted her shoulders much higher he was sure going to find out.

And precisely what, he mused tolerantly, did she think she could do to defend herself against him that he couldn't counteract and deal with before she'd even moved an inch? Kick-boxing, karate? He was trained and adept in each.

'Lanier,' he responded indolently.

So he was French. That explained the slight accent.

'Friend and neighbour.' One eyebrow slanted, and his mouth tilted fractionally. 'Requested by Vivienne to tell you in person news she felt would be too stark if penned in a written note left for you to read in the early-morning hours.'

Anneke was trying hard to retain a hold on her composure. 'So on the basis of good neighbourly relations you came over here at—' she paused to check her watch '—one-thirty in the morning, made me a cup of tea, and waited to tell me-*what*?'

'You're a mite ungrateful.'

His slow drawl held a degree of cynical humour, and it made her want to throw something at him. Surely would have if the sudden sharpness in those dark eyes and the subtle reassemblage of facial muscle hadn't warned her it would be infinitely wise not to follow thought with action.

'I've been on the road for eleven hours.' Her body stance changed, became more aggressive. 'I let myself in to my aunt's cottage and discover a strange, disreputable man calmly making himself at home in her kitchen, and I'm expected to smile and say, *Hi, my name is Anneke, what's yours? How nice, you've made some tea*?'

'And impolite,' he continued, as if she hadn't spoken at all.

'What do you object to? The "disreputable" tag?' Her eyes raked his lengthy frame, skimmed over broad shoulders, muscled chest, narrow hips, long, muscular legs, then slid back to his face. 'Sorry, Sebastian.' She gave his name faint emphasis. 'From where I'm standing, you hardly represent a trustworthy image.'

The eyes lost their tinge of amusement and acquired a

perceptive hardness that changed his persona into something dangerous.

He watched those splendid emerald depths dilate, and felt a moment's satisfaction. 'Vivienne is in Cairns.' The unadulterated facts. He gave them to her without redress. 'She had a call an hour after yours to say her daughter had gone into labour six weeks early. She caught the late-afternoon flight out of Coolangatta.'

Colour drained from her face. Elise was expecting a second set of twins. Six weeks premature. 'How is she?' The words whispered from her lips.

His eyes narrowed faintly. So she cared. Deeply. That was something. 'Vivienne said she'll ring early morning with an update.'

The exhaustion seemed more marked, the faint smudges beneath her eyes a little darker. She looked, he decided, as if she should sit down. He crossed to the small kitchen table and pulled out a chair, then transferred the cup and saucer from the buffet.

'Tea. Hot, white, one sugar.'

Just the way she liked it. Anneke owed thanks to her aunt. And an apology to this large, faintly brooding stranger.

Neighbour? There was only one cottage in close proximity, and that was owned, according to Aunt Vivienne, by a lovely author who kept strange hours. He was also something of a handyman who had, Anneke recalled sketchily from her aunt's correspondence, fixed her roof, replaced a blown fuse, lopped two overgrown trees, and undertaken some heavy garden landscaping.

Anneke regarded the man standing at the table with a faint frown. Not by any stretch of the imagination could she call him 'lovely'.

Mid to late thirties. Ruggedly attractive in a dangerous sort of way, with the type of physical frame that seamlessly melded honed muscle and leashed power together to present a formidable whole.

Let loose, he'd present a ruthless force no man in his right mind would choose to oppose. The woman, she perceived, who willingly stepped into his space would never be sure whether she'd dice with the devil in hell, or soar to heaven with a tutelary saint.

'Are you done?'

Anneke's lashes swept high at his quizzical query, but there was no confusion apparent, no embarrassment. Just analytical regard.

OK, so men weren't her favourite flavour of the month. Justifiable, according to Vivienne, whom he'd driven at speed to the airport that afternoon. *'Such a dear girl.'*

Familial beneficence tended to be biased, he mused. 'Dear' she might be…as a niece, a cousin, a friend. But the woman who stood before him was cool, very cool. With fire beneath the icy façade. He had a very strong desire to stoke the fire and watch the ice melt.

'It was kind of you to carry out my aunt's wishes,' Anneke said formally. It was the closest she intended to get to an apology.

Sebastian inclined his head in mocking acknowledgment. Given the circumstances, and the late hour, he should simply wish her goodnight and leave.

'I'll make fresh tea.' Suiting words to action, he easily dispensed with the cup's contents, flicked the kettle to reboil, and took another teabag from a glass container.

Damn him, did she have to spell it out? 'I'm quite

capable of making it myself.' She crossed to the refrigerator and extracted milk, then took it to the servery.

Big mistake. For it brought her within a hair's breadth of a hard male frame that seemed disinclined to move. Something that tripped the trigger on all her banked-up anger.

The silent rage she'd managed to contain all day burst free. 'You've more than done your good deed for the day.' Fine fury lent her eyes a fiery sparkle, and her knuckles shone white as she clenched her fists. 'I owe you one.'

He looked at her carefully, noted the thinly veiled anger, the exhaustion. 'So please leave?'

'Yes.' Succinct, with an edge of sarcasm.

'Gladly,' he intoned in a dangerously silky voice.

Something shifted in those dark eyes that she didn't want to define, and there was nothing she could do to avoid the firm hands which cupped her face, or prevent the descent of his head as he fastened his mouth over hers.

It was a hard kiss, invasive, with erotic power and a sweet sorcery that took what she refused to give.

No other part of his body touched hers, and he fought against leaning in and gathering her close.

A spark ignited deep inside and flared sharply to brilliant flame. For both of them. He could feel her initial spontaneous response before she refuted it. Sense her surprise, along with his own.

He softened his mouth, took one last tantalising sweep with his tongue, then slowly raised his head.

She looked—*shattered*. Although she recovered quickly.

He smiled, a slow, wide curving of his mouth as he regarded her stormy features, and he dropped his hands from her face. 'Now we're even.'

Then he turned and walked from the kitchen, trod a

path down the hall to the front door, then quietly closed it behind him.

It irked Anneke dreadfully that a few seconds of stunned surprise had rendered her immobile and robbed her of the opportunity to hurl something at him, preferably hard enough to do damage to any part of his anatomy.

Dulled reflex action, brought on by a degree of emotional, mental and physical exhaustion. Something that a good night's rest would do much to rectify, she perceived as she set the kettle to boil again and made fresh tea.

Men, she brooded as she sipped the delicious brew, were arrogant, heartless, self-oriented, entirely governed by their libido, and not worth a minute of her time.

A thought which persisted as she finished her tea, then she crossed to the bedroom and slid in between crisp, clean white sheets.

On the edge of sleep, one image invaded her mind, and it wasn't the sleekly groomed city lawyer in his three-piece business suit.

CHAPTER TWO

HAMMERING noises in close proximity were not conducive to restful slumber.

Anneke heard them in the depths of her subconscious mind and slowly drifted into wakefulness. Still the noise persisted.

What the hell…? She opened one eye and looked at the clock atop the bedside pedestal. Dammit, it was only *seven*. On Saturday.

Surely her aunt hadn't arranged for a contractor to do some work and forgotten to mention the fact?

Maybe if she buried her head beneath the pillow she could go back to sleep, she decided, suiting thought to action, only to groan out loud minutes later as the sound still penetrated with no seeming loss of intensity.

Annoyance had her sliding out of bed and pulling on a pair of shorts, and she paused briefly to drag a brush through the length of her hair before storming into the hall to assess where the hammering seemed loudest.

Rear, she decided, and made for the back door.

Quite what she'd expected to see when she opened it she wasn't sure. Certainly not Sebastian Lanier's tall, broad-shouldered, lean-hipped, jean-clad frame perched part-way up a ladder, wielding a hammer as he stroked in one nail after another.

'Just what the hell do you think you're doing?'

Well, now, there was a pretty sight to tempt a man's eye at this early hour. Nice legs. He followed the slender calves, the well-shaped thighs. Good muscle tone, he noted approvingly.

Narrow hips, neat waist, and the slight swing of her breasts made him itch to slide his hands beneath the oversize tee-shirt and see how well they fit his palms.

Slowly he lifted his eyes and took his time examining her mouth, and remembered the feel of it beneath his own.

He moved up a few inches and looked straight into a pair of bright, furious eyes whose emerald depths threatened nothing less than murder.

Sebastian smiled. A long, slow, curving movement that lifted the edges of his mouth and showed the gleam of white teeth. 'Good morning.' He positioned another nail and hammered it in.

Clean-shaven, his hair bound neatly at his nape, he looked almost respectable. It was the 'almost' part she had trouble coming to terms with. None of the men in the circles in which she moved resembled anything like *this* man.

Calm, she must remain calm. 'Do you know what time it is?'

Of course he knew what time it was. He'd been up since six, had orange juice, gone through his daily exercise routine, then assembled a high-protein drink in the blender and sipped it while he scrolled through his e-mail.

'Am I disturbing you?'

Oh, he was disturbing her, all right. Just how much, he was about to discover. A last attempt at civility, then she'd let him have it with both barrels blazing. 'Perhaps you'd care to explain what exactly it is that you're doing?'

She possessed a fine temper. He could see it in her eyes, the tilt of her chin, the way she stood.

'Yesterday I removed a section of worn guttering. Today I'm putting up new.' He held another nail in position and nailed it in. Then he turned his head to look at her. 'I arranged it with Vivienne.'

There was that faint smile again. Anneke gritted her teeth.

He moved down the ladder and shifted it, checked its stability, then stepped up again. And hammered in another nail.

'I suppose you're one of those irritating people who manage to get by on an indecently few hours of sleep?'

'Five or six.' He lined up another nail and rammed it home.

Anger coursed through her body, heating her veins, and erupted in voluble speech. 'You're doing this deliberately, aren't you?'

He cast her a long, measured glance, noted the twin flags of colour high on each cheek, the firm set of her mouth. 'Is that an accusation?'

'Damned right it is,' she bit out furiously.

Sebastian hooked the hammer into his toolbelt and descended down to the ground. 'Let's get one thing clear. I boot up my computer at one in the afternoon. Vivienne needs something fixed; I fix it for her. In the morning.'

His voice was quiet, almost too quiet. And silky, she decided. 'You have to start at *seven*?'

'I'm due in town at ten,' he explained reasonably. 'I won't have time to do anything when I get back from town except grab some lunch, and—''

'Go boot up the computer,' Anneke finished for him. 'And you just had to finish this section before you left.'

'Yes.'

'Today.'

'It could rain,' he responded solemnly.

Most unlikely. Her voice rose a pitch. 'You waltz over here and begin hammering shortly after dawn?'

'Dawn was five-thirty, daylight saving time,' Sebastian informed her mildly.

'I don't give a tinker's cuss when dawn was.' She advanced a step, and crossed her arms across her chest. 'I want you to stop hammering so I can get some sleep.'

'Ask me nicely.'

Her jaw went slack. 'I beg your pardon?'

His lips twitched. 'Ask me nicely,' he reiterated.

So he was amused. Well, she'd wipe that smile right off his face! 'You can go—' she enunciated each word carefully '—jump in the ocean.'

The phone rang, its peal issuing an insistent summons she chose to ignore. Temporarily.

'That'll probably be Vivienne.'

It didn't help any that he was right. Elise was stable; the unborn twins were fine. However, Elise would stay in hospital, probably until the twins' birth, anticipated prematurely. Naturally Aunt Vivienne would remain in Cairns.

'I'm so sorry.' The older woman's voice was achingly sincere. 'I feel a little easier in my mind knowing Sebastian is close by.'

A sentiment Anneke didn't share.

'You've met him, of course,' Aunt Vivienne continued. 'Such a thoughtful, caring man. And so handy. Oh, dear, I almost forgot—'' She broke off, paused, then launched into an explanation. 'I have an arrangement to prepare his evening meals. Anneke, could you?' A hesitant apology swiftly followed. 'I hate to ask, but would it be too much of an imposition?'

Yes, it would. If she never saw Sebastian Lanier again, it would be too soon! The thought of preparing a cooked meal for him every night was unbearable.

However, being Aunt Vivienne's guest, enjoying her aunt's home, made it difficult to refuse. 'I'll organise it with him,' she agreed, hiding her reluctance.

'Thank you, darling.' Aunt Vivienne's relief was palpable. 'You're such a good cook, far more adventurous than me. He's in for a gourmet feast.'

The word 'gourmet' struck a responsive chord, and Anneke allowed herself a slight smile. If Aunt Vivienne wanted her to prepare Sebastian's evening meals during her sojourn here, then she would. However, meat-and-potatoes-with-vegetables would definitely be off the menu.

A contemplative gleam entered her eyes. Sautéed brains, stuffed pigeon, pig's trotters. She gave a silent laugh. Maybe this might be fun, after all.

'I'll take care of it, Aunt Vivienne.' Oh, she would, indeed! 'Is there anything else you'd like me to do?'

'No, sweetheart. Thank you. I'll ring again in a day or two, or before if there's any news.'

'Give Elise my love.' Anneke replaced the receiver, and noticed the absence of hammering.

Had Sebastian finished? Or was he merely being courteous? She moved towards the back door and saw his lengthy frame bending over a stack of neatly piled wood.

Nice butt, she acknowledged. Some men looked good in tight, worn denim, and he was one of them. As she watched, he straightened and turned to face her.

'Good news?'

She was on the verge of retorting that it was none of his business, but managed to catch the words in time. 'Elise is stable; the twins are expected to deliver prematurely.'

Succinct, with just a touch of resentment, he mused, wondering how she would react if he took all that fine anger and turned it into passion.

Probably try to hit him. He banked down a silent laugh and deliberately drooped his eyelids so the gleam of humour was successfully hidden. It might even be interesting to allow her to score the slap.

Anneke regarded him through narrowed eyes, unable to read him. And the inability didn't sit well. Usually she had no difficulty in pegging the male species. Smooth, charming, vain, arrogant, superficial, blatant. Whatever the veneer, the motive remained
basic.

Yet instinct warned that *this* man didn't run with the pack, and that made him infinitely dangerous.

Damn his imperturbability. She wanted to shake that unruffled calm. 'Is six o'clock convenient for your evening meal?'

One eyebrow slanted, and she could have sworn she glimpsed a gleam of amusement in those dark eyes. 'Vivienne frequently shared dinner with me.'

She drew in a deep breath, then released it slowly. She even managed the semblance of a smile, albeit that it held a degree of cynicism. 'An example I have no intention of following.'

'You have an aversion to friendliness?'

Anneke could feel the anger rise, and didn't try to contain it. 'An aversion to *you*.'

His expression didn't change, although anyone who knew him well could have warned the stillness held ominous implications.

'You don't know me,' Sebastian intoned softly.

'*Believe* I don't want to.'

'Feel free to stow your bag in the boot of the car and drive back to Sydney.' His eyes were level, and resembled obsidian shards. 'The loss of a prepared evening meal won't negate my obligation to complete necessary chores for Vivienne.'

She drew in a deep breath, then released it slowly. She could, she knew, easily do what he suggested. Aunt Vivienne would accept she'd changed her mind, and be concerned about her ambivalence.

Except she didn't want to return to the city. Given a choice, she'd have preferred her aunt's company, her wisdom. And the solitude of a sandy stretch of beach in a gently curving bay where she could walk alone, meditate, and allow fresh emotional scars to heal.

A solitude she wouldn't gain if she went back to her small city apartment. Friends, concerned for her welfare, would ring and try to entice her to join them at any one of several parties, or attend the cinema, the theatre. Suggest lunch or dinner and attempt to play amateur psychologist.

Unburdening her soul and having her every word, every action dissected and analysed didn't form part of her agenda.

'I intend to stay,' Anneke responded with equal civility.

Sebastian hadn't been aware the small knot of tension existed until it suddenly dissolved in his gut. Nor could he explain the reason for its existence.

Sure, Vivienne's niece was a sassy, long-legged blonde whose captivating green eyes invited a second glance.

His mouth formed a slightly bitter twist. He'd known several sassy, long-legged women in his time, and bedded more than a few. Only to discover they'd coveted his wealth first and foremost. With the exception of Yvette, with whom he'd shared one precious year. In an unprecedented twist of fate, she'd been victim of a random road accident on the eve of their wedding.

For two years he'd buried himself in work, diced daringly in the world of high finance, only to wake one morning and opt for a complete change of lifestyle.

He owned apartments, houses, in several major capital cities around the world, and for a while he'd lived in every one of them.

It was in Paris, the country of his birth, where he'd first begun to pen a novel, the idea for which had niggled at his brain for months. The state-of-the-art computer which linked him to his various business interests had acquired a new file.

A file which had grown and totally absorbed him. His path to acceptance and publication had been a dream run. At a time when virtual reality teased the readers' senses, his futuristic upbeat plots had been a hit. International success soon followed, and in a bid for anonymity he'd returned to Australia, sought and found relative isolation in a picturesque bay in the Northern Rivers area, and snapped up a cottage he took pleasure in slowly renovating and refurbishing during the morning hours.

Once a year he flew to the States for the obligatory book launch. And each Christmas was spent in Paris. Occasionally he looked up old friends and joined the social set for a while, only to find the life palled, the new plot beckoned, whereupon he returned to the place he'd called home for the past five years.

Now he looked into the clear green gaze of the first sassy blonde who'd shown an active dislike of him, and relaxed his features as he proffered a faint smile. 'Six o'clock will be fine.'

Where had he been during that long minute of silence? Anneke told herself she wasn't interested. And knew she lied.

She inclined her head stiffly, and matched her voice to the gesture. 'I intend going back to bed.' Her eyes held his, fascinated by dark slate-grey depths whose expression was difficult to discern. 'I'd be grateful if you'd stop hammering so that I can catch up on some sleep.'

'OK.'

She couldn't believe he intended to comply. 'You'll stop?'

Those sensuously moulded lips curved slightly. 'You asked me nicely.'

Anneke opened her mouth, then closed it again.

She watched in silence as he removed the ladder and stored it, gathered up the used section of roof guttering and collected his tools.

Without a further word he turned and covered the distance to his cottage with an easy, lithe stride.

Denim hugged every curve, hinted at superb thigh and calf muscle, and emphasised the length of his legs. Lean waist, fluid muscular grace evident in the breadth of his shoulders denoted more than average strength.

Dammit, why was she standing here *watching* him, for heaven's sake? Men weren't her favoured species at the moment, and *this* man irritated her beyond measure.

She retreated indoors, paused long enough in the

kitchen to fill a glass with water and drink it, then she made for the bedroom and slid between the sheets.

The anger hadn't subsided; if anything it had intensified. Joined by the stinging realisation that she had no job, no salary, and running expenses to maintain on her apartment.

On the plus side, she had an annuity from inherited investments, sufficient to live quite comfortably until she found employment, and there was a reasonably healthy savings account from which she could draw funds to meet weekly expenses.

Anneke closed her eyes and deliberately summoned pleasant thoughts, employed meditation techniques, and resorted to counting sheep. Nothing worked.

With an angry jerk she tossed off the sheet, rose and pulled on a swimsuit. A swim, followed by a walk along the beach, then breakfast. After which she'd examine the contents of Aunt Vivienne's refrigerator and pantry, decide what to prepare for Sebastian's dinner, then drive into Byron Bay and collect everything she needed from the supermarket.

Anneke paused long enough to clean her teeth and run a brush through her hair, then she slid on a pair of sunglasses, caught up a towel, and made her way down onto the sandy foreshore.

The sun was warm, with the promise of increasing heat as the day progressed. A faint sea breeze teased the ends of her hair, and she inhaled the tangy salt air with pleasure.

There wasn't another person in sight, and she relished the solitude, choosing to explore the familiar shoreline for several minutes before opting to wade into the cool water.

Effecting a neat dive, she broke the surface and began a pattern of leisurely strokes parallel to the shore for a while, before emerging to towel the excess moisture from her skin and hair.

It didn't take long for the warm air to dry her swimsuit, and she wrapped the towel round her waist, then set out towards the outcrop of rocks at the furthest end of the bay.

Anneke could feel her body relax as the tension eased, and she increased her pace to a light jog, enjoying the exercise, the morning, the solitude.

It was almost an hour before she re-entered the cottage, and after a shower she dressed in casual shorts and a top, then caught up a pad and pen as she examined her aunt's pantry and refrigerator and noted what food supplies she'd need to collect from the supermarket.

CHAPTER THREE

BREAKFAST comprised cereal, toast and fruit, followed by ruinously strong black coffee.

Anneke tidied the few dishes, then she caught up her car keys, slid the strap of her bag over one shoulder, and made her way out to the carport.

Byron Bay was a pleasant seaside town, a popular holiday area, and the community centre for outlying banana, avocado and sugar cane farmers.

Parking the car wasn't a problem, and she took her time browsing through the supermarket as she selected her purchases and stacked them in the trolley.

It was almost midday when she returned to the cottage, and after unloading her various purchases she took time to have lunch before beginning preparations for Sebastian's evening meal.

At five she showered and changed into jeans and a singlet top, bound her hair into a single plait, then returned to the kitchen.

Artichokes stuffed and served with a rich cream sauce, marinated baby octopus, *risi e bisi*, two baby pigeons *confits aux raisins*, and, for dessert, her speciality—*bombe au chocolat*.

Anneke hoped he had a supply of antacid on hand, otherwise he was certain to be a victim of indigestion.

At precisely two minutes before six she trod the short path linking both cottages and knocked on Sebastian's back door.

She heard a deep bark, followed by a curt command, then the door swung open.

Anneke saw the dog first. A huge Alsatian with liquid brown eyes, a dark velvet pelt, and possessing all the qualities of a trained guard dog.

'Shaef,' Sebastian qualified. 'Let him become acquainted, then you'll never need worry about him again.'

Her eyes travelled over snug black jeans, a black open-necked shirt, to features that bore a faintly mocking expression.

He was an arresting man, compelling, and possessed of a leashed quality that some would find vaguely frightening.

Anneke didn't question his authority with Shaef. She had a healthy respect for canines, and the Alsatian was an awesome breed.

'Will you come in?'

'No,' she responded quickly. Too quickly, for she saw the sudden gleam apparent in his eyes, and caught the slight quirk at the edge of his mouth. 'Enjoy your meal.'

'*Merci.*'

No man had the right to look so darned sexy, or possess a voice that sounded like melted chocolate being dribbled over ice cream. Smooth, very smooth, she perceived. Yet there was tensile steel beneath the smoothness. The hardness of a man well-versed in the frailties of his fellow men.

Without a further word she turned and retraced her steps. In her aunt's kitchen she set about cleaning up, then when it was done she made herself a light, fluffy omelette, added a salad, and took the plate into the dining room.

Tomorrow night she'd serve him everything stuffed... carpet steak with an exotic sauce, stuffed mushrooms, zucchini, tomatoes and potatoes. She would even bake a vanilla sponge for dessert and stuff it with fresh strawberries and cream whipped with kirsch.

And Monday... She positively *glowed* at the thought of what she could do with seafood.

Anneke prayed fervently that if he didn't already have an ulcer, her epicurean offerings would soon provide him with one. Revenge, she determined, would be sweet.

Very sweet, she determined, upon waking next morning to the shrilling sound of an electric skill-saw cutting through wood.

Anneke spared a glance at her watch. Six-thirty. A half-hour earlier than yesterday. At least this morning she wasn't the victim of only a few hours' sleep.

If Sebastian Lanier was playing a game, then so, too, would she.

A slight smile played over her lips and she slid from the bed. A visit to the bathroom, then she pulled on briefs, shorts, and a singlet top. Her hair she deftly twisted into a single braid and let it fall between her shoulders. Then she slipped her feet into joggers and went to the back door with a ready smile in place.

He wore the same faded stonewashed jeans from the day before, and a different tee-shirt. Nice muscle structure, tight butt, firm waist, with no visible fat apparent on that mean frame.

'Good morning,' she greeted as she ran lightly down the

few steps. 'I had no idea Aunt Vivienne needed more repairs. What is it today?'

He pulled the switch on the electric saw and straightened as he turned to face her. The dark hair was neatly bound, but he had forgone the morning shave. It gave him a distinctly piratical look, and heightened the planes of his face, sculpted hard cheekbones and emphasised the strength of his jaw.

If he'd suffered a restless night due to indigestion, it didn't show.

'A section of the picket fence needs replacing. New posts, new palings.'

She widened the smile, and her eyes took on a sparkling gleam. 'How kind. Aunt Vivienne will be pleased.' She turned towards the path leading down to the beach, then cast him a backward glance over one shoulder. 'Have a nice day.'

Anneke broke into a leisurely jog, and on reaching the sand she crossed down to the water's edge and ran parallel to the shoreline until she reached the outward curve of the bay, then she slowed to a halt and went through her usual morning exercise routine.

She deliberately took her time, and when she returned to the cottage Sebastian was nowhere in sight. The carpenter's horse, any wood cut-offs had been cleared away, and a brief glance along the length of picket fence displayed the new section in place.

A muted throaty purr from an engine sounded loud in the morning's silence, and she turned towards its source. Reversing from Sebastian's garage was a late model Range Rover, with, she soon saw, Sebastian at the wheel.

So he was going out. Good, she thought happily as she let herself into the cottage. She had a few household chores to perform, then she'd shower and put a call through to Aunt Vivienne. After lunch she intended to curl up in a comfortable chair and read until it was time to begin preparing Sebastian's dinner.

Anneke had just finished lunch when the phone rang, and she crossed the room and lifted the receiver from its handset.

Her usual cheery greeting brought no response, so she repeated it. Still nothing. She was about to hang up when she heard the soft sound of human breathing.

Even, steady, it became louder and faster, until there could be no mistaking the implied simulation.

She cut the connection in one quick movement, then stood transfixed for several seconds before shaking herself free from momentary shock.

It was simply a random call, she attempted to rationalise. Perhaps some kid with too much time on his hands was getting his kicks from indiscriminate dialling.

Yet it gave her an eerie feeling, one that was difficult to dispel as she tried valiantly to lose herself in the plot of the current mystery she was reading.

Preparations for Sebastian's dinner didn't take overlong, and at a few minutes to six she took the loaded tray and carried it across to his cottage.

Sebastian appeared at the door seconds after she knocked. A white tee-shirt was teamed with black jeans, and both fitted snug on his frame.

He surveyed her with interest, caught the seemingly pleasant smile, and wasn't deceived.

His gaze flicked to the tray in her hand, and he didn't know whether to castigate or commend her.

Much depended on whether last night's meal had been a one-off, or if she'd duplicated dishes of which, while each separate one was a gourmet delight, the combination left something to be desired.

He thought of the rich *bombe au chocolat* reposing on a shelf in his refrigerator. Death by chocolate? Somehow he had the feeling the dessert was meant to be his *bête noir*.

'Enjoy.'

'Thank you,' Sebastian acknowledged as he took the tray, watching as she took a few seconds to fondle Shaef's ears. Then she turned towards Vivienne's cottage, and he viewed the elegant sway of her hips with male appreciation before taking the tray to the dining room table.

Shaef cast him an enquiring look and pricked his ears.

'That makes two of us,' Sebastian murmured as he placed dishes onto the table, caught up cutlery, and removed covers.

It only took a glance to interpret Anneke's meaning. Get stuffed. A slow, musing smile widened his mouth.

Vivienne's niece had gone to considerable trouble to exact revenge.

With deft movements he consigned the sponge, strawberries and cream concoction to the refrigerator.

Pride had prevented her from serving up burnt offerings, or the blandest of fare. Pride, and loyalty to her aunt.

Well, he wouldn't spoil Anneke's game.

He, too, could employ a little subterfuge. If most all of the minor repairs around Vivienne's property were completed within a week instead of the months she'd originally suggested, then so be it.

A slow smile curved his mouth, and the edges lifted in humour. And if he ran out of things to do, then he would invent some.

Sebastian sat down at the table and carefully removed

a portion of stuffing from each vegetable, then sliced into the delectable-looking steak.

A man would need to be wary around a woman like Anneke. His lips twitched and his eyes gleamed with cynical amusement. If each prepared meal provided an indication of her mood, then the next week or two could prove interesting.

Afterwards he scraped discarded stuffing into the refuse bin, made recklessly strong coffee, then carried it through to the office, turned on the computer screen and began to work.

Intrigued to discover within a short space of time that a minor female character of his creation had developed a few traits that changed stoic to sassy.

Anneke surveyed the number of pots and kitchen utensils atop the kitchen benchtop and wrinkled her nose at the folly of creating culinary mayhem.

Rinse and soak, she decided, then she'd attack the dishes when she'd eaten her own modest meal of salad greens with nuts, fresh cantaloupe, mango and feta cheese.

Afterwards, she'd thumb through Aunt Vivienne's numerous cookbooks and plot a menu for tomorrow evening's meal, then list the ingredients she needed to buy.

At nine Aunt Vivienne rang, with an update on Elise's health and the latest monitor results on the unborn twins. It was a case of 'no change' being good news.

Almost as soon as Anneke replaced the receiver, her mobile phone rang, and she indulged in a lengthy chat with a friend in Sydney before ending the call and retiring to bed with a book.

The morning brought a light rain, and after a leisurely breakfast Anneke showered and changed, then drove to Byron Bay to collect fresh seafood.

On impulse she opted to spend the day baking, and purchased ingredients to make a Christmas cake. Several small ones, she decided, would make excellent gifts for friends, wrapped in red and green Cellophane and tied with decorative ribbons. She could take them back with her, or, if she chose to lengthen her stay, then she could consign them via the postal service.

It rained on and off all day. Alternate heavy and light showers with very little time in between.

The kitchen was soon redolent with various aromas, as Anneke washed and soaked a variety of dried fruit in sherry and brandy.

By mid-afternoon shortbread, cut in fingers, lay cooling on baking racks. There was one tin filled with rumballs, another with fudge brownies. Tomorrow she'd bake Christmas cakes.

A quick glance at her watch determined it was time to begin preparing Sebastian's evening meal.

A secretive smile teased the edges of her mouth. She almost wished she could see his expression when he uncovered a platter containing miso soup thick with seaweed and tofu, grilled eel in a rich oyster sauce, sushi with slices of raw fish and seaweed delicacies, and *faux* caviare. Flavoured tofu with fruit comprised dessert.

Sebastian heeded her knock, caught her carefully composed expression, and was immediately on guard.

He mentally conjured the thick T-bone steak he'd removed from the freezer earlier in the day, the makings for a salad he could put together in minutes, and sought to protect his palate.

'Why not join me tomorrow night?'

'I wouldn't dream of interrupting your work,' she responded with extreme politeness.

'An hour or two won't cause much damage.'

'Damage' was the operative word, and she didn't covet an hour in his company, much less two. Besides, if she shared a meal with him she'd have to resort to conventional cooking, and that would definitely spoil the fun.

'Maybe another time.' Without a further word she turned and retraced her steps.

It was as well he liked Japanese food, although he conceded her choice of dishes was probably as deliberate as it was unusual. The dessert joined the chocolate *bombe* and the strawberry sponge sitting in his refrigerator.

Anneke checked the dried fruit, stacked shortbread into one of her aunt's cake tins, then cleaned up the kitchen.

After a day of preparing food, she opted for something simple for her own meal, and followed it with a bowl of fresh fruit. She added ice to a glass, filled it with water, then carried it through to the lounge and switched on the television.

The phone rang at nine. She remembered the time, as she glanced at her watch. Even as she picked up the receiver she had the instinctive feeling this was going to be a repeat of yesterday's nuisance call.

Bingo, Anneke registered as no one answered her greeting, and within seconds she could hear audible breathing on the line.

Who would do something like this? It couldn't be aimed at Aunt Vivienne, surely? Yet who knew Anneke was here?

She cut the connection and replaced the handset, then stood staring at the telephone as if willing it to divulge relevant information.

For five minutes she hovered in the kitchen, wiping down bench surfaces that had already been wiped, checking cupboards, the refrigerator, the pantry. Just in case the call was repeated.

The thought crossed her mind that perhaps she should report it. But what could the police do, except relay advice she was already aware of?

CHAPTER FOUR

SEVERAL friends were aware of Anneke's mobile listing, but she hadn't told anyone of her whereabouts or given out Aunt Vivienne's number. And no one she knew would make a nuisance, heavy breathing, non-speaking call then hang up.

She had no enemies, and no one she knew would wish her harm. So *who*? A frown creased her forehead. A mis-dialled number? Once, maybe. But *twice* indicated it to be premeditated.

The microwave digital display indicated a few minutes before six. Damn. There was no reason to front the day at such an early hour, and yet she felt too unsettled to simply sit around and do nothing.

A jog along the length of the beach followed by a swim in the cool, clear ocean would clear her mind, then she'd drive into Byron Bay and explore the shops for an hour or two. After lunch she'd mix the Christmas cakes and consign them into the oven.

This early there was a fresh newness to the day, apparent in the warmth of the sun's rays, the golden sand crisp from its tidal cleanse.

Anneke set a leisurely pace along the Bay's gentle curve to the outcrop of rocks before turning to retrace her steps.

It was then she saw a lone male figure closing the distance between them, his pace measuring hers in relaxed style but covering the sand more quickly due to a longer stride.

There was no disguising the tall, muscular frame, and if there was any doubt the dark hair sleekly bound at his nape provided recognition.

Sebastian.

Clad in dark sweat-shorts and singlet, he looked like something out of a health and fitness magazine. The sweatband round his head lent a credible likeness to an Apache brave.

The mental switch in image brought a smile to her lips and lit her eyes with a mischievous sparkle.

She watched with detached admiration as he drew close: the fluid flex of well-honed muscle and sinew, the lithe, animalistic grace of perfectly co-ordinated body movement.

At this stage most men would have bunched up their pectoral muscles, flung back their shoulders in an effort to impress a female of the species.

Sebastian merely slowed his stride and came to an easy halt. Lacking was the expected sheen of sweat; nor was there any evidence of shortness of breath.

'*Bonjour.*'

'Hi.'

The easy smile deepened the vertical crease in each cheek, and there was an appreciative gleam in those dark eyes.

'I didn't expect to see you out this early.'

Dammit, why did it take one glance at his mouth to bring vividly to mind how it felt to have it cover her own? And *why*, a silent voice taunted, should some internal flame ignite and flare into deep, pulsing life with anticipation that it might?

'I rarely sleep in.' She hadn't meant to sound defensive.

Touchy. Definitely touchy. And he wondered why. 'I wasn't aware I'd implied that you do,' he said quietly.

Oh, hell. She had the distinct feeling he could see inside her mind, and meaningful conversation at this hour of the morning wasn't her intention.

'Must keep the heart-rate up,' she indicated, preparing to sprint away from him.

'We could run together.'

'Sorry,' Anneke declared without compunction. 'I run for fun. You,' she said with certainty, 'adhere to a more professional pace.' She even summoned a slight smile. 'And I wouldn't suggest you alter it solely for my benefit.' She broke into a light sprint, then slowed her pace when she had put some distance between them.

It wasn't easy to ignore the faint prickle of awareness teasing the hairs on her nape.

His very presence irked her. He made her feel vulnerable, and she didn't like it any more than she liked him.

There were no messages on the answering machine, but her mobile showed one missed call, and when she checked voice mail all she heard was an indistinct whisper followed by the silent click of a replaced receiver.

Her stomach gave a small lurch, then settled.

Adam? Even as the thought intruded, she dismissed it. Adam Lloyd Chambers was a legal eagle of impeccable lineage, admired by his associates and a pillar within his social community.

The fact he had a penchant for sexual dalliances didn't alter the fact he was an unlikely candidate to make nuisance calls. Besides, she couldn't see him doing anything to jeopardise his career or his partnership.

Anneke made for the bathroom, showered and washed

her hair, then dressed in tailored shorts, added a cotton top. She cut up a selection of fruit, added cereal, then followed it with a poached egg on toast for breakfast.

She put a small load of washing through the machine, and after completing some essential housework she caught up her keys and drove into Byron Bay with the intention of browsing through the many craft shops, maybe taking time out to sip a cappuccino at one of several outdoor cafés before purchasing a selection of fresh fruit and a few staple vegetables.

The aroma of freshly baked bread was irresistible, and she entered the shop, purchased a baguette and a few savoury scrolls, then emerged out onto the pavement.

Some ham, a wedge of Brie, and a delicious salad would suffice as lunch. Then she'd curl up in the capacious cane chair on her aunt's porch and lose herself in a book until it was time to prepare dinner.

'Well, now, girl, what's that you've got there?'

She heard the voice, took in the thin face, the long, unkempt hair, the nose-stud, the eyebrow-ring, and a range of studs and earrings attached to each ear. The loose-flowing shirt looked as if it hadn't been washed in weeks, likewise the frayed and slashed jeans.

One glance at those eyes was enough for her to determine this was no peace-loving New Age devotee. They were dark, beady, and mean.

Trouble. Unless she handled him carefully.

Anneke lifted one shoulder in a careless shrug. 'Bread, fruit and vegetables.' She made to move past him, and saw the subtle shift of his body as he stepped close.

Damn. 'You're in my way,' she stated calmly.

'That's a problem?'

'It could be.'

'So, what you gonna do, pretty girl?' he mocked.

'Any one of a number of things.'

He leered at her, and ran the tip of his tongue over his lower lip. 'Such as?' His mouth parted in a soundless laugh. 'Scream?'

'How's your pain level?' Anneke countered matter-of-factly.

An arm curved along the back of her waist while another deftly removed a carry-bag. '*Chérie.* My apologies.' She felt the heat of Sebastian's frame as he leaned in close and brushed his lips to her cheek in a warm caress. 'Have you been waiting long?'

She turned her head and met a pair of steady dark eyes, glimpsed their warning flare, and controlled the unexpected flip her stomach executed as she became lost in the devastating warmth of his smile.

Only a fool would have ignored the hard-muscled body beneath the open-necked shirt and stonewashed jeans, or dismissed the ruthless intensity behind his deceptively mild expression.

Anneke had the distinct feeling he was poised for action. It was evident in his stance, the sharp stillness apparent in his eyes. For one infinitesimal second she almost felt sorry for her aggressor.

'Sebastian. *C'est opportun.*'

A split second to think. So, not fluent, he acknowledged. The accent was passable. His smile widened. Good. She would understand what he said when he made love to her.

His eyes were carefully bland. 'Should we effect an introduction?' He thrust out his hand and enclosed the young man's palm in a firm grip. 'Lanier. And you?'

'Go to hell.'

Sebastian's expression didn't change. 'What a shame, my friend,' he intoned with deadly softness. 'We're not going there.'

Anneke didn't blink at the blistering and very pithy response. 'Charming,' she murmured facetiously as her aggressor turned and ambled off along the pavement. 'Pity his suggestion was anatomically impossible.'

Sebastian's eyes narrowed fractionally. 'He intended to relieve you of whatever money you had in your wallet.' To fund the next fix.

'It would have been interesting to discover his threshold of pain.'

He cast her a sharp glance. 'What particular method did you have in mind?'

She told him, concisely, analytically, and had the satisfaction of evidencing a measure of respect.

'Reassuring,' he conceded, 'to learn you can take care of yourself.'

Anneke inclined her head. Dealing with the scruffy young creep wouldn't have posed a problem. However, she would have had to discard the carry-bags in a hurry, and to have her carefully selected purchases crushed or broken in a physical fracas would have been a terrible waste.

She turned towards him and raised an enquiring eyebrow. 'And your field of expertise?'.

He had trained beneath a well-respected master, practised in many a *dojo*, and occasionally fought in places no civilised self-respecting person would consider while serving his country for a time.

It was simpler to name one. 'Karate.'

Anneke considered him thoughtfully. Most men would

have launched into a string of achievements. However, Sebastian Lanier was not 'most men', and his simplicity intrigued her.

There was more to him than met the eye, she perceived. Entrepreneur, writer. What other vocation and skill did he possess?

Sebastian indicated the carry-bags. 'Anything likely to spoil in there for the next hour?'

'No. Why?'

He deftly turned her in the opposite direction. 'You can join me for lunch.'

She regarded him solemnly. 'It's polite to ask.'

His mouth curved to form a wolfish smile, and there was a gleam in those dark eyes she didn't quite trust. 'I feel it's the least I can do in light of the gastronomic feasts you've prepared for me over the past few nights.'

'Gastronomic' indeed. 'Feast' depended entirely on the interpretation, she decided with irreverent suspicion. 'Thank you.'

There were any number of cafés and restaurants from which to choose. Instead, he led her into a modern pub, the owner of which had gained recognition in the area for his brush with fame and the garnering of considerable wealth. A man's man, and one of the boys, local legend had it, who could sup beer at the bar with his friends equally as well as he'd cemented business deals in Hollywood and London.

'You don't object to a counter lunch?'

She searched Sebastian's features in an attempt to discern whether his choice was deliberate, and found nothing to indicate that it might be.

'It's ages since I had fish and chips.'

He cast her a musing glance. 'I think you'll find they manage something less basic.'

They did, and, although relatively simple fare, the freshly caught grilled schnapper was delicious, the salad superb, and it was obvious the licensee patronised the local bakery.

Sebastian noted her enjoyment, observed her healthy appetite, the precise but intensely feminine movements of her hands, the manner in which she sampled each mouthful.

Poetry in motion. There was no guile, no studied orchestration. He wondered what she would look like with her hair loose, and spread over his pillow as she slept. Or tossed and dishevelled in the throes of passion as she rode him hard and fast.

She possessed a beautiful mouth, even white teeth. Was she well versed in using both to drive a man wild and hold him on the knife-edge between pleasure and pain?

Confrontational, no artifice, he mused thoughtfully. What you saw was what you got.

Yet she wasn't above playing a diverse game. For the sheer hell of it, he suspected, as he mentally reviewed the exotic meals she'd delivered all three evenings. He'd expected unimaginative fare. Not the dishes she'd gone to a great deal of trouble to prepare.

His eyes acquired a gleam of dancing amusement. What did she have in mind for tonight?

Anneke sensed his gaze, caught the musing glint apparent, and spared him a level look. 'Nice to know I amuse you. Perhaps you could be specific?'

Sebastian banked down the laughter, broke off a piece of bread and ate it, then offered her a warm smile. 'How specific would you like me to be?'

She watched the powerful movement of his jaw, the

way his facial muscles clenched and relaxed, the smooth column of his throat. His hands fascinated her. Broad palms, strong wrists, tanned skin stretched over fluid sinew, long, tapered fingers that belied their strength, clean, well-shaped nails.

'Oh, the whole truth and nothing but the truth will do.'

'I'm curious to know where you learnt to cook.'

She effected a light shrug. 'A young chef rented the apartment next to mine for a while. I helped him perfect his English, and in return he shared his culinary skills.'

'Among other skills?'

She didn't pretend to misunderstand his meaning. 'He wasn't my lover.' She replaced her cutlery, then carefully pushed her plate aside and stood to her feet. 'Thanks for lunch.'

He'd offended her. Interesting. 'Sit down.'

'No.' Her eyes flared, darkening to the deepest emerald flecked with gold. Without a word she turned and walked from the room, out onto the pavement and into the sunshine.

She lifted a hand and slid her sunglasses down from atop her head, and walked along the street towards her car.

'You left these behind.'

Anneke heard Sebastian's faintly accented drawl, paused, then turned and threw him a fulminating glare.

He had her carry-bags secured in each hand, but made no effort to pass them to her.

'I'll take them.' She reached out, only to scream in silent frustration as he fell into step beside her. 'Don't,' she warned in a deadly quiet voice, 'think you're safe, just because we're in a public place.'

He looked at her with studied ease, aware from the set

of her shoulders, the slightly clenched fists, that she meant what she said.

'We're almost at the car park.'

'You don't need to play the gentleman,' she retaliated with heavy sarcasm.

'In this instance, I choose to.' He scanned the wide apron of bitumen with its lines of parked cars, identified hers, and crossed towards it.

Anneke walked ahead of him and unlocked and opened the passenger door, then stood aside as he placed the carry-bags onto the seat.

He straightened, and she was suddenly intensely aware of his height, his proximity, and the faint musky aroma of cologne and man.

He looked down at her, saw the tilt of her chin, the residue of anger that tightened her expression. Without a word he lifted a hand and trailed the tips of his fingers down one cheek and splayed them along her jaw.

Then he smiled and lowered his head down to hers, capturing her mouth with his own in a gentle evocative kiss that was all too brief.

'Drive carefully.' Without a further word he turned and navigated a line of cars to his own powerful Range Rover.

Frustrating, *irritating* man, she accorded, adding a few descriptive and vividly pithy curses as she crossed round and slid in behind the wheel.

She reversed, then eased her sedan out onto the street. By the time she arrived at her aunt's cottage she had devised numerous ways to render him grievous bodily harm, as well as concocting the most bizarre series of menus that she could summon to mind.

Anneke unpacked the carry-bags, poured herself a cold

drink, and checked her watch. Three hours until she needed to begin dinner preparations.

Housework, she decided. She'd clean and dust and polish. Busy hands, healthy mind. Well, hers was filled with vengeful thoughts, which somehow made a mockery of that particular saying.

When she'd finished, everything sparkled and the cottage was redolent with the smell of beeswax. And the richness of freshly baked fruit cake.

It was after five when her mobile rang, and without thinking she wiped her hands, then reached for the unit and activated it.

Nothing. Only an eerie silence echoed her customary greeting. Her fingers shook slightly as she disengaged the phone.

Rationale dictated it was just a crank call. She doubted it was Adam. Although she couldn't discount the possibility he might take a perverse delight in causing her a degree of nervous anxiety.

It was just after six when she delivered Sebastian's evening meal.

'Stay and have a drink with me.'

Anneke looked at him, saw the unbound hair and noted its unruly state—almost as if he'd raked his fingers through the length on more than one occasion.

Maybe the plot wasn't working out, or the characters weren't performing as they should. Or he was struggling through a bout of writer's block.

'Thanks, but I don't drink.' Not entirely true. She adored good French champagne, and reserved the partaking of it for special occasions. As this wasn't one of them, and she seriously doubted he had a bottle of Dom Perignon or

Cristal on ice, it was simpler to decline. 'Your meal will get cold, and so will mine,' she said easily, and turned towards the door.

He made no attempt to dissuade her, and when the door closed behind her he crossed to the table, removed the cover and examined the contents of the tray.

It could have been worse. He moved to the bank of cupboards, took out a skillet and reached into the refrigerator for a large T-bone steak.

When it came to the dessert, he scraped off the cream, took a tentative bite, then opted for fresh fruit. He washed it down with bottled mineral water, then spooned freshly ground beans into the coffee-maker, poured water into the cylinder and switched it on.

The glass carafe had just begun to fill when there was a crashing sound from the adjoining cottage.

He was out of the door and running, Shaef at his side, adrenalin pumping, his mind actively selecting one scenario after another as he covered the set of steps in one leap and pounded on the door.

CHAPTER FIVE

A MUFFLED and very explicit curse fell from Anneke's lips as she surveyed the mess at her feet.

Cut flowers were strewn in an arc across the floor, water pooled in a widening puddle, and Aunt Vivienne's prized Waterford crystal vase lay shattered in a hundred shards on the laundry's ceramic-tiled floor.

There was no one to blame but herself. Unless she counted a fractional second's distraction at the insistent and distinctive peal of her mobile telephone.

'Anneke.' Forceful, authoritative, *demanding*. Sebastian's voice penetrated the evening's stillness, accompanied by the heavy, insistent rap of knuckles on wood.

'OK, OK,' she responded in resigned exasperation. 'I'm in the…' Her voice trailed to a halt as he appeared at the screened laundry door.

'Hell,' he cursed quietly, taking in the scene at a glance. Her legs were bare, so were her feet.

'Apt,' she responded drily.

'Don't move. I'll be back.'

He was, within minutes, with a bucket, pan and brush.

'Don't throw out the flowers.'

'They're likely to contain hidden pieces of glass.'

'Crystal,' she corrected without thought, and incurred a dark, sweeping glance.

'Waterford, thirty-five years old, wedding gift. You want the pattern detail?'

'There's no need to be facetious.'

'Likewise, you don't need to be so particular.'

'Oh, go soak your head in a bucket!'

His smile held a certain grimness. 'Nice to have your gratitude.'

She wanted to burst into tears. She treasured beautiful things. Loved the art and symmetry of exquisite crystal and porcelain. To have a piece break by her own hand was almost akin to killing a living thing.

He glimpsed the momentary desolation, caught a flash of something deeper, and fought the temptation to pull her into his arms. Such an action, he knew, would only earn him the sharp edge of her tongue.

'Vivienne has plenty more flowers in the garden,' he offered mildly, ignoring her protest as he deftly swept everything into the bucket, then dealt with the water.

'Vacuum cleaner. Hall cupboard?' Had to be. Both cottages were similar in design.

Twice the vacuum hose rattled as the cleaner sucked up undetected shards of crystal, and she stepped onto a towel he spread on the floor while he completed the task.

'Thanks,' she added, aware she owed him that, at least. She could have coped, dispensing with the mess, but it was likely she'd have cut herself in the process.

Dammit, she didn't want to owe him. Nor did she particularly covet his company. He made her feel…uncomfortable, she conceded reluctantly.

As if he was all too aware of the sexual chemistry

between them, and content to wait and watch for the moment *she* felt it.

Well, she had news for him. She could pin it down to the precise moment she'd walked into Aunt Vivienne's kitchen the first night she arrived and found him there making tea. For her.

Sebastian watched the fleeting emotions chase across her expressive features, divined the reason for them, and kept his own expression deliberately bland.

She could tell him to go, or ask him to stay. There was always tomorrow, the day after that. And he was a patient man.

The tussle between politeness and impoliteness warred, and there was really no contest. 'Would you like some coffee?'

He studied her in silence for a few seconds. 'Thanks.'

In the kitchen she set the coffee-maker up, then extracted two cups and saucers, added a bowl of sugar, and took cream from the refrigerator.

Anneke was conscious of him as he leant one hip against the servery. His tall frame made the kitchen seem smaller, and she became aware of every move she made. Only sheer habit prevented the spoon clattering onto the saucer, and she was extremely careful with the glass carafe as she poured hot coffee.

Sebastian collected both cups and set them down on the dining room table, then he pulled out a chair and folded his length into it.

She crossed to the table and sat opposite him. Conversational skills were something she'd rarely lacked. Yet at this precise moment she had trouble summoning one topic to mind.

'How's the book going?'

An amused gleam momentarily lit his eyes before he successfully hid it by letting his eyelids droop fractionally. The inevitable question an author had to field from time to time. 'My answer would only seem a paradox.'

The dry response made it easy for her to resort to humour. 'You've hit a bad patch?'

He winced mentally. 'You could say I've dug myself into a hole and I can't see a way out.'

'Why not back up and avoid the hole altogether?'

Good point. 'I need to think about it a while.'

'So sharing coffee and conversation is really an excuse not to stare at a blank screen and curse beneath your breath?'

'Perhaps I couldn't resist your charming company.'

Icily polite. Furiously angry. Indignant, voluble, even sarcastic. At no stage could she recall being charming. Maybe it was time to try.

'Tell me why you write.'

'Curiosity, or genuine interest?'

'A bit of both,' she answered honestly.

'An obsessive need to create a story.' A statement which usually brought a non-committal response, indicating un-interest or lack of comprehension.

Anneke looked at him carefully. Glimpsed the fine lines fanning out from the corners of his eyes, the faint furrow creasing his forehead, as if he'd frowned in concentration too often in the past few hours.

'And the *how* of it?'

His mouth quirked. 'Matching the image in my head with words that allow the reader to capture my vision.'

An art form that wasn't always easy, requiring dedication and discipline, she perceived. There could be no doubt Sebastian Lanier possessed both qualities.

He waited for the inevitable comments relating to fame and fortune, the media circus he went to great pains to avoid. But none were forthcoming.

Inane questions weren't her practice. 'It must be a fascinating process.' Her eyes glinted with humour. 'And not without a degree of frustration when the words don't flow as you need them to.'

His smile held a warmth that made her stomach curl. And the eyes were dark, gleaming and steady. Assessing, analytical, almost as if he had calculated every move, every angle, and was waiting to see which one she would choose.

It gave her an uncanny feeling.

'Mind if I pour more coffee?'

His voice was husky and held a tinge of humour, almost as if he'd read her mind.

'Of course not. Help yourself.'

He indicated her cup. 'Want me to refill yours?'

It was strong, really strong. If she drank another, she'd be awake half the night. 'No, thanks. I'll have water instead.'

He crossed to the servery, helped himself from the coffee-maker, then reached into a nearby cupboard, extracted a glass and filled it with water. All with the ease of a man who was familiar with her aunt's kitchen.

She could almost imagine their easy friendship, and experienced a pang of envy.

He should get out of here. The computer beckoned, and he'd just had a fleeting but inspired flash as to how he could circumvent the current plot hole.

However, the coffee was good, really good. And Anneke's current mood intrigued him.

He placed the glass down onto the table in front of her, then slid into his chair.

'Your turn.'

Her eyes widened, the light, clear green darkening fractionally as comprehension hit.

Fascinating…eyes a man could drown in, and he discovered he wanted to, very much. Thread a hand through her silky hair and hold fast her head while he shaped her mouth with his own. Anchor her against him so she felt his need while he heightened her own. The slow erotic glide of hands, lips, until neither was enough and the barrier of clothes proved too much.

'You live in Sydney, and work in a legal office,' Sebastian prompted, banking down libidinous images.

'No longer work in one specific legal office,' Anneke corrected drily.

'Resigned?'

'Walked out.'

His eyes held a humorous gleam. 'Problems with the boss?'

She looked at him in measured silence. 'You could say that.' A statement she didn't intend to clarify.

At that moment the phone rang, its double peal insistent, and her eyes flared momentarily with apprehension.

Another nuisance call?

Sebastian unbent his lengthy frame and pushed in his chair. 'I'll let you get that.' He drained the remains of his coffee and carried the cup and saucer to the servery. Then he lifted a hand in silent salute and let himself out of the back door.

Anneke crossed to the phone, removed the receiver, and

experienced relief when she discovered the caller was one of her aunt's friends.

A relief which proved short-lived when the phone rang again minutes later.

She tossed up whether to answer it or not, for she couldn't discount the possibility it might be a legitimate call. Indecision warred for a few seconds, then she took a deep breath and unhooked the receiver.

Her heart sank. No answer, only heavy breathing. She resisted the temptation to crash the receiver down on its cradle. 'Damn you,' she said fiercely. 'Try this again, and I'll contact the police and have them put a trace on the line.'

There was the faint click of a receiver being replaced, then the hollow sound of a cut connection.

'Problems?'

Anneke whirled at the sound of that deep, faintly accented voice, and saw Sebastian, tray in hand, standing just inside the kitchen door.

Her heart was thumping in her chest, and her eyes, she knew, were stark and wide. Control kicked in, and she forced her voice into even tones.

'You heard.' There was no point in pretending he hadn't.

With ease, he crossed the room and deposited the tray on the servery. 'You didn't answer the question.'

Why fabricate? 'Someone seems to be having fun at my expense.'

He leant a hip against the cabinet and regarded her carefully, noting a face devoid of colour, eyes that were far too dark. 'How many such calls have you taken?'

'That was the sixth call in three days, if you count my mobile.'

'He's persistent.' He waited a beat. 'Abusive?'

Anneke shook her head. 'So far he hasn't said a word.'

'Tomorrow we notify the phone company and arrange an unlisted number.' His eyes hardened, and he kept them partially hooded. 'Shaef stays with you.'

'*We?* I can take care of it. And I don't need Shaef.'

'It's Shaef or me. Choose.'

She shot him a look of disbelief. 'Aren't you going just a tiny bit overboard with this?'

His eyes were obsidian, his gaze hard and unblinking. 'No.'

Anneke drew in a deep breath, considered telling Sebastian to go take a running hike, then thought better of it.

'It's probably a random call by some idle teenager who, hearing a female voice on the line, has decided to play a stupid game.'

'Maybe.'

'You think it's my ex-boss? If he's caught, and I press charges, the Law Society will suspend him from practice,' she qualified slowly. 'Why take the risk?'

Sebastian's gaze remained steady. 'Some men get their kicks skating close to the edge.'

'He already has my mobile number. Why not use that instead of the house phone?'

'It's too simple. He wants you to be aware he knows where you are.'

Her eyes darkened until they resembled the deepest emerald. Was Adam that cunning? That devious? She could recall telling him she had an aunt who lived in a cottage on a northern coastal beach, but she was willing to swear she hadn't mentioned Aunt Vivienne's surname, or *which* north-coast beach.

Get a grip, she mentally cautioned. You're not in any danger.

'Don't answer the house phone, and switch your mobile onto voice mail.'

'Any more instructions?'

'Don't be sassy.'

He loomed too close for comfort, and it took an effort not to step back a pace. 'You've done your good deed for the day. Twice over.'

'Is that a subtle hint for me to leave?'

'I'd hate to keep you from your work.'

'The computer can wait,' Sebastian drawled, moving forward a pace. 'This won't.'

'This' was his mouth on hers in what proved to be a devastating invasion. He possessed the touch, the instinctive mastery to make a kiss seem like an extension of the physical act itself.

Worse, to make a woman feel a kiss was nowhere near *enough*. That there was more, much more to savour in the realm of sensual delight.

A demanding lover, Sebastian Lanier would take everything a woman offered, and encourage her to give more.

Anneke suppressed a slight shiver. The reward would be magnificent, she acquiesced. Electrifying.

Her heart pounded, and her pulse raced almost out of control as he trailed his mouth to the edge of her jaw. She cried out as he savoured the column of her throat, and she arched her head to allow him greater access.

His hands were warm against her clothing as they moulded her close, and the barrier was something to be dispensed with as the need arose for skin against skin.

Sebastian was the first to move, tugging her blouse free, his fingers deft with buttons as he freed each and every one.

Her own sought purchase on soft cotton, and yanked hard until the tee-shirt slipped out from his waistband.

Dear Lord, he felt good. Hard ribs, corded muscles, broad back, wide shoulders. Her hands curved higher, then clung as he crushed her to him.

His mouth claimed, *staked* a possession that brooked no denial, and for one brief second she almost threw common sense out of the window.

Sebastian was aware the exact moment she began to retreat, and he reluctantly and very slowly broke the kiss, allowing his lips to brush hers, savouring each corner, then he pushed her gently to arm's length.

'I want to take you to bed.' A faint smile curved his lips. 'But I have the feeling you'd only hate me in the morning.'

As well as herself. Twisted sheets and an energetic coupling wasn't on her agenda. With any man.

'I'll write down my phone number. Should anything go bump in the night, call me.' He slid a hand to her cheek, cupped it, and traced her lips with his thumb. 'OK?'

Anneke inclined her head fractionally.

'I'll whistle up Shaef.'

Five minutes later the Alsatian was instructed who he had to guard, and how. Both doors were securely locked, and Anneke settled herself in bed with a good book.

It was after eleven when she put out the light, and on the edge of sleep it was Sebastian's image which came to mind. His sculpted features, the piercing grey eyes that saw too much.

Someone who had experienced more than his share, and had dealt with it. Only a fool would surmise otherwise.

She thought of his kiss, the way his mouth felt on her own, the familiarity of his hands as they moulded her body. And hated herself for wanting more.

CHAPTER SIX

ANNEKE woke early, stretched, then slid out of bed and almost stepped onto a sleek-coated animal curled protectively on the floor. A very large animal.

Oh, my God. *Shaef.*

Memory surfaced in one fell swoop, and a soft curse fell from her lips.

With considerable caution she skirted round the dog and crossed to the bathroom. The dog followed.

Five minutes later she returned to the bedroom, filching her swimsuit from the shower stall where she'd hung it over the taps to dry.

It fitted snug over her slender curves, and she pulled on sweat-shorts and top, then made her way into the kitchen.

Fresh orange juice added a certain zing to her palate, and she looked at the dog with a degree of doubt.

'OK, I guess you need to go outside. Water,' she declared decisively, and hunted for a bowl. 'Food.' The dog's ears pricked at the mention of it.

Dammit, she was a cat person. Dogs gnawed on bones, ate meat, and munched on dry food. A goodly amount of each, she surmised, judging by Shaef's size. None of which she had on hand.

'Sorry, fella.' She placed a bowl filled with water onto the floor. 'This will have to do for now, then you can go home for breakfast.'

When she let him out of the back door, he promptly lolloped to the nearest tree, then, considerably more comfortable, returned to sit on the step.

'Divided loyalties, pal. I'm going for a run along the beach. You get to choose whether you guard me or the house.' She smiled and leant down to fondle one silky ear. 'Personally, I'd go for the house.'

He didn't, of course. She hadn't moved more than half a dozen steps when he fell in beside her. 'Well, there's no doubt you take after your owner,' she said conversationally. 'He's every bit as stubborn as you are.'

Anneke reached the beach and sprinted down onto the sand. And saw Sebastian engaged in callisthenics. Waiting to join her?

Sebastian *plus* his dog? She sprinted towards him. 'Been waiting long?' she queried sweetly.

He wasn't deceived by the mildness of her tone. She was angry. Well, he could handle it. He drew himself up to his full height with ease, placed a hand on one hip and offered her a warm smile.

'Beautiful day.'

She'd slept well. It made the fact that he hadn't seem worthwhile.

'Should I put this down to chance? Or is your appearance on the beach at this hour a forerunner of things to come?'

My, she possessed a sharp tongue. He had an urge to take her mouth with his own and change tart to something smooth and sweet.

'You object to my company?'

She placed a hand on each hip, taking defiance to a new level. 'In the thinly veiled guise of bodyguard, *yes*.'

He had to work hard to prevent humour from entering his voice. 'Are you saying only one of us gets to share your run?'

Damn him, he was amused. 'Given a choice, Shaef wins out.' Her eyes searched his, saw the purposeful intent evident, and she released a deep sigh. 'But you're not going to give me a choice, are you?'

'No.'

'I just might have to hit you.'

'Think carefully before you do.'

There was a silkiness evident in his tone that sent a faint shiver down the length of her spine.

Without a further word she turned and broke into a run, aware of the moment he joined her, man and dog matching their stride to hers. Part of her wanted to set a punishing pace, but she knew she'd never outrun either of them.

A degree of resentment rose to the surface. Against Adam, if it was he who'd initiated a nuisance campaign, but primarily with Sebastian, for any number of reasons, she decided darkly. Foremost, for tugging at her emotions and turning them every which way but loose.

The sandy cove curved out to sea in a low outcrop of rocks, and Anneke turned when she reached that point and began retracing her steps without pause.

Shaef was having a wonderful time, bounding on ahead, then diverging down to the incoming tide to examine a shell or a piece of seaweed. Sebastian jogged steadily at her side.

It was a relief to draw level with her towel, and without saying so much as a word she pulled off her joggers, stripped down to her swimsuit, and sprinted lightly down to the water's edge.

She fully expected Sebastian to join her, and silently vowed as she dived into the cool sea that he'd regret it if he did. Quite *how* she'd ensure he regretted it, she wasn't clear.

Sebastian intuitively opted to engage Shaef in a game of throw-the-stick until Anneke emerged.

'Wise,' she muttered beneath her breath, and missed the amused gleam in his dark eyes as he called Shaef to heel.

'Share breakfast with me.'

She was sharing his dog, his protection. That was enough. She caught up the towel and wound it sarong-wise round her waist. 'Thanks, but no, thanks. I have a heap of things to do.'

He snared her wrist as she turned to walk away from him. 'Lock the cottage securely if you go anywhere. Drive with the central locking system in place. And make sure you park the car on a main thoroughfare.'

She began to steam with indignation. 'Anything else?'

'Carry your mobile phone at all times.'

'I'm amazed you haven't mentioned Shaef.'

'That's a given,' Sebastian intoned hardily. 'Where you go, he goes.'

The steam changed to smoke. 'Now just a tiny minute, here.' Anneke lifted a hand and poked his chest. Hard. 'If my heavy breather is Adam, he's hundreds of miles south in Sydney. A nuisance, but not a threat.'

'And if it's not Adam?'

Ice chilled her veins. 'I intend to find out one way or another. Meantime, stay off my back.' She poked his chest again for good measure, then tugged her hand free and marched back to the cottage.

Impossible, dictatorial, *stubborn* man. Who did he think he was? And by what right did he imagine he could tell her what to do?

Sebastian watched her retreating form, and that of Shaef, who, at a click of Sebastian's fingers, had taken a few bounding strides to fall in at Anneke's side.

A woman who would give as good as she got, and be passionate in giving it… Be it anger, or making love. The former he could handle with one hand tied behind his back. It was the latter that bothered him.

He could have done with cooling down in the ocean himself, and he measured the time it would take her to shower, make coffee, eat whatever it was she had for breakfast, then begin making phone calls.

At the very least he had ten minutes, even if she messed up the order of things.

Anneke entered the cottage and headed straight for the shower, where she sluiced off the salt water and shampooed her hair. Then, towelled dry, she dressed in sapphire-blue shorts and a matching sleeveless top.

Coffee, hot, sweet, strong and black, then she'd fill a bowl with cereal and fruit.

It was after eight when she crossed to the phone. Aunt Vivienne was first on her list, and, after eliciting news that Elise was fine, she gave her aunt relevant details and relayed the fact that until she contacted the police she had no idea whether they'd put a trace on the line or suggest she apply for an unlisted number. Either way, Aunt Vivienne's permission was essential.

Next came a call to the phone company, who, on receiving relevant details, promised to check their records and ring back.

Which left the police. Two 'on hold's and two transfers later, she connected with a very informative young man.

'Yes, ma'am. The complaint was logged in at twenty-o-five hundred hours last night by a Sebastian Lanier acting on behalf of Vivienne Sorrel, owner of the property. The duty officer advised appropriate action, which I understand is being taken, pending authority this morning from Vivienne Sorrel. Perhaps you might like to check with Sebastian Lanier?'

Check with him? She'd kill him! 'Thank you.' She replaced the receiver with care, then turned and marched from the cottage, closing the distance between both residences in swift, angry strides.

The back door was open, the screen door unlatched, and she knocked once, then entered to find Sebastian crisping bacon in the microwave while eggs simmered in a pan atop the stove.

'What God-given right do you think you have to log in a report with the police on my behalf?' Anneke demanded wrathfully.

The toaster popped up crisped bread, and he crossed to the servery, removed both slices and calmly buttered them.

'You're angry.'

Emerald fire flashed in her eyes, and she had to clench her fists to refrain from lashing out at him. 'You bet your sweet life I am.'

He glanced up, and shot her a direct look as he extracted a plate from the cupboard. 'I thought it wise to instigate immediate enquiries.'

'Just *who* in hell do you think you are?'

He placed the toast onto the plate. 'I promised Vivienne I'd keep an eye on you.'

'Well, you can take your damned eye off me, as of now.'

Sebastian deftly removed the pan, slid eggs onto toast, collected the bacon, and carried both plates to the table.

'Want to share?'

'No, I don't want to share *anything* with you!' She drew in a deep breath and released it. 'Nothing, *nada*, *niente*. Do you understand?'

He filled a mug with steaming aromatic black coffee, stirred in sugar, and savoured a mouthful. His shoulders lifted in a deliberate Gallic shrug. 'That's certainly specific.'

Anneke flung her arms in the air in a gesture of enraged despair. 'You're not going to do as I ask, are you?'

His eyes pierced hers, dark, dangerous and lethal. 'No.' He picked up cutlery and cut a neat slice from the corner of his toast. 'Not until the nuisance calls stop.'

'I'm twenty-seven years old, not seventeen. I've lived alone for seven years in a city known for its high crime rate. I can take care of myself.'

Sebastian forked a mouthful of toast and egg into his mouth, chewed and swallowed it, then proceeded to cut another slice.

'You've forgotten one thing.'

The anger was still evident, simmering beneath the surface. 'And what, pray, is that?'

'I gave Vivienne my word.'

'And your word is sacrosanct,' Anneke declared with marked cynicism.

'Yes.'

'So get used to it?'

'I'm simply telling you how it is,' he said calmly.

'In that case, there's nothing more to say.'

'No.'

There were *several* more words she could have uttered, many of them blistering and not in the least ladylike. However, restraint in this instance was a favoured option.

'Fine.' She turned towards the back door and walked from his kitchen, then crossed the stretch of lawn and garden separating each cottage.

Her car stood in the carport, and, making a split-second decision, she went indoors, changed her clothes, caught up her bag and mobile phone, then locked up the cottage, slid behind the wheel and reversed down the driveway.

Within minutes she gained the main road leading onto the northern highway. The Gold Coast was only two hours' drive away. Shopping centres, movies, glitzy boutiques. Just the place to escape to, Anneke decided.

She had travelled less than five minutes when her mobile phone rang, and she automatically activated it.

'Tell me where you're going, and what time you expect to be home.'

Her stomach performed a backwards somersault at the sound of Sebastian's voice on the line. It sounded impossibly deep, his accent more pronounced.

Anneke took a deep, steadying breath. 'Go to hell.' Then she cut the connection.

It should have made her feel better. Instead, she felt more and more like an angry juvenile kicking out against authority.

Examining the situation analytically, she was allowing emotions to overrule common sense.

Damn. She thumped a fist against the steering wheel. This contrary ambivalence was ridiculous.

Without further thought she slowed down and pulled off to the side of the road. She caught up her mobile phone and prepared to punch in digits she realised she didn't have. Sure, he'd written down his number, but that was on a piece of paper tucked into a teletex in her aunt's kitchen.

OK, all she had to do was ring directory service. Two minutes later she de-activated the call, and groaned with frustration. Sebastian Lanier's phone number was ex-directory.

One car passed, then another. She didn't notice the Range Rover ease to a halt behind her, nor was she aware as the driver slid out from behind the wheel and trod the bitumen to the passenger side of her car.

A firm tap on the glass was the first indication she had of anyone's presence.

Anneke's head swung towards the window, and even as her elbow moved in automatic reflex to punch down the central locking device the passenger door opened and Sebastian slid into the passenger seat.

His eyes were dark, almost black, his expression grim and unrelenting.

'Careless,' he drawled. 'Very careless.'

'My knight in shining armour,' Anneke mocked. Her eyes were sheer crystalline emerald.

One day soon he would take that spitting tongue of hers and tame it. Was she aware just how close he was to doing it now?

His eyes seared hers as he placed an arm along the top of her seat. 'Co-operate, Anneke, and we'll get along fine.'

It was impossible to ignore the clean male smell of him, the faint aroma of aftershave. Just as it was impossible to dismiss the way her pulse tripped and raced to a quickened beat in his presence.

'The moment the police discover the source of your nuisance calls,' Sebastian assured her with a degree of cynicism, 'you're as free as a bird.' His expression hardened. 'Now, tell me where you're going, what time you expect to return.'

Her chin tilted and her eyes assumed a fiery brilliance. 'What if I don't?'

'That was the first option,' Sebastian said hardily. 'The second is for me to tag along with you.'

'Don't be ridiculous!'

'Choose, Anneke.'

'And if I don't have any set plans?'

'The second option applies.'

Why was she fighting him? She couldn't win. He wouldn't allow it.

She took a deep breath, then slowly released it and handed him her mobile phone. 'Press "redial", and you'll discover I was trying to reach you for the sole purpose of relaying my whereabouts on the Gold Coast and estimated time of return.' When he didn't take the phone, she hit the 'redial' button and pressed the unit to his ear. 'Except your number is ex-directory, and not even the citing of an emergency would reveal it.'

She delved into her bag, pulled out a piece of paper and a pen and thrust them at him, watching as he stroked a series of digits, then handed back the paper.

'Satisfied?' she demanded.

'Ring me when you leave the Coast.'

It wasn't negotiable, and she didn't even bother to refuse him. Although it was impossible not to resort to sarcasm. 'Do we synchronise our watches?'

Sebastian cast her a look that was more expressive than mere words, then he reached for the door clasp and slid out from the seat. 'Drive carefully.'

He closed the door, then covered the distance to his Range Rover.

Anneke watched him in the rear vision mirror, then she activated the ignition, eased the car onto the road.

It should have been a wonderful day. The sun shone brightly in a clear azure sky. The temperature soared to a midsummer high. With only two weeks to go before Christmas, the shops bore colourful decorations and there was an air of expectancy among the many shoppers filling the malls and walkways.

Christmas carols, and a store Santa handing out lollies and balloons to eager children added festive anticipatory cheer.

Anneke had thought to spend Christmas with Aunt Vivienne, but now it appeared she'd be spending it alone.

She could fly to Seattle, join her mother and stepfather for a 'yours, mine and ours' family Christmas.

Or, alternatively, there was her father, happily ensconced in London, who would welcome her into *his* extended family.

A small body careened into her legs, and she held onto the runaway child, soothing the little boy until a harassed and very pregnant young mother caught up to him.

Within minutes her mobile phone rang, and after a moment's hesitation she answered the call. There was a sense of relief to discover it was a friend from Sydney, wanting to exchange mutual news. Difficult in the face of that friendship not to reveal her whereabouts, although 'the Gold Coast' was hardly a fabrication. She simply didn't add that she was only there for the day.

Lunch comprised a salad sandwich washed down by mineral water in an upmarket café, and afterwards she selected a number of Christmas cards.

Her mobile phone rang again while she hovered in a specialist boutique specialising in imported toiletries, and she gave the sales assistant a helpless shrug accompanied by a faint smile, then moved to one side to gain a little privacy.

'Anneke.' The familiar male voice was quiet, almost restrained, but very clear on the line, and her stomach flipped as she gripped the phone.

'Adam.' Calm, keep calm. Act nonchalant, a tiny voice persisted.

'Bitch,' he hissed before she had a chance to disconnect the call. 'No woman runs out on me.'

'There's a first time for everything,' she said crisply. 'Chalk it up to experience.'

'Didn't think I could find you, did you, sweetheart?'

Relief, revulsion…both washed over her in realisation that Adam had been the source. 'Making nuisance calls wasn't very smart, Adam.'

'Payback time,' he dismissed. His voice lowered to a seductive drawl. 'You should have played with me; we could have had a ball.' He proceeded to explain his sexual preferences in graphic detail. 'Pity, but I value my skin, and you've proven to be way too much trouble. *Ciao*, darling. Have a good life.'

Anneke closed the phone and replaced it in her bag. She should, she silently castigated herself, have cut the connection as soon as she heard his voice. Now she simply felt angry, sickened, as his words echoed and re-echoed inside her head.

CHAPTER SEVEN

THE impetus to continue shopping was sadly lacking. She needed a different image, something to distract her from dwelling on Adam's bitter invective.

There was a multiple number of cinemas within the shopping complex. She'd go buy a ticket and choose a film to view.

A film about the *Titanic* was currently showing, and it was after six when she entered the car park, located her car and slid in behind the wheel.

Her mobile phone message-bank listed that two calls had been received during her cinema sojourn. One was from Sebastian, the other from the police. She contacted the duty sergeant at the designated number, who relayed the fact that trace on her aunt's telephone had been successful, then contacted Sebastian.

He picked up on the second ring. 'Lanier.'

A concise, deep voice that had the ability to raise goosebumps on the surface of her skin.

'Anneke.' She barely paused a second. 'I'm leaving now.' She cut the connection, then switched on the ignition and eased the car down several floors to street level.

The drive to Byron Bay was uneventful, and soon after

crossing the Queensland-New South Wales border she passed paddocks high with mature sugar cane. Banana plantations dotted the distant rolling hills, and there were avocado farms, and rich, fertile soil revealing row upon row of pineapples.

Dusk fell swiftly, the shadows lengthening and deepening as light gave way to dark, and it was almost nine when she pulled in beneath the carport adjacent her aunt's cottage.

She switched off the ignition, left her numerous purchases in the boot, then locked the car and trod the path to Sebastian's back door.

Five minutes, ten at the most, then she'd leave.

The screen door was unlocked, and Shaef stood on the other side, tail swishing back and forth in welcome.

Anneke knocked and entered the kitchen, then moved down the hall. Sebastian had had part of the wall between two bedrooms removed. A large executive desk complete with a state-of-the-art computer sat in the middle of one room, and the other was lined from floor to ceiling with bookshelves. In the centre of the room was a large antique buttoned leather armchair, with a matching ottoman, and a standard lamp. Combined, it made a large office-cum-library.

He looked up from the sheaf of papers he was studying, and leaned back in his chair.

'Take a seat.' He indicated one of two sited on the other side of the desk.

'I'd really prefer to keep this short.'

He noted the weary curve of her shoulders, the faint lines of strain marring an otherwise smooth forehead.

Shaef moved forward, nuzzled her hand, then slumped at her feet.

Sebastian sent her a long, considering look. 'Sit down.'

'Still giving orders?'

He ignored the sally, his eyes dark and far too discerning. 'Have you eaten?'

Food, in any shape or form, would probably make her ill. 'I had something earlier.' It wasn't exactly a lie.

'I'll make some tea.' He rose to his feet, crossed round the desk, then moved into the hall.

Anneke could hear the distant sound of water flowing from a tap, the faint hum of an electric kettle as it heated, the chink of crockery.

She closed her eyes. It had been a hell of a day. And it wasn't over yet.

Sebastian re-entered the room, saw the fringe of lashes touching each cheek, the pale, translucent skin.

She was beat, and without doubt emotionally exhausted.

He placed the cup and saucer near the edge of the desk, and watched her nostrils flare slightly as the aroma of bergamot teased the air. Her lashes lifted, then swept upwards in a slow, curving arc.

'Thanks.'

It was hot, heaven, and sweeter than she preferred. She took another appreciative sip, then put the cup carefully back onto the saucer.

'I guess you know the police scored a positive trace to Adam's mobile phone?'

Sebastian leaned one hip against the edge of the desk. 'Yes.'

She tilted her head and looked at him. 'Thank you for your concern.' He deserved that. 'And your help.'

'As I recall, you weren't too keen to accept either,' Sebastian said drily.

No, she hadn't been. 'You were very controlling.'

One eyebrow rose, and his mouth curved with a tinge of humour. 'I'm surprised you don't add "manipulative".'

'That, too,' Anneke agreed.

'Did it ever occur to you to question *why*?'

With just a few words their conversation had taken a subtle shift, and she wasn't comfortable with the change. 'Maybe we can continue this another time.' She stood to her feet, and immediately wished she hadn't, for it brought her much closer to him than she would have liked. 'Although it really isn't necessary, is it?' She took a backward step, and missed the faint gleam of amusement apparent in those dark eyes.

'You think not? Perhaps I'd better clarify it.' He reached for her shoulders and pulled her forward until she stood anchored between his thighs. Then he slowly lowered his head and brushed his lips against her temple. 'Are you beginning to get the picture?'

One hand slid down her back and cupped her buttocks, while the other slipped up to hold fast her head.

'Sebastian—'

His lips feathered down to the edge of her mouth, lingered there, then teased a trail of light kisses along the full lower curve.

'I don't think this is a—'

'Good idea?' He slid his tongue between her lips and felt rather than heard her breath catch.

'No,' Anneke whispered, as her heart raced to a faster beat, and heat flared through her veins.

His mouth was a soft caress as his hands moulded her close.

A kiss, she told herself. That's all it is. Why, she could even persuade herself that it didn't mean anything. Nothing at all. Men had kissed her before, in friendship, affection, and with a lover's passion.

She lifted her hands and linked them together at his nape, then leant in against him to enjoy the sensation of closeness. And came seriously unstuck when his mouth firmed on her own.

He'd kissed her before, as a questing, seeking experiment, and as a form of angry punishment.

This, *this* was different. Very different. It was both possession and promise. And it made her feel terribly afraid.

He had the touch, the instinctive skill of a man well versed in a woman's needs. His hands, his fingers, knew when to glide, where to caress, to drive her wild.

It was as if every sensitive nerve-end quivered in anticipation, then shrieked at each teasing stroke, every light pinch.

Dear God, she was silk, her skin satin-smooth, and each erogenous zone reacted like fire to his touch. He wanted to free her beautiful body of the restriction of clothes, to explore each indentation, each curve, until she moaned with delight, then begged for release.

That it would be him, only him she saw when he drove himself into her and made her his own. And him, only him, who had the power to take her to the brink, then tip her over the edge. He who held her tight and caught her when she fell.

His fingers sought the clip fastening of her bra and deftly released it, then he slid his hand to cup the fullness of her breast, teased its hardened peak, then trailed his mouth down her throat to the creamy crest. And felt her resistance.

What was she doing? This had gone way beyond mutual exploration, or mutual gratitude.

Anneke could feel the evidence of his arousal, the hard potent shaft beneath the zip of his jeans as it pressed high against his belt. Sensual heat emanated from his skin, and the beat of his heart was hard and deep.

His mouth settled on hers, persuasive, evocative and devastatingly sensual.

It would be easy, so very easy to let him take her wherever he wanted to go. To give in to the magic he promised and just enjoy whatever the night might hold.

Yet, no matter what the enticement, casual sex wasn't her style.

It took considerable effort to retreat, to drag her mouth from his and push herself to arm's length. More to quieten her fast-beating heart and attempt to regain her breath.

'I think,' Anneke enunciated unevenly, 'it would be best if I left. Now,' she added, dropping her hands from his arms.

'Best for whom?'

'Me. You. Us,' she added for good measure. 'I mean, there is no *us*.' This was getting worse with every passing second. 'It's just—'

'Quit while you're ahead,' Sebastian advised gently, watching the fleeting change of expression chase across her features as she struggled for control.

He could pull her close, wreak havoc with that beautiful mouth, and take her here. On the desk, the floor. It didn't matter.

And that was the part that bothered him. He'd always displayed *finesse* with a woman. Wining, dining, flowers, pretty compliments. Sex by mutual consent, albeit that it might be wild or restrained. Rarely had he felt the urge to tear clothes from a female body, abrade her skin with his mouth, his hands, and join himself with her like a plundering conqueror.

He admired women...their strengths, their weaknesses, their passion. He respected their innate femininity. And he had enjoyed them. No serious commitment, no strings attached.

Until now.

Now he was captivated as never before by a smile, the way her mouth curved to tilt at the edges. The sweep of long lashes and the lure of a pair of green eyes which lightened or deepened according to mood.

She was fire and ice, passion and fury. And he wanted her in a way that he'd never wanted a woman before.

'Thanks for—' Her voice wasn't quite steady. 'Being there for me.'

He leaned forward and brushed a finger down the slope of her nose. 'My pleasure.'

'Really?' A faint smile teased the edges of her mouth as she moved back a pace. 'We've been at daggers drawn most of the time.'

It was his turn to smile. There was a dangerous quality evident in the darkness of his eyes, a latent passion which, unleashed, would sweep her way out of her depth. It was there in his expression, the forceful set of his features, the stance that was studiously relaxed. Like the watching eye of a tiger, just waiting to pounce.

Go, a tiny voice taunted. Don't linger.

Without a further word she turned and walked from the room, traversed the hall and let herself out of the back door.

Shaef shadowed her steps as she crossed the path connecting the two properties, and she leant forward to fondle his ears as she unlocked the cottage, then sent him on his way before she stepped inside.

The house was quiet, and she took a long, cool shower, slipped on a robe, then she delved into the refrigerator for a light snack.

Television provided instant visual entertainment, but there was little that captured her attention, even less that held her interest.

It had been a long day, and she took time to examine each and every incident in the hope that reflection would bring peace of mind.

Fat chance. All it did was prove she was too wired to simply fall into bed and covet sleep.

In desperation she selected a book, settled into an armchair, and tried to lose herself in the characters and plot of a favourite author.

Five minutes later she thrust it down. On impulse she went into the bedroom, discarded the robe and slipped into shorts and top.

Within seconds she left the cottage and made her way down onto the beach.

The moon was high in the sky, bathing everything with a pale opalescent glow. Shadows from a clump of palm trees cast long fingers over the sand, and the sea was a mass of silver and dappled pewter that stretched right out to the horizon.

Anneke walked along the damp sand left by an outgoing tide, and breathed in deeply of the clean night air.

There was a whimper, a short bark, then Shaef fell in step at her side.

'Unable to sleep?'

She should have known Sebastian would investigate Shaef's departure. Yesterday, even this morning, she would have resented his presence.

'I figured a walk might help.' It was impossible to detect his expression in the moonlight.

They walked in silence for a few minutes, and she was aware of him in a way she found vaguely frightening.

Somehow she'd known he was trouble from the moment she first caught sight of him.

At first she'd thought it was just chemistry. Sensual sexual magnetism at its most potent. An electric awareness that was both foolish and capricious.

'Want to talk about it?'

Anneke heard Sebastian's words, examined them, and took solace from the shadow of semi-darkness. How could she say that it was *he* who was on her mind, *him* disturbing her thoughts?

'Adam rang me this afternoon.'

Sebastian's voice became a silky drawl. 'Foolish of him.'

'Very,' she replied in succinct agreement.

'I imagine the conversation went from bad to worse?'

'You could say that.' She turned her head and looked out over the silver sea. There didn't seem to be any need to fill the gaps in between, or repeat the vicious personal attack. It was over. That was all that mattered.

By tacit consent they turned and began retracing their steps.

'Have dinner with me tomorrow night.'

Anneke directed him a faintly humorous glance. 'You want me to prepare a meal for two, then sit down at your table?'

'I had a seafood restaurant in mind, overlooking Byron Bay. Silver service, wine steward, waiters,' Sebastian indicated with unruffled ease.

'I get to wear stiletto heels, make-up?' She laughed, a

delightful light sound that held genuine mirth. 'OK. You're on. What time?'

'Six.'

When they reached Aunt Vivienne's cottage he stood aside while she inserted the key into the lock, then he turned and cut a leisurely stride to his own home.

She tried to tell herself she wasn't disappointed he'd made no attempt to touch her.

CHAPTER EIGHT

ANNEKE'S wardrobe of formal and semi-formal wear was reasonably extensive. The only problem being that most of that particular range of her clothes hung in the closet of her Sydney apartment.

In her rush to escape her job, Adam and the city, she'd simply dragged down a suitcase and pulled clothes off hangers, out of drawers, and flung them willy-nilly into the case.

Her proposed sojourn on an isolated beach had lent itself to including casual shorts and tops, jeans. Not elegant after-five wear, or extravagant high-heeled pumps.

It was a clear choice between a classic black dress, or a long floral slip.

The black dress won out, and she tended to her make-up with care, left her hair loose, and was about to catch up her purse when she heard Sebastian's Range Rover pull into the driveway.

Anneke reached the door as Sebastian trod the path, and the breath caught in her throat at the sight of him.

Attired in dark tailored trousers, matching jacket, and white shirt and tie, he was the antithesis of the man she was accustomed to seeing every day.

The image unsettled her. It was crazy to feel nervous, but she couldn't prevent the heavy thud of her heart, or the unwarranted apprehension which curled round her nerve-ends.

'Hi,' she greeted brightly. Too brightly?

Polite conversation had never been more difficult, and she waited until Sebastian reached the highway before querying, 'How long have you lived next door to my aunt?'

'Five years.'

'Yet during each of my visits I've never caught sight of you.'

He turned his head and cast her a quick glance. 'I travel around a bit in between finishing one book and starting the next.'

'Publicity tours?'

'Yes. And research.'

'You'd represent a publishing promoter's dream. The height, the arresting looks, combined with more than a hint of the dark and dangerous. The women would flock to the literary luncheons, the book-signings.'

'A compliment, Anneke?' he queried with deceptive mildness. 'Or a condemnation?'

She subjected him to a detailed appraisal, and took her time giving a considered opinion. 'Oh, a compliment.' Her eyes travelled up and met his briefly. 'I don't doubt you handle it all with consummate charm.' Except there would be an absence of ego, she determined silently.

She watched as he entered town and eased the vehicle into a car park. He cut the engine and removed the key from the ignition. 'Shall we go?'

The restaurant Sebastian had chosen specialised in seafood, and she ordered prawn cocktail as a starter, sea perch as a main course with vegetables, and she declined dessert.

Sebastian merely doubled her order, added prawns and scallops to his dish, then requested the wine steward bring champagne.

'We're celebrating?'

He dismissed the tasting ritual, and indicated both flutes be filled. Then he touched the rim of his flute to her own. 'To friendship.'

Friendship? Could a woman be *friend* to a man such as Sebastian Lanier? Somehow Anneke doubted there would be any half-measures. Sebastian might observe the court-ship dance, with its seeking manoeuvres, but when he'd staked his claim it would be all or nothing.

She had the strangest feeling that dinner this evening in semi-formal surroundings was the first step he intended she take to...*what*? His bed?

Their starter arrived, and she bit into the first of three succulent prawns doused with a delicate sauce and set on a bed of shredded lettuce.

It was difficult to sit opposite a man at a dinner table and not subconsciously observe the way he ate. Whether he stabbed his food with the fork, how he employed the knife. If his use of the cutlery was precise, or merely utilitarian. Body language, despite an adherence to good manners, tended to be revealing.

'Where will you spend Christmas?'

Anneke lifted her head and was unable to discern much from his gaze. 'I haven't made any definite plans.' She lifted her flute and sipped some champagne, then replaced it down onto the table. 'What about you?'

He pushed his entrée plate to one side and leaned back in his chair. 'Paris.'

The city of love. The Arc de Triomphe, Champs Elysées,

the Eiffel Tower, the Left Bank and the River Seine. Misty grey skies, drizzling rain; the cold. But the ambience…

Anneke stifled a sigh. 'You have family there?'

'Grandmère.' His expression softened, his mouth relaxed and his eyes held reflective warmth. 'Her eightieth birthday falls on Christmas Day.'

She could imagine the gathering, and felt vaguely envious. To be involved, to be part of it… The laughter, love. Gifts and giving.

'When do you fly out?'

'Friday week.'

A lump settled inside her stomach. In eight days he would leave, and when he returned she'd be gone.

The waiter appeared with their main course, and she viewed the grilled sea perch with its artistically displayed vegetables with perfunctory interest. All of a sudden her appetite seemed to have fled.

How long had she known this man? A week? Yet, while his presence had alternately annoyed and inflamed her, there was a pull of the senses, almost as if something was exigent, forcing recognition on some deep, primal level.

There was a part of her that urged compliance, a devilish spontaneity uncaring of anything except *now*.

And that was dangerous. Infinitely dangerous. Somehow she couldn't imagine it being easy to sample what Sebastian Lanier had to offer, then calmly turn and walk away.

It was better, far better not to engage in anything at all. Besides, what could happen in a week?

Anneke picked at the fish, sampled each of the vegetables, returned to the fish, then replaced her cutlery down onto the plate.

'The fish isn't to your liking?'

She glanced up and met Sebastian's perceptive gaze. 'No, it's fine. I'm just not that hungry.'

He speared a small scallop from his plate and held it temptingly close to her mouth. 'Try this. It's perfection.'

There was an implied intimacy in the gesture, and her eyes widened slightly, then stilled as she was held mesmerised by the sensual warmth apparent in the dark grey eyes of the man seated opposite.

Anneke felt as if she was damned if she took the morsel, and equally damned if she didn't.

'It's easy,' Sebastian said gently. 'Just open your mouth.'

She hesitated another second, then leant forward and took the scallop from his fork with her teeth.

Act, a tiny voice prompted. 'Superb texture,' she commented, and glimpsed the latent humour apparent.

'More?' The query was a soft, sensual drawl, and she shook her head as she reached for her glass.

What was the matter with her? Even the champagne tasted different.

The waiter appeared and removed both plates, queried their preference for tea or coffee.

'Tea—Earl Grey,' Anneke qualified, while Sebastian chose black coffee.

There was music, and a small dance floor, with two couples moving together as a slow ballad emitted from strategically placed speakers.

'Dance with me.'

She looked at him carefully, and knew she should refuse. There was something evident in his expression she couldn't quite define. Sensuality, intoxicating and mesmeric. Bewitching chemistry at its zenith.

Anneke gathered her napkin and placed it on the table,

then stood to her feet and allowed Sebastian to lead her to the dance floor.

He caught her close with natural ease, his steps fluid as he led her slowly round the small square.

She could close her eyes and pretend there was no one else around. Slide her hands up over his shoulders and link them together at his nape. Undo the leather clasp that bound his hair, then thread her fingers at will through its length.

The image remained with her of how he'd looked the first night she'd caught sight of him in her aunt's kitchen. A five o'clock shadow that had deepened into dark stubble, his hair loose and tousled. Even then she'd thought him lethal. *Shameless*, when he'd captured her head and bestowed a plundering kiss.

One ballad led on to another, and it was more than five minutes before the pace changed to something upbeat.

Sebastian led her back to the table. 'More tea?'

'No.' It was after ten. They'd eaten a leisurely meal, enjoyed a dance. There was no reason to linger. 'Would you mind if we leave?'

Sebastian settled the bill, and they walked to the car park. Within minutes the Range Rover eased its way onto the road, then picked up speed as they left the town behind.

Headlights shone twin beams into the encroaching darkness, and Anneke leaned her head back and focused on the road.

At this time of night there wasn't much traffic, and all too soon Sebastian reached the turn-off leading down to both cottages.

Anneke reached for the door-clasp as soon as he switched off the engine.

'Come in and share a drink with me.'

Every nerve in her body screamed an emphatic *no*. 'It's late, and I'm tired.' Did she sound as breathless as she felt? Dear heaven, she hoped not!

He caught hold of her hand and lifted it to his lips. 'You can sleep in tomorrow.'

'Sebastian—'

He stilled her voice by the simple expediency of pressing a hand over her mouth. 'Anneke.' His voice held a teasing quality. 'Are you afraid of me?'

She hesitated a fraction too long. 'No, of course not.'

His smile was warm and infinitely sensual. 'Then come share a coffee with me.'

Ten minutes, she compromised. She'd drink the coffee, then she'd go home.

Shaef greeted them at the door with restrained delight, and sank down at Anneke's feet as she chose the informality of the kitchen in preference to the lounge.

Sebastian shrugged off his jacket and discarded his tie, then he crossed to the sink and filled the coffee-maker with water, ground fresh beans and spooned them into the filter, then depressed the switch. 'Milk or cream?' He crossed to a cupboard and extracted two cups and saucers.

'Milk.'

He opened the refrigerator door, and she saw what looked suspiciously like her *bombe au chocolat*. Beside it was the sponge stuffed with strawberries and cream.

'You should throw them out.'

He shot her an amused glance. 'Not yet. I like to look at them.'

Her voice came out as a strangled sound. 'Why?'

He extracted a carton of milk and closed the refrigera-

tor door. 'Because it reminds me of how much trouble you
went to trying to kill me with indigestion.'

Of course he knew. How could he not?

'I was intrigued to know what you'd dream up to
serve me next.'

The coffeemaker completed its cycle, and Sebastian
took hold of the carafe and filled both cups.

'It was a challenge,' she conceded with a tinge of
humour. She spooned in sugar, stirred, then sipped the
contents. 'I owe you a meal. A decent one,' she qualified.

'An attempt to redeem yourself?'

'I'll go one better,' she said solemnly. 'Give me a menu,
and I'll prepare the food. Do you prefer vegetables or salad?'

'Vegetables. Buttered baby potatoes in their jackets,
asparagus with hollandaise sauce, honeyed carrots.'

'Dessert?'

'You.'

Anneke's eyes flew wide. 'Sorry, I don't decorate body
parts. Suggest something more conventional.'

He replaced his cup, removed hers, then captured her
hands and pulled her towards him. 'Will this do?'

She didn't have a chance to answer. His mouth closed
over hers in a gentle exploration that melted her bones.

Hands moulded her close as he deepened the kiss, and
she opened her mouth to him, slid the tip of her tongue
beneath the hardness of his own, and felt his breath catch.

Anneke wasn't quite ready for the long, sweeping
response as he took her from pleasure to possession, then
staked a claim.

It was all she could do to hang on and ride the storm of
his passion.

No one had kissed her with quite this degree of

hunger, and her whole body throbbed beneath his explosive touch as he began a trail of discovery of each and every pleasure pulse.

His mouth left hers and sought the vulnerable column of her throat, the delicate hollow, the edge of her neck, before slipping low to the soft curve of her breast.

Somehow the zip fastening at the back of her dress slid free, and the tiny shoestring straps were eased over each shoulder.

An indistinguishable moan died in her throat as deft fingers teased a sensitive peak to hardness, then rendered a similar supplication to its twin.

He took her to the brink between pleasure and pain, then trailed his mouth down to suckle each tender nub until she moved restlessly against him.

It wasn't enough, not nearly enough, and a soundless gasp escaped her lips as one hand slid to the apex between her thighs, teased the thin silk barrier of her briefs, only to retreat.

Anneke whimpered in protest, then she caught hold of his head and brought his mouth to her own in fierce possession, testing his control.

She'd thought to delight in his loss of it, but nothing prepared her for the deep, penetrating invasion that took hold of her emotions and tossed them high.

Her hands reached for his shoulders and she simply clung to him until the storm inside began to diminish. Slowly, ever so slowly, he lightened the kiss until his lips merely brushed against her own, then he linked his arms at the base of her spine.

His eyes were dark, so dark they were almost black, and there was a waiting quality evident beneath the sensual warmth.

The next move was hers. He was giving her the option to move away from him, say any words by way of excuse, then leave.

If she stayed, it would be because she wanted to, not due to any unfair persuasion on his part.

Indecision warred temporarily as she fought desire with sanity.

How could you know a man for months, a year, *longer*, yet not really know him at all? Then meet another, and see almost at once the heart of the man beneath the many layers fashioned by time and experience?

She could turn away and never know the joy he offered, or the depth of emotion they could share. Yet what was the price she might have to pay?

Sadly, she had the feeling it would be way too high.

'I think I'd better go.'

Sebastian leaned forward and brushed his lips against her forehead. 'I could tell you not to think. Just to feel.'

She lifted her head and met his steady gaze. There was a depth apparent that frightened her. Not out of a sense of threat, but something she was too afraid to define.

'I know.' Her voice came out as a husky whisper. She even managed a shaky smile. 'But you won't.'

He let his arms fall to his sides, and watched the fleeting emotions chase across her expressive features.

Then he watched as she took a backward step, then turned and walked to the door.

'Be ready at nine.'

Her hand froze as she reached for the latch, and she cast him a startled glance over one shoulder.

'Our picnic, remember?' A slow smile spread his mouth. 'I'll organise the food.'

Anneke recovered quickly. 'Nine.' Then she opened the door and closed it quietly behind her.

She'd left a light on inside her aunt's cottage, and it provided a welcoming glow as she crossed the path.

Sleep didn't come easily. Nor did peace of mind. But then she hadn't expected it to.

CHAPTER NINE

ANNEKE woke at dawn, opened one eye, groaned, then rolled over and tried to capture sleep. Two hours would be great, but she'd settle for one.

Ten minutes later she gave up on it and slid out of bed. An early-morning swim, then she'd shower, have breakfast, and package the small Christmas cakes designated as gifts ready to consign to the postal services tomorrow.

She expected to see Sebastian on the beach, but he was nowhere in sight. She ran the length of the cove, then stripped down to her swimsuit for a leisurely swim.

It was almost eight-thirty when Aunt Vivienne rang to report that Elise was progressing so well the doctors were confident she'd go close to full term.

'How are you getting on with Sebastian, Anneke?'

Oh, my, now there was a question! What would her kindly aunt think if Anneke went with total honesty and said she was on the verge of going to bed with him?

'Fine.' That covered a multitude of contingencies.

'Why don't you fly up and join us for Christmas, darling? I know Sebastian is going to Paris, and I don't like to think of you at the cottage alone.'

'That's thoughtful of you,' Anneke declared warmly,

grateful for the option of spending the festive season with family.

It was almost nine when she smoothed a hand down the seam of her designer jeans, then slid nervous fingers along the ribbed hem of the skinny top she'd chosen to wear.

A knock on the door heralded Sebastian's arrival, and she caught hold of her bag, collected her sunglasses, then crossed to open the kitchen door.

Clad in dark blue jeans and a black shirt with the sleeves rolled part-way up each forearm, he looked far too vibrant for any girl's peace of mind.

'Good morning.'

Sunglasses made it impossible for her to detect his expression, and she matched his smile with one of her own.

Sebastian headed the Range Rover north when they reached the open highway.

'Where are we going?'

'The Gold Coast hinterland. Lamington National Park, O'Reilly's.' He spared her a warm glance. 'We'll feed the lorikeets, have lunch, then maybe head down to Surfers Paradise for an hour or two.'

The sun was hot, tempered by a slight breeze, and Anneke was delighted by the friendly lorikeets. Feeding time was something else as the brightly coloured green and red plumed parrots settled on her arms then walked up onto her shoulders. Some even settled on her head, and she laughed when one became over-curious with the band confining her hair. His claws became tangled in the single thick plait, and his squawking brought Sebastian to the rescue.

'Hold still.'

'Believe me, I wouldn't think of doing anything else,' she assured him as he moved in close.

Too close. She was intensely aware of his shirt-clad chest and shoulders only mere inches from her cheek. Clean fabric mingled with the faint musky tones of his aftershave, and played havoc with her senses.

'He won't hurt you,' Sebastian murmured. 'He's just frightened.'

That makes two of us. But it wasn't the parrot she was afraid of.

'There,' Sebastian reassured. 'He's free.' He caught hold of her chin and lifted it. 'His claws didn't scratch you?'

'No.' Her mouth was inches away from his, and she had to control the temptation to reach up and pull his head down to hers.

'Hungry?'

'Yes.' It was true. The mountain air had given her an appetite.

'Come on, then.' He caught hold of her hand and tugged her towards the path leading to where the land cruiser was parked.

Sebastian unlocked the rear door and opened up a portable cooler. *'Voilà.'*

There were fresh steaks, crisp lettuce, fresh fruit, mineral water and a bottle of wine.

'You came prepared.'

His eyes challenged hers. 'Always.'

She doubted if anyone had managed to gain the element of surprise with this man. He was intensely vital, acutely alert, and far too discerning to be caught unawares.

Gas-fired barbecues were positioned at intervals on a grassed area adjacent the car park, and there were tables with fixed umbrellas to shade picnic-makers from the sun.

Sebastian took hold of the cooler. 'Let's grab a niche over there. I'll cook the steaks while you mix the salad.'

They drank a glass of superb Lambrusco with their meal, and washed the fruit down with mineral water.

Anneke rose to her feet and stacked plates and cutlery into a plastic bag ready to place in the cooler.

'Feeling energetic?'

She lifted both shoulders in a light shrugging gesture. 'Not particularly.'

So she hadn't slept much either. After an hour of tossing and turning, he'd pulled on a pair of jeans, booted up the computer and worked until three.

He collected the cooler and stored it in the rear of the Range Rover. 'Then let's head down to the Coast.'

More than an hour later they were seated at one of many tables overlooking the broadwater, savouring cappuccinos. It was a relaxed atmosphere, with numerous people wandering the boardwalk, admiring the many craft moored at the adjacent marina.

The physique, the hair, the dark, attractive features earned Sebastian more than a few covetous glances from the women who passed by their table.

'Oh, my,' Anneke declared, *sotto voce*. 'I think you have made a conquest. That's the second time one particular blonde has walked this way. Perhaps I should go powder my nose and leave a clear field?'

'Do that, and I'll take evasive action,' Sebastian drawled.

'You'll go powder *your* nose?'

He tipped his sunglasses further down his nose and speared her a level look over the rims. 'Kiss you in such a manner there'll be no doubt *you* are my only interest.'

'Wouldn't you be taking an enormous risk?' Anneke

queried sweetly. 'I might push you over the railing into the water.'

'Then we'd both look foolish,' he intoned lazily as he leaned forward and trailed light fingers down her cheek.

Her eyes dilated fractionally at his featherlight touch, and her lips quivered as he traced their fullness with his thumb.

'You've been treading on eggshells all day,' he said gently. 'Waiting for me to pounce?'

She held his gaze. 'I think you have a strategy,' she said with innate honesty. 'I just need to figure out which ploy you intend to use.'

Sebastian laughed, a soft, chuckling sound deep in his throat. He stood to his feet, anchored a ten-dollar bill beneath one saucer, then reached for her hand. 'Come on, let's walk.'

They explored the upmarket shopping complex, then wandered to the wharf market where fresh seafood was sold direct from the fish trawlers.

Anneke examined the prawns, the many varieties of crustaceans. They looked succulent, mouthwatering. 'I promised you dinner.' She shot him a teasing grin. 'Are you willing to trust me?'

'You want to take some of these home?'

'I'm buying,' she insisted as he extracted his wallet. 'I mean it,' she said fiercely.

He lifted both hands in the air. 'OK.'

She chose carefully, with the expertise of a market haggler, selecting, rejecting, until she was satisfied she had the best of the best.

'Let's get this into the cooler and head home.' Her mind was already busy with the preparation she needed to make, the time factor, a mental rundown of salad makings in the refrigerator.

It was almost seven when they reached the cottage. 'Give me an hour,' Anneke said as she extracted the seafood from the cooler. That would give her time to shower and change, and have the food ready on the table.

'I'll bring the wine.'

She managed it with five minutes to spare, and spent four of those minutes wondering if she should change blue jeans for black dress jeans, add blusher and eyeshadow or just stick with lipstick. Perfume?

A knock at the door precluded the necessity for either, and she crossed the kitchen and let him in.

Sebastian took the bottle of chilled white wine to the servery. 'Shall I open this?'

Anneke handed him the corkscrew. 'Please.'

He'd showered, shaved and changed into casual dark trousers and a pale blue shirt. Aunt Vivienne's kitchen wasn't large, and he seemed to fill it.

She extracted two glasses and set them on the table as he eased the cork out from the neck of the bottle.

'Anything I can do to help?'

'It's all done.' Did she sound as nervous as she felt?

He leaned forward and covered her mouth with his own, taking advantage of her surprise by bestowing an erotic tasting. He lingered a few seconds, then lifted his head.

She looked...momentarily startled, and her slight confusion pleased him. 'Shall we eat?'

Oysters mornay, chilli prawns, and crustaceans in their shells, split in half and the flesh coated with a delicate sauce and grilled. Fresh salad greens, and a baguette she'd heated to crunchy perfection in the oven.

'Magnificent,' Sebastian declared, with the pleasure of a man who had eaten well. 'More wine?'

'No,' Anneke refused quickly, and earned a slight smile.
'The need for a clear head?'

She didn't answer, didn't dare. 'I'll make coffee.'

Her movements were mechanical as she set up the
coffee-maker, and when she turned to open the cupboard
he was right there.

'Sebastian—' His lips settled over the vulnerable hollow
at the edge of her neck, and she lost track of whatever it
was she'd intended to say.

His mouth was warm, his tongue an erotic instrument as
he teased the pulsing cord, savoured it, then used the edge
of his teeth to take delicate nips from the sensitive hollows.

She made one last-ditch effort at protest, only to have
it die in her throat as he turned her fully into his arms and
covered her mouth with his own.

One hand lifted to cup her nape while the other slid
down her back and pressed her close against him.

His arousal was a potent force, and she felt her bones
begin to melt as liquid fire coursed through her veins. Each
sensory nerve-end was heightened to acute awareness, and
her body leaned in close to his as he deepened the kiss to
an imitation of the sexual act itself.

Anneke wanted to feel his flesh, taste him in a tactile exploration that would drive him wild. Her fingers slid to the
opening of his shirt, freed each button, then she trailed butterfly kisses across his chest, tangled her tongue in the whorls
of hair, took possession of one male nipple, and suckled.

His body shuddered, then tautened as firm hands
clasped hold of her waist, and it was she who cried out as
he lifted her onto the servery, then parted her thighs and
positioned himself between them.

His eyes were dark and impossibly slumberous as he

tugged her top free from her jeans, then pulled it over her head. The bra clip slipped open with ease, and he slid the straps down her arms and dispensed with the scrap of silk and lace.

Then he buried his face in the valley between her breasts and caressed the soft curves, tormented and teased each roseate peak, then trailed a path down to her navel.

Her jeans were a barrier he dispensed with with ease, tugging them free and dropping them onto the floor.

He kissed her, gently at first, then with an increasingly demanding possession, and when he at last lifted his head she could only look at him in shaken silence.

Sebastian didn't have to ask. The unspoken question was apparent in his stance, the liquid darkness of his eyes, the curve of his mouth.

A slight shudder ran through her body. If she turned away now, she'd never know his touch. And she wanted to, badly.

Not just the physical. She wanted more, much more than that. His heart, his soul. Everything.

Maybe, just maybe, she should take the gamble and run with it. Let emotions take her wherever he led.

A week could be a lifetime. And better to experience a week of heaven than never to experience it at all.

Slowly she reached out and slid her fingers to his nape, where a clip fastened the leather strip that bound his hair. Her eyes never left his as she slipped it free. Then she forked her fingers through the silken river of black, and spread it out so that it flowed onto his shoulders.

It gave him a rakish look that was pure pagan, primitive, and it was a gesture she'd wanted to make ever since she'd first stepped into this kitchen and found him making tea.

His smile was slow and infinitely sensual as he copied

her actions, releasing the thin elastic band at the base of her plait, then threading his fingers through the length of her hair.

It was the expression in his eyes that made her catch her breath and caused her pulse to quicken to a much faster beat.

'I think,' she said shakily, 'you'd better take me out of the kitchen and into the bedroom.'

He played the game, teasing her gently. 'You think so?'

'Otherwise I may never be able to cook or serve food in here again.'

Sebastian laughed. A deep, husky sound that curled into the recesses of her heart. 'Put your arms round my neck.'

Anneke did as she was told, and he kissed her long and deep, then he carried her through to the bedroom, switched on the light, and let her slide down to her feet.

In one easy movement he sought the pocket of his jeans, extracted a slim foil square and slipped it beneath one pillow.

Mesmerised, she stood still as he popped the studs on his jeans, then shucked them off. The thin covering of black silk sheathing his manhood followed, and her eyes widened at the sight of him.

His was a savage beauty. Primal, powerful. A man who could show great strength, even cruelty. Yet there was a tenderness apparent, an acute caring for those who were sufficiently fortunate to win his trust, his love.

Sebastian reached for her, pulling her in close as he tumbled them both down onto the bed. He was hungry for her, wanting, needing to sheath himself in the silken sweetness of woman. Not just any woman. *This* woman.

He needed to show her the difference. Knew, hoped, that she would *know*.

Anneke let her fingers splay over taut muscles at his

shoulders, trailed them to explore his ribcage, then slid down over his flanks to urge him close.

'*Non, mon ange*. We are just beginning.'

He took pleasure in the tasting of her skin, every inch of it, with the pads of his fingers, his lips. And felt her pulse quicken, her breath become erratic and fast.

Her body began to feel like the strings of a finely tuned violin, his touch creating magic that reverberated along each nerve fibre until her whole being *sang* to a tune that had never been played.

The feeling was so intense she could hardly bear it, and her hands became more urgent as she began to plead with him to ease the ache deep within.

He soothed her as she arched against him, caressing the moist heat with a touch that brought her to one explosive climax after another.

It wasn't enough, not nearly enough, and she became a wild wanton in his arms, pliant, bewitching, *his*.

He entered her slowly, allowing the silken tissues to stretch to accommodate him, then he drove forward with one powerful thrust.

Anneke gasped at the level of penetration, absorbed it, then met and matched his rhythm, unable to prevent the soft guttural cries that escaped her lips as he took her higher and higher to the brink, held her there, then caught her when she fell. And kissed the light tears as they trickled from her eyes.

Sebastian curled her close in the circle of his arms, and she dozed for a while, then stirred at the movement of a hand sliding low over one hip.

He was asleep. His breathing hadn't changed. She began a slow, tactile exploration of her own, skimming over warm skin, strong muscle and sinew to his pelvis, lightly examining the faint hollow, the keloid puckering of a surgical scar.

She let her fingers trail up over his ribcage to the dark smattering of hair on his chest. Hair that was light and springy, and different in texture from the glossy length he wore bound at his nape.

More than anything she wanted to explore the angles and planes of his sculpted features, the chiselled cheekbones, the hard jaw, the sensitive lines of his mouth.

Most of all she wanted to wake him. To feel again the power of his body as he joined it with hers. The acutely intense spiral of sensation that mixed pleasure with pain, then transcended both to rapturous ecstasy.

He'd shown her remarkable *tendresse*. Now she wanted his passion, unbridled, shameless and primitive.

A hand reached for hers, caught it, and brought it to his lips. Her heart almost stopped, then quickened to a faster beat as she raised her head and met a pair of dark eyes lambent with molten desire.

'You're awake.'

Without a word he kissed each finger in turn, savoured her palm, then grazed the fragile veins at her wrist.

One slight tug, and she lay sprawled across his chest.

She gained purchase on his shoulders and leant forward to kiss him, loving the feeling of power as he let her take control.

The sensual tasting tested his strength, and just when he thought he could stand it no longer she slid down onto him. Her movements were deliberately slow as she completed one erotic circle after another until it drove him wild. His hands bit into her waist, then splayed over her hips, holding her still as he drove into her again and again, until it was she who cried out, and their voices mingled in a mutual expression of wild, untamed passion.

Afterwards, when the spiralling subsided and their breathing returned to normal, he pulled her close and held her there.

Her hair was a mass of tangles from where he'd raked his hands through its length, and he soothed it gently, feeling its texture, the long silken strands that fell in a cloud over her shoulders.

He kissed her, long and deep, then he buried his mouth in the soft hollow of her neck as she slept.

Again and again they turned to each other in the night. As the light fingers of dawn filtered through the windows they rose from the bed and showered, only to return to bed to sleep until the shrill peal of the phone sounded loud in the morning stillness.

Sebastian kissed her briefly as she lifted her head and groaned. 'You'd better answer it, *mon amie*.'

Who could be ringing at this hour? She spared a glance at the bedside clock, and jolted upright. My God, *midday*!

She scrambled out of bed, grabbed the sheet and wrapped it round her naked form, then stumbled as the tucked-in portion stubbornly refused to part from the mattress.

Sebastian chuckled as she swore, and leaned forward to wrench it free.

Anneke raced into the kitchen, lifted the receiver and heard her aunt's anxious tones on the other end of the line.

Thinking quickly on her feet after a long night of loving and very little sleep was difficult. 'I was in the shower.' A necessary untruth, and she shivered as she felt Sebastian's lips nuzzle her neck. When his hands unbound the sheet, there was little she could do except shake her head at him in silent remonstrance.

'Is everything all right, darling?' Aunt Vivienne queried. 'You sound a little…strange.'

His lips sought her breasts, savoured the swollen peaks, then bit gently into the tender softness.

On a strangled note she ended the call, replaced the receiver, then allowed herself to be pulled into his arms.

'You're insatiable,' Anneke said unsteadily as his teeth nipped an earlobe.

'In a minute, I'm going to collect my clothes, go home, and spend what's left of the day at the computer.' His lips trailed to her temple, caressed the fast-beating pulse there, then travelled down to the edge of her mouth. 'I have a deadline to meet before I leave for Paris.'

She turned her mouth to meet his, and wondered if she'd ever be able to survive after he left. 'I'll bring dinner.'

'And stay.'

'Sebastian—'

'Stay, Anneke,' he repeated insistently. 'My bed, or yours. It doesn't matter.'

No, it didn't. To deny him was to deny herself.

CHAPTER TEN

THE days ran into each other, each one seeming more poignant than the last.

Sebastian rescheduled his work pattern from mid-morning to seven in the evening. Dinner was extended by an hour, and the nights were something else as their love-making took on a new dimension.

Anneke told herself she was happy, happier than she'd ever been. And she was. Except the dawn of each new day brought her one day closer to the time she'd have to bid Sebastian goodbye.

Wednesday they drove into Byron Bay township and consigned Sebastian's manuscript to his American agent via courier. Then they celebrated with champagne and dinner at the town's finest restaurant.

'Tomorrow we'll fly down to Sydney.'

Anneke heard the words, but didn't absorb them. 'What did you say?'

Sebastian's smile held a combination of humour and sensual warmth as he repeated the words.

Her heart flipped, then raced to a painful beat. 'We?'

'We,' he gently mocked. 'That will give you time to gather some clothes together, do any necessary shopping, and pack.'

'Pack?'

'You're coming with me to Paris.'

Her mind whirled at the implication, and her stomach began to compete with the erratic beat of her heart. 'What about a passport, visa—'

'Your passport is valid.' His eyes gleamed with humour as her mouth opened, then shut again. 'Vivienne,' he revealed succinctly.

'You've spoken to Aunt Vivienne?'

'I needed to check on your passport, make arrangements for both cottages, Shaef.' He paused for a second. 'And tell her you wouldn't be spending Christmas with her in Cairns.'

Christmas. She'd need to get gifts for his family; she couldn't possibly go empty-handed...

A strangled laugh rose and died in her throat with the realisation she didn't know any details at all, with the exception of his grandmother.

Sebastian caught each fleeting expression and accurately defined every one of them. He reached across the table and caught hold of her hand. 'It'll be fine,' he reassured her. 'Trust me.'

They arrived in Paris mid-morning on a cold, wet, typically grey mid-winter day, tired after a long international flight.

Sebastian collected their hire car, and drove to the gracious old home on Ile Saint-Louis where his grandmother had resided since the day she was born.

A very beautiful home, with exquisite carpets, antique furniture, and *objets d'art* worth a small fortune.

Anneke wasn't sure what she'd expected. Certainly it

hadn't been a very stylish and sprightly woman who could easily pass for fifteen years younger than her eighty years, and whose command of the English language was more than impressive.

'Your rooms are ready. I know you must want to shower, then change and rest.'

'Room, Grandmère,' Sebastian corrected. 'We share.'

'So.'

Anneke couldn't imagine such a little word could convey such meaning.

'Are you not going to introduce me to this young woman you have brought to meet me?'

'Grandmère…Anneke Sorrel.' His arm remained at Anneke's waist. 'Anneke…my grandmother, Madeleine Lanier.'

'Come here and let me look at you.'

'You will frighten her,' Sebastian declared with amusement.

'Indeed.' Madeleine Lanier drew herself up to her full height and glared at her grandson. 'I frighten no one. And if she belongs to you, she belongs to this family.'

A faint smile teased Anneke's lips. 'So you get to pass judgement.'

'She speaks.' Madeleine placed a hand to her heart.

'Indeed she does.' Sebastian leaned forward and gently brushed first one paper-thin cheek, then the other. 'And be warned, she also speaks passable French.'

'I think,' Madeleine declared, 'we should go into the conservatory and take coffee.'

'Tea,' Anneke said gently. 'Earl Grey, if you have it.'

'Has a mind of her own, hmm?'

'Yes, I do.'

'Good. I could not have borne it if Sebastian had brought me an airhead with designs on his money.'

'I do not think Sebastian would have dared do such a thing.'

That earned a quick glance from sharp brown eyes, and the beginnings of a musing smile. 'He has dared many things in his short lifetime. But crossing me is not one of them.' She moved forward and batted her grandson's arm away from Anneke's waist. 'Let her go. We shall get along very well, she and I.'

Madeleine Lanier was a pussycat. An aged, very fiercely loyal lady, who guarded her family with her life. But a pussycat, nonetheless.

Anneke spared Sebastian a mischievous smile, and met his gleaming gaze, saw the faint shrug of resignation that accompanied it.

'You are going to marry her, of course.'

'Of course, Grandmère. I just haven't got around to asking her yet.'

Madeleine stopped in her tracks, turned and directed her grandson a baleful glare. 'And why not?'

Anneke didn't know whether to smile or cry, for there was a very strong possibility jet lag had caused her to imagine the entire conversation.

The glare shifted to Anneke. 'You do *want* to marry Sebastian?'

This was the craziest discourse she'd ever entered into! 'If he asks me, I'll give it some thought.'

'Indeed!'

They took coffee in the conservatory. And tea. With tiny *petits fours* and dainty sandwiches. Then Madeleine shooed them upstairs.

'Your luggage will be in your usual suite, Sebastian. Breakfast,' she declared regally, 'is served at eight. Don't be late.'

The staircase was wide and curved gently upwards in a sweeping arc to the upper floor central landing, from which a wide corridor stretched in both directions.

Sebastian turned to the right and traversed the corridor to its end, then opened the door to an elegant suite with views out over the Seine.

Anneke slipped out of her shoes and crossed to the window. It was drizzling, and what she could see of the city was shrouded in damp mist.

In spring, in summer, it would be clear, the skies a delicate blue, and there would be colour instead of the grey of winter.

Hard, masculine arms closed round her waist and linked together over her stomach, and she leaned back against him.

She felt weary almost beyond belief. She wanted nothing more than a long, hot shower, and a comfortable bed.

'I love you,' Sebastian said gently. 'I planned to ask you to marry me over a candlelit dinner on Christmas Eve, with champagne, a single red rose, the gift of my mother's ring. To introduce you to the family on the day we present and open gifts. Noël.'

His lips touched the vulnerable spot just beneath her ear, and she turned to meet his mouth.

'Yes,' she said simply.

It had been that easy. His arms tightened fractionally. 'No qualifications?'

'Two. We do the Christmas Eve thing, and you bring me back to Paris in the spring.'

His smile stole her heart. 'You're beautiful, *mon ange*. My life.'

Anneke reached up and brought his mouth down to hers. *'Je t'aime, mon amour. Je t'aime.'*

Family, Anneke reflected as she stood within the circle of Sebastian's arms after breakfast on Christmas morning.

The elegant lounge was filled with various aunts and uncles, cousins. And children. Madeleine Lanier's great-grandchildren. Beautifully dressed, exquisitely groomed, and extremely well behaved. Madeleine would not have tolerated it otherwise.

She glanced across the room and met the eyes of the gracious old lady, and smiled.

Everyone together in peace and harmony. Sharing, caring. Hopes and dreams. Gifts and giving.

For Madeleine Lanier, this house, her family, represented a lifetime of memories.

And Anneke had gifted and been given the greatest gift of all.

Love.

THE MARRIAGE DEAL

HELEN BIANCHIN

CHAPTER ONE

'Cut,' the director called. 'That's a wrap.'

They were the sweetest words she'd heard all day, Sandrine decided as she lifted a hand to ease the weight of her elaborate wig.

Period costume was not the most comfortable wearing apparel, nor was the boned, tightly laced corselet worn to achieve an eighteen-inch waist and push her breasts impossibly high and bare them almost to the point of indecent exposure.

Add the heat of the studio lights, a lead actor who had an inflated ego and delusions of grandeur, the director from hell, and the axiom, 'One should suffer in the name of one's art', had never been more pertinent.

'A word, sweetheart.'

From Tony's lips, *sweetheart* was not a term of endearment, and she froze, then she turned slowly to face the aging director whose talent was legend, but whose manner on occasion belonged in a backstreet of Naples.

'Dinner tonight, my place. Seven.' Hard dark eyes speared hers. 'Be there.' He turned his head and swept an arm to encompass five of her fellow actors. 'Everyone.'

Sandrine stifled a faint groan. All she wanted to do was to change, shower, put on her own clothes and drive to the waterfront villa she called home for the duration of filming, catch a snack and read through her lines for tomorrow.

'Do we get to ask *why*?' the lead actor queried petulantly.

'Money. The film needs it. My guest has it,' the director declared succinctly. 'If his request to meet the cast will clinch an essential injection of funds, so be it.'

'Tonight?' Sandrine reiterated, and suffered the dark lance of his gaze.

'Do you have a problem with that?'

If she did, voicing it would do no good at all, and she affected an eloquent shrug in resignation. 'I guess not.'

He swung an eagle eye over the rest of the cast. 'Anyone else?'

'You could have given us more notice,' the lead actor complained, and earned an earthy oath for his temerity.

'Difficult, when the man only arrived in the country yesterday.'

'Okay, okay, I get the picture.'

'Pleased to hear it,' was the cryptic response. 'Continuity,' he commanded, and Sandrine gave a heartfelt sigh.

Fifteen minutes later she was done with wardrobe, and she crossed the car park and slid in behind the wheel of her hire-car. Dressed in casual shorts and top, her long sable hair wound into a careless knot atop her head made for comfort in the intense afternoon heat.

Sandrine activated the air-conditioning the instant the engine purred into life, and minutes later she gained the main southern highway.

Her leased accommodation was a two-level villa overlooking water at Sanctuary Cove, a prestigious suburb on Queensland's Gold Coast, only a ten-minute drive from the Coomera film studios.

She activated the CD player as she took the Hope Island–Sanctuary Cove exit ramp and let the funky beat ease the kinks of a rough day.

A tree-lined river wound its way towards a man-made canal system, a nest of beautiful homes and the lush grounds of a popular golf course.

A view that exuded peace and tranquillity, she conceded as she veered towards Sanctuary Cove, then, clear of the security gate guarding the entrance to one of several residential areas, she took the gently curved road leading to the clutch of two-level villas hugging the waterfront.

Cement-rendered brick, painted pale blue with white trim, pebbled gardens adorned with decorative urns provided a pleasant, refreshing facade, Sandrine acknowledged as she used a remote control to open the garage door.

Inside, there was an abundance of cool marble floors, sleek lacquered furniture, soft leather sofas and chairs, and the kitchen was a gourmand's delight with a wealth of modern appliances. The open-plan design was pleasing, encompassing a wide curved staircase at the far end of the foyer leading to a gallery circling the upper floor, where three large bedrooms, each with an en suite, reposed.

Wide, sliding glass doors opened from the lounge and dining room onto a paved terrace that led to a private swimming pool. There was also a boat ramp.

Sandrine discarded her bag, changed into a bikini and spent precious minutes exercising by swimming a few laps of the pool. She needed the physical release, the coolness of the water, in a bid to rid herself of the persistent edge of tension.

A shower did much to restore her energy level, and she towelled her hair, then used a hand-held dryer to complete the process before crossing to the large walk-in robe.

Basic black, she decided as she riffled through her limited wardrobe. A social existence hadn't been uppermost in her mind when she'd hurriedly packed for this particular sojourn, and most of her clothes were divided between three luxurious homes far distant from this temporary residence.

Don't even *think* about those homes or the man she'd shared them with, she determined as she cast a designer gown onto the bed, then extracted stiletto-heeled pumps and an evening bag in matching black.

Yet the image invaded her mind, his broad, sculpted features with their angles and planes hauntingly vivid. Slate-grey eyes seemed to pierce right through to her soul, and she shivered at the memory of his mouth, its sensual curves and the devastating skill of its touch.

Michel Lanier. Mid-thirties, and ten years her senior. Successful entrepreneur, patron of the arts, dark-haired, dark-eyed, with the features of a Renaissance prince and the skilled mentality of a street warrior. Born of French parents in Paris, he'd begun his education in France and completed it in America.

Husband, *lover*. A man who'd swept her into his arms, his heart, and made her his wife.

They'd met at the party of a mutual friend in New York. Sandrine had just completed a modelling assignment during a seasonal break and was due to return to Sydney the following week to resume the filming of a long-running Australian-based television series.

Sandrine flew in with Michel at her side, and within a week she'd introduced him to her family, announced her engagement and had the script writers rewrite her part in the series. As soon as the chilling episodes filming her character's accident and demise were completed, she accompanied Michel back to New York.

Two months later they were married quietly in a very private ceremony among immediate family, and divided their time between New York and Paris. Michel bought a luxury apartment in Sydney's prestigious Double Bay with magnificent views out over the harbour. Their Australian base, he explained.

For six months everything was perfect. Too perfect, Sandrine reflected as she selected black underwear and donned it, then pulled on filmy black hose before crossing to the mirror to begin applying make-up.

The problem had begun three months ago when they spent two weeks in Sydney and a friend gave her a script to read. The story was good, better than good, and she felt an immediate affinity with the supporting character. A vision of how the part should be played filled her head and refused to leave.

Sandrine had known the production time frame wouldn't fit in with Michel's European schedule. She told herself there was no way he'd agree to her spending four weeks in Australia without him.

On a whim she decided to audition, aware her chance of success was next to nil, and she'd almost dismissed it from her mind when, days later, they returned to New York.

Her agent's call confirming she had the part brought a mixture of excitement and trepidation. Production was due to begin in a month at the Coomera studios in Queensland.

She signed the contract when it arrived but delayed telling Michel, all too aware what his reaction would be. Each day that passed had made the telling more difficult, until there were too few days left.

A hundred times she'd rehearsed the words in her mind, yet none of them came out sounding right, and what began as a discussion rapidly digressed into an argument of such magnitude she'd simply thrown some clothes into a bag in the early hours of the morning and booked into a hotel until it was time to take her scheduled flight to Brisbane.

Sandrine had qualified that four weeks wasn't a lifetime, yet with every passing day the physical and spiritual distance between then widened to a point where she feared it might never be repaired.

Worse, Murphy's Law descended, and production had suffered one delay after another. An estimated four weeks extended to five, then six. Budget was shot to pieces as they went into their seventh week. The subtropical midsummer heat was a killer, and tempers frequently ran short as professionalism was pushed to the limit.

Sandrine stood back from the mirror, secured the last pin in the simple knot of hair atop her head, then slid her feet into the elegant black pumps, collected her evening bag and made her way downstairs.

The day's high temperatures had gone down a notch or two, and there was a slight sea breeze teasing the early evening air as Sandrine crossed the paved apron to the entrance of Tony's Main Beach apartment building.

Minutes later she rode the lift to a designated floor and joined the group of fellow thespians enjoying a cool drink on the wide, curved balcony overlooking the ocean.

A portable barbecue had been set up, and a hired chef was organising a selection of seafood, prawns and kebabs ready for grilling.

Sandrine accepted a wine spritzer and sipped it slowly as she cast the guests an idle glance. All present and accounted for, with the exception of the guest of honour, she perceived, and pondered his identity.

'Smile, darling. It's almost "show time" and we're expected to shine,' a husky male voice intoned close to her ear.

She turned slowly to face the lead actor, whose birth

name had been changed by deed poll to Gregor Anders. He was handsome in a rugged, rakish way and took his studio-generated image far too seriously, acquiring so many layers during his professional career it was almost impossible to detect the real man beneath the projected persona.

'Gregor,' Sandrine greeted coolly, and summoned a smile to lessen the sting of her words. 'I'm sure you'll shine sufficiently for both of us.'

It was easy to admire his ability as an actor. Not so easy to condone were the subtle games he played for his own amusement. Yet his name was a drawcard. Women adored his looks, his physique, his sex appeal.

'Now, now, darling,' he chided with a wolfish smile. 'We're supposed to share a rapport, *n'est-ce pas*?' One eyebrow slanted in mocking query.

'On screen, *darling*,' she reminded sweetly, and remained perfectly still as he lifted a hand and traced his forefinger down the length of her arm.

'But it is so much easier to extend the emotions beyond the screen for the duration of filming, don't you agree?'

Her eyes locked with his. 'No.'

'You should loosen up a little,' he cajoled, exerting innate charm.

'I play *before* the camera. Off the set, I suffer no illusions.'

'Strong words,' Gregor murmured. 'I could ensure you regret them.'

'Oh, *please*,' Sandrine protested. 'Go play Mr

Macho with one of the sweet young things who'll simply *swoon* at the thought of receiving your attention.'

'While you've never swooned over a man in your
life?'

You're wrong, she almost contradicted, but held her
tongue. Gossip ran rife and, in these circles, quickly
became embellished until only a grain of recognisable
truth remained.

'If you'll excuse me?' She lifted her empty glass a
few inches aloft, then turned and crossed to the bar.

Within minutes she was taking a refreshing sip of
orange juice. A waiter paused beside her and proffered
a tray of hors d'oeuvres. She smiled automatically,
selected one, then took a delicate bite. It was delicious
and brought an onset of hunger. A sandwich at lunch,
followed by an apple and mineral water wasn't much
in the way of sustenance.

Sandrine took a mini vol-au-vent and popped it into
her mouth.

'Where *is* the guest of honour?' a feminine voice
asked in bored tones, and she turned towards the attractive young lead actress.

'Bent on making a grand entrance, perhaps?'

'That's a woman's prerogative, sweetheart.'

The smile was a little too artificial, the voice a fraction too contrived. Cait Lynden had acquired *star*
status and wasn't about to let anyone forget it.
Especially a fellow actress playing a minor part,
Sandrine decided silently.

'No one seems to know who he is,' Cait mused. 'A
successful entrepreneur is all Tony will reveal.' An

acquisitive gleam darkened her beautiful blue eyes. 'Obviously rich. As long as he's presentable and under sixty, it could prove to be an interesting encounter.'

'And single?' Sandrine posed, only to hear the other's musical laugh.

'*Darling*, who cares?'

Not Cait, obviously.

Minutes later Sandrine detected a change in the buzz of conversation, a shift in tone definition that caused her to lift her head.

So he had finally arrived. Almost a half-hour late.

Some sixth sense alerted her attention, followed by a quick stab of apprehension.

'*Mine*,' Cait uttered, sotto voce.

Even as Sandrine turned slowly to conduct a sweeping appraisal of the room, a telltale prickle of awareness slithered down the length of her spine.

There was only one man who could generate this effect. One man whose soul was so closely attuned to her own they were almost twin halves of a whole.

Sandrine caught sight of a tall male frame, felt the familiar tug on her senses as she recognised the broad-boned, chiselled profile, the dark, conventionally groomed hair, which seven weeks ago had lain longer at his nape, adding a refined, untamed quality that was equally as dangerous as the man himself.

She'd adored threading her fingers through the silky thickness, the purchase it lent when she held fast his head and simply clung during the slow, exquisite torture of his lovemaking, the dazzling heat of their passion.

Those had been the wild, sweet days when there had been only love to guide them, she reflected. A time when she'd given him everything without thought of denial.

Now she watched Michel while he paused in conversation to lift his head as if he, too, sensed her presence. Dark grey eyes locked with hers, probing, intense, and totally lacking in any humour or warmth.

Time stood still as everything and everyone in the room faded to the periphery of her vision.

There was only Michel. The man, the moment, the exigent chemistry evident. She could sense it, *feel* its powerful pull as she became caught up in the magical spell of something so intensely primitive she felt raw, exposed and acutely vulnerable.

Then he smiled, and for an instant she was transported back to the time they first met. Almost a duplicate situation to this, where they'd caught sight of each other at the same time across a crowded room.

Except the past had little place in the present. She could see it in the sudden flare in those beautiful slate-grey eyes and sense it in his stance.

Body language. She'd studied it as part of her craft and she could successfully determine each movement, every gesture.

Did anyone else recognise the cool ruthlessness or define the latent anger that lurked beneath the surface of his control? They lent his features a dark, brooding quality and gave hint to a refined savagery, which unleashed could prove lethal.

He was a man who held no illusions and whose

youthful passage had moulded him, shaping a destiny many of his peers could only envy.

Sandrine watched in mesmerised fascination as he murmured an excuse to their host, then crossed the room and stepped out onto the terrace.

Fine Armani tailoring sheathed an awesome muscle definition in that powerful frame, and every movement held the lithe, flowing grace of a superb jungle animal.

Her heart thudded and quickened to a faster beat. Each separate nerve end became highly sensitised as he moved towards her, and she couldn't think of one sensible word to say in greeting. Considering the carelessly flung words they'd hurled at each other all those weeks ago, a simple hello seemed incredibly banal.

She didn't get the chance, for he captured her shoulders, slid one hand to hold fast her head, then his mouth took possession of hers in a kiss that sent her emotions spinning out of control.

It was claim-staking, she acknowledged dimly when she was able to breathe. Flagrant, seductive and hungry.

Worse was her own reaction as, after the initial shock, she relinquished a hold on sanity and opened her mouth to him.

She savoured the taste and feel of his tongue as it created a swirling, possessive dance with hers and lured her into an emotional vortex where time and place had no meaning.

When he lifted his head, she couldn't move. Gradually she became aware of the sound of background music, the indistinct buzz of conversation, as the room and its occupants filtered into her vision.

Dear heaven. How long had they remained locked in that passionate embrace? Thirty seconds, sixty? More?

All he had to do was touch her and she went up in flames. In seven weeks the passionate intensity hadn't lessened.

What did you expect? a tiny voice taunted. He's haunted your dreams every night since you left him and invaded your thought processes almost to the detriment of your work.

The emotional intensity shimmered between them, exigent, electric and mesmeric. Yet there was also anger, not forgotten nor forgiven.

'What are you doing here?'

Was that her voice? It sounded so cool, so calm, when inside she was a seething mass of conflicting tensions.

'I concluded my business in Europe.'

Important meetings where his presence was paramount. No opportunity for delegation there, she reasoned. What excuse had he given explaining her absence to family in Paris? To his elder brother Raoul, his *grand-mère*?

She experienced a moment's regret and banked down the edge of remorse she felt for the elderly matriarch who ruled with a fist of iron, yet had the heart of a pussycat and of whom she'd become very fond.

'And discovered I wasn't waiting in the New York apartment,' Sandrine voiced evenly. Her chin lifted fractionally and the topaz flecks in her eyes shone deep gold. 'Subdued and contrite at having thwarted you?'

'Difficult,' he acknowledged with wry cynicism. 'When a delayed filming schedule kept you here.'

Sandrine opened her mouth to refute that was something he couldn't have known, then she closed it again. All he had to do was lift the phone and instruct someone to report her every move. It angered her unbearably that he had.

'What's your purpose, Michel?' she launched with polite heat. If they were alone, she would have hit him. Or made every effort to try.

'You didn't answer any of the several messages I left on your message bank.'

She'd let every call go to voice mail and become selective in whose messages she returned. 'What was the point when we'd said it all?'

'Nothing is resolved in anger.'

So he'd let her go, sure in the knowledge that, given time, she'd come to her senses and run back to him? How many nights had she lain awake fighting against the need to do just that? Except pride and determined resolve had kept her firmly where she was. As well as loyalty to a project and a legally binding contract.

She looked at him carefully, noting the fine lines that fanned from the outer corners of his eyes, the faint shadows beneath. Unless it was her imagination, the faint vertical crease slashing each cheek seemed deeper.

Once, those dark grey eyes had gleamed with naked

passion...for her. Only her. She'd looked into their depths and melted.

Now there was only darkness and a hard quality that chilled her bones.

'You haven't explained why you're an invited guest in Tony's apartment,' Sandrine managed evenly, and saw one eyebrow arch.

'You mean you haven't guessed?'

There was soft mockery evident in his tone, an underlying hint of steel that tore the breath from her throat.

'Your sojourn in Europe is over and you've come to haul me home?'

Her facetiousness didn't escape him, and his mouth assumed a cynical slant. 'Try again.'

Anger overlaid fear. 'You want a divorce.'

His expression didn't change, but something in his eyes shifted, hardened. 'There hasn't been a divorce in the Lanier family for three hundred years.'

'You mean women have suffered the overbearing, arrogant, autocratic will of Lanier men for *centuries* without offering a word in complaint?'

'I imagine any complaints were soon—' he paused, the emphasis significant '—satisfactorily dealt with.'

She took his meaning and rode with it. 'Sex isn't the answer to everything.'

'Lovemaking.'

There was a difference. Dear heaven, such a difference. Even *thinking* about Michel's powerful body joining with hers brought a surge of warmth that raced through her veins, heating her body to fever pitch.

He saw the reaction in the subtle shading of her skin, the faint convulsive movement of her throat, the sudden, too rapid sweep of eyelashes as she sought to veil her response. And he experienced satisfaction.

'You haven't answered my question.'

'Which particular question is that?'

Her lashes flew wide, and the intensity of those deep brown, gold-flecked eyes held a brilliance that danced close to anger.

'What you're doing here, *tonight*?'

His gaze was direct, probing, and held a degree of cynical humour. 'Why, *chérie*, I am the guest of honour at this soiree.'

'The guest of honour touted to inject sufficient funds to rescue the film?'

Michel confirmed it with the faint inclination of his head. 'For a price,' he conceded with chilling softness.

Something inside her stomach curled into a painful knot. 'And that is?'

'A reconciliation.' Succinct, blatant and chillingly inflexible.

Dear God. Pious salutation had nothing to do with the words that remained locked in her throat.

From somewhere she dredged up the courage to confront him. 'A marriage certificate doesn't transform me into a chattel you own.'

Michel took in her pale features, the dark eyes that seemed too large for her face, the loss of a few essential kilos, and barely restrained himself from wringing her slender neck.

Sandrine became aware of the circumspect glances,

the ripple of curiosity Michel's action had generated. Cait Lynden's expression was composed, although her brilliant blue eyes were icy.

Their marriage hadn't been written up in any of the international society pages. It was doubtful anyone in this room knew the guest of honour's identity, much less his connection with a little-known supporting actress.

'This is hardly the time or place.'

Michel's smile was a mere facsimile and bore not the slightest degree of humour. 'No discussion, no negotiation. Just a simple yes or no.'

Simple? How could he deem something so complicated as *simple*? 'You can't demand conditions.'

'Watch me.'

'Blackmail, Michel?'

He gave an imperceptible shrug. 'Label it what you will.'

'And if I refuse?' Sandrine queried bravely.

Something moved in those dark eyes, making them appear incredibly dangerous. 'I walk out of here.'

And out of her life? As she'd walked out of his? Temporarily, she amended.

So why did she have the feeling she was poised on the edge of a precipice? One false move and she'd fall to unknown depths?

She could see the grim purpose etched in his features and she felt her stomach muscles clench in pain. 'You don't play fair.'

His expression didn't change. 'This isn't a game.'

No, it wasn't. Yet she hated him for employing manipulative tactics.

'Yes or no,' Michel reiterated with deadly quietness.

CHAPTER TWO

SANDRINE looked at Michel carefully, her eyes steady, her composure seemingly intact. Only she knew what effort it cost to present such a calm facade.

'I'm sure Tony has other sources available from which to raise the necessary money.'

'He has exhausted all of them.'

'How can you know that?' It didn't warrant an answer, she acknowledged wryly. The Lanier family consortium held immense holdings, and Michel was extremely wealthy in his own right. As such, he had contacts and access to otherwise privileged information.

Without the injection of funds, the film wouldn't be completed or make it into the cinemas, and the resulting financial loss would be disastrous.

The knowledge she held the film's fate in her hands didn't sit well. Nor did the fact that Michel had very skilfully planned it this way.

'With the possible exception of Gregor Anders, the film doesn't have the big-name leads to attract a runaway box office success,' Michel relayed with damning accuracy. 'The director and producer are both scrambling to resurrect their ailing careers with a period piece currently out of vogue.'

Add to that, she knew the film's financial backers

had set a limited budget that made little allowance for countless takes in a quest for perfection, delays, escalating expenses, and the result was a high-risk venture no sensible investor would touch.

Sandrine cast him a level look. 'That's your opinion.'

Michel's gaze remained steady, obdurate. 'Not only mine.'

'If that's true, why are you prepared to invest?'

His expression didn't change, and for several seconds she didn't think he was going to answer. 'Honesty, Sandrine?' he mocked lightly. 'You.'

Her eyes widened, then narrowed slightly.

'What did you think I would do, ultimately?' Michel demanded silkily. 'Just let you *walk*?'

She gritted her teeth, counted to five. 'I didn't *walk*,' she denied vehemently. 'I was committed to a signed contract. If I hadn't checked into the studio on the designated date, I could have been sued.'

'A contract you chose not to tell me you'd signed.'

'*You* were locked into meetings in Europe.'

'Aren't you going to introduce me, darling?'

Damn. Sandrine barely swallowed the vengeful curse as Cait placed an arm along the back of her waist in a gesture that indicated they were the closest of friends.

'Michel Lanier,' Michel interposed smoothly.

'Cait Lynden.' The smile, the voice, the actions, combined to provide maximum impact. 'So, you're our knight in shining armour.'

Sandrine watched an exquisitely lacquered nail trace

a provocative pattern down his suit sleeve and was overwhelmed by the desire to sweep it aside.

'And Sandrine's husband.'

Ouch. She felt Cait's slight intake of breath, glimpsed the coy smile and felt the faint increase of pressure as fingers bit into the back of her waist.

'Well,' Cait acknowledged as she turned to shoot Sandrine an icy glare, 'aren't you the secretive one.'

Michel took hold of Sandrine's hand and lifted it to his lips, then he spared Cait a level glance.

'If you'll excuse us? We were in the middle of a private discussion.'

Oh, my. He didn't pull any punches. She watched as the lead actress proffered a sizzling smile, then turned and walked away with a blatant sway of her hips.

'Another conquest,' Sandrine commented lightly.

'Let's focus on the immediate issue, shall we?'

The master manipulator. Dammit, why did she want to crack his cool facade when she knew what lay beneath the surface of his control?

His skill with words in the midst of her volatile diatribe had been chilling. Hell, he hadn't even raised his voice. *She* had been the one who'd lost it.

Now he was using that skill to employ invidious blackmail, cleverly positioning her between a rock and a hard place. She was the price, the film her prize.

'You leave me little choice,' she said with deliberate coolness, then waited a beat and added, 'For now.'

He reached out and brushed the back of his fingers down her cheek. 'No conditions.'

She felt her body's betraying response to his touch, the heated sensation that invaded her bones and melted them to molten wax.

Sandrine's eyes deepened, and her mouth shook a little. With anger, resentment and a need to swing into verbal attack mode. Except this wasn't the time or place if she wanted to retain any sense of dignity.

As it was, speculation undoubtedly ran rife among the cast members and fellow guests. Did Tony know that Sandrine Arnette was Michel Lanier's *wife*?

Michel watched as she fought to keep her conflicting emotions under wraps, and defined each and every one of them. With a degree of dispassionate anticipation, he was aware the fight between them had scarcely begun. He intended to win.

'I need a drink,' she admitted, watching as Michel's lips curved to form a musing smile.

He lifted a hand, and in an instant a waitress appeared at his side. Michel had that effect on women. All women, of any age. It was an inherent charm, one he used quite ruthlessly on occasion.

He lifted two flutes of champagne from the tray and handed one to Sandrine.

'*Salut.*' He touched the rim of her flute with his own.

She ignored the temptation to drain the contents in one long swallow and deliberately sipped the chilled aerated wine, savoured the taste, then let the liquid slide down her throat.

'Shall we join our host?'

Sandrine's eyes clashed momentarily with his, then

she veiled their expression. There would be an opportunity later to unleash the verbal diatribe seething beneath the surface. Round one might be his, but she had every intention the next would be hers.

She summoned a slow smile, her acting ability prominent as she tucked a hand into the curve of his elbow.

'Having provided the guests with an unexpected floor show, don't you think introductions are somewhat overdue?'

Minutes later Michel moved easily at Tony's side, displaying an interest in each guest's professional background as he posed questions with practised charm.

Working the room, Sandrine recognized with cynicism. A retentive and photographic memory ensured he was never at a loss in the business arena or among the social set.

'As secrets go, yours is a doozey.'

She turned slightly and encountered a slender young woman whose name temporarily escaped her.

'Stephanie Sommers, marketing.'

'Yes, of course,' Sandrine responded, warming to Stephanie's faintly wicked smile.

'I can understand you keeping him under wraps. Where did you find him?'

'New York. We married in Paris.'

'Ah, the universal city for lovers.'

Sandrine felt a shiver slither its way over the surface of her skin as she experienced instant recall of the city, the ambience. The magic. Paris in the spring, when the grey skies cleared and everything came alive. As her heart had when she first met Michel.

An ache centred in the region of her diaphragm, intensifying as memories surfaced. Memories that had held such promise, so much love, she'd imagined their lives together were inviolate and forever entwined.

The stuff of which fantasies are made, she reflected wryly. With little basis in reality.

'Tony is on his best behaviour.'

Sandrine summoned a quick smile. Something that was becoming a habit as the evening progressed. 'The future of the film is at stake.'

'Is it?'

The query bore a certain quizzical humour as if Stephanie had already concluded the injection of essential finance was a done deal.

It was, although Sandrine wondered what the marketing manager's reaction would be if she discovered the reason for Michel's investment.

'Okay. So the rest of us get to sweat it out a little longer.'

Sandrine looked suitably enigmatic until Stephanie gave a low, throaty chuckle.

'You can't say I didn't try.' The attractive blonde spared a glance at her watch. 'I'm going to have to leave soon.'

'A date?'

'With a baby-sitter who can only stay until ten,' the marketing manager replied with a touch of cynicism.

'Divided loyalties?'

'No contest. My daughter wins out every time.' She

quickly scanned the room, then lowered her voice to a confidential tone. 'Your husband has escaped from Tony and is heading this way. Impressive beast, isn't he?'

Beast was an apt description. Although not in the context Stephanie implied. 'Tony, or Michel?'

She met Stephanie's direct look with equanimity, glimpsed the momentary speculation before it was quickly masked and cast her a wicked smile.

'Surely you jest?'

Sandrine refrained from responding as Michel loomed close.

She felt her body stiffen in anticipation of his touch and she unconsciously held her breath, only releasing it when he made no attempt at physical contact.

'Michel, you've met Stephanie?' she managed smoothly.

'Yes. We shared an interesting discussion on marketing techniques.'

'Albeit that it was brief.'

'Something we will correct, *n'est-ce pas*?'

Oh, my, he was good. The right amount of interest, the desired element of charm, with hard business acumen just visible beneath the surface.

'It will be a pleasure,' Stephanie accorded, then she excused herself, and Sandrine watched as she talked briefly to Tony before exiting the room.

'She is a friend?'

The mildness of Michel's voice didn't deceive her. 'Actors have little to do with the business heads.'

'Am I to assume, then, that tonight is the first time you've met?'

She cast him a mocking glance. 'Would you like me to give you a run-down on everyone at this soiree? Whom I speak to, touch?' She paused a beat. 'Kiss?'

'Careful,' Michel warned silkily. 'You're treading dangerous ground.'

'In the name of one's craft, of course,' she added, and derived a degree of personal satisfaction at the way his eyes narrowed.

'If I thought otherwise,' he drawled, 'I'd carry you kicking and screaming onto the first plane out of here.'

'Neanderthal tactics belong to a distant civilisation.'

'Neanderthal and civilised do not mesh, *chérie*. Persist in baiting me, and I'll show you just how un-civilised I can be.'

Her chin lifted, and her eyes remained remarkably steady as they clashed with his. 'Too late, *mon amant*. I've already been there, remember?'

'I retain a vivid memory of a little wildcat who threw a few objects at me in temper.'

Expensive Waterford crystal. An inkwell, a paper-weight and a small clock decorating the antique desk in his study.

At the time she'd been too angry to care, but after-wards she'd experienced a pang of regret for the exquisite crystal items that formed part of a desk set. And the panelled wall they'd collided with before falling to the marble floor to shatter in glittering shards when Michel deftly moved out of the line of fire.

Now, as she reviewed her explosive reaction, she

felt ashamed for having displayed such a lack of control.

'You provoked me.'

'It was reciprocal.'

Words. His, cool and controlled, whereas hers had been the antithesis of calm. Yet equally hurtful, uttered in frustrated anger.

'Space and time, Michel?' Sandrine queried with a trace of bitterness. 'In which to cool down and pretend it never happened?'

'I imagined we'd already resolved the situation.'

The gold flecks in her eyes became more pronounced as she held on to her anger. Twin flags of colour highlighted her cheekbones as the memory of the very physical sex they'd shared immediately afterwards came vividly to mind. On top of his magnificent antique desk. Hard, no-holds-barred sex, libidinous, barbaric and totally wild. Afterwards he'd cradled her close and carried her upstairs, bathed and gently towelled her dry, then he'd taken her to bed where he made exquisite love long into the night.

She'd waited until he'd fallen asleep, then she'd dressed, thrown clothes into a suitcase, penned a hastily scrawled note and left as the new day's dawn was lightening a shadowed grey sky.

'No.' The single negation emerged with quiet dignity. Sex…even very good sex, she amended, didn't resolve anything.

He had never felt so frustrated in his life when he discovered she'd left. If he could have, he'd have boarded the next Australia-bound flight and followed her. Except Raoul was in America, and Sebastian, youngest of the three Lanier brothers, was honey-mooning overseas. He'd had no option but to attend scheduled meetings in various European cities, then conclude them with a brief family visit with his *grand-mère* in Paris.

'An empty space in bed, a brief note, and a wife on the other side of the world who refused to take any of my calls.' For that, he could have shaken her sense-less.

'If you're through with the interrogation,' Sandrine said stiffly, 'I'd like to leave. I have an early call in the morning.'

His features hardened and his eyelids lowered slightly, successfully masking his expression. 'Then let's find our host and thank him for his hospitality.' He took hold of her arm, only to have her wrench it out of his grasp.

'I'm not going anywhere with you.'

One eyebrow arched in a deliberately cynical ges-ture. 'Are you forgetting our bargain so soon?'

'Not at all,' Sandrine declared bravely. 'But I'm damned if I'll allow you to share a house with me!'

His smile bore no humour at all. 'Separate resi-dences aren't part of the deal.'

'Go to hell,' she vented, sorely tried.

'I've been there,' Michel said with dangerous soft-ness. 'I don't intend a return trip.'

'I think,' she declared with controlled civility, 'we should save any further discussion until later.'

'I haven't even begun,' he stated with deliberate

emphasis. 'And the guests are free to speculate as they like.' He curved an arm around her waist and anchored her firmly to his side. 'Place one foot in front of the other and smile as we bid Tony goodnight.'

'*Or else*?' Sandrine countered with controlled anger.

'It's a matter of dignity. Yours,' Michel declared in a silky smooth tone. 'You can walk out of here or you can exit this apartment hoisted over my shoulder. Choose.'

Her stomach turned a slow somersault. One glance at his set features was sufficient to determine it wouldn't be wise to oppose him.

Her eyes held a chill that rivalled an arctic floe. 'I prefer the first option,' she said with icy politeness.

It took ten minutes to exchange pleasantries and have Michel confirm a business meeting with Tony the following morning. Sandrine didn't miss the slight tightness of Tony's smile or the fleeting hardness evident in his eyes.

'He's sweating on your decision,' she inferred as they rode the lift down to the ground floor. 'A calculated strategy, Michel?'

He sent a dark, assessing look in her direction, and she glimpsed a faint edge of mockery beneath the seemingly inscrutable veneer.

The query didn't require a verbal affirmation. The three Lanier brothers, Raoul, Michel and Sebastian, controlled a billion-dollar corporation spearheaded by their father, Henri, who had ensured each of his three sons' education encompassed every financial aspect of business.

The lift slid to a smooth halt, and they crossed the foyer to the main external entrance.

Sandrine extracted her cell phone and flipped it open. 'I'll call you a taxi.'

The streetlight nearby provided a luminous glow, the shadows highlighting the strong planes of his face.

'I have a hire-car,' Michel informed her silkily. 'I'll follow you.'

'You can move in tomorrow—' She broke off as the connection engaged. 'Could you send a cab to—'

Michel ended the call by the simple expediency of removing the small unit from her hand.

'How *dare* you?' The words spilled out in spluttered rage, and she made a valiant attempt to snatch the cell phone from him, failing miserably as he held it beyond her reach. 'Give it to me!'

One eyebrow arched in silent cynicism as she stamped her foot in wordless rage.

'Where are you parked?'

She glared at him balefully, incensed that much of her visual anger was diminished by the dark evening shadows. 'Aren't you booked in somewhere?'

She had tenacity, temper and *tendresse*. The latter had never been so noticeably absent. A faint twinge of humour tugged at the edge of his mouth. 'I checked out this morning.'

Damn, *damn* him, she silently vented. 'My car is the white Honda hatchback,' she told him in stilted tones. She turned away, only to have his hand snag her arm, and she whirled back to face him in vengeful fury. 'What now?'

'Your cell phone,' Michel said mildly as he held it out to her. She snatched it from him as if his fingers represented white-hot flame.

She would, she determined angrily as she slid in behind the wheel and engaged the engine, drive as fast as she dared and hope to lose him. Fat chance, Sandrine silently mocked minutes later as she ran an amber light and saw, via the rear-vision mirror, his car follow.

Knowing Michel's attention to detail, it wouldn't surprise her if he had already discovered her address and was therefore quite capable of reaching it with the aid of a street map. It was a sobering thought and one that relegated her actions to a foolish level.

No more taking risks with the traffic lights, she determined as she settled down to the twenty-minute drive and tried to ignore the twin set of headlights following several metres to the rear of her car.

Sandrine switched on the radio, selected a station at random and turned up the sound. Heavy rock music filled the interior, and she tried to lose herself in the beat, hoping it would distract her attention from Michel.

It didn't work, and after several minutes she turned down the sound and concentrated on negotiating a series of traffic roundabouts preceding the Sanctuary Cove turn-off.

A security gate guarded the entrance to the road leading to her waterfront villa, and she activated it, passed through, then followed the curving ribbon of bricked road past a clutch of low-rise apartment buildings until she reached her own.

After raising the garage door by remote control, she eased the car to a halt as Michel slid a sleek late-model sedan alongside her own.

The garage door closed, and Sandrine emerged from behind the wheel to see Michel pop the boot of his car and remove a set of luggage. She wanted to ignore him, but Michel Lanier wasn't a man you could successfully ignore.

Something twisted painfully in the pit of her stomach as she unlocked the door leading from the garage into the villa.

Pausing, she turned back towards him. 'There are three bedrooms upstairs,' she informed in a tone resembling that of a hostess instructing a guest. 'Choose one. There's spare linen in the cupboard.'

He didn't answer, and the silence was enervating. Without a further word, she stepped through to the hallway and made her way towards the kitchen.

The villa's interior was light and modern, with high ceilings and huge glass floor-to-ceiling windows. Large urns painted to blend with the muted peach-and-green colour scheme held a variety of artificial flowers and greenery, adding a tropical ambience to the expanse of marble-tiled floors.

The only sound was the staccato click of her stiletto heels as she crossed into the kitchen, and within minutes the coffee machine exuded an exotic aroma of freshly dripped brew.

Sandrine extracted two cups and saucers, sugar,

milk, placed them on the counter, then she filled one cup and took an appreciative sip.

It was quiet, far too quiet, and she crossed into the lounge and activated the television, switching channels until she found something of interest. The images danced, her vision unfocused as her mind wandered to the man who had invaded her home.

Temporary home, she corrected, aware that filming would wrap up within a week or two. Less for her, as she was only required in a few more scenes. Then what? Where would she go? There were a few options, and she mentally ticked them off. One, return to Sydney. Two, find modelling work. Three… No, she didn't want to think about the third option. A marriage should be about equality, sharing and understanding each other's needs. Domination of one partner by another was something she found unacceptable.

Sandrine finished her coffee, rinsed her cup, checked her watch, then released a heavy sigh. It was late, she was tired, and, she decided, she was damned if she'd wait any longer for Michel to put in an appearance. *She* was going to bed.

The silence seemed uncanny, and she found herself consciously listening for the slightest sound as she ascended the stairs. But there was none.

If Michel had showered, unpacked and made up a bed, he'd achieved it in a very short time.

The curved staircase led onto a semicircular, balustraded gallery. Three bedrooms, each with an en suite, were positioned along it, while the double doors at the head of the stairs opened to a spacious sitting room.

Sandrine turned right when she reached the top and entered the bedroom she'd chosen to use as her own. Soft lighting provided illumination, and her nostrils flared at the scent of freshly used soap and the lingering sharpness of male toiletries even as her eyes swivelled towards the large bed.

The elegant silk spread had been thrown back, and a long male frame lay clearly outlined beneath the light covering.

Michel. His dark head was nestled comfortably on the pillow, his eyes closed, his breathing slow and even.

Dammit, he was in *her* bed! Asleep!

Well, that would soon change, she decided furiously as she marched across the room. Without hesitation she picked up a spare pillow and thumped it down onto the mattress mere inches from his chest.

'Wake up,' she vented between clenched teeth. 'Damn you, wake up!' She lifted the pillow and brought it down for the second time. 'You're not staying in my room!'

He didn't move, and in a gesture of sheer frustration she pounded the pillow onto his chest.

A hand snaked out as she made to lift the pillow for another body blow, and she gasped as his fingers mercilessly closed over her forearm. Dark eyes seared hers.

'This is my room, my bed. And you're not occupying either.'

'You want a separate room, a separate bed?' His eyes seemed to shrivel her very soul. 'Go choose one.'

'You're doing this deliberately, aren't you?' she demanded, sorely tried. Pain focused behind each temple, and she lifted her hands to soothe the ache with her fingers. 'I'm not sleeping with you.'

'*Sleep* is the operative word,' Michel drawled.

She controlled the urge to hit him…by the skin of her teeth. 'You expect me to *believe* that?'

He looked…magnificent, and dangerous as hell. The brooding sexuality he exuded sent warning flares of heat racing through her veins.

Sandrine shifted her attention to his face and settled fleetingly on his mouth. Her lips quivered in vivid memory of how they'd moved beneath his own only a few hours ago. A traitorous warmth invaded her body, and she almost waived controlling it. *Almost.*

'Afraid to share the bed with me, Sandrine?'

Yes, she longed to cry. Because all it will take is the accidental brush of skin against skin in the night when I'm wrapped in sleep to forget for a few essential seconds, and then it'll be too late.

'Sex isn't going to make what's wrong between us right.'

'I don't recall suggesting that it would.'

'Then perhaps you'd care to explain why you've chosen my room, my *bed*?' she sputtered, indicating the bed, *him*. She drew in a deep breath, then released it slowly. 'If you had any gentlemanly instincts, you would have found another room!'

'I have never pretended to be a gentleman.'

Sandrine glared at him. 'No,' she agreed. 'Barbarian is more appropriate!'

'Careful, *chérie*,' Michel warned silkily.

A small decorative cushion lay within easy reach, and she swept it up in one hand and hurled it at him. 'I hate you.'

Two seconds later she lay pinned to the mattress as Michel loomed close above her. 'Let us put this *hate* to the test, hmm?'

She fought him, vainly twisting her body beneath his own as she attempted to wrench her hands free. 'Don't do this.'

It was a statement, not a plea, and he noted all her fine anger, her fearless tenacity and her passion. All it would take was subtle persuasion and sensual skill to have her become pliant in his arms.

'Then you should have thought before you pounded me with a pillow.'

'If you bait me, expect a reaction,' she launched in pithy response.

His expression didn't change although she could have sworn she glimpsed a glimmer of amusement.

'So...do you want to continue with this game of one-upmanship, or shall we bring it to a halt? Your call, Sandrine.'

She wanted to yell *Fight to the death*, and be damned. Except it would be *her* death. Emotionally, mentally, physically. And she didn't want to offer him that power.

'If you'll *move* yourself,' she suggested with expressive intonation, 'I'll go change and shower.'

'*Oui*, but first…' He took her mouth in a fleeting soft kiss, lingered at the edge, then swept his tongue into the silky interior to wreak brief and devastating havoc before easing his lengthy frame back onto the mattress. '*Bonne nuit, mignonne.*'

He rolled onto his side, pulled the covering to his waist and closed his eyes.

Sandrine lay frozen for a few seconds as she savoured the taste of him. Warm, musky and wickedly erotic. Damn him, she swore silently. He might have allowed her to call the tune, but he'd managed to have the last word.

With extreme care, she slid off the bed and crossed to the en suite, undressed, then took a leisurely shower, allowing the hot spray to ease the tension tightening her neck and shoulder muscles. Then she closed the dial, reefed a towel and, minutes later, donned a cotton nightshirt.

It seemed ironic and, she perceived wryly, probably owed something to her rebellious streak that she possessed complete sets of exquisite satin-and-lace French lingerie, yet alone she chose to wear something plain and functional to bed.

Michel lay still, his breathing deep and even as she crossed the room to snap off the light.

Afraid to share the bed with me? His words whispered in an unspoken challenge, taunting her.

Maybe she should turn the tables on him and do the unexpected. He'd sleep for hours, and although she wouldn't be there to witness it, she'd give almost anything to glimpse the look on his face when he woke and saw she'd occupied the other half of the bed.

A secret smile curved her lips as she slipped under the covers. He wanted to play games, huh? Well, let the games begin!

It gave her satisfaction to devise one scheme after another until sleep claimed her and tipped her into a world of dreams where Michel was alternately lover and devil, the location changed from one side of the world to another and became a film set where she was centre stage without any recollection of her lines.

CHAPTER THREE

SANDRINE came sharply awake to the shrilling sound of her digital alarm and automatically reached out a hand to turn it off. Except she was on the wrong side of the bed, and her fingers came into contact with a hard, warm male shoulder.

Michel. She tore her hand away as he uttered a muffled Gallic curse and reared into a sitting position.

'My alarm,' she explained sweetly as she slipped out of bed and crossed round to still the strident sound. The illuminated numerals registered four-thirty. 'Sorry if it woke you.'

She wasn't sorry at all. It was payback time for last night, and victory was sweet.

Drapes covered the wall of glass, filtering the early dawn light. This was Queensland, and the height of summer when the sun rose soon after four in the morning.

Sandrine crossed to the walk-in robe, selected jeans and a sleeveless ribbed top, then she collected fresh underwear and stepped into the adjoining en suite.

Ten minutes later she emerged, dressed, her face completely devoid of any make-up and her hair twisted into a loose knot at her nape.

She didn't give the bed or its occupant a single glance as she caught up her bag and exited the room.

In the kitchen she extracted fresh orange juice, drank it, then picked up a banana and made her way through to the garage.

Fifteen minutes later she was in make-up, mentally going over her lines while the wizard in cosmetic artistry began transforming her for the camera.

On reflection, it was not a happy day. Everyone was edgy, tempers flared as the temperature rose, and professionalism was strained to the limit.

It hadn't helped when Michel put in an appearance on the set after the lunch break. He stood in the background, his presence unquestioned given his possible investment, an apparently interested observer of the film-making process as the actors went through their paces...again and again as Tony sought perfection in his quest to impress.

No matter how hard Sandrine tried to ignore her indomitable husband, he was *there*, a constant on the edge of her peripheral vision, ensuring that her total focus was shot to hell.

'What are you doing here?' she demanded sotto voce during a break from filming.

Michel leant forward and brushed his lips to her temple. '*Chérie*, is that any way to greet your husband?'

'Please. Go away.'

She caught a glimpse of humour lurking at the edge of his mouth and bit back the need to scream.

'If I'm going to invest a considerable amount of money in order to salvage this venture,' he drawled, 'I think I should check out the action.'

'This is supposed to be a closed set.'

'I'm here at Tony's invitation.'

'Very cleverly baited, I imagine, so that our esteemed director took the hook?'

His smile didn't reach his eyes. 'You know me so well.'

No, she wanted to refute. I thought I did, but now I feel I hardly know you at all.

'How long do you intend to stay?'

'On the set? Until you finish for the day.' He lifted a hand and brushed gentle fingers across one cheek. 'Why? Does my presence bother you?'

She sharpened her verbal claws. 'Isn't that your purpose?'

'Shouldn't you read through your lines?' Michel countered, watching as she turned without a word and crossed to pick up her copy of the script.

It didn't help any that Cait Lynden chose that moment to exert her considerable feminine charm or that Michel appeared responsive, albeit politely so.

A ploy to make her jealous? It's working, isn't it? a wretched little imp taunted.

She watched them surreptitiously beneath veiled lashes and had to admit the blood simmered in her veins as Cait flirted outrageously with the deliberate touch of her hand on his sleeve, the wickedly sensual smile, the brazen *knowledge* evident in those glittering blue eyes.

Sandrine felt the knot in her stomach tighten as she sightlessly scanned the upcoming scene in her copy of the script.

Damn Michel. For every darn thing. And especially for invading her professional turf.

'Okay, everyone. Places, please.'

Thank heavens for small mercies, Sandrine accorded as she mentally prepared herself to be in character and silently rehearsed her few lines.

It was late afternoon before Sandrine was dismissed from the set with the news she wouldn't be required until Tuesday. The person responsible for continuity took the requisite Polaroid, and Sandrine went through the process of discarding the elegant costume and wig with help from the wardrobe assistant, then she removed her make-up and shook her hair free from the confining hairnet.

The comparison between screen actress in character and the modern jean-clad girl was remarkable. So remarkable, she decided ruefully, that it was unlikely anyone would recognise her as being one and the same person.

It was after five when she emerged into the parking lot, and she filched keys from her carry-bag as she walked towards her car.

'Hoping to slip away undetected?'

Michel fell into step beside her, and she quickened her pace, choosing not to answer him.

A minute later she slipped the key into the lock and opened the door, then slid in behind the wheel and fired the engine.

A great exit line would have been *Eat my dust*, except the moment was dramatically reduced as her tyres squealed faintly on smooth bitumen, and she was forced to adhere to the low speed limit.

However, once she hit the highway she put her foot down and let the speedometer needle soar as far as she dared without risk to life or limb or threat of a speeding ticket. It provided some release for the build-up of tension.

Sandrine reached Sanctuary Cove in record time, and inside the villa she ran lightly upstairs, changed into a maillot, grabbed a towel, retraced her steps and went out to the pool.

The water was refreshingly cool, and she stroked several lengths of the pool before turning onto her back and lazily allowing the buoyancy of the water to keep her afloat.

It was all too easy to allow her thoughts to wander and reflect on the day's events.

And Michel.

She hadn't slept well and had spent much of her waking hours wondering at her sanity in sharing the same bed. It was madness, an act that amounted to masochism. For to lie so close, yet be so far from him, attacked her emotional foundation and tore it to shreds.

What would he have done if she'd reached out and touched him? If he'd ignored her, she'd have died. Yet if he'd responded, how could she hope to handle the aftermath?

Such an act could only amount to sexual gratification and achieve nothing except provide mutual satisfaction. Akin to scratching an itch.

The attuning of heart, mind and soul would be missing, and somehow just *sex* wasn't enough.

She was mad. Insane, she added mentally. Any other woman would catch hold of Michel's coat-tails, exult in all that his wealth and social prestige could provide and hang in there for the ride.

And what a ride! Even the thought of it sent warmth flooding through her body. Each separate nerve end quivered in anticipation, and sensation wreaked havoc with her equilibrium.

It had been bad enough when they were oceans apart. Now that he was here, it was a thousand times worse.

Magic, she thought. Highly sensitised, sensual sorcery of a kind that defied valid description. Transmuted in the touch, the look, the promise...and the anticipation.

To part after a long night of loving and count each hour until they could be together again. To counter and feed that need with a phone call, a softly spoken promise. The delivery of a single red rose. That special look lovers exchange in a room filled with people. And the waiting, the wanting.

Was it love? The to-die-for, till-death-us-do-part kind of loving? Or was it sexual satiation, a sensual nirvana?

She'd thought it was both until their first serious argument. Now she wasn't so sure.

'Pleasant thoughts, I trust?'

The faintly inflected drawl caused her to jackknife

and turn towards the tall male figure standing close to the pool's edge.

Michel had discarded his jacket and tie and loosened the top two buttons of his shirt. His hair looked slightly ruffled, as if he'd dragged impatient fingers through its groomed length.

'How long have you been standing there?' she demanded.

'Does it matter?'

Watching her unobserved almost amounted to an invasion of privacy, and she didn't like it one bit.

A few strokes brought her to the side of the pool, and she levered herself easily to sit on its edge. Her towel lay out of reach on a lounger, and she rose to her feet, then caught it up in one quick movement.

His faint amusement didn't go unnoticed, and she determinedly blotted the excess moisture from her body before tending to her hair.

'I've booked a table for dinner at the Hyatt.'

Sandrine heard the words but momentarily chose to ignore them.

'I'm sure you'll enjoy the meal,' she managed calmly. 'I've heard the chef has an excellent reputation.'

'For two,' Michel informed her. 'At seven.'

'I shan't wait up.'

'You have an hour to shower and get ready.'

She looked at him steadily. 'I'm not going anywhere with you.'

'Damn, you try my patience!'

'And you try mine!'

'Is it unacceptable to want to share a meal with my wife in pleasant surroundings?'

'No,' Sandrine said sweetly. 'Providing your wife is willing. And in this instance, she's not!'

'Sandrine—'

'Don't threaten me, Michel.' She tried for quiet dignity but didn't quite make it. Her eyes speared his, dark and intense with emotion. 'I refuse to fall in with every suggestion you make.'

'You prefer to eat here?'

'Don't you get it? I don't want to share a meal with you. *Anywhere*.' A faint tremor shook her body, and she tightened her grip on the towel.

His eyes narrowed. 'You're shivering.'

'How perceptive,' she mocked. 'If you'll excuse me, I'll go take a hot shower.' As she moved past him, she endeavoured to ignore the sheer magnetism of the man. And her body's traitorous reaction.

Two more weeks, she reasoned as she ran lightly upstairs. Maybe less. And filming would be over. At least, her participation would finish. Could she go the distance, living in the same villa, sharing the same bed as the man who was bent on using any advantage he could gain?

Sandrine reached her bedroom and crossed into the adjoining en suite. A swift turn of the dial and warm water cascaded onto the tiled floor of the shower.

It took only seconds to strip the wet Lycra from her body, and she stepped into the large cubicle, reached for the bottle of shampoo, then began the task of lathering it through her hair.

Ten minutes later she emerged into the bedroom and came to a sudden halt at the sight of Michel in the process of discarding his clothes.

'Finished?'

Sandrine's left hand flew to the towel carelessly caught in a knot between her breasts, and with her right she steadied the towel wound high on her head.

'There are two other bathrooms on this level,' she pointed out in a slightly strangled voice.

'You object to sharing?'

Oh, my, he was good. Reasonable, faintly teasing beneath the edge of cynicism.

'Yes,' she returned, regaining her equilibrium as she crossed the room to collect fresh underwear. 'Considering your main purpose is to unsettle me.'

'An admission I'm succeeding, Sandrine?'

She'd fallen straight into that one, hadn't she? 'Not at all,' she responded calmly, and knew she lied. Her entire nervous system jangled at the very thought of him.

Watching Michel as he crossed the room to the bathroom created a havoc all of its own as she took in his broad frame, the muscular set of his shoulders, superb pectorals, the hard-packed diaphragm and firm waist.

She controlled a faint shiver at the thought of what it felt like to be held close, to feel the strength in those arms as he enfolded her firmly within them.

It was almost possible to breathe in the musky aroma of his skin, the clean freshness of the soap he used, the male cologne. Sense the way he tasted when her mouth joined with his, the faintly abrasive and moist slide as their tongues caressed and explored in an erotic mating dance.

The essence of his sex, the degree of power she experienced in taking him to the brink of his control, the way that large male body shook as he tumbled over the edge. Man at his most vulnerable.

Sandrine tried to restrain the way heat flared through her body, but she failed as the image of his lovemaking rose to taunt her.

He had the look, the touch, the power to drive a woman wild. And much to her chagrin, there was a part of her that wanted him badly. Without question or recrimination.

She heard the faint buzz of his electric razor, followed minutes later by the fall of water in the shower stall.

She immediately visualised Michel's naked form, his potent masculinity, the impressive power sheathed at the apex of his thighs.

Focus, concentrate, *remember* the accusations they'd exchanged seven weeks ago, she silently raged as she discarded the towel and stepped into briefs, then fastened her bra before pulling on a pair of jeans and a cotton top.

That fateful night she had looked at Michel... someone she'd loved with all her heart, in whom she had implicit trust, and believed their lives, their love, were forever entwined...and now it was like looking at a stranger.

With an irritated gesture, Sandrine unwound the

towel from her head and shook out hair that fell in a
cloud of sable silk onto her shoulders.

How did the axiom go? *Marry in haste, repent at
leisure*?

She reached for the hair dryer, plugged it in, then
began combing the warm air through her hair.

What would have happened if she'd stayed? If she'd
cancelled her flight and risked a breach of contract?
Would they have resolved anything? Or had her abrupt
departure merely precipitated their separation?

Seven weeks. Weeks that could be viewed as a brief
respite, or a lifetime, depending on the interpretation.

'You intend wearing casual gear to dinner?'

Sandrine reached forward and switched off the hair
dryer. Via mirrored reflection, she saw him discard the
towel, step into briefs, then pull on tailored trousers
before crossing to the wardrobe and extracting a shirt.

'I hadn't planned on dressing up.' She caught her
hair and began winding it into a knot.

'Leave it loose.'

Her hands didn't falter as she fastened the knot with
pins. 'It's cooler if I wear it up.'

Michel buttoned his shirt, fastened his trousers, then
pulled on socks and shoes.

'No make-up?'

'Why?' Sandrine countered. 'I'm not planning on
going anywhere.'

His expression didn't change, but his eyes hardened.
'I leave in five minutes, Sandrine. With, or without
you. Your choice.'

She turned to face him. 'You could always ring

Cait. She'd just *die* to share anything with you.'
Without a further word, she walked from the room and
made her way downstairs to the kitchen.

A tin of salmon and a tossed salad were poor sub-
stitutes for the appetiser, main course, fruit and cheese
board Michel would no doubt enjoy with table service,
a fine wine, subdued lighting and soft background music. She told herself she didn't care as she heard him
exit the house, followed by the start of a car engine.

Half an hour later she rinsed the few plates she'd
used, placed them in the dishwasher, then filled a glass
with bottled water and crossed into the lounge to
watch television.

At ten she dimmed the lights and went upstairs to
bed. For a few minutes she dithered over *which* bed,
rationalising that the main bedroom was *hers*, and if
Michel was determined to make it *his*, then he could
damn well *suffer* because she didn't intend to move.

Yet sharing the bed was akin to playing with fire,
and no way did she want to get burned. To slip into
the convenience of pleasurable sex wasn't on her
agenda.

With that thought in mind she collected linen and
made up the bed in a room farthest from the one
Michel had designated his own. Then she moved a few
essentials in clothes and toiletries and determinedly
slid between cool percale sheets, then turned out the
light.

Moonlight shone through in between the painted
wooden shutters, and after what seemed an intermi-

nable length of time spent tossing and turning, she padded across to the window to adjust them.

Sleep was never more distant, and she did the yoga thing, counted sheep and endeavoured to think pleasant, relaxing thoughts. Except the image that rose to taunt her belonged to Michel, and she rolled onto her stomach and punched the pillow.

Her room faced the water and was therefore at the opposite end of the house to the garage. Was he home yet? She hadn't heard so much as a sound to indicate he'd returned.

Maybe some gorgeous female had insisted on sharing his table and right this minute they were caught up in a web of harmless seduction. Or would it be harmless? Michel was a practised raconteur, and charm personified. He also possessed an indefinable sensual aura that had most women conjuring up every ploy in the book to attract his attention.

Sandrine played numerous different scenarios in her mind, damning Michel in every one of them until her subconscious mind took her deeper into vivid dreams that seemed no less real.

It was after eleven when the powerful car whispered to a halt in the garage. Michel entered the house and turned out lights as he gained the upper floor.

The empty bed gave him a bad moment, then he systematically conducted a quiet search of the remaining rooms and experienced an enormous degree of relief when he discovered his wife's recumbent form caught in a tangled twist of sheets.

He stood in the open doorway for several long minutes, then crossed to the bed.

She was beautiful. So fiercely independent and possessed of so much spirit. He wanted to smooth the hair back from her forehead and brush his lips across her temple.

Damn. He wanted more, so much more than a gesture of tenderness. He craved what they'd once shared. The mesmeric magical heat that culminated in shameless passion and encapsulated them as twin halves of a whole. Complete, inviolate, *one* on every level... spiritually, mentally, emotionally.

Another curse whispered from his lips, one that would have scorched the ears of anyone who chanced to overhear it. Directed entirely at himself for allowing the strictures of business to take precedence over love for his wife.

Instead of taking the next flight in pursuit, he'd thrown himself into resolving extremely delicate financial negotiations in a takeover bid integral to the family's overflowing coffers. And ensured Sandrine's safety by employing a pair of highly reputable professionals to watch over her twenty-four hours a day.

His manipulative skill in the business arena was highly regarded among his peers. Women actively pursued him for his wealth and social position. They pandered to his ego, made all the right practised moves in an existence that he'd come to consider artificial. Experience had made him both cynical and wary.

Until Sandrine.

Sandrine, with her lack of guile and artifice, whose

laughter was both infectious and earthy. Her smile could light up her whole body so that her skin glowed and her eyes gleamed with a reflected warmth that came straight from the heart.

He'd wanted her from that first moment, not just in the biblical sense. Instinct warned it would be more than that. Much more.

She was his most precious possession, and from the beginning he'd wanted to shield and protect her.

There was no way he could sanction her flying off to the other side of the world without him. Or staying there alone. The timing, given his professional responsibility, couldn't have been worse.

A wry smile twisted his mouth. Financial wizardry was his speciality, and fate had been on his side. He could rescue a movie on the brink of foundering and employ emotional blackmail to salvage his marriage. What was it they said? *Kill two birds with one stone.*

The movie didn't present a problem. Sandrine, on the other hand, would be no easy victory.

It was a challenge. The most important of his life, and one he was determined to win.

A slight sound caught his attention, and he watched as she turned restlessly onto her back.

She looked defenceless in sleep, he mused. Her skin smooth and translucent in the reflected hall light. Her eyelashes impossibly long, and her mouth soft and lushly curved.

His emotions stirred into life, and he determinedly tamped them down as he gathered her into his arms and carried her back to the room they'd shared the previous night.

She stirred slightly as he lowered her into bed, then she settled, and he removed his clothes and slid in beside her to lie silent and unmoving in the darkness until sleep finally claimed him long after the witching hour of midnight.

CHAPTER FOUR

SANDRINE woke slowly as gradual awareness dispensed one layer of unconsciousness after another, bringing with it the reality of a new day.

Sunday, she determined with a restful sigh. No early-morning call, no studio.

Then she remembered, and with memory came the realisation that she wasn't in the bed or the room she'd retreated to last night.

What's more, she wasn't alone.

A masculine arm held her anchored closely against a very male frame. A very aroused male.

Michel's hand splayed over her stomach, and she could feel his steady, rhythmic heartbeat against her shoulder.

Dear God.

Seeking help from the Deity didn't work. Nor did the fervent but faint hope she might be dreaming, for no one dreamed with their eyes open.

Her thoughts reflected a kaleidoscope of conflicting emotions as she rationalised what action she should take.

If she kept her breathing even and she moved slowly, an inch at a time, maybe Michel wouldn't notice, and eventually she'd be able to slip free from his grasp and the bed.

A ridiculous strategy, she silently castigated herself seconds later when the slightest movement resulted in an involuntary tightening of his hold.

What now? Jab her elbow into his ribs? Thump a fist against his forearm? Maybe both? Yes, that might work.

'Planning your method of attack?' a deep voice drawled far too close to one ear.

'You got it in one,' she responded thickly, aiming a vicious jab with her elbow...and missed as he successfully deflected the manoeuvre. Kicking her heel against his shins didn't make an impression at all, and she uttered a growl in rage. 'Let me go!'

'*S'il vous plaît*?' he queried musingly.

'Go to hell.'

'If you want to play...'

'You're enjoying this, aren't you?' she retorted vengefully as she twisted helplessly to free herself.

'Not particularly. I prefer a woman to be pliant and willing in my arms.'

'Fat chance!'

'You would like me to prove how easily I can change your mind?'

Sandrine lay very still as she attempted to control the sudden hitch in her breathing. All too easily, she agreed silently, much to her chagrin.

He buried his mouth in the soft curve of her neck, then trailed a path to her temple. His hand moved up to cup her breast, and her stomach muscles tightened against the onslaught of sensation.

'Is this where you insist I fulfil my part of the bargain?'

With one easy movement he rolled onto his back and carried her with him to straddle his waist. His features were dark, accentuated by the visible evidence of a night's growth of beard. His eyes held a watchful quality, assessing and vaguely analytical.

This, *this*, she qualified shakily, could prove highly dangerous.

He resembled a lazy tiger, supine, visually content, but exuding a primitive degree of power. One wrong word or move on her part and she entertained no doubt his indolent facade would swiftly vanish.

Her position was extremely tenuous, to say the least.

He lifted a hand and brushed the back of his fingers down her cheek, then slid them forward to cup her chin. 'Your definition, not mine.'

He pressed his thumb against the centre of her lower lip, and acute sensation quivered through her body. 'I moved into another room by choice.'

'And I brought you back here.'

'Because you don't like sleeping alone?' she queried with deliberate sarcasm.

'Sex isn't necessarily a prerequisite to sharing the nuptial bed.'

'You expect me to believe that? Of *you*?'

He was silent for several telling seconds, and when he spoke his voice was so silky it sent shivers scudding down the length of her spine. 'I have a vivid memory of the long nights we shared, *chérie*.'

So did she. Nights when she became a willing wanton in his arms as she embraced a sensual feast so erotic there were times when she wept from the joy of it.

'That was then,' Sandrine said slowly, and glimpsed his wry smile.

'And this is now, hmm?'

'Yes.'

'In that case, let's get dressed and go downstairs for breakfast.' In one smooth movement he lifted her to stand on the floor, then he swept aside the covers and slid to his feet.

Clothes, bathroom, she decided, in that order, gathering jeans and a stretch rib-knit top. Seconds later she was safely ensconced behind a closed door with, she hoped, total privacy.

There were no locks on the internal doors, and she took a quick shower, dressed, then emerged to find the bedroom empty.

Sandrine descended the stairs and followed the aroma of freshly brewed coffee to the kitchen, where Michel looked completely at ease breaking eggs into a bowl while a skillet heated on the stove top. Dressed in black designer jeans and a white polo-neck knit shirt, he looked indecently male.

His actions reminded her of the breakfasts they'd shared and their easy camaraderie. Then, she would have teased him mercilessly, applauded his skill and uttered a husky laugh as he carried her back to the bedroom.

Now, she silently filled two glasses with orange

juice, poured the coffee and transferred everything onto the table.

Michel placed one plate with a steaming omelette before her, then settled in the seat opposite.

Her stomach felt as if it were tied in knots, and it irked her considerably that his appetite didn't appear in the least affected.

Sandrine forked a few morsels into her mouth, bit off a segment of toast, then sipped the strong black coffee.

Michel refilled his cup, added sugar, then pushed his empty plate to one side and sank back in his chair. 'We have the day. What do you suggest we do with it?'

She replaced her cup on its saucer and met his steady gaze with equanimity. 'I plan to go shopping.'

'Specifically?'

'Food,' she answered succinctly. 'Staples such as bread, milk, eggs, fruit.'

'And then?'

'Take the car and explore a little.'

Michel rose to his feet and began clearing the table. 'I'll drive. You can play navigator.'

'Excuse me?'

He cast her a musing glance that held a hint of patient forbearance. 'We'll take in the supermarket, then explore.'

'Since when did *I* become *we*?'

His silence was telling, his expression equally so, and she was the one to break his gaze as she gathered up a few spreads and carried them to the refrigerator.

'What if I'd prefer to be alone?'

'Don't push it, Sandrine.'

It took only minutes to rinse and stack the few plates in the dishwasher, then Sandrine collected her shoulder-bag, slid sunglasses atop her head and walked through to the garage, uncaring whether Michel followed or not.

Sanctuary Cove village comprised a wide variety of up-market stores and trendy boutiques, numerous cafés and restaurants and was accessed via two bricked lanes whose median strip held immaculately trimmed palm trees. The adjoining grounds fringed a lush green golf course, which seasonally hosted international competitions.

The few grocery staples required to boost supplies could have been selected in five minutes, but Sandrine deliberated over the choice of fruit, the varieties of lettuce, and opted to visit the local bakery rather than select packaged sliced bread.

Michel added a few selections of his own and appeared mildly amused when she rejected more than one.

Half an hour later they retreated to the villa, stored their purchases and returned to the car.

'Where to?'

'There are mountains, beaches, theme parks,' Sandrine responded as Michel eased the car through the security gate. 'Your choice.'

'Noosa.'

She cast him a startled glance. 'That's more than a two-hour drive north.'

He gave a slight shrug. 'Is that a problem?'

'No, I guess not.'

He reached a large roundabout and circled it. 'Navigate, Sandrine.'

She directed him onto the multilane highway where they joined the swift flow of traffic travelling north, and after an hour they took the Sunshine Coast bypass.

Soon they were driving through farmland devoted to sugarcane, avocados, pineapples, strawberries and a variety of fruit trees. Small country towns reflected a slower-paced lifestyle, old-style buildings mingling with modern, and in the distance lay the brooding range of bush-clad hills, a deep blue-green against the azure skyline.

'The Glasshouse Mountains,' Sandrine revealed, studying the tour-guide booklet. 'Montville, Maleny. Craft ware, quaint teashops, picturesque.'

'We'll go there tomorrow.'

She frowned and cast him a quick glance. It was difficult to determine anything from his expression for his eyes were shaded by dark sunglasses and his focus was on the road ahead.

'What do you mean...*tomorrow*?' she demanded.

'We'll detour through on the way back to the Coast,' Michel explained patiently.

'You intend for us to stay overnight in Noosa?'

'Is that a problem?'

'You're darn right it's a problem. I don't have a change of clothes for a start,' she said heatedly.

'It's a tourist strip. The shops will be open. We'll buy what we need.'

She turned on him with ill-concealed anger. 'Did you plan this?'

'It seems foolish to travel back to the Coast tonight, only to turn around and return again tomorrow,' he said reasonably.

'You could have asked me!'

'And given you the opportunity to refuse?'

She shot him a fulminating glare. 'I dislike being hijacked.'

'Look on it as an adventure.'

Some adventure! If she managed to get through the next thirty-six hours without hitting him, it would be a miracle.

'If I'd known you had this in mind, I'd have brought along the script. It might have escaped your attention, but I'm due on the set Tuesday and I need to study my lines!'

'I have it on good authority the lines are few, and unless the scene needs to be reshot, you should be done by midday.'

'I hate you.'

'Hate is a strong emotion and, as such, better than indifference.'

'You just missed the turn-off.'

'Caused by a navigational distraction?' he mocked as he decelerated, then swung the car into a wide turn.

Her lips tightened, and she refrained from uttering a further word except for curt, explicit instructions.

Michel chose the most up-market hotel resort on the main Hastings Street strip, relinquished the vehicle for valet parking, then led her into the main foyer to register.

It would serve him right if the hotel was fully booked, she reflected vengefully. Luck wasn't on her side as Michel completed the necessary paperwork and accepted a card folder with their room security tags.

Their suite overlooked the river towards a bank of riverfront mansions, Sandrine discovered on crossing to the window. The tranquil vista exuded a different ambience from that of the Gold Coast.

'Lunch,' Michel declared. 'Let's go find a place to eat.'

Sandrine turned towards him. 'I don't want to be part of a game you've chosen to play.'

'Specifically?'

'You're a superb tactician, Michel,' she acknowledged dryly.

'Is that a compliment, or a condemnation?'

'Both.'

'*Merci*,' he returned with wry humour. 'What game is it you imagine I'm playing?'

'One of revenge.'

He didn't pretend to misunderstand. 'Choosing to keep you in suspense as to when I begin collecting on our deal?'

'Yes.'

He wanted to cross the room and shake her until she pleaded for mercy. Instead, he thrust a hand into his trouser pocket and controlled the timbre of his voice. 'What if I said *tonight*?'

Something inside her stomach curled into a hard, painful ball. 'Why wait? Why not now?'

She reached for the buttons on her blouse and slowly undid one, then the other, forcing her fingers to remain steady until all the buttons were freed.

'Do you have any specific requirements?' Dear heaven, how could she sound so calm when inside she was shaking like a leaf?

'Enlighten me.'

'You're the one calling the shots.' She slid the blouse off one shoulder, then the other, and draped it carelessly over a nearby chair. As her fingers went to the snap fastening on her jeans, she looked over at him. 'Aren't you going to get out of your clothes?'

How far would she go? 'When you're done,' Michel drawled, calling her bluff, 'you can undress me.'

Pain arrowed through her body, so acute it almost made her wince. *Act*, a tiny voice prompted. You're good at it.

Sandrine managed a faint shrug. 'If that's what turns you on.' She slid the zip down on her jeans and slowly eased the denim over her hips. She slipped off her joggers, lifted one leg free, then the other, and tossed the jeans on top of the blouse.

He wasn't going to let her go through with this, was he?

She stood in briefs and bra, and although they covered her more adequately than a bikini, she felt vulnerable and exposed.

He stood perfectly still, his gaze steady and unblinking as she looked at him.

Damn him, he wasn't going to help her out.

With slow, sure steps she crossed to where he stood. His shirt was short-sleeved with three buttons at the neck. She caught hold of the knit fabric on either side of his rib cage and pulled it free from his waistband. Then she tugged upwards with little success until he obligingly raised his arms and lowered his head to accommodate the shirt's easy removal.

Too much. He really was much too much, she muttered silently. The spread of his shoulders, the breadth of chest, the strong musculature that rippled and bunched with every movement.

She threw the shirt in the path of her blouse and jeans, then turned back and reached for the snap on his jeans, pulled it open, then stifled a soft curse.

Buttons. No zip for easy unfastening.

Each one presented a fresh torture. Her fingers fumbled, and she felt totally inadequate for the task. It didn't help any that the denim was stretched tight against a hard male arousal.

She could, she reasoned, literally throw up her hands and tell him to complete the task himself. Except she was darned if she'd allow him the satisfaction of winning a challenge. She could almost hear his musing drawl, see the faint mockery in those dark eyes as he finished discarding his clothes.

As he would, if only to witness her discomfort, she determined as she dealt with another button.

How things had changed, she reflected wryly. In the not-too-distant past she'd have laughed and delighted in the task, taking pleasure in teasing him outrageously and exulting in his reaction.

Now, he had control while she slipped into such a state of nerves she couldn't even manage something as simple as undoing a series of buttons!

Just do it, the tiny voice urged. Slip into pretend mode and imagine he's someone who means nothing to you.

There, it was done. Stretch fashion jeans possessed one inescapable flaw. They were the very devil for someone else to remove! Tailored trousers wouldn't have presented any problem, but jeans were a different story, she decided, gritting her teeth as she tugged the fabric down over powerful thighs.

The action brought her face close to a vulnerable part of his anatomy, and she entertained the brief vindictive thought that with one quick movement she could cause him considerable pain. The consequences, however, wouldn't be worth it.

In a few swift movements he slid off his joggers, then stepped out of his jeans and kicked them to one side. Fine black silk skimmed his hips and couched his manhood, emphasising olive skin roughened by hair and a male frame in superb physical shape.

Sandrine momentarily closed her eyes, then opened them again. Michel wasn't an unknown lover. Why hesitate?

There was a part of her that longed for the feel of his mouth, the tactile skill of those clever hands as they created havoc with each separate pleasure zone. She wanted to lose herself in the wealth of emotional and spiritual sensations, to go to that special place where there was only *him*...and the unique alchemy they shared.

It had been good. Better than good, she amended.

A hand caught hold of her chin, lifted it so she had to look at him. His thumb traced the edge of her jaw, lingered there, then slid slowly down the column of her throat.

Sandrine swallowed compulsively, wanting to move away but held mesmerised by the darkness of those deep grey eyes as he forced her to hold his gaze.

Then he lowered his head and angled his mouth over hers in a kiss that was hard and mercilessly plundering as he took what she wouldn't willingly give.

Just as she thought her jaw would break, the pressure eased, and his tongue caressed and cajoled in a teasing dance that almost made her weep.

Not content, he savoured the taste of her lips, their soft, swollen contours throbbing beneath his touch. He nipped the full centre with the edge of his teeth, caught her indrawn breath, then angled his mouth to hers in a kiss that tore at the very threads of her soul.

With considerable ease his lips trailed a path down her neck, lingered as he explored the hollows at the edge of her throat, then travelled to the soft fullness of her breast.

In one easy movement he freed the twin hooks of her bra and dispensed with it before returning his attention to the rounded curve.

A soft flick from the tip of his tongue brought a

surge of sensation, and she arched her neck, allowing him access.

Her whole body began to melt as heat flowed through her veins, warming her body until she was on fire with a passion so strong, so tumultuous, there was only the man and the aching, wanting *need*.

His hand slid down to her waist, then splayed low over her stomach, his fingers slipping beneath the satin and lace of her briefs, seeking, probing, *teasing*, until she scaled the heights, clung, then descended in a free-falling spiral.

He caught her as she fell, held her, then took her on a return journey that was even more devastating than the first.

This time she was unable to still the soft, throaty cries or stop the flow of tears as they trickled slowly down her cheeks.

Michel brushed a thumb against each rivulet in turn, dispensing the dampness with a tenderness that brought a lump to her throat. His lips settled at the corner of her mouth, caressing the soft fullness of her lower lip with the edge of his tongue.

He paused to nibble the moist inner tissue, then conducted a seductive foray, tracing her tongue with his own, before taking possession with claim-staking action.

Sandrine was barely conscious of her hands creeping up to link together at his nape as he folded her close, and she kissed him back, giving, taking, in what became a storm of sensual exploration.

It wasn't enough. Not nearly enough, and she

moved against him, instinctively seeking more. Her hands shifted to his shoulders, then slid down over his back, urging him closer as she unconsciously raked her nails over muscled flesh to emphasise her need.

Without missing a beat, Michel swung an arm beneath her thighs and swept her into his arms, then tumbled with her down onto the bed. In one easy movement he rolled her beneath him, caging her body as he tore his briefs free.

It was as if every pore of her skin became highly sensitised to his touch, and an exigent sexual chemistry was apparent—vital, electric, lethal—for it melted her mental resistance, leaving only the craving for physical release.

Now, she urged, unaware whether the word left her lips or not. She was burning up inside, on fire with a primal heat so intense she lost sight of who and where she was in the need to have him deep inside her, matching each primeval movement until that deep, rhythmic possession transported them both simultaneously to exquisite sensual sensation.

Sandrine almost cried out loud when his mouth left hers and began a slow, tortuous descent, pausing to savour delicate hollows at the base of her throat before trailing a path to her breast, suckling first one acutely sensitised peak before delivering a similar assault on its twin.

Her stomach tensed as he explored the delicate indentation of her navel, and she gasped as he moved low to caress the most sensitive pleasure spot of all.

Her body arched as she became consumed by a

wicked ecstasy so acute she began to plead, muted guttural sounds she didn't recognise as being her own voice.

She reached for his head, seeking purchase on his hair, and she pulled it mercilessly in a bid to have him desist. Only to have him catch hold of her wrists and effortlessly clamp them to her sides.

'Michel.' His name emerged endless minutes later, accompanied by a mindless, tortured sob. 'Please.'

Seconds later he slowly raised his head and gave her a long, impassioned look. His eyes were so incredibly dark they were almost black.

Her breath came in ragged gasps, and her pulse seemed to beat so fast it was almost out of control. Her eyes felt too big for her face, their expression wild, dilated with an emotion she didn't care to define.

When his head lowered, she gave an anguished cry and felt her flesh quiver uncontrollably as he began bestowing an agonisingly slow trail of soft, open-mouthed kisses to her navel, the soft slope of her breasts, their tender aureoles, the slender column of her neck, before taking possession of her mouth.

Timeless minutes later he freed her hands, and the breath stilled in her throat as he entered her with one powerful thrust.

She could feel herself stretching to accommodate his length, the tightness as she enclosed and held him, followed by the primitive rhythm that he kept erotically slow at first, so measured and deep she was aware of every muscle contraction.

She was almost falling apart when he quickened the

pace to a heavy, pulsating action that took her so high she became wild with the force and strength of it.

Her body felt as if it were a finely tuned instrument played by a virtuoso until it was wooed to such a fine crescendo that the only possible climax was to fracture and splinter into a thousand pieces in the accompanying electric silence.

He remained buried deep inside her as he cradled her face and kissed the teardrops trickling slowly down each cheek, trailing their path to the edge of her lips.

How was it possible to weep with such a combination of acute pleasure and sadness? Sadness, she rationalised, for an awareness that the pleasure had been all hers.

Michel supported his weight, then bestowed a series of butterfly kisses to the contours of her mouth before lifting his head to gaze down at her.

'Okay?' he queried gently.

What could she say? There wasn't one adequate word that came readily to mind. 'Speechless,' she managed at last.

'I meant *you*,' he qualified slowly.

'Fine.' You lie, the tiny voice chastised. Your body still vibrates from the feel of him, and you ache with a hurt that has little to do with physical pain.

Michel saw the faint clouding evident in those beautifully luminous brown eyes and glimpsed the rapid pulse beat at the base of her throat.

He leant forward and placed his lips to that frenetically beating hollow, felt her tremor and gently tucked a stray swath of hair from her cheek.

Sandrine wanted to close her eyes and block out the sight of him, but that wasn't an option. Instead, she wrinkled her nose at him in silent, mocking remonstrance.

'Lunch,' she declared, 'I'm hungry.' In one easy movement she slid off the bed and crossed the room to the en suite.

Michel followed and merely arched an eyebrow when she lifted a hand in mute denial that he share her shower.

'Modesty is inappropriate,' he drawled as he stepped in beside her, caught up the soap and began lathering it over her body.

'Give it to me,' she said in a strangled voice as she attempted to take the soap from his hand.

'No.'

She didn't want to fight. Dammit, she didn't possess the energy or the inclination right at this moment to do more than submit to his ministrations.

When he finished, she let the fine needle spray rinse the soap from her body, then she slid open the glass door and reached for a towel. By the time Michel emerged she was dressed, her hair was swept into a knot on top of her head, and she was applying colour to her lips.

He pulled on his clothes, ran his fingers through his dampened hair, then he inclined his head in bemused mockery and swept an arm towards the door. 'After you.'

CHAPTER FIVE

THEY selected a small intimate restaurant with an appealing blackboard menu, chose an outdoor table shaded by a large umbrella, ordered seafood pasta, *focaccia* and white wine, and were impressed by the quality of the food and the service.

Sandrine declined anything to follow and settled for strong black coffee.

'You enjoyed the food?'

She looked at the man seated opposite and fought against an enveloping wave of sensation.

How was it that he had this cataclysmic effect on her? He exuded an unfair share of sensuality, an inherent quality that was both mesmeric and magical.

'Yes, thank you.'

His mouth curved into a faint smile. 'So polite. More coffee?'

She shook her head, then watched as he gestured to the waiter to bring the bill.

'Shall we leave?' Michel queried minutes later, and Sandrine rose to her feet in acquiescence.

Together they strolled along the main street, pausing every now and then to examine a shop window display. Sandrine purchased a few postcards, added moisturiser and sun-screen cream, insisting on paying for them herself. Use of her credit card took care of a bikini and sarong wrap in glorious turquoise.

'The resort pool or the ocean?' Michel asked as they deposited an assortment of carry bags in their hotel suite.

She didn't hesitate for a second. 'Ocean.'

It took only minutes to change, collect a towel and cross the street to the beach.

A number of people inhabited the clean white sand; children laughed and squealed as they played while adults were bent on improving their tans or relaxing beneath large beach umbrellas.

The sea looked peaceful, with the gentle waves of an incoming tide encroaching on the foreshore. The curved bay was picturesque with its outcrop of rocks, a steep, bush-clad hill that led to a Natural Reserve.

There were many such beaches, coves and bays along the eastern coast, but Noosa held a reputation all its own.

Bliss, Sandrine silently reflected as she spread her towel beneath the beach umbrella Michel had erected. First, she'd sunbathe, then she'd swim.

Applying sun-screen cream was a sensible precaution, given the strength of the summer sun, and it took only minutes to cover her legs, arms and midriff.

'What do you think you're doing?' she demanded as Michel extracted the plastic bottle and squeezed a generous portion onto his cupped fingers.

'Applying cream to your back.'

Her mouth pursed at the amusement apparent as he

began smoothing the protective cream onto her shoulders.

He was thorough. A little too thorough, she decided as he ensured every centimetre of exposed skin was covered. He even went to the extent of loosening the clip of her bikini top, then refastening it. And his fingers caused havoc with her nervous system as they conducted a firm, circling massage across her back, over her waist and down to the line of her bikini briefs. Controlling her breathing became an effort, and she was grateful her expression was hidden behind dark glasses.

'Thanks.' Her voice was husky, almost indistinct.

'You can return the favour,' Michel instructed her indolently, handing her the bottle.

His request was deliberate, she was sure of it. Part of a strategy to test the effect such an action would have on her. Well, she'd show him just how easy it was to touch him. It wouldn't trouble her at all.

Ten seconds in and she knew she lied. He could have done the macho thing and flexed every muscle. Instead, he simply sat with his knees raised, his back to her, and his breathing didn't alter a fraction as she completed the application in record time.

Sandrine didn't want to think about the way her pulse raced into overdrive or how every nerve end uncurled in sensitive anticipation. An ache began deep inside, radiating from her central core until it encompassed her whole body.

'All done,' she managed evenly as she recapped the

bottle, mirroring his movements as he stretched out, face down, on the towel.

Twenty minutes later she strode across the sand to the water's edge, took a few steps, then dived into the cool blue-green sea, emerging to the surface to cleave the waves with leisurely strokes parallel to the shore.

There was something infinitely tranquil about the unlimited expanse of an ocean and the sensation of being at one with nature. Quite different from using a swimming pool, she mused as she trod water and admired the exotic landscape with its many brightly painted, low-rise apartment buildings and houses dotting the foreshore.

It was—how long since she'd last holidayed in Noosa? Years, she perceived wryly. A midyear school break with her parents in the days before divorce had torn the family in two, introduced bitterness and a division of loyalties with the advent of step-parents and step-siblings.

Exclusive boarding schools had effectively ensured a safe haven when she no longer fitted easily into one family or the other. There had always been love and welcome whenever she visited. But there had also been an awareness she was a reminder of another life, another time. An awkwardness, she reflected, that had resulted from her own sensitivity. Something that could have had a detrimental effect.

Instead, she had learnt to be self-sufficient, to strive and succeed on her own merits. And she had, utilising her talent with speech and drama by channelling it into acting, initially in school plays. Part-time modelling with an agency resulted in her appearance in a television commercial, and the rest, as they say, became the substance of dreams when she was offered a character role in a long-running Australian television series.

A modelling assignment in New York during a seasonal filming hiatus had garnered an invitation to a party where Michel numbered one of several guests. Two linked events that had changed her life.

'Intent on solitude?'

Sandrine's eyes widened at the sound of that familiar drawl, and she turned to see Michel within touching distance. Wet hair and water streaking his face did nothing to detract from the chiselled perfection of his features or lessen the degree of power he managed to exude without any effort at all.

'No.'

'Care to try your hand at something more adventurous?'

She was unable to read anything from his expression, and his eyes were too intently watchful for her peace of mind. 'Such as?'

'Hang-gliding, parasailing, jet-skiing?'

'Surely you jest?'

'Hiring a boat and exploring the waterways?' Michel continued as if she hadn't spoken, and she scooped up a handful of water and splashed him with it. 'I could retaliate,' he warned.

'I'm trembling.'

His lips formed a musing smile. 'It can wait.'

It wasn't the words but the implication that sent a

shivery sensation feathering the surface of her skin. His eyes held a warm, purposeful gleam that did much to melt through a layer of her resolve.

Her eyes remaining locked with his, she was aware of him to a degree that was vaguely frightening. Magnetic sensuality. She didn't want to be held in its thrall, for it clouded logic and decimated any rationale.

Michel divined her ambivalence, successfully attributed its cause and chose to cut her a little slack. 'Race you in to shore.'

He even held back, matching his strokes to meet hers, and they emerged from the water together. On reaching their shaded location, he caught up his towel, blotted off the excess moisture, then wound and secured the towel low on his hips.

'Feel like a drink?'

'After a shower and I've changed into something a little more respectable,' Sandrine parried as she copied his actions.

Michel pulled the beach umbrella from the sand and returned it to the hire stand en route to their hotel. 'Go on up,' he directed when they reached the entrance. 'I'll be there in ten minutes.'

She inclined her head, then crossed to Reception to collect their room card. Inside their suite, she made straight for the shower and emerged into the bedroom to discover Michel in the process of discarding several glossy signature carry bags onto the bed.

'You've been shopping.'

'Something to wear to dinner,' he declared as he divided and emptied the bags. 'Here.' He picked up a tissue-wrapped package and tossed it onto the pillow. 'This is for you.'

This, she discovered, was a pair of black silk evening trousers, together with a silk camisole in soft antique gold. There was also a pair of exquisite, lacy black briefs.

'Thanks,' she murmured appreciatively, watching as he shook free a pair of black slacks and a deep blue, short-sleeved silk shirt.

If only he'd relayed his intention to stay overnight, she could have packed a few clothes and he'd have saved some money. Although money was hardly an issue, she decided as she discarded the towel and quickly donned underwear.

The evening trousers and camisole were a perfect fit, and she was in the process of applying make-up when Michel re-entered the room.

Sandrine glanced away from the mirror and met his gleaming gaze. 'They're lovely,' she complimented.

'*Merci*,' he acknowledged with mocking amusement as he discarded the towel.

She returned her attention to applying eye shadow, willing her fingers to be steady as she brushed a soft gold to one upper lid.

The mirror proved her worst enemy, for it reflected heavily muscled thighs, smooth hips and buttocks and a fleeting glimpse of male genitalia as he stepped into briefs. The action involved in pulling on the pair of dark trousers emphasised an impressive display of honed muscle and sinew, and she was unable to glance away as he shrugged into his shirt and tended to the buttons.

Get over it, she derided in silent chastisement, and determinedly focused her attention on completing her make-up. It was something of a relief to enter the en suite minutes later, and she activated the hair dryer, opting to leave her hair to fall loose onto her shoulders.

'Beautiful,' Michel complimented when she re-entered the bedroom. 'But there's something missing.'

She felt on edge, jittery in a way that could only be attributed to acute sensitivity to this particular man. All her fine body hairs seemed to stand on end, quivering like miniature antennae, and her stomach didn't belong to her at all.

This was madness. Why did she feel as if she were being stalked by a prowling predator waiting for the right moment to pounce?

'What is that?' she managed lightly, and felt her body tremble slightly as he moved towards her.

'These.' He took hold of her left hand and slid first her wedding ring, then the magnificent pear-shaped diamond onto the appropriate finger.

Sandrine looked down at her hand, saw the symbols of his possession and didn't know whether to laugh or cry. 'Michel—'

Anything further she might have uttered was stilled as he pressed a finger to her lips. 'Let's go have that drink, shall we?'

The hotel lounge held a mix of patrons, and Michel quirked an eyebrow when she insisted on orange juice.

'The need for a clear head?'

'Definitely!'

'Afraid, Sandrine?'

Of you? 'No,' she responded evenly. Her reaction to him was something different entirely.

His husky chuckle was almost her undoing, and she could have hit him when he raised his glass in a silent, mocking gesture.

'How is your grandmother?' A safe subject, surely, she considered as she took a sip of the refreshing juice.

Michel's eyes held hers as he settled back in his chair. 'She expressed regret that you were unable to join me.'

Not so safe, she mentally corrected. 'She's an incredible lady.'

'Who regards you with affection.'

What could she say to that? After a few seconds she settled with 'How kind.'

'I promised we'd visit her after our return to New York.'

She didn't want to think that far ahead. It was enough just to get through each day.

'Would you like another drink?'

Sandrine shook her head, then watched as he set his empty glass down on the table. 'Shall we go have dinner?'

They chose Italian, the best restaurant, they were assured, in town. Michel ordered a smooth vintage Lambrusco to accompany a gnocchi starter, and they both settled for veal scallopini as a main, with an exquisite lemon tart for dessert.

The ambience was definitely European, the waiters

were Italian, and the food...*perfetto*. Sandrine expressed her pleasure as the waiter served them with a liqueur coffee.

'I don't think I'll eat a thing until at least midday tomorrow,' she declared as they walked out onto the street.

One shoestring strap slipped down over her shoulder and she absently slid it back in place. It had been a great few hours, reminding her far too vividly of previous evenings they'd shared over good food and fine wine.

'That was nice,' she said, offering him a warm smile. 'Thank you.'

His expression was equally warm, and those brilliant grey eyes bore a gleam she didn't care to define. 'My pleasure.'

'Let's walk,' she suggested on impulse. Hastings Street ran parallel to the foreshore, and it wasn't late. A number of tourists were enjoying the evening air, walking, drinking coffee at pavement tables adjoining numerous cafés and restaurants.

Michel caught her hand loosely in his, and she didn't pull free.

Did they look like lovers? Somehow she didn't think so. Their body language wasn't right.

He traced an idle pattern across the delicate veins at her wrist and felt the sudden surge in her pulse as it leapt to a faster beat.

When she attempted to tug her hand free, he forestalled the action by lifting her hand to his lips and kissing each finger in turn, aware of the slight tremor that shook her slender frame.

Sandrine lifted her head and met his steady gaze. 'Are you trying to seduce me?'

'Am I succeeding?'

Only too well.

'Resorting to the neutrality of silence, *mignonne*?'

She offered him a stunning smile. 'Of course.'

'On the grounds that anything verbal might give me a swelled head?'

'Something like that.'

They strolled along one side of the street, pausing every now and then when something in a shop window caught their attention, then they crossed over and wandered back to their hotel.

It was after eleven when she preceded him into their suite, and she automatically stepped out of her shoes, then reached for the waistband of her evening trousers.

Only to discover he'd already beaten her to it. She stood perfectly still as he slid the garment down past her thighs and she didn't move when he slipped the camisole over her head.

It was difficult to retain much dignity clad only in lacy black briefs, and she retreated into the en suite as Michel began divesting his clothes.

The lack of a nightgown caused her a moment's consternation, then she plucked a towel free and wound it sarongwise round her slim form. She might have little option but to sleep nude, but she was darned if she'd walk naked into the bedroom!

Misplaced modesty, she decided ruefully as she met

the dark, gleaming gaze of the man settled comfortably against a nest of pillows. The expanse of sun-kissed olive skin covering honed muscle and sinew was impossible to ignore, so she didn't even try.

His faintly quirked brow didn't help any, nor did his slow, teasing smile as she slid between the sheets before discarding the towel.

'It's a little late to play shy, *chérie*.'

'Perhaps I don't feel comfortable parading nude.'

'Do you?'

A slight frown creased her forehead. 'Do I—what?'

'Feel uncomfortable with me,' Michel pursued patiently as he rolled towards her and supported his head with a propped elbow.

He was too close, and much too dangerous. She became conscious of her breathing and monitoring every breath she took. The beat of her heart seemed loud in her chest, and she was willing to swear the pulse at the base of her throat was visible and far too fast.

'*I* feel uncomfortable with me when I'm around you,' Sandrine admitted with husky honesty, and her eyes widened as he lifted a hand and stroked a forefinger lightly down the length of her nose.

'And that's bad?' He pressed the pad of his thumb against her lower lip, then slowly traced its curve.

Heat suffused her body and pooled between the apex of her thighs. Sensation flared deep within, and her fingers clenched in an effort to control the aching need that made her want to reach for him.

'You're doing this deliberately, aren't you?' Sandrine queried in a slightly strangled voice.

'What am I doing, *mignonne*?'

'Seducing me.'

His head lowered and his lips brushed against her own. 'Mmm,' he teased, his breath warm as it mingled with her own. 'Want me to stop?'

She nearly said *yes*. Then his mouth was on hers, gentle at first, then the pressure increased as he took her deep.

Unbidden, her arms lifted as she linked hands at his nape, and she held on during the sensual storm that followed, giving, taking, in a manner that left her weak-willed and malleable. *His*.

It was a long time before they lay spent, and curled in each other's arms they drifted easily into a blissful sleep from which they stirred in the early dawn hours to shower, then make exquisitely slow love until the waiter delivered their breakfast.

'What to you want to do with the day?' Michel queried as he drank the last of his orange juice, then poured strong black coffee.

Sandrine spooned muesli and fruit, added milk into a bowl, then looked enviously at the plate of bacon, eggs and fried tomato. She was famished. And filled with a languid warmth that owed everything to sensual and sexual satiation.

'Maleny, Montville, the Glasshouse Mountains.'

'I was afraid you would suggest that.'

'Why?' she asked, feigning innocence. 'What else did you have in mind?'

'We could stay here, order a late lunch, then drive back to the Coast.'

The thought of spending several more hours in bed with him would weaken her defences, and they couldn't afford to be weakened further! 'It's a new day,' she proffered solemnly. 'Let's make good use of it.'

'My intention precisely.'

'Let's not go for overkill. We scratched an itch, and it was great.' Better than great. There weren't the words to even begin a satisfactory description for what they'd shared.

His gaze sharpened. 'That's all it was for you? Scratching an itch?'

Sandrine lifted her cup, sipped the dark, sweet brew, then replaced it on the saucer. 'You want to conduct an analysis, Michel? Should I determine a points system and rate you accordingly?'

He wanted to drag her to her feet, sweep her back into the bedroom and change that tepid warmth into blazing heat.

She'd been with him every inch of the way, through the night and in the morning. He was prepared to stake his life on it. He'd felt the tremors shake her body, the sweet tug of her muscles as she took and held him in a fit so snug he grew hard at the very thought of it.

She was slipping into self-protection mode in the clear light of day. He could cope with that as long as he had the nights.

'I don't recall your confiding too many comparisons,' he drawled. 'And as we never did indulge in the Was-it-as-good-for-you-as-it-was-for-me? scenario, I see no reason to begin now.'

'Confidence is a fine thing.'

'Knowledge,' Michel corrected with a tinge of mockery. 'Of you.'

Oh, yes, he had that, she admitted wryly. He knew precisely which buttons to push, and where and when. It gave him an unfair advantage.

They finished breakfast in silence, then showered and dressed before checking out of the resort and collecting the car.

It was a beautiful day, the sky a clear azure with only a few wispy clouds in sight. Warm sunshine promised high summer temperatures as they left Noosa and headed towards the mountains.

Soon there were roadside stalls selling a variety of fruit and vegetables, and as they ascended, the ground undulated with acre upon acre in a patchwork of green pasture. It was a visual vista Sandrine found relaxing.

Not so relaxing were the events of last night. It was all too easy to reflect on the heaven of being in Michel's arms, savouring his taste, his touch, exulting in the sheer sensation of two lovers in perfect accord.

Even now, her body ached in places, and all it took was one glance, a vivid memory, and the heat began to simmer deep inside, flaring acutely until Michel became her total focus. Intense sexual chemistry, and ruinous to her peace of mind.

It brought a lump to her throat for a few long seconds and made swallowing difficult.

Dear heaven, think of something else! There, in the

paddocks, were cattle, and overhead a helicopter swung east. On a rescue mission, perhaps?

The car braked suddenly and an arm shot out in front of her, providing a barrier as she was flung forward against her seat belt simultaneously with Michel's muffled oath.

'What on earth?' Sandrine queried in startled surprise as the car came to a screeching halt, only to see the answer for herself as a small dog streaked from the road into the opposite paddock.

'Idiot animal. It could have been killed,' Michel muttered angrily as he directed her an encompassing glance. 'Okay?' She nodded wordlessly, and his gaze sharpened. 'Sure?'

He caught hold of her chin between thumb and forefinger and turned her head towards him, subjecting her to a sweeping appraisal.

'Yes.' It would never do for him to guess her shaken composure was due to *him*, and not the near accident.

She lifted a hand to her throat to hide the fast-beating pulse thudding in the hollow there, and she breathed a silent sigh of relief when he released her and turned his attention back to the road.

It was almost midday when they reached Montville, and Sandrine was captivated by the quaint buildings, the cafés and tearooms, the abundance of craft shops.

Together they browsed in a few of the shops, and she selected a few gifts for her step-siblings, then they enjoyed a delicious lunch in a café overlooking the valley before heading back to the Gold Coast.

It had been a pleasant break, and she said so as they entered the Sanctuary Cove villa just after six.

'All of it?' Michel drawled with a distinctly wicked smile.

'Most of it,' Sandrine qualified, and heard his faint laugh.

'Let's change and eat out.'

'I could make something,' she prevaricated, mentally assessing the contents of the refrigerator. It held steak, sufficient greens to make a salad, and fresh fruit.

'I'll book a table at the Hyatt,' Michel determined firmly.

'I have lines to study,' Sandrine warned as he placed the heel of his hand at the back of her waist and propelled her towards the stairs.

'We'll be home by nine. You can curl up in a chair and go through them then.'

Sandrine chose a casually elegant cream pant suit, dressed it up with gold, stiletto-heeled sandals, then fixed a long, matching cream fringed scarf at her neck so that half its length trailed down her back.

The Hyatt was well patronised, and the maître d' escorted them to a table close to a window with a pleasant view out over the river.

Michel ordered wine, then they selected their starter and main course, but deferred dessert.

Sandrine was enjoying her prawn starter when she heard a familiar light voice exude an affectionate greeting, and there was Cait Lynden, a veritable feminine siren dressed in black, looking like a model who'd just stepped out of *Vogue*, hair and make-up the picture of perfection. With Gregor at her side.

'*Darling*,' Cait effused, proffering an air kiss to one cheek. 'Fancy seeing you here.'

Sandrine spared Gregor a quick glance, glimpsed the slight roll of his eyes and deduced that Cait was on a mission. A mission named 'snaring Michel'.

'The long arm of coincidence,' Sandrine agreed, and sent Michel a mocking glance beneath partly veiled eyelashes.

'You won't mind if we join you?' Cait slipped into a chair without waiting for an answer.

Oh, *great*. This held the promise of turning into quite an evening.

'I'll order another bottle of wine,' Gregor insisted as the wine steward and the waiter hovered attentively while Cait and Gregor perused the menu and gave their order.

Cait turned towards Sandrine. 'Are you not feeling well, darling?' False concern coloured her voice, and Sandrine silently applauded Cait's acting ability. 'You look a little pale.'

Sandrine summoned a sweet smile. 'Do you think so?'

'Gregor is hosting a party Saturday night. You must both come.'

'Unfortunately we'll be in Sydney,' Michel drawled, and lifted his glass to take an appreciative sip.

Really? Sandrine queried silently. She certainly intended to visit her family there, but she hadn't given a thought to whether Michel would join her.

Cait hid her disappointment well. 'What a shame.'

The waiter removed their plates and returned in minutes with Cait's and Gregor's starters.

'It should be an interesting shoot tomorrow.' Sandrine could almost sense Cait's sharpening figurative claws as she sought to scratch. 'Sandrine has this intimate scene.' She paused, then went for the kill. 'Knowing she's with other men must be difficult for you to handle.'

'I don't have a problem with it.' Michel's smile was deadly, his voice dangerously soft. 'Considering I'm the one who gets to take her to bed.'

Sandrine watched with fascination as Cait fluttered her lashes. 'I adore a proprietorial male.'

'Really, darling?' Gregor interposed. 'You surprise me. I had you pegged as calling the shots in a relationship.'

If looks could kill, Gregor would be dead and Cait would be up on a murder charge, Sandrine mused.

Well versed in the subtle games some women felt compelled to play, on one level she found Cait's behaviour amusing. On another, she wanted to scratch her eyes out! Jealousy, she reflected wryly, was not an enviable trait.

She spared Michel a quick glance and caught the faint gleam evident in those grey eyes. Was she that transparent? He had acquired the ability to read her mind with remarkable accuracy almost from the beginning, whereas his was mostly a closed book. As a poker player, he would be superb.

The waiter appeared with Cait's and Gregor's main dishes, and Sandrine concentrated on doing her salmon justice.

'How long will you stay in Sydney?'

Sandrine had to hand it to Cait…she was persistent. 'I'm—' not sure, she was going to add, except Michel intercepted.

'Until the film wraps up and the publicity is done.'

'And afterwards?' Cait persisted with light coquetry.

Michel proffered a polite smile. 'New York. Then Paris.' He turned towards Sandrine, caught hold of her hand and lifted it to his lips.

Careful, Sandrine silently warned. This is definitely overkill.

Except there was nothing she could do to still the tide of warmth sweeping through her body. It was as if his slightest touch activated a switch, leaving her with little or no control over her emotions. Something she found difficult to bear, given the state of their relationship.

'French is such a romantic language,' Cait said with an envious sigh. 'To have a lover so lost to passion in my arms he lapses into his native tongue…it drives me wild.'

'There have been so many,' Gregor drawled. 'One imagines you must be multilingual.'

'Beast.'

'Just telling the truth as I know it, darling.'

Cait transferred her attention to Sandrine. 'I've auditioned for the lead in a new Lucas film. I think I'll get it.' She smoothed a hand over her hair. 'Do you have anything in mind?'

Sandrine replaced her cutlery and sipped the contents of her glass. 'Congratulations.'

'You didn't answer my question.'

She was conscious of Michel's intent interest in her response and deliberated for several seconds. 'I don't have any immediate plans.'

'Coffee, *chérie*?' Michel queried smoothly, and he summoned the waiter as she shook her head. 'You'll excuse us if we leave.' He made it a statement. 'I need to check some computer data, and Sandrine has to study her lines.' He signed the credit slip, then rose to his feet. 'Good night.'

They reached the main entrance and within minutes the concierge had summoned their car. Sandrine slid into the passenger seat and laid her head against the cushioned rest.

'No comment?'

She turned her head slightly as Michel eased the car onto the bricked roadway and negotiated the roundabout. 'None whatsoever,' she offered wryly, and heard his low, husky laugh.

Within minutes Michel activated the security gate leading to the waterfront villas, and in no time at all he drew the car to a halt inside the garage.

'Where would you prefer to study?' he asked as they entered the lounge.

'Here.' She wanted to kick off her shoes and curl up in one of the cushioned chairs.

'I'll set my laptop up on the dining-room table.' He shrugged off his jacket and hooked it over one shoulder. 'Will you make coffee, or shall I?'

'You,' she delegated. 'I'm going upstairs to change.'

Michel was still bent over the laptop when she reentered the bedroom a few minutes before midnight, and she fell asleep within minutes of her head hitting the pillow.

She didn't hear him slip into bed beside her, nor was she aware of his arm drawing her close.

CHAPTER SIX

SANDRINE breathed a sigh of relief. Seven takes wasn't bad. The scene had come together, no one had fluffed their lines, and the electric intensity had been achieved at a level even Tony could applaud.

She was tired, hot, and the boned corselet pulling her waist into an impossibly small measurement was killing her. The heavy make-up felt as if it was a mask of greasepaint about to slide off her face, and if she didn't get rid of the elaborately coiffed wig *soon*, she'd scream.

Added to which, it was late, and she was impossibly thirsty and hungry. The instant she discarded the heavy period costume, she intended to drink half a litre of water, follow it with a powdered protein drink, then sink her teeth into a fresh, crisp apple.

'You look fragile, darling,' Gregor murmured. 'Too many late nights catching up on time lost between the sheets?'

'Yes.' She was in no mood to participate in his game of verbal thrust and parry.

'Lucky you.'

She offered him a stunning smile. 'Aren't I just?'

'Our esteemed investor looks immensely *physical*. Tires you out, does he?'

'Wrong, Gregor,' she responded sweetly.

His eyes gleamed. 'Mmm, hidden talents, darling?'

She merely smiled and crossed to join the wardrobe assistant.

Twenty minutes later she felt considerably better, dressed in jeans and a T-shirt, her feet encased in heeled sandals, her hair twisted into a careless knot at her nape. All she had to do was check what time she had to report on the set the next day, then she was free to go home.

Seven was an improvement on the early hour of five, and she turned towards the exit, caught sight of Michel deep in conversation with a man whose tall frame seemed familiar.

Both men glanced up at the same time, and Sandrine's eyes widened in surprise at his identity. What on earth was Michel's elder brother doing here? She'd last seen Raoul Lanier three months ago in Paris. Then, he'd regarded her with warmth and affection.

Sandrine was aware of his veiled scrutiny as she crossed to where they stood.

'Finished for the day?' Michel queried.

'I was just checking tomorrow's filming schedule.' She turned towards the man at his side. 'Raoul,' she greeted evenly. 'How are you?'

'Well. And you?' he returned smoothly.

'Fine.' Such polite formality. Her smile was overbright. 'When did you arrive?'

'This morning.'

Ask a direct question and she might get a direct answer. 'A social visit?'

'Not entirely.'

'Raoul is joining me in meetings with marketing,' Michel informed her in a voice that held a faint sardonic edge. 'Then he's due in Sydney to initiate negotiations on another matter.'

'Taking care of business,' Sandrine mocked lightly, aware of Raoul's level scrutiny.

'Yes.'

'I didn't ask Michel to inject finance to rescue the film.'

'I'm aware of that.'

'You mean to ensure he's not making a foolish investment.' It was a statement, not a query.

'Michel makes his own decisions.'

'Obviously.'

Raoul's gaze didn't falter. 'I understand you've reconciled?'

'We're working on it,' Michel drawled.

'And you, Sandrine,' Raoul posed. 'Are you working on your marriage to my brother?'

'Michel is sharing my villa, and my bed.' She'd wanted to shock him, but there wasn't a flicker of emotion evident on those chiselled features.

'That doesn't answer my question.'

'It's as much as you're going to get.' She turned on her heel and walked away. One Lanier brother was enough. Two was one too many!

Sandrine was halfway to Sanctuary Cove when her mobile phone rang, and she automatically engaged it.

'Raoul is meeting Stephanie Sommers, the film's

marketing representative, for dinner,' Michel informed her. 'He has invited us to join them.'

'No.'

'I'll be home in an hour.'

'*No*, Michel.' The stressed negative went unheard for he'd already ended the call.

She depressed the button and tossed the phone onto the passenger seat. Damn him. She cursed him again as she garaged the car and ran lightly upstairs.

An hour later she had showered, dressed, and was applying the finishing touches to her make-up when Michel walked into the bedroom.

He gave her a long, considered look, then quirked one eyebrow. 'Dressed to do battle?'

Black did things for her. It highlighted the texture of her skin, accented the burnished sheen of her sable-coloured hair and emphasised her luminous brown eyes.

Sandrine capped the mascara wand and tossed it into her make-up bag. 'You could say that.' She turned towards him. 'What time and where is this momentous dinner taking place?'

'At the Mirage Hotel, in an hour.'

She tossed a lipstick into her evening purse and snapped it shut. 'It'll take twenty minutes to reach Main Beach.' She slid the long chain strap over one shoulder and walked to the door. 'I'll be in the lounge catching the evening news.'

She descended the stairs and moved into the lounge, switched on the television and prowled the room, too restless to sit.

Mindful that she'd eaten very little all day, she filled a glass with water and drank it, then she splashed a small quantity of excellent Chardonnay into a crystal goblet.

It was half an hour before Michel entered the lounge, and the sight of him adorned in black evening suit, crisp white shirt and dark tie made the breath catch in her throat.

He possessed an exigent sexual chemistry that melted her bones. Dear heaven. How was it possible to want something so badly with your heart, yet conversely deny it with the dictates of your brain?

With a faintly mocking gesture she lifted the goblet in a silent salute, then raised it to her lips and took a small sip. 'This is solely for Stephanie's benefit.'

'The wine, or your attendance at dinner?'

A slow smile curved her generous mouth. 'Dinner. It isn't fair to pitch her alone among the wolves.'

'*Wolves*, Sandrine?' he queried with ill-concealed mockery. 'Isn't that a little extreme?'

'No.'

His voice held a certain dryness. 'I'm sure Stephanie can take care of herself.'

'Against Raoul? Are you kidding?'

It would be interesting to see how Stephanie reacted to the elder Lanier brother. A single mother raising a child alone had to have more than her share of courage and perspicacity.

'I'm sure you'll enjoy playing the role of her protector,' Michel mused as he crossed the room.

With one hand he extracted the goblet from her fin-

gers and placed it on a nearby side table. At the same
time he slid his other hand to cup her nape, drawing
her close as his mouth fastened over her own in a kiss
that tore at the restraints of his control.

He felt a slight tremor slither through her slim frame
and he deepened the kiss to something that resembled
possession.

It was several minutes before he slowly lessened the
intensity, trailing the soft, swollen curve of her lower
lip with a touch as light as a butterfly's wing.

'We'd better leave or we'll be late,' Michel murmured as he eased her to arm's length.

Sandrine stood motionless for a few seconds, her
eyes wide in a face that was pale beneath its cosmetic
enhancement. Then she extracted a lip pencil from her
evening purse and crossed to the ornate mirror to effect repairs to a mouth devoid of colour.

Her fingers shook slightly, and she cursed beneath
her breath at the level of emotional helplessness
Michel was able to achieve.

When she was done, she replaced the lip pencil in
her purse and preceded him through to the garage,
slipping into the passenger seat as he slid in behind
the wheel.

The Sheraton Mirage resort was built on a narrow
peninsula, a luxury low-rise facing the ocean. It was
renowned for its innovative design, extensive use of
marble, an elegant waterfall and tranquil views out
over a wide pool with its island bar to the ocean beyond.

Michel relinquished the car to the valet to park, and

Sandrine entered the magnificent foyer at his side. Raoul rose to his feet from one of the large cushioned sofas and moved forward to meet them. Of Stephanie there was no sign.

'Punctuality appears not to be Ms Sommers's forte,' Raoul indicated dryly. 'Shall we go into the lounge for a drink while we wait?'

'Maybe she's caught up in traffic.'

'Or the baby-sitter didn't show or the child was sick,' Raoul added with thinly veiled mockery.

So he'd had Stephanie investigated. Undoubtedly initiated before he left Paris as part of the Lanier modus operandi, Sandrine concluded cynically.

'I imagine if Stephanie is going to be delayed for any length of time, she'll call,' she felt impelled to defend.

At that moment a cell phone rang, and Raoul extracted a slim compact model from inside his dinner jacket. Two minutes and two curt words later, he cut the connection.

'It appears Ms Sommers has been held up with a flat tyre. She'll be another ten minutes.'

Stephanie entered the lounge one minute ahead of time, and Sandrine had to admire her cool unruffled demeanour as she crossed to where they sat.

'I must apologise. I hope there wasn't a problem holding the booking?' She glanced from one man to the other and offered Sandrine a warm smile. 'Shall we go in?'

Sandrine silently applauded Stephanie's style. The

young marketing executive had panache. What's more, she wasn't averse to taking control.

Something Michel would soon alter in his favour, Sandrine perceived as the maître d' seated them at their table and beckoned the drinks waiter. To whom Stephanie made it clear *she* was hostess.

Michel's features were inscrutable, while Raoul opted for chilling politeness.

Perusing the menu and selecting a starter and main required deliberation, and when their orders were placed Michel eased back in his chair and regarded the attractive strawberry blonde seated opposite with studied ease.

'Perhaps you'd care to relay your marketing strategy, Ms Sommers.' He paused a beat. 'For this film in particular.'

'Stephanie,' the marketing executive corrected with a faint smile. 'When we receive the finished film from the studio, it will be viewed in a private cinema by about thirty people. We'll then arrange meetings to discuss the target market and determine to what age group the film will have most appeal.'

Sandrine watched as Stephanie paused to lift her glass and take a measured sip of chilled water. Her hand was steady, her actions carefully controlled, and she displayed admirable poise as she replaced the glass and subjected both men to a level gaze.

'Further discussions will follow on which segments should be selected for the trailer, the shots to appear in press releases overseas and locally, and which of these will be released to the television stations and other media, including the entertainment pages in newspapers and magazines.'

'Worldwide?' Michel queried, and Stephanie inclined her head in silent acquiescence.

'Of course,' she confirmed. 'We'll also push to heighten public awareness of the film by organising a fashion shoot with one of the prestige fashion magazines to ensure coverage in the major national weekly magazines.'

'In which only the lead actors appear?' Raoul posed.

'Not always,' Stephanie qualified, and Sandrine successfully hid a faint smile at the other woman's ability to cover all the angles. 'We can arrange to include focused shots of local actors to draw their attention to their involvement in the film. Press shots of Michel and Sandrine at a social gala would draw public attention and highlight the film.'

'Sandrine's involvement in professional modelling would also be of interest, would it not?'

The waiter arrived with their starters, and there was a pause as the wine steward made a production of opening a bottle of wine, which he mistakenly proffered to Raoul for tasting.

Sandrine watched with interest as Raoul deferred the sampling to Stephanie and she could only admire her very skilled acceptance. For a moment she even thought she caught a glimpse of amusement in Raoul's gaze, only to decide it was her imagination.

'We organise press interviews in the star's hotel,' Stephanie elaborated, 'or if they've stipulated private leasing, we arrange a mutually agreeable venue for the interview.'

'Simultaneously?'

'In an intense push to raise public awareness.'

'Impressive,' Michel commented, and began on his starter.

'It's my job to impress.'

'Tell me,' Raoul interjected in a deceptive drawl. 'Don't you have family obligations that might interfere with total dedication to optimum marketing of this film?'

Sandrine wanted to kick his shin *hard* beneath the table. What game was he playing, for heaven's sake?

'I'm sure you're already aware I'm a single mother with a three-year-old daughter,' Stephanie responded smoothly. 'Should there be a crisis, I'd deal with it in the best way possible.' She fixed Raoul with a penetrating look. 'And my daughter would always take precedence.' Her chin lifted fractionally. 'Does that answer your question?'

Oh, my, Sandrine breathed. It was possible to cut the air with a knife!

'Yes.'

'Good.'

Michel cast his brother a brief, considering glance, then returned his attention to his starter.

'Were you able to get a baby-sitter for tonight without difficulty?' Sandrine posed conversationally.

'Given that I had very short notice, yes.'

'The Lanier brothers expect instant action in re-

sponse to their slightest whim.' She was conscious of
Michel's swift glance but ignored it.

'Really?' Stephanie's voice was dry. 'And you married one of them?'

'I thought it was a good idea at the time.'

'Total bewitchment, followed by a reality check?'

'Something like that,' Sandrine said with a wicked
smile. She was beginning to enjoy herself!

'More wine, Ms Sommers?' Raoul queried silkily.

'Stephanie,' the marketing executive corrected with
equal smoothness. 'And no, thank you. I get to drive
home after this.'

'Pity.'

'For declining the wine?'

Sandrine watched as Raoul leant back in his chair.
She seriously doubted any woman of his acquaintance
had challenged him on any count.

'For endeavouring to treat this as other than a business meeting.'

'That's unfair,' Sandrine protested quickly.

'And unjustified,' Stephanie added, folding her napkin and placing it beside her plate. 'You insisted on
meeting tonight.' She picked up her evening purse and
focused her attention on Michel. 'I've already relayed
our marketing strategy. Therefore my presence here is
no longer necessary. Enjoy the rest of your meal.'

Sandrine watched the attractive blonde turn from the
table and step quickly towards the main desk, pause
briefly as she presented a credit card, then disappear
through the door.

'A slight case of overkill, Raoul?' Michel mocked,

raising one eyebrow at his brother's narrowed gaze, then added thoughtfully, 'Are you going to let her get away?'

Raoul shifted his napkin onto the table and rose to his feet. 'No, I don't believe I am.'

'That was extremely—'

'Inappropriate,' Michel completed with dry cynicism.

'Yes, it was.'

'I hope he catches her.'

'Even if he does, I doubt it'll do him any good,' Sandrine opined, annoyed at Raoul's inexplicable behaviour and Michel's subsequent amusement.

'You don't think Raoul will be able to mend fences?' He lifted his glass and took an appreciative sip of the excellent wine.

'Not easily.'

His eyes gleamed with humour as they swept her expressive features. 'You don't think my brother would benefit from the love of a good woman?'

'Whatever happened to the reverse side of the coin?' Sandrine parried. 'Shouldn't a woman benefit from the love of a good man?'

'Of course.'

'It's unfortunate the Lanier men have their thinking locked into another century.'

Michel's gaze narrowed fractionally. 'Specifically?'

The waiter removed their plates and summoned the wine steward to replenish their glasses.

'You're amused by Raoul's reaction to Stephanie. What if it progressed into something serious?' She lifted a hand in an expressive gesture. 'Do you imagine Raoul would countenance Stephanie's continuing with her career?'

He subjected her to an unwavering appraisal as he leant back in his chair with indolent ease. 'As you are determined to do?' he riposted with deceptive mildness.

'You don't get it, do you?'

'Get what, precisely?'

'It's not about a *career* as such.' She should have a script, dammit! She'd carefully thought out everything she wanted to say. Hell, she'd had enough time! Where were all those fine words now? Out the window, along with her sanity.

She took a slow, calming breath. 'It's about seizing an opportunity and striving to achieve the best possible result. Not for fame and fortune, but to satisfy a creative need.' She waited a few seconds before adding, 'Because there's a depth, an inner feeling so in tune with the part that you feel *you* are meant to be the medium to convey the written words, actions and emotions on film for the audiences to appreciate the true depth of the character.'

Michel remained silent. The silence stretched into minutes as the waiter brought their main course and made a production out of flourishing a gigantic pepper-mill, explaining the intricacies of the chef's skill before bidding them *bon appétit* in appalling French.

Michel picked up his fork and speared an artistically carved carrot rosette. 'You didn't pause to consider that if you got the part, it would involve your being in Australia at a time when I was locked into important business meetings in Paris?'

'Do you know how many actresses auditioned for that part?' she demanded. 'My chances of succeeding were as hopeful as a snowflake surviving in hell.'

He was calm, his movements controlled, but she sensed leashed anger beneath the surface. 'Yet you did succeed,' he reminded her with deceptive mildness. 'You also signed a contract, confirmed flight arrangements and waited to tell me coincidentally two days prior to my being due in Paris.'

He pressed his fork into a baby potato, slid it into the small pool of hollandaise sauce and sampled it with evident enjoyment, then he lifted his head and his gaze pierced hers, steady and unblinking. 'You expected me to say, ''That's fine, darling. Call me. See you next month''?'

The nerves in her stomach tightened and curled into a painful knot. 'The timing was wrong. So was the film location.' She ran the tip of a fingernail along the hemmed edge of her napkin. 'I knew you'd protest, but I hoped you'd understand.'

'Enough to agree to your being apart from me for a considerable length of time?'

'It was only a few weeks.'

'At a time when I couldn't delegate in order to join you,' he reminded her. 'If you remember, we opted against an open relationship for the commitment and permanency of marriage, determining to arrange our lives so we could be together.'

'Are you implying I placed more importance on an acting part than *you*?'

'Deny your actions confirmed it.'

'You reacted as if I were a *possession*, someone who should be available whenever you happened to snap your fingers!' Sandrine accused, and saw his eyebrow lift in silent mockery. 'I wasn't referring to the bedroom!'

'I'm relieved to hear it,' Michel drawled.

'Am I interrupting something?'

Sandrine turned towards the owner of the faintly accented voice and summoned a wry smile. 'Only a current battle in the continuing war.'

Raoul slid into his seat. 'Want me to play mediator?'

'No,' she responded sweetly.

'Michel?'

'It'll keep.'

A devilish imp prompted the words that slipped easily from her tongue. 'We have a capricious airhead opposing a dictatorial tyrant.'

'A moment ago I was labelled possessive,' Michel relayed with marked cynicism, flicking his brother a dark glance. 'You caught up with Stephanie?'

'Yes.'

'I assume you offered an apology.'

'Which she refused to accept,' Raoul indicated dryly, and Sandrine proffered a musing grin.

'Verbally flayed you, did she?'

'You could say that.'

'So, when do you intend seeing her again?' Michel asked archly.

'Not at all, if she has anything to do with it.'

'Let me guess,' Sandrine posed. 'Tomorrow? On what grounds?'

Raoul lifted one eyebrow. 'Do I require any?'

No, of course he didn't, she dismissed. All he had to do was exert a measure of innate charm and women fell at his feet. Stephanie, she perceived, could prove to be an exception.

The waiter came with his main course and appeared affronted when Raoul dismissed his spiel before he even had the chance to begin with it.

'How long will it take to wrap up filming?' Raoul queried as he sliced into a succulent fillet of beef.

'I have another day scheduled. Maybe two at the most,' Sandrine told him. 'Tony is hopeful two weeks will do it.'

'I understand you have to remain on call for the possibility of retakes, publicity, promotion?'

'Yes.'

Raoul turned towards Michel. 'You intend remaining on the Coast?'

'Sydney,' Sandrine interjected. 'I have family there. If the studio calls me in, I can take the next flight out and be here the next day.'

'Aren't you forgetting something, *chérie*?' Michel queried silkily.

'You?' Her smile was a little too wide and too bright.

'So brave,' he mocked lightly.

Foolish, she amended silently, for thinking she could best him. Verbally, physically, or mentally.

'Dessert?'

'Coffee,' she said firmly, aware of the need to be decisive. 'Liqueur. Kahlua.'

Michel beckoned the waiter, conferred with Raoul, indicated their order, then requested the bill.

'The account has been settled, *m'sieur*.'

'I think you're mistaken.'

'No, *m'sieur*. The lady who was dining with you instructed the account be billed to her credit card.'

Sandrine hid a smile. Stephanie had managed to score on two counts. She'd walked out on Raoul Lanier and she'd added insult to injury by taking care of the bill.

'It appears Ms Sommers is a young woman to be reckoned with,' Michel commented dryly.

'Indeed.'

She detected mockery in Raoul's drawled response and was unable to suppress a grin. 'I'm with Stephanie.'

Both men sent her a level glance.

'Take her home,' Raoul instructed as he rose to his feet. 'And hush her mouth.'

Michel's eyes gleamed with humour. 'I intend to,' he said, suppressing a laugh.

Raoul accompanied them through the foyer to the main entrance and stood while the concierge summoned their car.

'Sweet dreams,' Sandrine teased as she bade Raoul goodnight, then slid into the passenger seat.

His expression was unreadable, and she gave a soft chuckle as Michel eased the car down to street level. Unless she was mistaken, Raoul had met his match, and she, for one, was going to enjoy watching the game!

CHAPTER SEVEN

SANDRINE focused her attention on the scene beyond the windscreen as the car entered the flow of north-bound traffic.

The night was clear, the air sharp, and the lighted windows of various high-rise apartment buildings vied with far distant stars in an indigo sky.

'Shall we continue where we left off?'

She cast Michel a steady glance, aware that the night's shadows were highlighting the angles and planes of his face.

Her voice assumed unaccustomed cynicism. 'It won't change the fact that we had a major fight over my decision to fulfil an acting contract.'

He smote a clenched fist against the steering wheel, and she looked at him in startled disbelief.

'*Mon Dieu*. This is not about you pursuing a career.' He paused at a roundabout, waiting for two cars to circle and exit. 'It's about us being together. Not me being forced to spend time in one city while you're on the other side of the world in another. *Comprends*?'

'It was unavoidable.'

'It need not have been if you'd enlightened me about the audition at the time,' Michel enunciated with restraint. 'Thus giving me the opportunity to implement a contingency plan.' He directed her a dark look that spoke volumes before returning his attention to the road. 'I won't allow it to happen again.'

She drew in a deep breath and released it slowly. 'Excuse me? You won't *allow* it?'

'No,' he reiterated hardily. 'In future there will be no misunderstandings, no assumptions. We communicate and leave nothing in doubt.'

'I'm not sure we have a future,' she countered wretchedly, and could have bitten her tongue for uttering the foolish words.

'Oh, yes, we do, *mignonne.*' His voice was deadly soft.

'How can you say that?'

'Easily.'

'What about unresolved issues?'

'Name them,' Michel challenged.

'*You,*' Sandrine began, crossing each of his sins off on her fingers. 'Keeping tabs on me, investigating everyone to do with the film, conspiring to come up with a financial rescue package and making *me* a condition. Blackmail,' she asserted finally, 'is a criminal offense.'

'You're the wife of a wealthy man whose access to a family fortune makes anyone associated with me a prime target. Ransom, extortion, kidnapping. Of course I had someone watch over you.'

'You could have told me! How do you think I'd have reacted if I saw someone following me?'

'You refused to take or answer any of my calls, remember?' he retorted. 'And I pay for the best. Not some amateur who'd frighten you by being visible.'

'What did he do?' she demanded, immeasurably

hurt. 'Report whom I spoke to, where I went, what I did...every minute of every day?'

'It wasn't about my lack of trust in you,' he bit out angrily. 'It was about protection. *Yours*.'

'It was an invasion of privacy. *Mine*.' She was on a roll and couldn't seem to stop. 'I hate you for it.'

'So hate me, *mignonne*. At least I knew you were safe.'

'I guess the film running overtime and over budget played right into your hands. It gave you a lever, a figurative gun to hold to my head. *Do what I say, or else*.' She directed him a fulminating glare. 'I'll never forgive you for that.'

'"Never" is a long time.'

'It's as long as my lifetime.'

'Tell me,' Michel drawled. 'What did you intend to do when filming was completed?'

'Visit my family.'

'And afterwards?'

That was in the hazy future and something she'd deliberately not given much thought.

'I don't know,' she admitted honestly, and grimaced at the husky oath that rent the air.

'*You don't know*.' He raised both hands off the wheel, then gripped it hard. 'Next you'll tell me you intended contacting me through a lawyer.'

'I suppose it was a possibility.'

'Not telephoned me? Or caught a flight home?'

'Where *is* home, Michel?' she queried wryly. 'You have a residential base in several cities. I'd have had to have your secretary check on your whereabouts at the time.'

'*Sacré bleu.* You have my personal cell phone number where you can reach me anywhere at any time!'

'Maybe I wouldn't have wanted to!'

'Did it not occur to you that I might have taken all that into consideration and put, as you so cynically called it, "a figurative gun" to your head?'

The car slowed almost to a halt, and Sandrine was startled to see Michel activate the security gate permitting access to the Sanctuary Cove residential suburb. Seconds later the gate slid open and they drove through.

'Believe me, I would have used any weapon I had.'

'Blackmail, Michel?'

'You wouldn't answer my calls. If I arrived on your doorstep, would you have let me in?'

'Probably not.' At least, not at first. Her initial instinct would have been to slam the door in his face. The next...call the police? No, she refuted silently. She wouldn't have gone that far.

Was he right insisting on an enforced reconciliation? Putting them in the same residence, giving her no choice in the matter?

Within minutes they reached the villa, and once inside she crossed to the stairs and made her way up to the main bedroom.

For weeks she'd been so angry with Michel, herself, the circumstances that had caused the dissent between them. Now there was a degree of self-doubt, a measure of regret...and pain.

In the bedroom she slipped off her shoes and crossed to the floor-to-ceiling window. She made no attempt to draw the drapes as she looked out across the bay to the brightly lit restaurant cantilevered over the water.

Within a few days she'd leave here and probably not return. Sydney beckoned, and family. Her mother would be pleased to see her, likewise her father. But on separate occasions at different venues. She'd visit, take gifts, greet each of her step-siblings, and pretend she belonged.

She closed her eyes and tried to ignore the loneliness deep inside. An ache behind her eyelids culminated in tears that escaped and slid slowly down each cheek.

A faint sound, a slight movement, alerted her to Michel's presence, and she prayed he wouldn't turn on the light.

Sandrine sensed rather than heard him cross to stand behind her, then his hands closed over her shoulders as he drew her back against him.

'We made a deal, remember?'

'What deal are you referring to?'

'Never to spend a night apart. Except in circumstances beyond our control.'

So they had. And somehow taking a bit part in a movie being shot on the other side of the world didn't come close in the qualifying stakes of circumstances beyond our control.

'Where do we go from here?' she queried quietly, and he didn't pretend to misunderstand.

'Let's just take it one day at a time, hmm?'

For several minutes he didn't move, then his hands slid down her arms and linked together at her waist. She felt his lips brush against her ear, then trail slowly down the sensitive cord of her neck to nuzzle the soft hollow there.

It was heaven to lean her head into the curve of his shoulder and just *be*. To absorb the warmth of that large pulsing body, to take comfort in the shelter it afforded her, and to luxuriate in the touch of his hands, his lips.

He didn't offer a word, nor did she. They didn't move, just stood there for what seemed an age.

Then Michel gently turned her to face him, and she lifted her arms to encircle his neck as he lowered his head down to hers.

His mouth explored the soft lower curve of her own, grazing it with the edge of his teeth before sweeping his tongue to test the delicate tissues and tease the sensitised ridges in an erotic tasting that made her want more than this gentle supplication.

He'd removed his jacket and tie, but his shirt was an impossible barrier she sought to remove. She needed to touch his skin, to feel the heavy pulse of his heart beneath his rib cage and to explore the very essence of him.

By tacit agreement, they divested each other's clothes in a leisurely, evocative fashion, the slither of silk over skin arousing and heightening the senses to fever pitch.

Now. She wanted him *now*. Hard and fast. She needed to feel his strength, his unfettered passion.

Her mouth met his hungrily as he tumbled her down onto the bed, and she was aware of uttering small sounds of encouragement as he explored her, then she groaned out loud with pleasure as he entered her in one long thrust, stilling for timeless seconds as she absorbed him.

He withdrew and she lifted her hips as he plunged deep inside. She clung to him, urging him harder, closer, until pleasurable sensation reached an almost unbearable intensity.

Sandrine cried out, beseeching him with a litany of pleas as she became helpless beneath an emotion so treacherous it almost succeeded in destroying her.

Afterwards she could only lie there and attempt to regain control of her ragged breathing. And her sanity.

His eyes never left hers, and she felt as if she were drowning as he traced a finger over the soft curve of her mouth, probing the inner skin with erotic sensitivity.

Not content, he trailed a path down the length of her throat, then lowered his head to her mouth to create fresh havoc with her senses as he kissed her, thoroughly, mindlessly, then feathered his lips to the sensitive hollows beneath her throat, her breasts, savouring each peak in turn with devastating eroticism.

As he travelled lower, her body quivered, then tautened against an invasion so blatantly intimate she began to burn with the intoxicating heat of his touch.

After play merged into foreplay as passion reignited, and she was driven by a hunger so intense she became a willing wanton in his arms, taking intimate liberties that had him groaning beneath her as they both became lost in mesmeric rapture.

They took the late-morning flight out of Coolangatta airport, approaching the outskirts of Sydney just over an hour later.

The jet banked towards the ocean, providing a panoramic view of the harbour and city. Tall skyscrapers vied with elegant homes dotting numerous coves and inlets. Scenic landmarks such as the Sydney Harbour Bridge and the Opera House were distinctive from this height, and Sandrine felt the familiarity of home as they began their descent.

This was where she'd been born, raised and educated. Her family, her friends were here. For a while she could relax, visit family, meet friends and indulge a penchant for shopping.

The benefit of travelling first class was the speed of disembarking, and in no time at all Michel had collected their bags from the luggage carousel and organised a taxi.

It was a bright sunny day, with hardly a cloud in the sky. In some ways it seemed an age since she'd left Sydney; in others it was as if it were only yesterday.

Nothing had changed, she noted as the taxi took the customary route from the airport. Industrial areas gave way to semi-industrial, then residential. The terrace houses looked the same, although a few had received a fresh coat of paint. Traffic hurtled along the busy road at maximum speed, accompanied by the hydraulic hiss of heavily laden trucks, the occasional squeal of hastily applied brakes as a driver attempted a risky switch of lanes and miscalculated.

A turn-off led towards wide, tree-leafed roads, older-style homes, most lovingly restored and some still standing in palatial grounds.

Double Bay housed an eclectic mix of homes and apartment buildings. It was an inner suburb where old-money status sat next to new, where Porsches, Bentleys and BMWs parked nose to tail with Ferraris, Audis and Rolls-Royces. It housed one of the city's most exclusive shopping centres where trendy cafés nestled between designer boutiques, classy restaurants and a ritzy hotel.

Michel's apartment was situated atop a three-level, spacious old home that had been gutted and architecturally designed to resemble the original homestead. Pale lemon stucco with a white trim and black-painted, iron-lace railings provided a gracious exterior. Each floor housed a separate apartment, reached by a lift instead of the original staircase, and modern materials had been crafted to resemble the old, thereby retaining a sense of timeless grandeur that was complemented by exquisite antique furniture.

Sandrine had fallen in love with it at first sight, and now she crossed the spacious lounge to wide glass doors guarding the entrance to a long veranda that offered panoramic views over Port Jackson Harbour.

'Penny for them,' Michel teased with measured indolence as he joined her. He linked his arms around her waist and drew her back against him.

'Nothing in particular,' she said reflectively. 'Just a feeling of satisfaction at being home again.'

'You'll want to ring your family and make arrangements to meet them.'

'Yes,' she agreed. But not collectively. There was definitely a *yours* and *mine* definition apparent, and she'd learnt from an early age not to shift the line between the two!

'Lunch or dinner, whatever suits,' Michel offered. 'As long as I can put in a few hours on the laptop each day.'

She watched a ferry glide across the harbour and glimpsed a freighter on the horizon. 'You want to work this afternoon?'

'Unless you have a better idea.'

The temptation to tease him was irresistible. 'Well, it's ages since I had a manicure, my hair could do with a trim, and I need to replenish some make-up.'

'I work, you shop,' he quipped with a musing drawl.

'Are you sure you don't mind?'

His hands slipped up to cover her breasts, the touch light, tantalising, and she caught her breath at the sensual promise evident as his lips settled in the sensitive curve of her neck.

'Go, *chérie*. Be back by six, and we'll eat out.'

Unpacking could wait until later, and with a light laugh she slipped from his arms, caught up her shoulder-bag, then blew him a cheeky kiss before heading for the front door.

Sandrine enjoyed a wonderful few hours. The manicure proved to be no problem, and the hair salon readily fitted her in between appointments. Tempted by a trendy café, she ordered a cappuccino, a salad and sandwich, then she browsed among several boutiques lining a narrow street of converted old-fashioned cottages.

An arcade in the Ritz-Carlton Hotel housed several exclusive shops, and in one she discovered a perfect pair of shoes.

It was almost six when the taxi pulled into the kerb adjacent to the apartment, and she cleared security, then rode the lift to the top floor.

Michel was seated at an antique desk in one corner of the lounge, and he glanced up from the laptop as she entered the room. He'd changed out of his suit and wore dark chinos and an ivory chambray shirt.

He caught sight of the brightly coloured carry bags, glimpsed the beautifully styled hair and offered her a warm smile as he closed down the computer.

Sandrine deposited the bags on a nearby chair. 'I bought shoes.' She wrinkled her nose at him. 'Very expensive shoes.'

A husky laugh escaped his throat as he crossed to her side. 'Hmm, new perfume?'

'You noticed.'

'I notice everything about you.'

Just as she'd developed a keen sixth sense about him. The clean male smell of his soap and cologne, freshly laundered clothes and a masculine scent that was his alone.

'What time did you book the restaurant?'

'Seven.'

'Then I'd better go unpack, shower and dress.'

He slid a hand beneath her hair and cupped her nape as he lowered his head down to hers. The kiss held passion and promise, and she felt vaguely regretful as he let her go.

It was a warm summer's evening, and she selected black silk evening trousers, a jewelled singlet top, then added a sheer black evening blouse. Stiletto-heeled pumps, a matching jewelled evening bag completed the outfit. Make-up was understated, with emphasis on her eyes.

Michel had chosen a restaurant specialising in sea-food, and they each selected a prawn starter and ordered grilled fish to follow. The wine steward presented a bottle of Dom Pérignon champagne.

'Did you get in touch with your parents?'

She felt guilty that she hadn't. 'I'll ring them both in the morning.'

He lifted his flute and placed the rim against her own. '*Salut.*'

Their starter arrived, and she bit into a succulent prawn and savoured the taste. Heaven. The sauce was perfect.

'With both you and Raoul in Australia, who is minding—'

'The store?'

'Figuratively speaking.'

'Henri heads a very capable team in our absence.'

'When is Raoul returning to Paris?'

His smile held a faint wryness. 'Twenty questions, Sandrine?'

She gave a slight shrug. 'Curiosity, I guess.'

'His plans are less flexible than mine.'

'And you, Michel?' she queried fearlessly. 'How long will you stay in Australia?'

His gaze was direct, unwavering. 'As long as it takes.'

She didn't pretend to misunderstand. Something curled inside her stomach and tightened into a painful ball. 'I might be called back to the Gold Coast studios to reshoot a scene. Then there's the publicity promotion…'

'I've been working, myself, every day since I arrived in Australia.'

The laptop. In this electronic age it was possible to access and transmit data at the touch of a button.

'It isn't necessary for—'

'Yes,' Michel interrupted. 'It is.'

The waiter removed their plates, and the wine steward refilled their flutes with champagne.

'Michel…' She trailed to a halt, and although her eyes searched his, she was unable to gain much from his expression.

'We promised to take each day as it comes, remember?'

Yes, so they had. But with every day that passed she realised how hard it would be to have to live without him. And she knew she didn't want to. It should be so simple to mend an emotional bridge. You just said the words, and everything was fixed.

Except they had to be the right words, and it had to be the right time and the right place.

When they made love, she freely gave him her body, her soul, and prayed he knew what he meant to her. But she was a wordless lover, and ''I love you'' hadn't passed her lips since the night before she left New York.

The waiter presented their main dish, and Sandrine looked at the succulent barramundi, the artistically arranged salad and discovered her appetite had fled.

So, too, had her conversational skills. For how did

you talk banalities with someone you'd soon share sexual intimacy?

She had only to look at him, and in her mind she could feel the touch of his hands, his lips, *know* the reaction of her traitorous body as he led her towards sensual fulfilment. Just as she knew *he* was equally as aware.

It was akin to a silent game they played. Except there was no deliberation, no premeditation. Intense sensual chemistry sizzled between them, ready to ignite as easily as dry tinder at the toss of a lighted match.

It had always been the same. Had she confused sexual attraction with love? *And what is love?*

If you took away sexual desire, what was left? A solid friendship? She would have said yes, until he forbade her to take the movie role. A friend would have been pleased she'd auditioned successfully.

Still, although friendship was important in marriage, a legal union was about commitment, honesty and trust. Because if you love, you want to commit, and there needed to be trust and honesty for the union to succeed.

When it came to honesty, she'd shifted the boundaries, signed a contract without his knowledge and against his wishes, confronted him at the eleventh hour, taken the flight, the job, regardless.

At the time she'd been so angry over his inflexibility she hadn't really given anything else coherent thought. There was a part of her that cherished the sanctity of marriage. And her feelings for Michel weren't in question.

Yet she was an independent young woman. She'd

owned her own apartment, her own car; she had not one, but two great jobs she loved, and for the past seven years she'd been a free spirit, answerable only to herself.

Why had she imagined marriage to Michel wouldn't change that?

Be honest, a small voice taunted. *Love* was the prime moving force in this union. She'd been so caught up in the wonder and magic of it all that she hadn't focused too much on the future.

Carpe diem. Seize the day. And she had, only too willing to allow Michel to sweep her off her feet, exultant with joy at the thought of sharing her life with this man, and confident love would conquer all.

In a world where women had fought and won equality with men in the business arena, she'd taken it for granted she would combine her career with marriage. Michel hadn't objected to her participating in a few modelling assignments. Why should he object to her taking a part in a film?

Yet he had. Warning irrevocably that he didn't view marriage as two partners pursuing separate careers and leading separate lives.

'The fish isn't to your liking?'

Sandrine glanced up quickly. 'No. I mean, yes.' She gave a helpless shrug. 'I'm not that hungry.' She forked a mouthful of salad, alternated it with the succulent fish, then took another sip of champagne in the hope it would renew her appetite.

'I've managed to get tickets for *Les Misérables*,' Michel remarked, and she offered him a smile.

'That's great.' She'd seen two different productions and loved both. 'When?'

'Tomorrow night.'

There was also a popular movie she wanted to see, and she mentioned it. 'Perhaps we could ask Angelina to join us?' she posed, aware how much pleasure it would give her stepsister. In which case she'd have to even things out by issuing a similar invitation to her stepbrother.

'Of course. But first, ascertain which night suits your mother and your father for dinner. As our guests.'

Step-family politics, she mused, required delicate handling.

It was almost ten when they left the restaurant, and within minutes Michel hailed a taxi to take them home.

Sandrine felt pleasantly tired as they entered the apartment, and she slid off her shoes and hooked the sling-back straps over one finger.

'Coffee?'

'I'll make it,' Michel offered as he shrugged out of his jacket. 'I need to go on-line and check some data.'

'Okay.' She tried to stem a feeling of disappointment. A part of her wanted to curl up in his arms and enjoy a leisurely lovemaking. Maybe she wouldn't be asleep when he came to bed, or if she was, he'd wake her. 'I'll go to bed and read.'

Except she only managed one chapter before the book slipped from her fingers and hit the carpeted floor, and she didn't stir when Michel slid quietly in beside her two hours later.

CHAPTER EIGHT

SANDRINE took the cordless phone into the bedroom after breakfast and rang her mother, had the call diverted to a mobile number and interrupted Chantal at the manicurist.

'Dinner, darling? Love to. How long are you in town?'

'A week, at least.'

'The weekend is out. Thursday?'

'Thursday's fine,' she agreed.

'Cristal. Seven o'clock? We'll meet you there.'

Her father was in a business meeting, but Lucas took the call, his conversation equally as brief as that of her mother.

'Friday,' Sandrine wrote in her diary planner.

That left Angelina and Ivan, step-siblings and arch-rivals for her attention. They were both in school and couldn't be contacted until late afternoon.

There were a few close friends she wanted to communicate with and she spent the next hour glued to the phone.

Michel was seated at the desk in the lounge when she emerged. The laptop was open, and he was speaking rapid French into his cell phone.

Sandrine wandered into the kitchen, poured herself

some fresh orange juice, then sat down at the dining-room table and leafed through the daily newspaper.

'What do you want to do with the day?' Michel queried when he finished his call.

'Me as in *me*?' she posed with a faint smile. 'Or me as in *you and me*?'

'You and me,' he drawled, reaching across to catch hold of her chin.

'Too much togetherness might not be wise.'

'You have me at your mercy. Choose.'

She pretended to consider as she ticked off each option on her fingers. 'The beach, a movie, shopping, wander around Darling Harbour, the Rocks, visit the Chinese Gardens, visit a few art galleries, the museum. Hmm,' she deliberated, then added without changing her voice, 'Or I could tie you to the bed and have my wicked way with you.' She sent him a stunning smile. 'Darling Harbour, I think. I'll go get changed.'

He tilted her chin and settled his mouth on hers in an all-too-brief evocative kiss. 'I'll take a raincheck.'

'On Darling Harbour?'

His eyes gleamed with latent humour. 'The bed.'

She slipped from his grasp. 'You did say I get to choose.'

It was a lovely day, with just enough of a breeze to take the edge off the summer's heat. Together they strolled along the boardwalk stretching the length of the Darling Harbour complex, enjoyed an excellent lunch at a waterfront restaurant, then browsed through the shops and crossed the pedestrian bridge. On impulse they took in a two-hour harbour cruise, then caught the monorail into the city.

It was almost six when they re-entered the apartment, and after a quick shower they each changed into elegant evening wear and took a taxi into the city.

There wasn't time for a leisurely meal, so they skipped the starter, settled for the main and forewent coffee in order to take their seats in time for the first act of *Les Misérables*.

It was a magnificent production, and Sandrine was lavish with her praise as they emerged into the foyer after the final act.

They chose a trendy café in which to have coffee, then hailed a taxi to the apartment.

Michel curved an arm round her waist as they stepped into the lift, and Sandrine rested her head against his shoulder. It had been a pleasant day, followed by a lovely evening, and she told him so.

'Thank you,' she added simply as they entered the lounge.

'For what, *chérie*? Spending a day with my wife?'

'For taking the time.'

He pulled her into his arms and kissed her, gently at first, then with increasing passion as she lifted her arms and wrapped them round his neck.

It was a while before he released her, and she stood there, his arms linked loosely around her hips. 'You're not going to check the laptop for messages?'

'There's nothing that can't wait until morning.'

She crossed to the wide hallway and made her way to the main bedroom, where she removed her shoes, the slim-fitting black gown and the beautifully crafted sequined jacket, then she reached to take the pins from her hair and encountered Michel's hand in the process of undoing the elegant French pleat.

When he was done, she helped him remove his jacket, the dress shirt, then the trousers. His eyes held hers as he slipped out of his shoes and peeled off his socks.

All that remained between him and total nudity was a pair of black hipster briefs, and she let her hand slide over his chest, teasing one male nipple, then the other, before skimming her fingers down to his waist.

She didn't tie him to the bed, but she did tease and tantalise him in a wicked exploration that tested the limit of his control. With her lips, the soft feather-light stroke of her fingers, the brush of her skin against his.

Sandrine lost track of time as she played the role of seductress, and just as he reached for her, she sank onto him and took his length in one exultant movement that shattered both of them.

What followed became a sweet, savage lovemaking that broke through the barriers of ecstasy and took them to a place where sensation ruled the mind, body and soul.

They went to sleep in each other's arms, and the last thing Sandrine remembered was the touch of Michel's lips against her temple, the deep, heavy tempo of his heart as it beat strongly in his chest.

Dinner with her mother, stepfather and Angelina carried undertones she was loath to pin down. Chantal was so incredibly vivacious it hurt, Roberto overdid the charm, and Angelina barely touched her food. Consequently the evening became something of a strain.

A call to her mother the next day brought an assurance Sandrine didn't buy for a second. It would do no good to question her father, and she didn't even bring up Chantal's name during dinner the following evening.

A shopping expedition on Saturday with Angelina brought forth a confidence that settled the question.

'Mum and Dad are getting a divorce,' Angelina blurted out as they shared lunch.

Sandrine experienced a gamut of emotions but managed to school most of them as she took in her stepsister's pinched features and lacklustre expression. 'How do you feel about it?' she queried gently.

'I hate it.'

I'm not that rapt, either, she echoed silently. Roberto may not be the ideal husband, but he was a caring father.

'She's seeing someone else,' Angelina informed her morosely.

'*She's* the cat's mother,' Sandrine corrected absently.

'*Mother*,' her stepsister declared with mocking emphasis, 'has a toy boy. I doubt he's thirty.'

Hell, that put a slightly different complexion on things. 'Maybe she's just—'

'Using him for sex?'

'Taking time out,' she continued, and wondered why she was trying to play down Chantal's behaviour to a sixteen-year-old who was more au fait with the situation.

'He drives a Ferrari, has oodles of money and looks like he stepped out of *GQ* wearing a Versace suit.'

Some contrast, when Roberto was on the wrong side of fifty, three stone overweight and losing his hair.

'And you hate him,' she deduced, and saw the younger girl work herself into a hissy fit.

'I hate *her*. What does she think she's *doing*? Dad practically lives at work, and I may as well not have sat my exams, the marks were so bad.'

Sandrine finished her *latte*. 'How long has this been going on?'

'Six months.'

'Okay.' She rose to her feet. 'Let's go.'

'Let's go? *That's it*?'

'Shopping.' She cast Angelina a purposeful smile. 'When the going gets tough, women go shopping.' She made a beckoning gesture. 'On your feet, girl. I'm about to indulge your wildest fantasy.'

Her stepsister's face was a study in conflicting emotions. 'You are?'

'Indeed.'

Sandrine was as good as her word, and when she had the taxi drop Angelina home early that evening, her stepsister was weighed down with a wide assortment of emblazoned carry bags.

'Thanks, Sandrine.' Angelina planted a kiss on her cheek before sliding out from the taxi. 'You're the best.'

No, Sandrine silently denied as the taxi swung back

into the flow of traffic. I merely trod the same path when Chantal and *my* father broke up, and I'd have given anything to have someone understand my pain.

She'd rung Michel from her cell phone to say she'd be late, and it was almost seven when she entered the apartment.

Michel met her at the door, saw her apparent tenseness and immediately cancelled plans he'd made for the evening. Instead, he brushed his lips across her forehead, then pushed her lightly in the direction of their bedroom.

'Go change, and I'll order in.'

Sandrine shot him a grateful glance. 'Pizza?'

'Okay.'

She kept walking, and in the bedroom she went into the en suite, took a leisurely shower, then she slipped on a short silk robe and pinned up her hair.

Michel sat sprawled on one of several sofas in the lounge, and he patted the seat beside him as she crossed the room. 'Come here.'

It would be heaven to receive some comfort, and she slid down onto the seat and curled her feet beneath her as he pulled her into the curve of his body.

'Want to tell me what's bothering you?'

Was she that transparent? Or was it because this man was so attuned to her that very little escaped him?

She told him briefly, wondering how anyone who hadn't shared a similar experience could possibly understand the breakdown of the family unit.

'You're concerned for Angelina.'

'The emotional upheaval has a far-reaching effect,'

Sandrine said slowly. 'It made me very aware of my own survival. I became very independent and self-contained. I guess I built up a protective shell.'

Yes, Michel agreed silently. She had at that, removing it for him, only to raise the barrier again at the first sign of discord. Self-survival... He was no stranger to it himself.

The intercom buzzed, and Michel answered it, releasing security for the pizza-delivery guy, and afterwards they bit into succulent segments covered with anchovies, olives, capsicum, mushrooms and cheese, washing them down with an excellent red wine while watching a romantic comedy on video.

The days that followed held a similar pattern. Michel divided the first half of each day to business via his laptop and cell phone, while Sandrine caught up with friends over coffee. Most evenings they dined out, took in a show or visited the cinema.

Sandrine's stepbrother, Ivan, chose the premiere screening of the latest *Star Wars* episode, and they indulged his preference for burgers and Coke.

Pinning down Chantal for a mother-and-daughter chat proved the most difficult to organise, with two lunch postponements. Third time lucky, Sandrine hoped as she ordered another mineral water from the waitress and half expected a call on her cell phone announcing Chantal's delay.

Fifteen minutes later Chantal slid into the chair opposite with a murmured apology about the difficulty of city parking and an express order for champagne.

'Celebrating, Chantal?' She hadn't called Chantal *Mother* since her early teens.

'You could say that, darling.'

'A new life?'

'Angelina told you,' Chantal said without concern, and Sandrine inclined her head.

'The news disturbed me.'

'It's my life to lead as I choose.'

'With a man several years younger than yourself?'

Chantal gave the waitress her order, then she leant back in her chair and took a long sip of champagne. 'I thought I was meeting my elder daughter for a chat over lunch.'

'I think I deserve some answers.'

'Why? It doesn't affect you in any way.'

That stung. 'It affects Angelina.' *Just as your break-up with Lucas affected me.*

'She'll get over it,' Chantal said carelessly. 'You did.'

Yes, but at what cost? It had succeeded in instilling such a degree of self-sufficiency that she thought only of herself, her needs and wants. And such a level of self-containment had almost cost her her marriage.

A slight shiver shook her slim frame. She didn't want to be like Chantal, moving from one man to another when she was no longer able to live life on her own terms. That wasn't love. It was self-absorption at its most dangerous level.

'This new man is—how old? Thirty?'

'Thirty-two.'

'Which means when you're sixty, he'll only be forty-four.'

'Don't go down that path, Sandrine,' Chantal warned.

'Why? Because you refuse to think that far ahead?'

'Because I only care about *now*.'

I don't, she noted with silent certainty. I care enough about the future to want to take care of every day that leads towards it. And I care about Michel enough to *want* a future with him. Desperately.

It was as if everything fell into place. And because it did, she chose not to pursue Chantal's indiscretions. Instead, she asked a string of the meaningless questions Chantal excelled in answering as they ate a starter and a main, then lingered over coffee.

They left the restaurant at three, promising to be in touch *soon*, and Sandrine took a page out of her own advice to Angelina. She went shopping. Nothing extravagant. A silk tie for Michel, despite the fact he owned sufficient in number to be able to wear a different one each day for several months. But she liked it and paid for it with a credit card linked to her own account and not the prestigious platinum card Michel had given her following their wedding.

'For you,' she said, presenting it to him within minutes of entering the apartment.

'*Merci, chérie.*'

'It's nothing much.'

His smile held a warmth that sent the blood coursing through her veins. 'The thought, *mignonne*, has more value than the gift itself.'

He pulled her into his arms and kissed her with such slow eroticism she almost groaned out loud when he released her.

'A call came through this afternoon. Tony wants you back on the set to reshoot a scene.'

Damn. Having to reshoot was something she'd been hoping to avoid. 'When?'

'Tomorrow. I've booked an early flight and accommodation at the Sanctuary Cove Hyatt.'

For the next few days the pace would be frenetic, she perceived. After the film wrapped, the publicity promotion would follow.

'Go change,' Michel bade her. 'We'll eat out, then get an early night.'

They chose an intimate French restaurant that served exquisite nouvelle cuisine, then afterwards they strolled along the street, pausing now and then to admire a shop window display. Michel threaded his fingers through her own, and with daylight-saving providing a late-evening dusk, the magic of pavement cafés and ornamental street lighting provided an illusory ambience.

Darkness fell, breaking the spell, and Michel hailed a cruising taxi to take them home.

CHAPTER NINE

IT HAD been a fraught day, Sandrine reflected as she garaged the car. Her final scene had to be shot again and again, and instead of being able to leave the set around midday, it was now almost seven.

She was tired, she had a headache, she was past hungry, and all she wanted to do was sink into a hot spa bath, slip on headphones and let the pulsing jets and music soothe her soul. For an hour.

Heaven, she breathed, entering the villa.

'I was just about to embark on a rescue mission,' Michel drawled as he strolled towards her. He took in her pale features, darkened eyes, the slight droop of her shoulders, and withheld an imprecation. 'Bad day?' he queried lightly. His hands curved over her shoulders as he drew her close. His mouth touched hers, lightly, briefly, and emotion stirred as she turned her face into the curve of his neck.

'Tony insisted the scene be shot so many times. I lost count after fifteen.' He smelt so good, *felt* so good, she could have stayed resting against him for ages. After a few timeless minutes she lifted her head and moved out of his arms. 'I'm going to soak in the tub.'

Warm water, scented oil, an Andrea Bocelli CD on the Walkman. Sandrine closed her eyes and let the tension gradually seep out of her bones.

She didn't hear Michel enter the bathroom, nor did she see him step into the tub, and the first indication she had was the light brush of fingers down her cheek.

Her eyelids flew wide and her mouth parted in unvoiced surprise as Michel positioned her in front of him.

She lifted a hand to remove the headphones only to have his hand close over hers holding them in place, then both hands settled on her shoulders and his fingers bit deep in a skilful massage that went a long way to easing the knots and kinks out of tense muscles.

She sighed blissfully as Michel handed her a flute of champagne, and she took a generous sip of the light golden liquid.

A slow warmth crept through her body, and with each subsequent sip she began to relax. Even her head felt light. Probably, she decided hazily, because she hadn't eaten a thing since lunch.

Sandrine had no idea how long she stayed in the gently pulsating water. It seemed ages, and she uttered a mild protest when the jets were turned off.

Michel lifted her from the tub, then caught up a large fluffy towel and dried the excess moisture from her body.

'You didn't have any champagne,' she murmured as he swept her into his arms and carried her into the bedroom.

'How do you feel?'

'Relaxed.'

He switched on the bedside lamp, hauled back the

bed covers and deposited her onto the sheeted mattress, then joined her.

All she wanted to do was curl into his arms, rest her head against his chest and absorb the strength and comfort he could offer her.

She felt his lips brush her own and she whispered his name in a semiprotest.

'Just close your eyes,' he bade huskily, 'and I'll do all the work.' His mouth grazed the edge of her jaw, then slipped down the slope of her throat.

What followed was a supplication of the senses as he embraced her scented skin with a touch as light as a butterfly's wing. With his lips, the pads of his fingers, he trailed a path from one sensory pleasure spot to another, lingering, savouring, until the warmth invading her body changed to slow-burning heat.

He lifted her hand and kissed each finger in turn, stroking the tip with his tongue, then when he was done he buried his mouth in her palm.

It was an evocative gesture that brought her response, only to have her touch denied as he completed a sensual feast that drove her wild.

He entered her slowly, and she groaned out loud as he initiated a long, sweet loving that was exquisite, magical. It left her weak-limbed and filled with languorous warmth.

Afterwards he folded her close into the curve of his body and held her as she slept. Her hair, loosened from its confining pins, spilled a river of silk over his pillow.

Michel waited a while, then carefully eased out of

bed, showered, dressed in jeans and a cotton shirt, then went downstairs to the kitchen and began organising the evening meal. He'd give her an hour, then wake her.

When he returned to the bedroom, she lay precisely as he'd left her, and he stood quietly at the foot of the bed for several minutes watching as she slept.

She possessed a fierce spirit, an independence that was laudable. It had been those very qualities that had drawn him to her, as well as her inherent honesty. His wealth didn't awe her, any more than *he* did. It was a rare quality to be liked for the man he was and not the Lanier family fortune.

Was she aware just how much she meant to him? She was the very air that he breathed, the daytime sun, the midnight moon.

Yet love alone wasn't enough, and he wasn't sufficiently foolish to imagine a ring and a marriage certificate were a guarantee of lifelong happiness.

Sandrine stirred, opened her eyes, focused on the man standing at the foot of the bed and offered him a slow, sweet smile.

'You shouldn't have let me sleep,' she protested huskily. 'What time is it?'

'Almost ten. Hungry?'

She didn't have to think about it. 'Ravenous.'

'I've made dinner.'

Surprise widened her eyes. 'You have?' She pushed herself into a sitting position and drew the sheet over her chest, then grinned at his teasing smile. 'Give me five minutes.'

She made it in seven, after the quickest shower on record, and slipped on a silky robe rather than dress.

'Oh, my,' Sandrine mused with pleasure as she sat down at the table. 'You do have hidden talent.'

'Singular?' Michel queried mockingly.

'Plural. Definitely plural,' she applauded as she sampled a sip of wine with a sigh of appreciation.

Filet mignon, delectable salad greens, a crusty baguette, and an excellent red wine, with a selection of fresh fruit.

Sandrine ate with pleasurable enjoyment, finishing every morsel on her plate, and she watched Michel cross to the stereo and insert a CD. Then he moved towards her and drew her up from the chair.

'What are you doing?' she queried with a faint laugh as he led her to the centre of the room and pulled her close.

The music was slow, the lyrics poignant, vocalized in the husky tones of a popular male singer.

Mmm, this was good, so good, she silently breathed as he cradled her body against his own. His hands stroked a sensuous pattern down her spine, then he cupped her bottom as she lifted her arms and linked her hands together at his nape.

The warmth of his body seemed to penetrate her own, and she melted into him as they drifted as one to the seductive tempo.

His lips settled at her temple, then slid down to the edge of her mouth, and she angled her head, inviting his possession in a kiss that was slow and so incredibly sweet she never wanted it to cease.

Sandrine gave a soundless gasp as he swept an arm beneath her knees and lifted her into his arms, then held on tight as he carried her through to the bedroom.

'Move, darling. Just a little closer now. Smile.'

If the photographer said *smile* one more time, she'd scream!

It was the end of what had been a very long day. Newspaper interviews and photographs from nine until eleven this morning, followed by a fashion shoot for the Australian edition of a top fashion magazine. Then an appearance at a high-profile charity luncheon held at the Sheraton Mirage, with a brief turn on the cat-walk.

There had been photographs at *Movieworld*. One of the prime television channels was videotaping coverage for a spot on the evening news.

Tonight was the gala black-tie event to publicise the movie. Dignitaries would be present, and the city's wealthy socialites would have paid handsomely to mix and mingle with the producer, director and actors.

It was all a planned marketing strategy to provide maximum impact in the publicity stakes. Gregor and Cait had given interviews in their hotel, and advertising trailers would run on television and in the cinemas.

Sandrine didn't have star status in the film, but as a home-grown talent in acting and modelling, she gained attention. As Michel Lanier's wife, she was guaranteed media coverage.

'Pretend, darling,' Cait murmured with a mocking edge. 'You're supposed to be an actress, so act.'

'As you do, *darling*?' she responded sweetly.

'She really is a barrel of laughs,' Gregor muttered to Sandrine sotto voce. 'Desperate, dateless and deadly.'

'I can have any man I want,' Cait ventured disdainfully.

'No,' he denied smoothly. 'Most, darling. But not all.'

'Go get stuffed.'

'I don't participate in anatomically impossible feats.'

'You could always try.'

'We'll move it over there,' the photographer called, indicating the marina and one luxury cruiser in particular, whose owner had generously lent it for publicity purposes.

How much longer before she could escape? Surely they didn't require her much longer?

'Okay, Sandrine, you can go. Cait, Gregor, I want a few inside shots.'

Thank heavens. She'd almost kill for a long, icy cold drink with just a dash of alcohol to soothe the day's rough edges.

'Lucky you,' Cait voiced cynically. 'You're off the hook.'

For now. She stepped off the cruiser and quickly cleared the marina. The adjoining luxury condominiums of the Palazzo Versace were spectacular in design, resembling a precious jewel set in a sparkling sapphire-blue sea.

Their hotel was reached via an overhead footbridge

from the shopping complex, and Sandrine went directly to their suite.

Michel was seated at the small desk, his shirt sleeves turned back, studying the screen on his laptop as she entered. He glanced at her, then raised an eyebrow as she moved straight to the bar fridge, extracted a bottle of sparkling fruit spritzer and rummaged through the assortment of miniature bottles in the minibar.

'That bad?' he queried as he rose to his feet and crossed to her side.

'Oh, yes.' She broke the seal on the gin, added a splash, then filled the glass with spritzer and took a long sip. 'And tonight will be worse.' She felt his hands on her shoulders and sighed as he skilfully worked the tense muscles there. 'Remind me we're flying out of here tomorrow.'

She heard his husky chuckle and leaned back against him. He felt so good she just wanted to close her eyes, absorb his strength and have the immediate world go away.

'Two days in Sydney,' he drawled, and brushed his lips to her temple. 'Then we fly home.'

Home had a nice ring to it. She pictured their New York apartment overlooking Central Park and sighed again, feeling some of the tension subside.

'I have a few things to tie up there, which will take a week, maybe longer, then we'll spend some time in Paris.'

'I think I love you,' Sandrine said fervently.

'Only *think, chérie*?'

She opened her mouth to protest, then closed it again. 'I was being facetious.'

'So one would hope.'

She turned slowly to face him, saw the gleam of humour evident in those dark eyes and aimed a loosely clenched fist at his chest. The next instant she cried out as he removed the glass from her fingers and hoisted her over one shoulder.

'What are you *doing*?'

He walked towards the adjoining en suite, released her down onto the tiled floor, then began removing her clothes, followed by his own.

'Michel?'

'Taking a shower.'

She glimpsed the slumberous passion evident and shook her head. 'We don't have time for this.'

He reached into the glassed shower cubicle and turned on the water, adjusted the temperature dial, then stepped inside and drew her with him. 'Yes, we do.'

The water beat down on her head, and she heard his husky chuckle as she cursed him. Then she stilled as he caught up the soap and ran it over her slim curves.

He was very thorough. Too thorough, Sandrine decided as heat flared through her body at his intimate touch, and she moaned out loud as his mouth closed over hers in an erotic tasting that almost sent her over the edge.

When he raised his head, she looked at him in dazed disbelief as he handed her the soap and encouraged her to return the favour.

She did, with such sensuous, lingering skill he lifted her high against him and plunged deep inside, again and again while she clung to him.

Afterwards he caught up the plastic bottle of shampoo and washed her hair, then rinsed it before shutting the water and reaching for both towels.

Dry, he pulled her close and kissed her with unabated passion, then put her firmly at arm's length.

Sandrine looked at him with musing suspicion. 'You planned that.' It was a statement, not a query.

'Guilty.'

She pulled the hair dryer from its wall attachment and switched it on. 'We'll be late.'

'No, we won't.'

Five minutes didn't count, Sandrine acknowledged less than an hour later as they entered the large downstairs foyer.

Michel looked striking in full evening dress, and she felt confident in encrusted ivory silk organza with a scooped neckline. Elegant evening pumps in matching ivory completed the outfit, and she'd swept her hair high in a smooth French pleat.

The function-room doors were open and guests were beginning to enter. The Gold Coast's social glitterati were evident in force, Sandrine perceived, noting the elegant gowns, expensive jewellery, exquisitely made-up and coiffed women present. Without exception, the men were in full evening dress and bow tie.

Sandrine sighted Stephanie, who returned her smile and joined them within seconds.

'I've seated you with Cait Lynden, Gregor Anders,

the charity's chairwoman and her husband, and myself. The mayor and his wife are at Tony's table immediately adjoining yours. There'll be two tables seating the studio heads and various representatives from the marketing team.'

Sandrine saw Stephanie stiffen slightly and soon determined the reason as Raoul joined them.

'The photographer was happy with everything today,' Stephanie continued, ignoring Raoul after offering him a fleeting polite smile. 'There will, of course, be more taken tonight. However, we'll try to contain it so it doesn't become too intrusive. Now, if you'll excuse me?'

'You appear to have a disturbing effect on that young woman,' Michel observed to his brother.

'I'll settle for disturb rather than disinterest,' Raoul drawled in response, and Sandrine wrinkled her nose at her husband, then turned to Raoul.

'Like that, is it?' she teased.

'She doesn't want to talk to me and she avoids my calls.'

'I imagine you've arranged a few meetings with marketing?' she posed musingly, and glimpsed the gleam of humour evident in his expression. 'In Michel's absence, in the name of business, of course.'

His smile held a certain wry amusement. 'Of course.'

'Another rare young woman uninfluenced by the Lanier wealth and social status?'

'I think we should go inside and take our seats,'

Michel indicated quizzically. 'Naturally you've arranged to sit at our table?'

'*Oui*,' Raoul agreed dryly, and Sandrine suppressed a chuckle as a committee member checked their tickets and indicated their table location.

The chairwoman's husband was the sole occupant, and upon introduction he explained that his wife was busy with last-minute details. Of Cait and Gregor there was no sign, and Sandrine suppressed the uncharitable thought that Cait was probably aiming to stage-manage a dramatic entrance.

She wasn't wrong. Just as the lights flickered, indicating the formalities were about to begin, Cait swept into the function room with Gregor and a photographer in tow.

In a gown that was backless, strapless and appeared moulded to her figure, the actress stepped towards them, pausing every now and then to pose as the camera lens focused on her.

'We're not late, are we?' The beautiful, sultry smile was at variance with the breathless little-girl voice.

Cait, the actress, playing to the audience, Sandrine perceived wryly. Of the remaining empty seats, Cait slid into the one between Raoul and Michel.

Sandrine kept a smile in place with difficulty and took a sip of chilled wine.

Stephanie slipped into her seat seconds before the evening's master of ceremonies stepped on stage to take the microphone.

There were introductions and speeches as the spotlight focused on Cait, Gregor and Tony, followed by a studio representative. The mayor said his piece, then a small army of waiters began serving the starter as music beat through sound speakers and a singer provided entertainment on stage.

Sandrine was supremely conscious of the man seated at her side. His enviable aura of power combined with a dramatic measure of primitive sensuality had a magnetic effect.

Cait resembled a feline who'd just swallowed a saucer of cream, Sandrine observed as she forked a morsel of the artistically arranged starter.

'Darling, you don't mind if I have a few photos taken with Michel, do you?' Cait queried, managing to make the request sound like a statement.

The female star and the man who'd rescued a movie from financial disaster, Sandrine reflected cynically, and wondered why she should feel like a possessive tigress. Protecting your interest, a tiny voice taunted. And her interest was Michel, her marriage.

'Mr Lanier has specified any photographs in which he appears must also include his wife,' Stephanie informed her with businesslike candour.

'A group photo, perhaps?' Raoul suggested in a slightly accented drawl. 'Including the marketing manager?'

Stephanie cast him a level glance. 'I don't think that's necessary.'

'Oh, but I think it is,' Raoul argued smoothly. 'Marketing is an integral part of any film production, *non*?'

Careful, Sandrine cautioned silently. Stephanie is a

steel magnolia, not a fragile violet. Baiting her won't achieve a thing.

'Marketing as a whole,' Stephanie agreed.

The chemistry between them sizzled, Sandrine mused. Raoul was a persistent and determined man. While Stephanie gave every indication of wanting to avoid him at any cost. Who would win?

Michel reached out a hand and threaded his fingers through her own. She turned towards him and caught the smouldering passion evident beneath his veiled gaze.

'My money's on Raoul,' she said quietly.

'Indeed,' Michel agreed. 'Although I doubt it'll be an easy victory.'

His thumb began a disturbing pattern across the sensitive veins inside her wrist, an action that played havoc with her equilibrium. As he intended it to do.

'I think I need to repair my make-up,' Sandrine ventured, and caught Michel's knowing smile. He realized the effect he had on her and precisely why she wanted a temporary escape.

'You look beautiful just the way you are.'

'Flattery won't get you anywhere,' she responded with a teasing smile, aware that she lied. She was so incredibly susceptible to everything about him. His voice, the softly spoken French he frequently lapsed into whenever he became lost in the throes of passion. The fluid movement of his body, his limbs, the way he smiled and those chiselled features softened when he looked at her.

She'd thought independence was important, but

nothing in her life held a candle to her love for Michel. He'd been right from the start. Why choose to be apart unless circumstances made it impossible to be together?

All those lonely nights she'd spent in her empty bed she'd longed for him to be beside her, to feel his touch. She'd enjoyed the part she'd played in the film, but that satisfaction didn't come close in compensation for being away from her husband.

Sandrine pushed open the door to the powder room and freshened up. Just as she was about to leave, Cait entered the vestibule.

One eyebrow slanted in recognition, and her mouth curved into a petulant smile. 'Really, darling, I'm surprised you could bear to leave Michel's side.'

Sandrine was heartily sick of the actress's game playing. 'It's a challenge, is it, Cait, to seduce another woman's husband?'

'Forbidden fruit, darling, tastes much sweeter than any that's readily available.' She raised a hand and placed the tip of a finger in her mouth. 'And it's always interesting to see if I can pluck the fruit from the tree.' She deliberately licked her finger, removed it, then offered Sandrine a sultry look. 'So to speak.'

Sandrine had had enough. She replaced her powder sponge and lipstick in her bag and closed the clasp. 'If you can succeed with Michel, you can have him.' She moved towards the door and paused momentarily at the sound of Cait's sultry drawl.

'Aren't you going to wish me good luck?'

'The hell I will,' she said inelegantly, and stepped quickly to the function room.

The buzz of voices hit her the moment she re-entered the large room, and she forced herself to walk slowly across the carpeted floor.

The chairwoman and her husband were absent from their table, as were Stephanie and Gregor. Only Michel and Raoul remained, and they appeared deep in conversation as she rejoined them.

Michel cast her a quick glance, glimpsed the faint edge of tension and accurately defined the reason for it.

'Cait?'

She managed a wry smile. 'She made it clear you're the target of her affections.'

'Indeed.'

He seemed amused, damn him.

'If you choose to play her game, then she can have you.'

He picked up her hand and lifted it to his lips, then kissed each finger in turn. 'Now why would I do that, *chérie*, hmm?' He grazed his teeth against her thumb, and saw her eyes flare. 'When all I want is you.'

'Perhaps you should tell Cait that.'

He brushed his mouth across the delicate veins inside her wrist, and Sandrine barely controlled the shiver that threatened to scud the length of her spine.

She could feel herself slowly drowning when she looked at him. The liquid warmth evident in his gaze rendered her bones to jelly, and she had to physically stop herself from leaning forward to place her lips against the sensuous curve of his mouth.

As crazy as it seemed, she could almost feel him inside her, relive the strength and the power of him as muscles deep inside clenched and unclenched in intimate spasms.

He knew. She could see by the glint of those dark eyes that he'd somehow detected the way she was inwardly reacting to him. She lowered her lashes and attempted to pull her hand free. To no avail, as he merely carried her hand to rest on his thigh.

An equally dangerous move, and she pressed the tips of her fingernails into hard muscle in silent warning.

'We've been invited to party on at the hotel's nightclub,' Michel relayed. 'Everyone else associated with the film and marketing will be there.'

She almost groaned out loud. 'Tell me our flight isn't the early-morning one,' she pleaded, and he gave a husky laugh.

'Eleven-thirty.'

'Breakfast before nine isn't an option,' she warned.

'Plan on sleeping in, *chérie*?'

She wrinkled her nose at him. '*Sleep* is the operative word.'

The photographer got his shots, several of them. Raoul very cleverly positioned himself beside Stephanie while Cait insinuated herself between Raoul and Michel. Gregor, bless him, wriggled his eyebrows at them all and flanked Stephanie.

It was after eleven when the evening began to wind

down, and half an hour later they wandered in groups towards the nightclub.

The DJ was spinning loud, funky music, the air was thick with noise, a cacophony of voices straining to be heard, and flashing strobe lighting provided a visual disturbance.

'Let's party, darling,' Gregor invited as he swept a glass of wine from the tray of a passing waitress.

'Why don't you ask Sandrine to dance?' Cait queried with a contrived pout. 'I want to play with the big boys.'

'Both of whom have their own women,' Gregor warned, regardless of her careless shrug. 'Don't do it, sweetheart.'

'Oh, stop trying to spoil my fun.'

Raoul turned towards Stephanie and indicated the crowded dance floor. 'Are you game to enter the fray?'

'With you?'

'Of course with me.'

'I'm not really into dancing.'

Cait placed a hand on Michel's forearm and used her fingers to apply a little pressure as she tilted her head and offered a provocative smile. 'Sandrine won't mind if I drag you away.' She turned towards Sandrine, openly daring her to object. 'Will you, darling?'

Michel covered Cait's hand with his own and transferred it to her side. His expression was polite, but there was an inflexible hardness apparent in his gaze. 'Regrettably, I do mind.'

Cait didn't bat an eyelash. 'I think the idea is for

everyone to loosen up a little now the film is in the can.'

'Define "loosen up",' Michel drawled.

Sandrine recognised the faint inflection in his voice and almost felt sorry for Cait.

'There's the party after the party, if you know what I mean,' the actress intimated with deliberate coquetry. 'A very *private* party.'

Was she aware just how brazen she sounded? And how damning? There was an edge apparent, a hyped overbrightness that hinted at substance enhancement. It left a sick feeling in Sandrine's stomach and provoked a degree of sadness.

'No.'

Cait's mouth formed a perfect bow. 'No?'

If she stayed another minute, she'd say something regrettable! 'Please, excuse me for a few minutes?'

'Do you mind if I join you?' Stephanie asked.

It took several minutes to weave their way through the nightclub patrons and locate the powder room. Once inside, the noise level diminished to a bearable level as they joined the queue waiting to use the facilities.

'Ten minutes, fifteen tops,' Stephanie commented as she examined her nails. 'Then I'm out of here, business and social obligations completed.'

'The suits won't have reason to complain,' Sandrine agreed with a quizzical smile, then saw the marketing manager visibly relax.

'It's all coming together well. The trailers are good, and the media blitz will gain the public's attention.'

The queue shifted, and they moved forward a few paces.

'I understand you're returning to Sydney tomorrow.'

Sandrine inclined her head. 'Just for a few days, then we fly home.'

'New York,' Stephanie murmured. 'I visited there once. Very fast, very cosmopolitan.'

'It has a beat all its own.'

'Distinctive.'

'Like the Lanier men.'

'One of them in particular,' Stephanie declared dryly.

Sandrine shot her a teasing smile. 'Persistent, is he?' she queried, and caught the other woman's wry grimace.

'You could say that.'

'Naturally, you don't like him.'

'He makes me feel uncomfortable.'

'Uncomfortable is good.'

'No,' Stephanie refuted. 'It's a pain in the neck.'

A light bubble of laughter rose to the surface. 'Good luck.'

'For Raoul to catch me? Or for me to escape unscathed?'

'Oh, I'll take a gamble and go for the first option,' Sandrine said wickedly.

'Not in this lifetime.'

There was a finality about those few words, and she wondered what, or rather *who* had damaged Stephanie's trust in men.

The music hit them in waves as they returned to the nightclub, and Stephanie joined a representative group from the marketing team as Sandrine crossed to rejoin Michel.

As she approached, Cait wound an arm round his neck and placed her mouth to his. It was a deliberate and calculated action, she knew, but one that angered her unbearably.

Michel showed restrained dignity as he broke the contact, and the actress turned towards Sandrine with a tantalising smile.

'You said I could have him, darling.'

'From where I stood, it didn't look as if he wanted you,' she managed in a remarkably even voice.

'Bitch.'

'I could say the same.'

Michel caught Sandrine's hand and linked his fingers through hers, applying a slight warning pressure. Which she ignored.

'Perhaps we should leave,' he suggested indolently, and suppressed a degree of amusement as Sandrine shot him a stunning smile.

'Why? I'm having so much fun.' She lifted his hand and brushed her lips across his knuckles. 'Ask me to dance.'

His eyes darkened and acquired a wicked gleam as he led her onto the dance floor. 'Minx,' he murmured close to her ear.

'Confrontation,' she mocked lightly. 'Works so much better than retreat.' A light gasp escaped her lips as he drew her in close. 'That might be a bit of overkill.' One hand cupped her bottom while the other slid to clasp her nape.

'You think so?' he drawled, enjoying the way her heart thudded into a quickened beat, the slight huskiness in her voice.

The music slowed, and they drifted together for several long minutes, only to break apart as the DJ switched discs and tempo.

By mutual consent they began circulating between the various business heads from marketing, the studio. Something that took a while, until they came at last to Raoul.

'Sleep well,' she bade as he brushed his lips to her cheek.

Minutes later they entered their suite, and Sandrine slipped off her shoes, then unfastened the zip and stepped out of her gown.

It had been a long day, and there was a sense of satisfaction that everything had come to a close.

She crossed to the en suite, removed her make-up, slipped on a silk nightshirt, then re-entered the bedroom and slid into bed.

Within seconds Michel joined her, snapped off the bedlamp, then caught her close.

It was heaven to lean against him, to feel the reassuring beat of his heart beneath her cheek. His lips touched her temple, then slid to her mouth to bestow a brief, warm kiss.

His chin rested against the top of her head, and she simply closed her eyes and drifted off to sleep within seconds.

CHAPTER TEN

SYDNEY looked achingly familiar, and the Double Bay apartment particularly welcoming. There were several things she wanted to do, a few loose ends she needed to tie up, and she wanted some time alone with her father.

Michel's cell phone rang as Sandrine began unpacking the few necessities required during the next day or two, and his voice faded into a muted sound as he took the call in the lounge.

He returned to the bedroom minutes later and began unpacking. 'Raoul has set up a meeting with the Enrique Corporation for tomorrow afternoon.'

A new deal, initiated by Raoul who had flown into Sydney the previous day, which, if it proved successful, would see a Lanier Corporation link in Australia.

'I'll ring Lucas and see if he's free to meet me for lunch.'

Michel handed her his cell phone. 'Do it now. We're meeting Raoul for dinner, and it might be late when we get back.'

She punched in the relevant numbers, greeted her father's availability with enthusiasm and agreed on a time and place to meet.

'All done,' Sandrine said with satisfaction. She had

twenty minutes in which to change and repair her make-up, and she managed it with a minute to spare.

Deep red evening trousers and a matching cropped evening jacket worn over a black silk camisole highlighted the texture of her skin and emphasised the lustrous colour of her hair. She left it loose to fall onto her shoulders, simply because there wasn't sufficient time to pin it up.

Raoul was booked into the Ritz-Carlton in Double Bay, and they joined him in the lounge at seven for a drink before entering the restaurant.

The maître d' led them to a table and snapped his fingers for the wine steward.

'Too premature for champagne?' Sandrine queried with a quizzical smile.

'Who needs a special occasion to drink champagne? Dom Pérignon,' Raoul instructed, and she observed the smooth approach of the waiter. Such synchronisation in service deserved a reward.

After they ordered a starter and main, deferring dessert, Sandrine spared a cursory glance at the room and its occupants as she sipped champagne from a crystal flute.

Michel and Raoul discussed strategy for the next day's meeting and finetuned arrangements over the starter.

They were part way through the main dish when something caught Sandrine's attention. The stark light of a flashbulb, followed by the glimpse of a familiar figure combined with a trill of laughter she'd hoped never to hear again.

For a moment she thought, *hoped*, she was mistaken, but no, there, making a grand entrance, was none other than Cait Lynden.

I don't believe this. She had known Cait and Gregor were due to fly out to the States this week, but of all the hotels in Sydney, was it coincidence Cait had chosen this one...or had she done some careful sleuthing?

Perhaps she wouldn't notice they were here?

Fat chance, Sandrine acknowledged in wry silence as she viewed Cait's performance. For it was a piece of superb acting, which didn't fool her in the slightest. Any more than it deceived Michel or Raoul as Cait approached their table.

'For heaven's sake,' Cait greeted with delighted enthusiasm, 'who would have thought we'd run into each other, *here*, of all places.'

The maître d' hovered, well used to the presence of celebrities in this exclusive hotel. He aimed to please and to serve, and Cait took flagrant advantage of his position.

'You don't mind if I join you?' She slid into the chair held out for her, then waved her hand in an elegant gesture to the wine steward. 'Bring another bottle of champagne.' When the waiter presented her with a menu, she scanned it quickly, then handed it back to him. 'Just a starter. The Caesar salad.'

'You're alone?' Raoul drawled in query, and Sandrine watched Cait weigh up which Lanier brother she'd attempt to captivate.

Just try it with Michel, she warned silently, and I'll scratch your eyes out!

The famous pout was a touch overdone. 'Gregor deserted me, the rat.' Her mouth formed a moue. 'I could have ordered room service, but I didn't feel like being alone.'

Cashing in on national publicity and revelling in the limelight, Sandrine perceived, then mentally chastised herself for being cynical.

'So, what are we celebrating?'

'Life,' Michel stated with studied indolence as he took hold of Sandrine's hand and lifted it to his lips. 'And love.' He kissed each fingertip in turn, then curled her hand within his.

Oh, my, that was about as blatant as you could get. Add to that the passionate gleam apparent in his eyes, the sensual curve of his lips. It was a combination that succeeded in melting her bones.

'Quite a change from when Michel first appeared on the scene a month ago,' Cait imputed with thinly veiled sarcasm. 'At Tony's apartment I could have sworn you were enemies instead of husband and wife.'

'If husbands and wives didn't experience a difference of opinion on occasion, the marriage would become boring,' Sandrine offered.

'Really?'

'Anyone for coffee?' Raoul intervened. 'I have a few calls to make.'

'Likewise I need to go on-line.' Michel succeeded in attracting the maître d's attention, then turned towards Cait. 'By all means stay on and finish the champagne.'

They weren't able to escape quite so easily. The

photographer appeared out of nowhere and reeled off
a few shots, which, unless Sandrine was mistaken,
would be sold to at least one of the national newspapers.

Michel muttered an imprecation beneath his breath,
signed the proffered credit slip, then rose to his feet
and pocketed his wallet.

'Safe flight, darlings,' Cait bade, again looking like
a cat who'd just finished a bowl of cream.

'*Merci.*'

Michel curved an arm round Sandrine's waist as
Raoul accompanied them to the main entrance, then
waited as they slid into a taxi.

'Coincidence, do you think?' she posed as the taxi
swiftly joined the traffic.

'Extremely doubtful,' Michel said dryly.

'Coffee?' Sandrine offered on entering the apartment five minutes later. 'We didn't have any, and if
you need to work on-line…'

'The only thing I want to work closely with is *you*.'

A lazy grin widened her mouth, and her eyes sparkled as she turned towards him. 'I'm not sure I like
being referred to as a *thing*.'

He crooked a finger in a beckoning gesture. 'Come
here.'

Laughter bubbled up inside her, emerging as a delightful throaty sound. 'You'd better have a good reason for issuing orders.'

'Oh, I don't think you'll have reason to complain.'

She moved into his arms and felt them enfold her
close. 'Really?'

'*Really*,' he mocked lightly, then proceeded to kiss her with such passion she went up in flames.

They made it to the bedroom, discarding clothes as they went, and it was a long time before she found the energy to do more than murmur her appreciation as she slipped close to the edge of sleep.

The taxi eased to a halt outside the Ritz-Carlton, and Michel paid the driver as Sandrine emerged from the vehicle.

Together they entered the main lobby, shared a coffee with Raoul, then Sandrine rose to her feet and brushed Michel's temple with a light kiss.

'Three o'clock?'

Michel's answering smile held warmth as he inclined his head. 'Have fun.'

Her mouth assumed a wicked curve. 'I intend to.' She wanted to select a special gift for his grandmother and she was due to meet her father at one.

Double Bay was a delightful place to browse and shop, and she found a beautiful Hermès silk scarf that was just perfect.

It was almost one when she entered the restaurant Lucas had recommended, and she was barely seated when the maître d' showed him to their table.

'Sandrine,' Lucas greeted with affection, 'this is a pleasure.'

She ordered wine, and they settled on a starter and main.

'It's regrettable this has to be brief, but I have a scheduled meeting at two-fifteen.'

'That's okay,' Sandrine voiced without hesitation.

He surveyed her over the rim of his glass. 'You have something on your mind you want to discuss with me?'

'Chantal.'

Lucas replaced his glass down on the table. 'You know your mother and I no longer maintain contact.'

She was aware of all the reasons why and had accepted them. 'I'm concerned for her.'

'And you expect me to share that concern?'

'She's my mother,' she said simply.

'Chantal is an emotional butterfly, always seeking something different and new. When life becomes boring, she moves on without too much thought for those left behind.' He paused as the waiter removed their plates. 'I rebuilt my life with a loving woman.'

A loving woman who was civil and superficially affectionate to her husband's daughter from his first marriage, but one who'd made it clear Sandrine had no place in her home or her heart.

Lucas placed a hand over hers. 'Your mother will never change. She's *Chantal*,' he declared with wry cynicism, as if that explained it all. 'You have Michel. Treasure that love and treat it with care.'

There was no point to pursuing the conversation, and she didn't even try. Instead, they spoke of Ivan's academic achievements and aspirations.

It was after two when they emerged from the restaurant, and Sandrine gave her father an affectionate hug in farewell.

She needed to make a few calls to friends, and she

strolled towards the hotel, settled herself comfortably in the lounge, ordered a cappuccino and punched a series of numbers into her cell phone.

She temporarily lost track of time, and it wasn't until she glanced at her watch after concluding the last of her calls that she realised it was after three.

Where was Michel? Sandrine checked her watch for the third time in fifteen minutes. It wasn't like him to be late.

'Can I get you anything else, ma'am?'

She cast the waitress a brief smile and shook her head. 'Thank you.'

A slight frown creased her forehead. She hadn't got the meeting place wrong because Michel had dropped her off outside this hotel more than three hours ago.

Perhaps he'd been held up. Yes, that was it. His meeting had run overtime.

The frown deepened. If that were true, why didn't he ring? She slipped the cell phone from her bag and checked it for any messages. There were none.

Okay, she'd ring him on his cell phone. A few words of reassurance were all she needed. Without further hesitation she punched in the numbers and waited, only to have the call switch to voice mail. She left a message, then slipped the phone into her bag.

Raoul. Maybe she could call Raoul, she thought, only to remember she hadn't keyed his number into her memory bank.

Business lunches were notorious for running late. Any minute now Michel would call, apologise and explain. Except he didn't, and a fist closed over her heart.

Several different scenarios played through her mind and she examined and discarded each of them.

The peal of the phone interrupted her increasing apprehension, and she plucked the unit from her bag and activated it.

'Raoul, Sandrine.'

'Michel—'

'Is okay,' Raoul assured her. 'There was a slight car accident, and the officers who attended the scene insisted everyone involved receive a medical examination.'

Dear heaven. 'Where?'

He named a private city hospital. 'Take a cab. I'll be waiting for you.'

A chill invaded her bones. 'I'm on my way.'

The ensuing fifteen minutes were the longest minutes of her life as she imagined a plethora of possibilities regarding Raoul's description of events.

'Okay, he's okay,' she repeated several times beneath her breath as the cab negotiated heavy city traffic.

What if Raoul wasn't telling her the truth? Dear Lord in heaven, what if the accident had been severe?

Sandrine froze. Images of horrific televised accident scenes flashed before her eyes. She pictured bodies being cut from crushed vehicles and transported by ambulance to hospital.

How much longer? She checked the location and estimated another five minutes should do it, providing there were no unexpected traffic snarls.

The cab made it in seven, and she hurriedly thrust

a note into the driver's hand, opened the door and waved away his move to give her change.

She ran down the concrete path and paused impatiently as she waited for the automatic glass doors of the main entrance to open.

Sandrine was oblivious to the nurses' station, the collection of waiting patients. All she saw was Raoul crossing the room towards her, and she rushed to his side.

'He's with the doctor,' Raoul soothed, taking hold of her elbow as he led her down a corridor. 'He's fine. The wound needs a few stitches.'

Her stomach clenched at the thought of torn flesh being stitched together. 'How bad is it?'

Raoul gave her arm a reassuring squeeze. 'A few scratches, some bruising.' He indicated a doorway to the right. 'He's in here.'

Sandrine's heart missed a beat, then thudded loudly in her chest as she stepped into the room. The attending doctor partly obscured Michel from her view, and she moved quickly to his side, her eyes sweeping over his features, his lengthy frame, in a bid to determine the extent of his injuries.

'*Michel*,' she breathed raggedly as she took in those flawless, broad-boned facial features, then roved over his bare chest.

No scratches, no visible bruising, she noted with relief. The doctor was working on Michel's left arm, stitching what looked to be a deep gash, and she paled at the sight of the needle suturing the wound.

'My wife,' Michel drawled as the doctor paused in his task to give her a quick glance.

'Your husband is fine. A few bruised ribs from the restraining seat belt, plus a gashed arm. I'll be done in a few minutes, then you can take him home.'

Sandrine felt the blood drain from her face as her vivid imagination envisaged the car screeching as Michel applied the brakes, the sickening crunch as two cars collided, the reflexive action at the moment of impact.

For one brief, infinitesimal second she experienced a mental flash of how it might have been, and the thought of what *could* have happened almost destroyed her. A life without Michel in it would be no life at all.

A hand curved round her nape as Michel pulled her towards him, and her hands instinctively clutched hold of his shoulders. Then his mouth was on hers in a brief, hard kiss that almost immediately softened to a light caress before he released her.

'Don't, *chérie*,' he chastised huskily, and uttered a muffled curse as he saw her lips tremble.

She tried to smile but didn't quite make it.

Michel's eyes darkened, and he caught her hand and held it. His thumb lightly caressed the veins inside her wrist, moving in a rhythmic pattern that stirred her senses. Just looking at him made her want to fling her arms around him and hold on tight.

Relief flooded her veins, closely followed by love. The deep, abiding-forever kind. Her heart, her emotions, belonged to this man, unequivocally. Nothing else held any importance.

'There, all done,' the doctor declared as he applied a dressing and secured it. 'Those stitches need to be removed in a week.'

Michel rose to his feet, grabbed his shirt from the back of the chair, shrugged it on and attended to the buttons before slipping into his jacket. 'Let's get out of here.'

'I'll organise the cab and drop you off on my way to the airport,' Raoul stated as they exited the building, and Sandrine gave him a brief, keen glance.

'You're flying back to the Gold Coast?'

He offered her a wry smile. 'Yes.'

'I see.'

'Do you?'

Her eyes held musing humour. 'Oh, yes.' Stephanie was in for a battle if she thought she could easily dismiss Raoul. The Lanier men fought for what they wanted. 'I recognise the signs.'

'Then wish me luck, Sandrine.'

'Do you need it?'

His expression assumed a faint bleakness.

So he wasn't so sure after all. Good, she decided silently. He'd appreciate Stephanie all the more for not providing him with an easy victory.

She lifted a hand and brushed her fingers down that firm cheek. 'You have it, Raoul.'

He offered her a smile that held warmth and affection. '*Merci.*'

CHAPTER ELEVEN

THERE was a rank of taxis outside the main entrance, and one moved forward at a flick from Michel's fingers.

Twenty minutes later the cab slid to a halt outside their apartment building, and they bade Raoul a quick farewell, then made their way through the foyer to the lift.

The instant the lift doors closed behind them, Michel punched the appropriate panel button, then he pulled her close and fastened his mouth over hers in a kiss that was all too brief as the doors slid open at their designated floor. They walked the few steps to their door and then entered the apartment.

For a few seconds she stood in dazed silence, her eyes large as she looked at him. There was so much she wanted to say, yet the words seemed caught in her throat.

He was so dear to her, so very special. Life itself. Without him, the flame within her would flicker and die.

Something flared in his eyes, and she stood perfectly still as he threaded his fingers into her hair and tilted her head.

'I couldn't bear to lose you,' she said simply, and saw his lips curve into a gentle smile.

'It isn't going to happen.'

'Today, just for a while, I thought it might have.'

As long as he lived, he'd never forget the expression in her eyes, the paleness of her features when she entered the emergency room. His thumb caressed the firm line of her jaw. 'I know.'

She swallowed, the expression in her eyes mirroring her emotions. 'You probably should rest,' she voiced huskily.

'You think so?'

'Michel…' She paused as his head lowered down to hers and his lips settled on one cheekbone, then began trailing a path down the slope of her jawbone to settle at the edge of her mouth.

'Hmm?'

'I can't think when you do that.'

'Is it so important that you think?'

One hand moved to the vee of her top and slid beneath it.

'I want…' Her breath hitched as his fingers brushed the slope of her breast, the touch infinitely erotic over the soft silk and lace of her bra.

His lips teased hers, light as a butterfly's wing, as they stroked over the sensuous lower curve, then he swept his tongue to taste the sweetness within.

This, *this*, was where she was meant to be. Held in the arms of the man who was her soul mate. Nothing else mattered.

'What is it you want, *chérie*?' Michel drawled gently.

'*You*,' she said simply. 'But first…' Her voice

climbed a few notches, then came to a sudden halt as his fingers slid to unfasten the clip of her bra. The sensitive peaks burgeoned in anticipation of his touch, and heat arrowed from deep within as he began an erotic, evocative stroking. It drove her wild, and she groaned out loud as he pulled the knit top over her head, discarded her bra, then lowered his mouth to one highly sensitised peak.

She could feel herself begin to melt as her body melded to his, aligning itself to allow him access as her hands crept round his neck.

A long, heartfelt sigh whispered from her lips as he shifted his attention to render a similar salutation to its twin. For what seemed an age she exulted in the sheer sensation his touch evoked, feeling every pore, every nerve cell pulse into vibrant life.

It wasn't enough, and she murmured encouragement when his fingers slipped to her waist and attended to the zip fastening.

His clothes were an impossible barrier she sought to remove with considerable care, and his gentle smile almost completely undid her as he put her at arm's length and finished the task.

Sandrine took in his muscled frame, the olive-toned skin stretching over superb bone structure and honed sinew. His shoulders were broad, his chest tightly muscled and liberally sprinkled with dark, curling hair that arrowed down to his waist, then flared into a geometric vee at the juncture of his thighs.

He was an impressive, well-endowed man, a skilled and exciting lover whose degree of *tendresse* melted her bones, while his passion had the power to awe and overwhelm.

With one easy movement he swept an arm beneath her knees and lifted her high against his chest.

'Your arm,' she protested, and heard his husky laughter.

'Afraid it might hinder me?' Michel teased as he strode through to the bedroom.

'Hurt you,' she corrected as he pulled back the bedclothes and drew her down with him onto the sheets.

He kissed her, deeply and with such soul-destroying intensity she lost track of time and place until he slowly released his mouth from her own.

She looked *kissed*, he saw with satisfaction. Her mouth was slightly swollen, and her eyes resembled huge liquid pools a man could drown in.

He wanted to savour the taste of her, skim his lips over every inch of her skin, suckle at her breasts with the ferocity of a newborn infant seeking succour. Except a man nurtured his woman's breasts to give her pleasure, for some of the most sensitised nerve endings were centred at those peaks.

Most of all he wanted to bury himself deep in her moist heat and become lost in the sweet sorcery that was *Sandrine*. His woman, his wife. His life.

From the moment he met her, he had only one agenda. It was instant, breathtaking desire. Yet it had been more than that, much more. Deep within the raw, primitive emotion had been the instinctive knowledge they were meant to be. Almost as if they'd known each other in a former existence.

Crazy, he dismissed with a mental shake of his head. He possessed a logical, analytical mind. Yet he was frighteningly aware of the timing and how, had he not been at a friend's home attending a party, he might never have met her. Equally, the slender thread of chance that led her to be persuaded to tag along to something she freely admitted hadn't been her first choice of an evening's entertainment.

Of the many women he'd met socially and in the business arena, there had been none who'd come close to the magic that was Sandrine.

Beautiful, with a gently curving slenderness that made her frame perfect for displaying designer clothes on various European catwalks. Fine-boned facial features, lovely, wide-spaced dark brown eyes, a generous mouth.

Rather than her physical appearance, it had been the genuine warmth of her smile, the expressive eyes and her *joie de vivre*. The way her chin tilted when she laughed, the faint twist of her head as she tossed her hair back over her shoulders. The sound of her voice, its faint huskiness when she became emotionally aroused. And because he was a man, the feel of her body in his arms, her mouth beneath his. The scent and essence that made her unique.

Destined to be, he mused, like two halves of a whole that fitted perfectly together as one.

'Michel?'

He looked down at her and tried to control the slight tremor that threatened to destroy the slim hold on his libido. 'You get to talk *after* we make love,' he teased mercilessly, and felt his body go weak at the languorous humour evident in those beautiful dark eyes.

'You could make an exception.'

He trailed a finger down the slope of her nose. 'So what is it you want to say that can't wait, hmm?'

She reached up a hand and pressed a finger to his lips, stilling any words he might have added. '*I love you*.' There was the prick of unshed tears, an ache deep inside her heart.

He kissed each of her fingers in turn, and she almost melted from the warmth evident in his gaze. '*Merci, chérie*,' he said gently.

'I always have,' she assured him with such a depth of feeling two tears materialised, clung to her lashes, then spilled to run down her cheek in twin rivulets. 'I always will.'

His thumb stroked away the dampness. 'Are you done?'

She inclined her head and made an attempt to restore her composure. Her gaze speared his, and there was a depth apparent that made him catch his breath.

'I have something for you.' He reached out and slid open a drawer of the bedside pedestal, extracted something, then turned back to her and caught hold of her left hand.

It was an exquisite diamond-studded ring, a perfect complement to her existing rings.

'It's beautiful,' Sandrine breathed. 'Thank you.' A circle symbolising eternity. She wanted to cry. 'I have nothing for you.'

The passionate warmth evident in his gaze succeeded in melting her bones. 'You're wrong,' Michel said tenderly. '*You* are my gift. Infinitely more precious than anything you could give me. *Je t'aime, mon amour*.' His voice was husky as he curved her close against him. '*Je t'adore*.' His lips hovered fractionally above her own. 'You are my life, my love. Everything.'

Love was understanding, compassion and trust. And more, much more.

She linked her hands behind his head and pulled him down to her. '*Merci*,' she teased, and heard his husky growl an instant before his mouth closed over hers.

After the loving, she lay spent, curled in against his side, one arm flung across his midriff, her cheek resting on his chest.

The sun had shifted lower in the sky, and soon dusk would fall. Shadows danced slowly across the pale wall, creating an indecipherable pattern.

At last everything had fallen into place, she decided dreamily. The film was finished, publicity completed. Tomorrow she would board a flight with Michel bound for New York. A week later they'd embark on a holiday in France.

Paris in winter, drizzle, grey skies. But nothing would dull the magic of love in a city made for lovers. It was the appropriate city in which to try to conceive a child.

'Are you awake?'

She felt him shift slightly towards her. 'Want me to order in something to eat?'

'How do you feel about children?'

'In general?'

She waited a few seconds. 'Ours.'

Now she had his attention. 'Are you trying to tell me something?'

'There's nothing to tell…yet.'

He propped up his head as he leant towards her. 'The thought of your being pregnant with my child overwhelms me.'

She wrinkled her nose at him. 'Too overwhelming?'

He kissed her with lingering thoroughness. 'I think we should work on it.'

'Now?'

'You object?'

She didn't answer. Instead, she showed him just how she intended to work on it.

THE HUSBAND
ASSIGNMENT
HELEN BIANCHIN

CHAPTER ONE

RAOUL LANIER inclined his head in silent acknowledgment as the attractive airline hostess extended a customary farewell to passengers leaving the aircraft.

Her mouth curved a little wider, and the expression in her eyes offered numerous sensual delights should he choose to extend an invitation to share a drink during her stopover.

The attention she'd bestowed on him during the long international flight had included a friendly warmth that went beyond the courteous solicitousness proffered to his fellow travelers.

It could have proved an interesting diversion, if fleeting sexual encounters formed part of his personal agenda, Raoul mused as he cleared the aircraft and entered the concourse.

As the eldest son and part heir to a billion-dollar fortune, a sense of caution coupled with cynicism had formed at an early age.

Good European genes had blessed him with enviable height, superb bone structure and ruggedly attractive facial features that inevitably drew a second glance. Physical fitness and fine clothes completed a combination that proved magnetic to women of all ages.

A quality that was both an advantage and a curse, he acknowledged with rueful humor as he rode the escalator down to ground level and crossed to the appropriate luggage carousel.

Raoul checked his watch. He had two hours in which to clear customs, take a cab to the hotel at Double Bay, shower and change, before he was scheduled to appear at a business meeting.

Primarily his Australian visit was intended to target the possibility of setting up a Sydney base for the multinational Lanier conglomerate. Wheels had already been set in motion, and if all the details met with his satisfaction, he was prepared to clinch the deal.

Not easily, for he was a skilled tactician whose strategy was recognized and lauded by his peers and associates.

He spotted his luggage, hefted it from the carousel and then strode out of the terminal to summon a taxi.

Brilliant summer sunshine had him reaching for protective sunglasses as he provided the driver with the name of his hotel, then he sank back against the seat in contemplative silence.

The meeting this afternoon held importance. He planned to present a noncommittal persona, and absent himself from the scene for several days, reachable only by cell phone during a sojourn on Queensland's Gold Coast.

Checking up on family. His mouth thinned slightly as his expression assumed reflective thought.

He held filial affection for both his brothers. The

youngest, Sebastian, had recently married and was at present taking an extended holiday in Europe with his new wife.

However, it was Michel who was providing concern, with his marriage of six months in apparent crisis. Seven weeks ago Michel's wife had left New York and flown to Australia to take part in a movie being filmed at the Gold Coast Warner Brothers' studios.

Michel had concluded important European meetings, then followed Sandrine with a view to negotiating a reconciliation. The fact the movie had developed financial problems merely added a bargaining dimension Raoul suspected Michel intended to use to his advantage.

Each of the Lanier brothers possessed a considerable personal fortune, and sinking a few million dollars into a floundering movie wouldn't put a dent in Michel's assets.

A sudden screech of brakes, a muffled curse from the taxi driver, followed by an offered apology captured his attention, and he caught the buildup of traffic, the terrace houses, as the driver swung into the outer lane.

Raoul caught a glimpse of tall buildings stretched skyward in the distance, and estimated it would take ten minutes, fifteen at most, to reach the Ritz-Carlton hotel in Double Bay.

He was no stranger to this large southern hemispheric city, and he held a certain affection for its scenic beauty and stunning architecture, albeit that it was very young in terms of his native France.

Home was a luxury two-story apartment in Auteuil filled with antique furniture, marble-tiled floors, oriental rugs, objets d'art.

He had been born and raised in Paris, graduated from one of its finest universities, then was absorbed into the Lanier corporation as a junior executive.

Raoul gave a grim smile in memory of those early days beneath his father's eaglelike tutelage. Henri Lanier had been a hard taskmaster. Ruthless, Raoul conceded, but fair.

Today, Henri presided as the figurehead of a multinational conglomerate, with Raoul and Michel holding equal power. Sebastian, on the other hand, had chosen law, graduated, practiced, then he penned and sold his first novel, and the rest as they say was history.

The taxi slid to a halt outside the entrance to a gracious well-established hotel a short distance from the waterfront.

Raoul handed the driver a folded note, then stepped from the vehicle while the concierge collected his bags from the boot.

Checking in was a simple procedure, and in his room he took bottled water from the bar-fridge and drank it, ordered room service to deliver lunch at midday, then he unpacked a few essentials, showered, shaved, donned a complimentary robe and replaced the receiver on the last of a few calls less than a minute before a steward presented lunch.

Afterward he dressed, checked his briefcase and took the lift to the main lobby. His meeting was scheduled for two. It was now three minutes past the hour. Essential minutes that gave him an edge, unless the man he was due to liaise with was also well-versed in tactical game-playing.

Eagerness inevitably bred punctuality, Raoul acknowledged, especially when the possibility of a large investment was at stake.

The meeting could easily have stretched to an hour. Raoul cut that time in half with clear instruction and assertive demand, leaving no shred of doubt as to who held command.

Afterward he returned to his room, snagged bottled water from the bar-fridge, then he opened his laptop and spent time keying in data and directing it via e-mail to Paris. He made two calls, the second of which was to Michel, alerting him to his arrival the following day.

Raoul flexed his limbs, then stretched his lengthy frame. He needed exercise. The gym? First, he'd exchange the business suit for sweats and sneakers, and take a walk in the fresh air. His plans for the evening encompassed nothing more than ordering in a light evening meal, followed by an hour or two on the laptop, then he intended to fall into bed and catch up on sleep.

The intercom buzzed, and Stephanie reached out to activate it.

'Michel Lanier is here.'

She winced at the receptionist's attempt at a French pronunciation, and stifled a faint smile at the girl's obvious effort to impress. Michel Lanier was, she had to concede, an impressive man. If a woman was susceptible to a tall, dark-haired, attractive male.

'Give me a minute, then show him in.'

It was an integral part of Stephanie's job as a marketing manager to initiate discussions and venture opinions. She liked what she did for a living, it paid well and the rewards were many.

There was satisfaction in utilizing her expertise in film, together with an instinctive grasp of what attracted and titillated public interest, thus improving cinema attendance, and profitability for the film studios, the investors.

This particular movie had gone over budget, over time, financial avenues had been exhausted and a week ago it had been destined not to be completed.

The crux had been Sandrine Lanier, part-time model and actress, who had a minor role in the film, and her husband's willingness to inject a considerable amount of money to salvage it.

Stephanie shuffled the papers she'd been perusing into a folder at the sound of a double knock on her door, and hit the Save button on her computer.

'Michel and Raoul Lanier.'

She successfully hid her surprise as she registered both names, and she stood and summoned a friendly smile as Michel Lanier entered the room.

'Please take a seat,' she instructed, indicating a pair of comfortable leather chairs.

'My brother requested he sit in at this meeting,' Michel Lanier revealed smoothly. 'You have no objection?'

What could she say? 'No, of course not.'

Michel made the introduction. 'Stephanie Sommers. Raoul Lanier.'

In his late thirties, she surmised, and the elder, if only by a few years.

Raoul Lanier stood an inch, maybe closer to two, taller than his brother. His broad frame held a familial similarity, as did his facial features. Except his hair was darker, almost black, and his jaw had the dark shadow of a man who was forced to shave night and morning.

Wide-set gray eyes, dark as slate, were far too knowledgeable for a woman's peace of mind. As to his mouth…its curve held a sensuality that hinted at great passion. Equally she imagined those lines could thin, perhaps become almost cruel if he was so inclined.

His presence in her office hinted *business,* which raised doubt in her mind that Michel Lanier held the sole stake in a financial package aimed at rescuing the film in which his wife played a minor part.

'Stephanie.' He extended his hand in formal greeting, and she took it, choosing to ignore the faint tinge of mockery evident.

His handshake was firm, his touch warm, and she told herself the sensual awareness pulsing through her veins was merely a figment of her imagination.

'Mr. Lanier,' she acknowledged coolly.

One eyebrow rose, and his mouth curved slightly. 'Raoul.' He lifted a hand and indicated Michel with an expressive gesture. 'Otherwise an adherence to formality will prove confusing.'

His accent was slight, but evident nonetheless, and the depth and intonation of his voice curled around her nerve endings and tugged a little, setting her internal protective mechanism on edge.

Charm, he had it. There was also knowledge apparent in those dark eyes, a knowledge that was wholly sensual, sexual, coupled with contemplative interest.

He would be lethal with women, she deduced wryly. Given his looks, his physique, his wealth, he wouldn't even have to try.

With deliberate movements, she crossed around her desk and sank into the leather chair. It was a position of power, and she used it mercilessly.

'I have the figures you requested.' She looked at Michel, and chose to ignore Raoul entirely. 'Together with a rundown of proposals we intend to use in promoting the film.' She picked up a manila envelope and slid papers into it. 'I'm sure you'll find it satisfactory. Of course, we can't begin with promotion until the film is completed. The marketing people will have a private viewing, then discuss which aspects should be highlighted to attract the attention of the viewing public.'

She kept her attention on Michel. 'I believe the producer anticipates another week should wrap up filming, with perhaps a further few days scheduled for reshooting. It would be of added interest to include you in the publicity campaign...both as an investor, and Sandrine's husband.' Her smile was purely professional. 'I trust you'll be agreeable?'

When he didn't respond, she explained, 'It's all part of the bid to protect your investment.' Did she sound cynical? She hadn't meant to, but it had been a long day. 'Do you have any questions?'

'You have another appointment?' Raoul queried silkily.

'Yes, I do.' Stephanie glanced at her watch, and stood. 'I'm sorry I can't spare you more time.' She met Michel's enigmatic gaze, then picked up the manila envelope and held it out to him. 'When you've examined these, please feel free to call me with any queries.'

'I'd like the opportunity to continue this discussion,' Raoul indicated. 'Shall we say dinner, tonight? Michel and Sandrine will join us. I'm staying at the Sheraton Mirage. Six-thirty in the main lobby?'

It annoyed her unreasonably that he took her acceptance for granted. 'I'm sorry, I won't be able to make it.'

'A date you can't break in the interest of business?'

Important business. Or was Raoul Lanier merely employing undue influence in his own interest?

'With my daughter, Mr. Lanier, whom I'm due to collect from the day care center in half an hour.' Her personal file was easily accessible to anyone with the right connections. Eliciting such details would be a breeze for someone of Michel or Raoul Lanier's standing.

His eyes narrowed fractionally. 'It isn't possible for you to hire a baby-sitter?'

She wanted to hit him for attempting to infringe on her personal life. 'Difficult, at such short notice,' she responded stiffly.

'Make the call, Stephanie.'

She disliked being controlled, and she resented this man's aura of power.

There was the temptation to tell him to go to hell, and she barely managed to bite her tongue. Michel Lanier was a wealthy man in his own right, although she couldn't be certain part of his investment wasn't being funded by the Lanier conglomerate. In which case, Raoul Lanier had a legitimate claim.

She could insist on another evening. In fact, she was sorely tempted to do just that. Except it seemed foolish to be irksome just for the sake of it.

Her expression was cool and composed as she inclined her head. 'If you'll excuse me?' She walked to the door and opened it, waiting as both men filed past her and exited the room.

One pair of dark gray eyes held a glimmer of amusement, and her own sharpened, then deepened with silent anger.

He was enjoying this, and didn't appear to give a second's consideration to what it would cost her in time and effort.

She closed the door behind them, then she crossed to her desk and pressed the required digits to connect with the teenage student she relied on to baby-sit. A few minutes later she replaced the receiver, gave a heavy sigh, then walked out to reception.

Michel Lanier was using his cell phone, and she was acutely conscious of Raoul's studied appraisal as she crossed to his side.

'Six-thirty, the Sheraton Mirage foyer,' she confirmed, adding with a certain cynicism, 'I shall look forward to it.'

He withdrew a slim billfold. 'My card, with my cell phone number.'

She wanted to ignore the courtesy, and add with cutting sarcasm that Hell could freeze over before she'd willingly choose to contact him.

Stephanie caught the quick gleam of amusement apparent, and deliberately arched an eyebrow in silent query, held it, then she accepted the card from his outstretched hand, careful to ensure their fingers didn't touch.

Was that an imperceptible quirk of mockery at the edge of his lips? She told herself she didn't give a damn.

Without a further word she turned and retraced her steps.

It was almost five, which allowed her one hour and ten minutes to collect Emma from the day care center, drive to Mermaid Beach, feed and bathe her daughter, then shower, dress, brief the baby-sitter and leave.

Do-able, provided there were no hiccups or delays.

An added bonus was that Sarah, her baby-sitter had offered to arrive early and take up any slack.

Something for which Stephanie was immensely grateful as she stepped into a slim-fitting black dress and slid the zip home. A few strokes of the brush to her strawberry-blond hair restored order to the stylish bob, and she examined her makeup, added a touch of blusher to her cheeks, spritzed her favorite Hermés perfume to several pulse points, then she slid her feet into stiletto-heeled black pumps, caught up a black shoulder bag and stepped quickly into the lounge.

'Bye, darling.' She leaned down and gave Emma a hug. 'Be a good girl for Sarah.' She turned toward the baby-sitter. 'Any problems, ring me on my cell phone. I won't be late. *Thanks,*' she added with heartfelt sincerity.

'Anytime. Enjoy yourself.'

That was debatable, Stephanie perceived as she crossed the path and slid in behind the wheel of her car.

Business, she reminded herself as she reversed out from the driveway, and eased the sedan down the quiet suburban street. Tonight is strictly business.

Why, then, did she have the feeling that she'd been very cleverly manipulated?

The distance between Mermaid Beach and the Sheraton Mirage hotel at Main Beach represented a fifteen-minute drive...slightly less, if she was fortunate enough to strike a green light at every traffic controlled intersection.

It was a beautiful summer evening, the sun reflected the day's heat, and Stephanie reached forward to adjust the air conditioning.

High-rise buildings stood like tall sentinels, vying with luxury hotels lining the long gently curved stretch of oceanfront.

The Gold Coast had been her home for almost four years. Years in which she'd mentally fought to put a broken relationship behind her and deal with the bitterness of knowing the man in her life had expected...no, begged, her to terminate an accidental pregnancy on the grounds a baby would represent too much responsibility and wreck his plans. With icy calm she'd handed back his engagement ring and walked out of his life.

It hadn't been easy. Yet Emma made it all worthwhile. She was a dear child, Stephanie's image with soft blond curls with the merest tinge of reddish gold.

A horn-blast shattered Stephanie's introspection, and a slight frown creased her forehead as the car developed a faint bump. Seconds later she didn't know whether to curse or cry as she pulled into the side of the road and brought the vehicle to a halt.

Just what she needed. A puncture, when she hadn't allowed herself a minute to spare. Dammit. She reached forward and popped the boot, then she slid out of her seat and prepared to change the tire. Left front, she determined as she removed the jack and set it in position.

Stiletto heels and a figure-hugging dress didn't make for ideal maneuvering. Nor did she relish wrestling with unfamiliar tools as she attempted to loosen stubborn wheel nuts.

This was one occasion when she was more than willing to put feminine self-sufficiency to one side and welcome male assistance.

Except no car stopped, and she battled with the task, completed the wheel change, replaced tools and then cleaned up as best she could with a packet of moist wipes and a box of tissues.

A quick glance at her watch confirmed she was already ten minutes late, and she reached for her cell phone, extracted Raoul Lanier's business card and keyed in the appropriate digits.

He answered on the second ring, and she identified herself, offered an explanation, an apology, and ended the call before he had the opportunity to say a further word.

Five minutes later Stephanie slid the car to a halt in the Sheraton Mirage hotel underground car park and took the lift to the main lobby.

She saw Raoul at once, his height and breadth of shoulder emphasized by superb tailoring, his dark hair well-groomed.

As she drew close he turned toward her, and he stood watching her approach with an unwavering scrutiny that made her want to check if there was a smudge on her nose or cheek, and wonder whether her hasty cleaning-up had removed every speck of grease and dust.

Stephanie mentally squared her shoulders as she summoned forth a warm smile. She was practiced in the social graces, and adept at handling any situation. It was very rare for her to allow anything or anyone to ruffle her composure.

All she had to do, she assured herself silently, was get through the next hour or two with her dignity intact.

'Sandrine. Michel,' she greeted with ease as she joined them. 'Raoul,' she acknowledged civilly. 'I'm sorry about the delay.'

Take control, a tiny voice prompted. 'Shall we go in?'

She didn't miss the faint narrowing of his dark eyes, nor did she mistake the deceptive indolence apparent, and she ignored the slight shiver that feathered its way down her spine.

Raoul Lanier was just a man whose wealth and power were enviable assets in the business arena. She had no interest in him on a personal level, she assured herself.

Why, then, did she feel on edge and about as confident as a seven-year-old child, instead of the twenty-seven-year-old woman she was?

CHAPTER TWO

THE maître 'd led them to a table with a splendid view out over the pool and ocean. He seated them with reserved politeness, then summoned the drinks waiter.

Stephanie perused the wine list with practiced ease. Her knowledge of Australian wines was comprehensive, and she conferred over a choice of red or white, sparkling or still.

'What would you suggest?' Raoul drawled, mildly amused by her determination to play hostess.

'The hotel carries a selection by a multigold medal vintner. I can recommend their Chardonnay or the Pinot Noir.'

Raoul ordered a bottle of each, and when the wine steward uncorked and presented the wine, Stephanie declined, opting for mineral water.

'The need for a clear head?'

'Of course,' she returned coolly. 'The evening's purpose is focused on discussions about marketing strategies for the movie.' She turned her attention to Michel. 'I trust you've had an opportunity to examine the paperwork?'

'Perhaps we could leave any business discussion until after we've ordered our starter and main?' Raoul suggested imperturbably.

Stephanie directed him a studied glance, and met his level gaze. 'If you'd prefer, Mr. Lanier.'

'Raoul,' he insisted silkily.

'Raoul,' she conceded, imitating his slightly accented intonation. If he wanted to play a game of verbal thrust and parry, she'd prove she could be his equal.

Her resolve deepened the color of her eyes and lent a slight tilt to her chin.

It amused and intrigued him. Most...no, *all,* he mentally amended, women of his acquaintance tended to assume a mantle of coquetry, some subtle, others distinctly blatant, in his presence. Cynicism acquired at a young age had taught him that wealth and social status provided the attraction. Experience hadn't changed his opinion.

A waiter approached their table, conferred over the choice of starters, and at a request from Michel, provided a knowledgeable dissertation regarding the merits of each main dish on the menu before taking their order.

Stephanie lifted her glass and sipped the contents. Despite the apparent social implications, this evening was *business,* and she intended to relay the pertinent aspects of marketing strategy, outline the precise course it would take for this particular film, then she would leave.

If Raoul, Michel and Sandrine chose to linger or move on to the bar, that was their choice.

She replaced her glass onto the table and directed her attention toward Michel. 'I've already outlined the major facets of film marketing strategy in an appendix among the paperwork handed to you this afternoon,' she began formally. She was aware of Raoul's studied gaze, and chose to ignore it.

'Briefly to recap, when the completed film is delivered to us from the studio, it receives a private viewing by several people, about thirty in all. Various meetings are held to discuss the target market, what age group the film will most appeal to, which segments should be selected for the trailer.' It was an involved process, and one in which she excelled. 'We need to determine which shots will appear in press releases to television and the media, overseas and locally.'

Raoul noted the way her skin took on a glow beneath the muted lighting, the small gestures she used to emphasis a point. The liking for her job seemed genuine, and her enthusiasm didn't appear to be contrived. Unless he was mistaken, this was no hard sell by a corporate executive intent on personal success at any price.

'In order to heighten public awareness of the film, we'll organize a fashion shoot with one or more of the prestige fashion magazines, and arrange coverage in at least two of the major national weekly magazines. As well as local and interstate newspapers.'

The waiter approached the table and set down their selected starters, and almost on cue the wine steward appeared to top up their drinks.

'It would be advantageous to utilize Sandrine's modeling connections to the fullest extent,'

Stephanie continued as she reached for her cutlery. 'We'll also arrange for you to be present at a few social events and organize media coverage. Press interviews will be set up with the main actors and a few of the cast, the release of which appear simultaneously to draw public attention to the film.'

'Impressive,' Michel drawled, incurring a sharp glance from his wife.

'Laudable,' Raoul inclined in agreement. 'Perhaps you'd care to elaborate—your degree of dedication to this particular project?'

'Total,' she responded, then qualified evenly, 'With one exception. In terms of personal family crisis, my daughter Emma takes precedence.'

'Not optimum,' Raoul discounted, employing an edge of ruthlessness.

A deliberate strategy to place her behind the eight ball? 'You have no obligations whatsoever, Mr. Lanier?' she posed smoothly. 'No wife or mistress who has license to your time?' Her gaze lanced his, level, unwavering, undeterred by the warning glint apparent. 'Or does *business* consume your life to the exclusion of all else?'

It was possible to hear a pin drop within the immediate vicinity of their table. No one, she imagined, had dared to confront Raoul Lanier in such a manner.

'A subtle query on your part?' Raoul posed with hateful amusement. 'As to whether I have a wife?'

'Your marital status is of no interest to me whatsoever,' she responded evenly. It was the truth. 'And you didn't answer the question.'

Would she be so brave if they were alone? Perhaps, he accorded silently, sufficiently intrigued to discover if the bravado was merely a facade.

'I allow myself leisure time.'

His drawled response set her teeth on edge, and she summoned a sweet smile. 'Sensible of you.'

She had no answer for the sensual tension electrifying the air between them. Or for the insane desire to challenge him to a verbal fencing match. It was almost as if some invisible imp was prompting her into battle, and putting words in her mouth she would normally never utter.

'I hope you weren't too inconvenienced in locating a baby-sitter at such short notice?' Sandrine queried in what Stephanie perceived as a skilled attempt to switch the subject of conversation.

'Fortunately not.'

Sandrine offered a wry smile. 'The Lanier brothers tend to snap their fingers and expect immediate action.'

'So I gather,' Stephanie responded dryly.

'Can I persuade you to try some wine, Stephanie?' Michel intervened smoothly. 'Half a glass won't affect your ability to drive.'

'Thank you, no.'

The waiter unobtrusively removed their plates, inquired if the starter was to their satisfaction, then retreated.

Raoul leaned back in his chair and subjected Stephanie to an analytical appraisal. The subdued lighting emphasized delicate bone structure, lent a soft glow to her skin and accentuated the blue depth of her eyes.

She possessed a lush mouth, full and softly curved, and he watched it draw in slightly, caught the faint tightening of muscles at the edge of her jaw as she became aware of his deliberate assessment.

For one infinitesimal second her eyes blazed fire, and he noted the imperceptible movement as she attempted to minimize a convulsive swallow.

Not so controlled, he decided with satisfaction, aware that it would provide an interesting challenge to explore the exigent chemistry between them.

How would that mouth feel beneath the pressure of his own? There was a part of him that wanted to ruffle her composure, test the level of her restraint, and handle the aftermath.

Stephanie barely restrained the impulse to *hit* him. He was deliberately needling her, like a supine panther who'd sighted a prey within reach and was toying with the decision to pounce, or play. Either way, the result would be the same.

Raoul Lanier was in for a surprise if he thought he could try those tactics with her, she decided in silent anger.

She held his gaze deliberately, and saw one eyebrow lift in a slow arch, almost as if he had read her mind. Mental telepathy? Somehow she doubted he possessed that ability. More likely it stemmed from an innate and accurate knowledge of women.

The appearance of the waiter with their main course temporarily diverted her attention. She looked at the plate placed before her, and felt her appetite diminish to zero.

'The meal isn't to your liking?'

Stephanie heard Raoul's deep drawl, sensed the double entendre, and for a brief moment she entertained tossing the contents of her glass in his face.

Smile, a tiny voice urged. This isn't the first occasion you've had to deal with male arrogance, and it sure won't be the last. Business was the purpose for this meeting, albeit that it was being conducted in luxurious surroundings with the accompaniment of fine food and wine.

'Do you have any queries?' she asked of Michel, and incurred his thoughtful gaze.

'You appear to have covered everything for the moment.'

'Perhaps Stephanie would care to give us her personal opinion on this film,' Raoul drawled as he toyed with his wineglass.

'My expertise is with marketing strategy, Mr. Lanier,' she said with grave politeness, whereas underneath that superficial veneer she was seething.

His gaze seemed to lance through every protective barrier she erected, and she hated him for it.

'Surely you have an opinion?' he queried mildly.

'Nothing is a guaranteed success,' she voiced steadily. 'And there are varied degrees of success. I understand both director and producer have a certain reputation in their field, the cast comprises relatively high profile actors, the theme will attract public interest.' Her gaze was unwavering as she held his. 'I can only assure you marketing will do a commendable job with promotion.'

She glimpsed his cynical smile, saw the hardness in those powerful features and refused to allow either to unsettle her equilibrium.

'A standard response,' Raoul acknowledged silkily. 'That conveys precisely nothing.'

She'd had enough. 'You're talking to the wrong person, Mr. Lanier. But then, you know that, don't you? This so-called business dinner is merely a social occasion initiated by you for your own amusement.' She removed her napkin and placed it beside her plate, then she stood to her feet and collected her evening purse. Ignoring Raoul, she focused her attention on Michel. 'Enjoy your meal.'

Without a further word she turned from the table and made her way to the main desk. Requesting the bill, she produced her corporate card, instructed the maximum estimated amount for the total be written in, then she signed the credit slip and pocketed her copy.

Stephanie moved into the foyer and crossed to the lift, jabbing the Call button with more force than necessary.

Damn Raoul Lanier. He'd succeeded in getting beneath her skin, and she hated him for it. Hated herself for allowing him to affect her in a way that tore at the foundations of unbiased *professional* good manners.

For heaven's sake, where was the lift? Another five seconds, and she'd take the stairs. Almost on command, the doors slid open, four people emerged and Stephanie stepped into the cubicle, then turned toward the control panel.

Only to freeze at the sight of Raoul Lanier on the verge of entering the lift.

'What do you think you're doing?' she managed to ask in a furious undertone.

'Accompanying you down to your car.' He reached forward and depressed the button designating the car park.

An action which galvanized Stephanie into jabbing the button that held the doors open. 'Something that's totally unnecessary. Get out.'

He didn't answer. Instead he leaned forward, captured both her hands and held them firmly while he depressed the appropriate button.

Stephanie wrenched against his grasp in an attempt to get free, without success, and she watched with mounting anger as the doors slid closed and the lift began to descend.

'Let go of me.' Her voice was as cool as an arctic floe.

'When the lift reaches the car park,' Raoul drawled imperturbably.

'You are the most arrogant, insolent, insufferable man I've ever had the misfortune to meet.'

'Really? I'm flattered. I expected at least ten damning descriptions.'

'Give me a few seconds,' she threatened darkly.

She was supremely conscious of him, his physical height and breadth, the aura of power he exuded, and this close his choice of cologne teased her senses, notwithstanding the essence of the man and the electric tension evident between them.

The heightened sensuality was almost a tangible entity, powerful, primeval, riveting. It made her afraid. Not only of him, but herself and the long dormant emotions she'd deliberately tamped down for four years.

The lift came to a smooth halt, and she wrenched her hands free, then exited the cubicle the instant the doors slid open.

'Where is your car?'

She began walking toward the glass doors that led to the car park. 'There's no need to play the gentleman. The area is well-lit.'

She may as well have not spoken, and she drew in a deep breath, releasing it slowly as she deliberately ignored him and increased her pace.

It took only minutes to reach her car, and she extracted her keys, unlocked the door, then stilled as a hand prevented her from sliding in behind the wheel.

'Whatever you're thinking of doing,' she said tightly, searing him with a look that would have felled a lesser man. 'Don't.'

'I was going to offer an apology.'

'For initiating an unnecessary social occasion in the guise of *business,* then conducting a deliberate game of cat and mouse with me?' Her tone was deceptively soft, but her eyes resembled crystalline sapphire. 'An apology is merely words, Mr. Lanier, and I find your manner unacceptable.' She looked pointedly at his hand. 'You have three seconds to walk away. Otherwise I'll alert security.'

'And request you rejoin me at dinner,' he continued as if she hadn't spoken.

'I'm no longer hungry, I don't like you, and—' she paused fractionally, and aimed for the kill '—the last thing I want to do is spend another minute in your company. Is that clear?'

Raoul inclined his head in mocking acceptance. 'Perfectly.' He attended to the clasp and held open the door. *'Au revoir.'*

Stephanie slid in behind the wheel, inserted the key into the ignition and fired the engine. 'Goodbye.'

The instant he closed the door she reversed out of the parking bay, then without sparing him a glance she drove toward the exit.

Minutes later she joined the flow of traffic traveling toward the center of town, and it wasn't until she'd cleared the three major intersections that she allowed herself to reflect on the scene in the hotel car park.

She'd managed to have the last word, but somehow she had the feeling Raoul Lanier had deliberately contrived his apparent defeat. And that annoyed the heck out of her!

'You're home early,' Sarah said with surprise when Stephanie entered the house just before nine.

'Everything all right?' Stephanie asked as she placed her bag down onto the table, and began removing her earrings.

'Fine. Emma is never any trouble. She had a glass

of milk at seven-thirty, and went to bed without a murmur.'

She looked at the textbooks laid out on the table, the empty coffee mug. 'Another coffee? I'm making myself some.'

Sarah stood, closed and stacked her books, then slid them into a soft briefcase. 'Thanks, but I'll take a rain check.'

'I appreciate your coming over at such short notice.'

'It's a pleasure,' the baby-sitter declared warmly. 'You have a lovely quiet house, perfect study conditions.' She grinned, then rolled her eyes expressively. 'Two teenage brothers tend to make a lot of noise.'

Stephanie extracted some bills from her purse and pressed them into the girl's hand. 'Thanks, Sarah. Good luck with the exams.'

She saw her out the door, then she locked up and went to check on Emma.

The child was sleeping, her expression peaceful as she clutched a favorite rag doll to her chest. Stephanie leaned down and adjusted the covers, then lightly pushed back a stray lock of hair that had fallen forward onto one soft cheek.

The tug of unconditional love consumed her. Nothing, *nothing* was as wonderful as the gift of a child. Emma's happiness and well-being was worth any sacrifice. A stressful job, the need to present cutting-edge marketing strategy, estimating consumer appeal and ensuring each project was a winner.

The necessity, she added wryly, to occasionally entertain outside conventional business hours. She was familiar with an entire range of personality traits. In her line of business, she came into contact with them all.

Yet no man had managed to get beneath her skin the way Raoul Lanier did. She dealt with men who'd made flirting an art form. Men who imagined wealth condoned dubious behavior and an appalling lack of manners. Then there were those who had so many tickets on themselves they no longer knew who they were.

She'd handled each and every one of them with tact and diplomacy. Even charm. None of which qualities were evident in the presence of a certain Frenchman.

He unsettled her. Far too much for her own liking. She didn't want to *feel* insecure and vulnerable. She'd tread that path once before. She had no intention of retracing her steps.

Stephanie entered the main bedroom, carefully removed her dress and slipped off her shoes, then she cleansed her face free of makeup, stripped off her underwear and donned a long cotton T-shirt before returning to collect her mug of coffee and sink into a deep-cushioned chair in front of the television.

At ten she turned out the lights and went to bed, only to lay awake staring into the darkness as she fought to dismiss Raoul Lanier's disturbing image.

*   *   *

The in-house phone buzzed, and Stephanie automatically reached for it, depressed the button and endeavored to tame the frustrated edge to her voice. 'Yes. What is it, Isabel?'

It wasn't shaping up to be a good day. That little Irish gremlin, Murphy, had danced a jig on her turf from the moment she woke. Water from the shower ran cold from the hot tap, necessitating a call to a plumber. Emma wanted porridge instead of cereal, then requested egg with toast cut into soldiers, only to take two mouthfuls and refuse to eat anymore. Depositing her daughter at day care resulted in an unprecedented tantrum, and she tore a nail wrestling the punctured tire from her boot at the tire mart en route to work.

'I have a delivery for you out front.'

'Whatever it is, take care of it.'

'Flowers with a card addressed to you?'

Flowers? No one sent her flowers, except on special occasions. And today wasn't one of them. 'Okay, I'm on my way to reception.'

Roses. Tight buds in cream, peach and pale apricot. Two, no three dozen. Long-stemmed, encased in cellophane, with a subtle delicate perfume.

'Stephanie Sommers? Please sign the delivery slip for this envelope.'

Who would send her such an expensive gift? Even as the query formed in her mind, her mouth tightened at the possible answer.

He wouldn't…would he?

'They're beautiful,' Isabel breathed with envy as

Stephanie detached an accompanying envelope and plucked out the card.

"A small token to atone for last night. R."

Each word seemed to leap out in stark reminder, and she wanted to shove Raoul Lanier's *token* into the nearest wastepaper bin. *Atone? Twenty* dozen roses wouldn't atone for the studied arrogance of the man.

'Shall I fetch a vase?'

Stephanie drew a shallow breath, then released it. 'Yes.' She handed the large cellophane sheaf to her secretary. 'Place these on the front desk.'

'You don't want them in your office?'

'They'll make me sneeze.' A slight fabrication, but she didn't want to be constantly reminded of the man who'd gifted them. 'Take messages on any of my calls for the rest of the afternoon, unless they're urgent, or from Emma's day care center.'

She stepped back into her office, closed the door, then crossed to her desk, picked up the letter opener and slit the envelope.

Quite what she expected to find, she wasn't sure. Certainly it had to be relatively important to warrant special delivery.

Stephanie extracted the slim piece of paper, saw that it was a check, made out to her and signed by Raoul Lanier for an amount that covered the cost of dinner the previous evening. To endorse it, just in case she might be in doubt, there was a hotel business card attached with his name written on the reverse side.

How dare he? The dinner was a legitimate business expense. Raoul Lanier had chosen to make it personal.

Well, she knew just what to do with his check. Her fingers moved automatically, and seconds later the torn pieces fluttered into the wastepaper bin.

Stephanie sank into her chair and turned on the screen on her computer. *Work.* She had plenty of it. All she had to do was immerse herself in the electronic checking of pertinent details to dispense the omnipotent Frenchman from her mind.

Except it didn't quite work out that way. His image intruded, disrupting her focus, minimizing her concentration.

It was something of an endurance feat that she completed the day's schedule without mishap, and she closed down the computer as Isabel entered with a sheaf of messages. Three of which she returned, two were put to one side for the morning, and one she discarded.

Raoul Lanier could whistle *Dixie,* she decided vengefully as she slid papers into her briefcase and caught up her bag.

Her gaze skimmed the office in a cursory check before leaving for the evening. She caught sight of the special delivery envelope that had contained Raoul Lanier's check, and she reached for it, flipped it idly between her fingers, then on impulse she bent down and caught up the torn check she'd consigned to the wastepaper bin.

Stephanie took an envelope from her stationery

drawer, placed the torn check into it, dampened the seal, then wrote Raoul Lanier in bold black ink, followed by the name of his hotel.

The Sheraton wasn't that far out of her way, and a wry smile teased her lips as she anticipated his expression when he opened the envelope.

Tit for tat wasn't an enviable modus operandi, but she was darned if she'd allow him to have the upper hand.

It was a simple matter to drive up to the main hotel entrance and hand the addressed envelope to the concierge. Difficult to hide a vaguely exultant smile as she eased the car onto the main road.

Traffic was heavy, consequently it took at least three light changes to pass through each main intersection as she headed for the day care center.

Emma looked slightly flushed, and her eyes held a brightness that foreshadowed an increased temperature. 'I'll see how she fares through the night,' Stephanie declared quietly to the attendant nursing sister. 'I may keep her home tomorrow.'

'Give me a call in the morning.'

An hour later she'd bathed and changed Emma, encouraged her to eat a little dinner, only to have her throw up soon after. Something that occurred with regularity throughout the night.

By morning they were both tired and wan, and at eight Stephanie made a series of calls that gained a doctor's appointment, the office to relay she'd be working from home and to divert any phone calls to her message bank and finally, the day care center.

'Sick,' Emma said in a forlorn voice, and Stephanie leaned down to brush her lips across her daughter's forehead.

'I know, sweetheart. We'll go see the doctor soon, and get some medicine to make you better.'

Washing. Loads of it. She took the second completed load out and pushed it into the drier, then systematically filled the washing machine and set it going again.

A gastro virus, the doctor pronounced, and prescribed treatment and care. Stephanie called into the pharmacy, collected a few essentials from the nearby supermarket, then she drove home and settled Emma comfortably on the sofa with one of her favorite videos slotted into the VCR.

A sophisticated laptop linked her to the office, and she noted the calls logged in on her message bank, then settled down to work.

Emma slept for an hour, had some chicken broth, a dry piece of toast, then snuggled down in the makeshift bed Stephanie set up on the couch.

By evening Emma was much improved, and she slept through the night without mishap. Even so, Stephanie decided to keep her home another day as a precaution.

Work was a little more difficult with a reasonably energetic child underfoot, and when she'd settled Emma into bed for her afternoon nap she crossed to the phone and made a series of necessary calls.

One revealed the information she sought, in that Michel Lanier was investing personal, not Lanier corporate funds. Therefore it was solely Michel to whom she owed professional allegiance.

Stephanie opened her laptop, and began sourcing the necessary data she needed to complete a report. Although film was her area of expertise, she worked on other marketing projects and liaised with several of her associates.

It was almost three when the doorbell rang, and she quickly crossed to open the door before whoever was on the other side could ring the bell again.

Security was an important feature for a single woman living alone with a young child, and aluminum grills covered every window and both doors.

Possibly it was a neighbor, or a hawker canvassing door-to-door.

Stephanie unlocked the paneled wooden door and was temporarily unable to contain her surprise at the sight of Raoul Lanier's tall frame beyond the aperture.

He looked vital, dynamic, his broad-boned features portraying a handsome ruggedness that was primitive, compelling. Almost barbaric.

Words formed to demand how he'd discovered where she lived. Then they died before they found voice. All Raoul Lanier had to do was lift the telephone and make a few inquiries to elicit the pertinent information.

CHAPTER THREE

'WHAT are you doing here?'

Raoul arched an eyebrow. 'Do you usually greet everyone this way?'

'No,' she managed to say coolly.

'And keep them standing on the doorstep?'

He bothered her more than she was prepared to admit. On a professional level, she had no recourse but to suffer his presence. However, this was *her* time, her *home,* which made it very personal.

She was safe. The outer wrought-iron security door was locked. He couldn't enter unless she chose to release the catch.

'I conduct business in my office, Mr. Lanier. I suggest you contact my secretary and make an appointment.'

'In case it slipped your mind, you refused to take my call.'

'I had to do some urgent work on the computer,' she explained, determined not to sound defensive. 'My secretary took messages.'

'I gave her one. You didn't return it.'

She regarded him carefully. 'There was no need, given Michel is investing personal, not Lanier company funds, into the film.'

'As a matter of interest, did the roses make it into your office?'

Stephanie's eyes flared, then assumed cool control. 'I had Isabel put them in reception.'

'And tore up my check.'

'It was a business dinner,' she reminded firmly.

'Business was on the agenda,' Raoul granted in measured tones.

'It was the sole reason I accepted your invitation.'

There was cynical amusement lurking in the depths of his eyes. 'You have since made that remarkably clear.'

'I'm not into playing word-games, nor do I indulge in male ego-stroking.'

He laughed. A deep throaty sound that held a degree of spontaneous humor, and something else she didn't care to define.

'Invite me in, Stephanie.'

'No. Emma is due to wake from her nap anytime soon.'

'Have dinner with me tonight.'

'I don't date, Mr. Lanier,' she added icily.

'Raoul,' he insisted evenly. 'The sharing of a meal doesn't necessarily constitute a date.'

He really was too much! 'What part of *no* don't you understand?' she demanded, and saw his eyes narrow slightly.

'Are you so afraid of me?'

Fear had many aspects, and while her personal safety wasn't in question, her emotional sanity was something else entirely. She'd turned the lock on her emotional heart and thrown away the key. This man saw too much, sensed too much, and was therefore dangerous.

'You're wasting your time,' she said quietly.

One eyebrow arched. 'You think so?'

'We have nothing to discuss.'

'Yes,' Raoul argued silkily. 'We do.'

His gaze seemed to sear right through to her soul, and it took enormous willpower to keep her eyes level, *emotionless.*

'In your dreams,' Stephanie reiterated with pseudo sweetness.

His expression didn't change, although his voice was a soft drawl that conveyed innate knowledge. *'Oui.'*

She drew a deep breath, and released it slowly. 'If you don't leave immediately, I'll make a call and have you charged with harassment.'

Stephanie closed the door, and leaned against it for several long minutes, then she drew in a deep breath and moved toward the kitchen. Crossing to the refrigerator she took a can of cola, popped the tab, then she extracted a glass and filled it with the sparkling dark liquid.

Her skin felt heated, and her pulse beat fast at the edge of her throat. Damn him. Who did he think he was?

A hollow laugh escaped into the silence of the room. Raoul Lanier knew exactly who he was. What's more, she had the instinctive feeling he would stop at nothing to get what he wanted.

The question was, *what* did Raoul Lanier want with her?

Sex. Why else did men pursue women, if not to indulge in intimacy?

Hadn't she discovered that to her cost? Ben had said the sweet words and pushed all the right buttons. Until she fell pregnant. Then he became someone she didn't know at all, and she'd walked away, vowing never to trust a man again, ever.

There were men she dealt with in the course of her business life, and despite numerous invitations she'd held steadfast to her rule not to date.

However none had affected her as Raoul Lanier did. Instant awareness. Sexual chemistry at its zenith, she added with silent cynicism.

Electric, primeval, *shocking,* she acknowledged, remembering vividly the moment their gazes met when he'd walked into her office.

Within seconds, it had seemed as if her life came to a standstill and there was only *him.* Invading her senses, warming her blood, staking a claim. As if he possessed a blueprint to her future. It had unnerved her then. It disturbed and unnerved her now.

Her fingers clenched until the knuckles shone white, and she crossed to the sink and discarded the glass.

Do something. Anything. The ironing, she decided. Heaven knew she had enough of it. By then Emma would be awake, and she'd entertain her until it was time to cook dinner.

Two hours later Stephanie settled Emma in front

of the television and slid an educational video into the VCR.

'I'll start dinner, sweetheart.' The house favored open-plan living, and the lounge adjoined the dining room, both of which were visible from the kitchen.

There was chicken and vegetable broth left from yesterday, and she peeled potatoes, carrots and added broccoli to go with the steamed chicken. Better to stick to something fairly bland for the next day or two.

She had just added water to the saucepan when she heard the singsong peal of the doorbell. She reached for the kitchen towel, dried her hands and crossed into the lounge.

'Doorbell,' Emma announced solemnly as Stephanie moved into the hallway.

The only person who popped in without forewarning was her neighbor, and she opened the door with a ready smile, only to have it fade as she recognized the man on the landing.

'What are you doing here?'

'I believe we've already done that,' Raoul said with musing mockery. He held out two brown paper sacks. 'I brought dinner.'

'Why?' she demanded baldly.

'Why not?' he posed lightly.

'Mommy?'

Stephanie closed her eyes, then opened them again, spearing him with a look that spoke volumes before turning toward her daughter. 'It's okay, darling,' she said gently. 'Go back into the lounge. I'll be there in a minute.'

'Hello, Emma.'

His voice was calm, soothing...friendly, *warm,* damn him!

'Hello.' Emma was openly curious, and not at all intimidated. 'Who are you?'

Raoul sank down onto his haunches in one fluid movement. 'A friend of your mother's.'

'What's your name?'

'Raoul.'

'Are you having dinner with us?' the little girl queried solemnly.

'Would you like me to?'

Oh my, he was good! Stephanie shot him a glance that would have felled a lesser man.

'Yes.'

Unfair, she wanted to scream.

'Mommy?'

'I'm sure Raoul—' she hesitated fractionally over his name '—has plans for the evening.'

'Do you?' Emma asked, her eyes wide with curiosity.

'No plans,' Raoul assured.

Dammit, he was enjoying this!

'You can watch my video,' Emma invited, offering a generous smile.

'I'd like that.'

Stephanie met his eyes, glimpsed the silent query lurking there and wanted nothing more than to close the door in his face. 'I don't think it would be a good idea.'

'I promise to be on my best behavior,' Raoul declared solemnly.

Don't you get it? she wanted to demand in anger. You're *not* welcome. And never will be, a silent voice echoed.

He inclined his head, aware that she was teetering on the edge, and anything he said at this point could work to his disadvantage.

'Please, Mommy.'

Blind trust. To a child, everything was simple. If only it was as simple for an adult!

Stephanie inserted the key and unlocked the security door. 'Come in.' Her voice was polite, but lacked any pretense of enthusiasm or graciousness.

'You're big,' Emma declared as he entered the lobby, and he smiled.

'Maybe it's because you're small.'

'I'm three,' the little girl pronounced proudly.

Raoul indicated the paper sacks. 'If you lead the way, I'll deposit these in the kitchen.'

It was a comfortable one-level house, relatively modern with average-size rooms. Raoul's presence seemed to diminish them, and she was supremely conscious of him as he followed her down the hallway.

It was almost as if all her fine body hairs stood on end in involuntary protection. Which was crazy, she silently chastised. Already she was fast becoming a mass of nerves, and he hadn't even touched her.

What would you do if he did? Don't think about it. It's not going to happen.

She crossed around behind the kitchen counter in an unconscious attempt to put some space between them.

There was already two saucepans simmering on the stove, and she indicated them as he placed the sacks down. 'I usually feed Emma about this time.'

'Then perhaps we can eat together.'

Stephanie opened one sack, and removed plastic containers that revealed tandoori chicken, steamed rice and a selection of vegetables. The second sack contained a crusty baguette, a selection of cheeses and a bottle of wine.

It offered a tasty feast, and surpassed the broth, boiled chicken and plain vegetables she'd intended to share with Emma.

'I'll fetch an extra plate and cutlery.'

'Tell me where they are, and I'll attend to it while you set out the food.'

'You can sit next to me,' Emma said in a bright voice.

Oh Emma, *don't*. This is a one-off, not the beginning of a friendship.

'It will be a pleasure.'

'I'm a big girl now. I can eat all by myself.'

It was meaningless chatter, and Stephanie didn't know whether to smile or sigh as her daughter regaled their reluctantly invited guest with the names of her friends at the day care center, her swimming lessons, a recent birthday party, videos she liked to watch and the much anticipated event…a trip to the theme park Movieworld on Saturday.

'Mommy's got tickets,' Emma assured as she finished the last of her vegetables. 'You can come, too.'

Oh, no, he can't. 'Mr. Lanier is a very busy man, darling. Besides, you may not be well enough to go,' Stephanie qualified quickly. 'We'll have to wait and see.'

She didn't want to spend time with him, even in the company of her daughter. And he knew. She could sense the faint amusement evident as she stood to her feet and began collecting plates and cutlery together.

'You can watch my video with me while Mommy does the dishes.' Emma began to hop down from the chair, then she paused. 'Please leave the table, Mommy?'

Stephanie felt her heart tug at Emma's earnest attempt to remember her manners. 'Yes,' she said gently, watching as her daughter unhesitatingly accepted Raoul Lanier's hand.

How could Emma be so friendly with someone she'd only just met? A man, when Emma came into contact with so few men. *Especially a man of Raoul Lanier's caliber.* Someone Stephanie had disliked on sight.

Dislike wasn't an adequate description, she decided cynically as she crossed to the sink and began rinsing plates.

His mere presence attacked the protective wall she'd built around herself. She liked to think she had total control, and responsibility for her life and everything in it rested solely with *her*. She didn't need a man invading her space, her time, her emotions.

Unless, of course, a woman was sufficiently fortunate to find the right man. Someone who would recognize and respect a woman's needs, who would give as well as take.

Get a grip, a skeptical voice derided silently. You're content with the status quo, remember? You have a home, a good job and a child who is the light of your life. What more do you want?

Nothing, she assured herself, and knew she lied.

The rinsed plates and cutlery were consigned to the dishwasher, and she dealt with the saucepans with more diligence than was necessary.

Stephanie reentered the lounge and almost halted midstep at the sight of Emma seated beside the man she wished was anywhere else but *here*.

They looked *comfortable* with each other, and she wasn't sure she liked it. Be honest, and admit you hate it, an inner voice taunted.

What's more, Emma was giving Raoul a running commentary on the video as it played, drawing his attention to the various figures in and out of costume.

A glance at the screen was sufficient for Stephanie to determine the video had only a few minutes left to run, and as the credits rolled Stephanie reached for her daughter's hand as she deactivated the VCR. 'Time for your bath, sweetheart.'

For a moment it seemed Emma might object, then she slid off the cushioned seat and stood.

'I'll come back and say good-night,' she assured Raoul with childish earnestness as he unwound his length in one fluid movement.

'Mr. Lanier has to leave,' Stephanie said firmly, willing him to do just that. Her voice gentled, 'You'd better say good-night now.'

Emma looked at him with unblinking solemnity for all of twenty seconds. 'Good night.'

Stephanie began to lead her daughter from the room, only to have Emma pause and ask wistfully,

'Will you come and see us again?'

Raoul looked from the child to the mother, and back again. His smile was gentle. 'I'd like that.'

Emma grinned unabashedly, and broke into a skipping gait as she followed Stephanie from the room.

Oh hell, Stephanie cursed silently as she ran water into the bath and began undressing her daughter. How did you tell a three-year-old not to like someone? Explain that adult judgment was based on more than superficial appearance? And the reason for her mother's dislike was seeded in distrust and fear?

It was far beyond the comprehension of a child, and because of that it would be unfair to issue a reprimand.

Raoul focused his attention on the number of picture frames lining a mahogany dropped table, and moved close to examine them.

Emma as a baby; sitting clutching a teddy bear that was almost of a similar size to the child; standing; perched on Santa Claus's knee in a store studio shot; seated on a tricycle.

There was a photo of an older couple whom he deduced were Stephanie's parents, but nothing of the man who was Emma's father.

He lifted a hand and threaded fingers through his hair. If he had any sense he'd let himself out of the house and drive back to his hotel where at least three hours' work awaited him on the laptop. He had international telephone calls to make, data to check. He'd be lucky if he got to bed before midnight.

Not that it mattered much, he reflected wryly. The past few nights hadn't been given to peaceful sleep. His mind had centered too often on a strawberry-blond blue-eyed young marketing executive who held no qualms in challenging him to a verbal sparring match at the slightest provocation.

His gaze strayed to the television, caught the moving images in color and endeavored to focus his attention on a geographical program featuring a safari park in Africa.

The sound of a childish voice had him turning toward the door, and seconds later Emma skipped into the room ahead of Stephanie.

'I'm going to bed now.'

She was her mother in miniature. The hair was a few shades lighter, but the eyes were bright blue, and the features held the promise of fine bone structure.

'Good night, Emma.'

'I'll see you out before I put Emma down,' Stephanie ventured coolly.

'If you trust me in your kitchen, I'll make coffee

while you put Emma to bed. There's something I want to discuss with you.'

She didn't believe him. He could see the faint wariness, the doubt. And the need not to make an undue fuss in front of her daughter.

'I'll be back in ten minutes,' she accorded with resignation. 'Coffee and sugar are in the pantry. Milk in the refrigerator. I take mine white with one sugar.'

She reentered the lounge to find two cups filled with steaming coffee set on the occasional table, and the aroma of freshly ground coffee beans teased her nostrils.

'You've made a conquest,' Stephanie indicated as she picked up a cup.

Raoul inclined his head. 'With Emma,' he acknowledged in an accented drawl. 'But not her mother.'

'Nor are you likely to,' she assured coolly. There was a part of her that silently screamed for him to leave, *now*. She didn't want him in her house, her lounge, and she especially didn't want him creating havoc with her emotional sanity.

He didn't shift position, yet there was a stillness evident in his stance, an intense watchful quality that sent prickles of alarm scudding down the length of her spine. 'No?'

One single word that held a wealth of meaning she didn't want to explore. 'Why don't you cut to the chase?' A bald suggestion that evoked a cynical smile.

'Your unbiased opinion on the projected success of the movie Michel is investing in.'

'I wouldn't hazard a guess,' Stephanie offered evenly. 'There are too many dependent factors.' Her gaze speared his. 'Now, if you don't mind, I must ask you to leave. I have a report I need to work on.'

A lazy smile curved his mouth. 'A businesslike indication the evening is at an end?'

'Yes.' She wrestled with her conscience, and added, 'It was thoughtful of you to bring dinner. Thank you.'

'How polite.'

She detected mockery in his tone, and ignored it as she led the way toward the front door. There was a heightened awareness that played havoc with her nerve endings. Dammit, she could almost *feel* his presence as he walked in her wake, and she hated her reaction as much as she hated *him*.

Stephanie slipped the latch, opened the door and stood to one side to allow him clear passage. 'Good night, Mr. Lanier.'

'Raoul,' he insisted quietly. 'There is just one more thing.'

'What?' she managed to ask with remarkable steadiness.

'This.'

His hands captured her face and his head lowered down to hers before she could utter any protest, and then it was too late, for his mouth had taken possession of her own in a kiss that was so incredibly evocative it stirred her emotions and sent them rocketing out of control.

Dear heaven. It was all she could do not to lean in against him as he deepened the kiss to something so intensely sensual her whole body quivered in reaction.

This is *insane,* a tiny voice cautioned. What in hell are you *doing?*

With determined resolve she reached up and wrenched free of his hands, his tantalizing mouth, at the same time taking an unsteady step backward in an attempt to put some space between them.

Her breathing came in ragged gasps, and she could only stand looking at him with a combination of dismay and shock.

She wanted to scream *how dare you?* Twin flags of color tinged her cheeks, and her eyes darkened to the deepest sapphire. 'Get out.'

The words emerged in a damning whisper, and he pressed a finger to her mouth, tracing its slightly swollen curves with a gentleness that almost undid her.

'Au revoir, cherie.'

He stepped past her, and she closed the door, attached the safety chain, then she turned and leaned her back against the solid wood.

She closed her eyes against his image, then opened them again. As much as she blamed *him,* she also apportioned herself some of the blame. For not only responding, but *enjoying* the feel of that skillful mouth as it possessed her own.

Stephanie pushed herself away from the door and collected the empty coffee cups from the lounge and carried them into the kitchen.

Menial chores completed, she entered the small room she'd set up as a home office, activated her laptop and spent three hours on the report.

It was late when she went to bed, and after two hours spent tossing and turning, she switched on the bed lamp and read for an hour before falling into a deep sleep filled with a vivid dream about a nightmarish character who bore a striking resemblance to Raoul Lanier.

CHAPTER FOUR

THE weekends were strictly devoted to mother-and-daughter time. Saturday morning Stephanie put Emma in the car and drove to a park with a play area, grassy banks bordering a meandering ornamental lake where children could feed the ducks.

For more than an hour Emma ran and played with some of the other children, scrambled over the jungle gym and had several turns on the swing.

Then it was time to drive to the local shopping center, collect the week's groceries before returning home for lunch. While Emma had her afternoon nap, Stephanie caught up with the housework, after which Emma engaged in swimming lessons held at the local pool.

Stephanie inevitably planned something special for dinner, and when the dishes had been cleared away and Emma was bathed and in bed, she'd curl up in a chair and slot a rented video into the VCR.

The pattern rarely changed, and she told herself she was content. Or she had been, until five days ago when a tall ruggedly attractive man with a fascinating French accent invaded her life.

Last night his touch had awakened feelings and emotions she didn't want to think about. Yet conversely, they infiltrated her mind and upset her equilibrium.

Stephanie let her thoughts wander from the actors on screen depicting unrequited love between two people from opposite ends of the social structure.

Another week, she determined, then the film would wrap. That was when her job would step into a higher gear as she organized television interviews, photo and fashion shoots, and the pièce de résistance, the gala dinner and dance.

Her involvement with Michel and Sandrine would be at a premium. Her contact with Raoul would hopefully be minimal.

Then Michel, Sandrine and Raoul would fly out from the Gold Coast to New York, Paris…and her life would revert to normal.

Sunday brought the coveted visit to Movieworld, and Stephanie took pleasure in seeing all the sights, experiencing the acted thrills and spills through the eyes of her daughter. Emma could barely keep awake toward the end, and after such an exciting day she willingly had her bath, ate an early dinner, then climbed into bed.

Monday brought a return to their weekday routine, and Stephanie focused on her schedule as she checked and wrote up her diary.

A cocktail party on Tuesday evening, followed by the gala dinner Saturday night meant she needed to enlist Sarah's baby-sitting services, and she made the call.

The day fled swiftly, the afternoon proving fraught

as last-minute checks revealed a few glitches she needed to chase up and eliminate. Her car, which she'd dropped in for its customary service, needed a replacement part that hadn't arrived by courier in time for the mechanic to finish the job. A temporary loaned vehicle sufficed, and when she arrived home it was to discover a stray dog…a very large dog, she surmised, had somehow gained entrance through the day and had dug up nearly all of her garden plants. He'd also scared their cat half to death judging by his perch high up a tree.

Adding insult to injury, the dog had had a ball trying to drag washing from the clothesline.

It should have been Friday the thirteenth, Stephanie muttered beneath her breath as she set about rescuing the cat, gathering up broken plants, then she retrieved the washing and sorted clothes into Mend, Discard, Wash.

Surprisingly she slept well and woke to a beautifully sunny day with the promise of soaring temperatures and high humidity.

Stephanie favored slim-fitting stylish business suits for office wear, and she owned several that she mixed and matched with a variety of silk blouses. She coveted a sophisticated look, actively promoting an image of skilled efficiency, knowledge, nous.

This morning she selected a tailored skirt and jacket in deep sapphire blue. No blouse, black stiletto heels, her only jewelry a watch and slender neck chain.

The day progressed without a hitch, and she arrived home with forty minutes in which to bathe and feed Emma, shower, dress, then leave at six to attend an invitation-only cocktail party held in a very prestigious penthouse apartment at Main Beach.

Speed and organization were of the essence, and not for the first time she wished she had an eight-hour-a-day job that began when she walked through the office door in the morning and ended when she left late afternoon. And after-hours social obligations didn't form part of her salary package.

If that were the case, she wouldn't be able to afford this pleasantly furnished brick and tile house with its swimming pool, situated a short walk from the beach and a major shopping center. Nor would she own a relatively late-model car, or possess such a fashionable wardrobe of clothes.

For some reason she viewed the evening's cocktail party with unaccustomed reluctance. She need only stay a short while, she reminded herself as she put the finishing touches to her makeup, then she added earrings, a matching pendant, and slipped her feet into black stiletto-heeled pumps.

Basic black in a classic design, Stephanie accorded as she checked her appearance in the long cheval mirror. Short sleeves, scooped neckline, smooth-fitting, with black lace overlaying the skirt and finishing in a scalloped hemline a modest few inches above the knee.

She flicked a glance at her wristwatch, caught up her evening purse and walked out into the lounge where Sarah was entertaining Emma with a new picture storybook.

The little girl had already been bathed and fed, and Stephanie crouched low to bestow a hug. 'Be a good girl for Sarah. Love you.'

'Yes. Love you, too,' Emma responded, tightening her arms around her mother's neck for a long minute.

Special, Stephanie accorded silently. The love of a child was unconditional, and therefore something to treasure.

'Okay,' she issued as she kissed her daughter's cheek and broke contact. 'Time to go.'

She could handle the daily routine of leaving Emma in care, for there was no other option. However, leaving her at night proved a wrench every time, no matter how she rationalized that she only socialized when the job demanded it.

Tonight's soiree was being held in a penthouse apartment situated opposite the Sheraton Mirage to celebrate soaring sales of an imported line of luxury lingerie. Successful advertising, publicity, promotion and marketing had attracted the eye of the Gold Coast's glitterati, resulting in a runaway success. The firm's European director had opted to fly in from Milan to inspect the firm's first Australian boutique and, rumor had it, to inspect his recently acquired apartment in the luxurious Palazzo Versace.

Stephanie reached Main Beach at six-thirty, parked in the underground car park beneath the complex, then rode the lift to the main foyer. Directions to the designated penthouse were easy to follow, and minutes later she'd cleared security and was led by a hostess into a large formal entertaining area filled with mingling guests.

A waiter appeared almost instantly and proffered a tray containing a selection of hors d'oeuvres. They were bite-size, and Stephanie took one, then at the waiter's encouragement, she selected another. There was champagne, which she declined in favor of flavored mineral water.

'Isn't this something else?'

She turned at the sound of a familiar voice, and offered the advertising executive a warm smile. 'Something,' she agreed, following his gaze as it encompassed the luxurious furnishings, magnificent tiling, the expensive paintings adorning the wall, each of which appeared to be genuine originals.

The million-dollar view out over the Broadwater, the many high-rise apartment buildings to the hills in the distance was picture-perfect by daylight. In another hour, when darkness fell, it would provide a fairyland of light against the backdrop of an indigo sky.

'It would appear lingerie does very well.'

'It's high-quality luxury, exceptional workmanship,' Stephanie stated, and incurred a slightly cynical smile.

'And ruinously expensive.'

'It has the name,' she said simply.

'Which we help promote.'

She inclined her head. 'Successfully.' Her gaze skimmed the room, touching on the occasional familiar face. A waiter proffered a tray of savories, and she accepted one, aware of hunger pangs and the knowledge she wouldn't eat dinner.

'If you'll excuse me,' she indicated minutes later. 'There's someone I want to talk to.'

During the next hour she mixed and mingled with fellow guests, some of whom she knew, others who clearly represented the cream of Gold Coast society.

Their host was a charming Italian whose attractive good looks caused more than one female heart to flutter in anticipation of gaining his attention.

Stephanie found it mildly amusing to observe the subtle, and not so subtle, attempts to flirt and charm him into more than a fleeting conversation. Some of it was merely harmless game-playing, which he dealt with the ease of long practice.

Anytime soon an announcement would be made, the host would deliver a gratifying speech, there would be the obligatory champagne toast, coffee would be offered, then she could leave and drive home.

Her gaze shifted, made restless by some indefinable shift in the room's occupants. Her skin's surface contracted in an involuntary shiver, almost a gesture of self-defense, and a slight frown creased her forehead. What on earth...

Then she glimpsed a tall broad-shouldered frame, and the breath caught in her throat at the sight of a familiar dark well-groomed head.

It couldn't be...could it? Her attention was riveted

as she watched the man turn toward her, and had her worst fears confirmed.

Raoul Lanier.

His features were unmistakable. The sculpted bone structure, broad cheekbones, the slant of his jaw, the wide set of those dark gray eyes. And the mouth.

Her eyes honed on that sensuously curved mouth, and remembered how it felt to have it close over her own. A slight tremor shook her slender frame, and she controlled it, barely.

With a sense of mesmerized fascination she watched as he paused to utter a few words to the person he was speaking to, then he turned and began making his way toward her.

For one wild moment she considered leaving. And she almost did, except instinct warned he would probably follow.

As he drew close she ignored her body's reaction and consciously took a slow steadying breath, aware the room and its occupants faded into obscurity.

There was only him, and an acute awareness she was loath to acknowledge.

'Stephanie.'

'Don't tell me,' she began in a voice edged with cynicism. 'Our host is a friend of yours.'

Raoul's eyes assumed a musing gleam. 'We attended the same university.'

'Sheer coincidence, of course,' she continued wryly. 'That you both happen to be in Australia at the same time. Staying not only in the same state, but the same city.'

He inclined his head, and moved in close to make room for a guest intent on beckoning the waiter.

Their bodies almost touched, and she instinctively moved back a pace.

Had he known she'd be here? 'I wouldn't have thought feminine lingerie would interest you.' She'd meant it to be a cutting remark, but as soon as the words were out of her mouth she realized their implication.

'It depends on the woman,' he intoned with dry amusement. 'And whether I'm sufficiently fascinated to want to remove it.'

The very thought of those clever hands easing a bra strap off a smooth shoulder, fingers skillfully manipulating a clasp, then lingering at the curve of a feminine waist before sliding lacy briefs down over slender hips…

Stop it. Wayward thoughts and a vivid imagination could only spell trouble.

'If you'll excuse me,' Stephanie said firmly, intending to remove herself as far away as possible from this disturbing man.

'No.'

She looked at him in silent askance, unaware that her eyes deepened in color and assumed a warning sparkle. 'What do you mean—*no?*'

His fingers closed over her elbow. 'Let me introduce you to Bruno.'

She shot him a fulminating glare. 'Get your hand off me.'

'*Merde,*' he swore softly. 'You try my patience.'

'Should I offer to mediate?' an amused male voice intruded.

Stephanie turned and came face to face with her host. A man whose eyes held wisdom and astute knowledge.

'Are you not going to introduce me to this young lady?'

'Bruno Farelli,' Raoul indicated smoothly. 'Stephanie Sommers.'

Bruno took her hand in his and lifted it to his lips. 'Stephanie,' he acknowledged. 'A pleasure.' His dark eyes gleamed with latent humor as he indicated Raoul. 'You do not like this man?'

'He irritates the hell out of me.'

Bruno's amusement was barely restrained. 'Interesting. Women usually fall at his feet.'

'How—' she paused deliberately, then continued with pseudo sweetness '—foolish of them.'

'Raoul must bring you to dinner,' Bruno drawled. 'My wife will enjoy your company.'

'I don't think—'

'Adriana was unable to join me tonight. My daughter did not travel well on the long flight.'

'I'm sorry,' Stephanie said with genuine sympathy.

He regarded her for several long seconds. 'Yes, I do believe you are,' he accorded quietly, pausing as his personal assistant drew close and murmured a brief message. Bruno nodded, then cast Stephanie and Raoul an apologetic glance. 'We will talk later. Now I must say a few words to my guests.'

The words were practiced, but sincere, and the

small surprise was a sneak preview of next season's new lingerie designs, which three models displayed to perfection. Expertly choreographed, the brief parade provided a tantalizing glimpse of what would appear in the boutique a few months from now.

It was a masterly stroke, and a successful one, judging by the buzz of voiced approval. Many of the women would purchase to titillate their husbands, whilst some of the men would designate a gift to a mistress, Stephanie deduced with a degree of cynicism.

'Can I get you another drink?'

Her glass was almost empty, and she surveyed it speculatively, not wanting to offer any encouragement for Raoul to remain at her side. 'I think I'll wait for coffee.'

'Which probably won't be served for another half hour,' Raoul drawled, and she offered him a witching smile that didn't reach her eyes.

'Then you mustn't let me keep you.'

Amusement tinged his expression. 'A politely veiled directive?'

'However did you guess?'

He was silent for several seconds, then he ventured with dangerous softness, 'Did Emma's father hurt you so badly?'

She met his gaze with fearless disregard, aware he saw more than she wanted anyone to see. It unsettled her, and attacked the carefully constructed wall she'd erected guarding her emotions.

A mix of emotions warred with each other as she

sought to control them. 'It's none of your business,' she managed to say with equal quietness.

There was a ruthlessness evident in those compelling features she found disconcerting.

'Does it not occur to you that I might choose to make it my business?'

'And if I choose not to let you?'

He was silent for several long seconds. 'Do you think you can stop me?'

She deliberately raked him from head to toe, and back again. 'You'd be a fool to even try.'

'I've been accorded many things,' Raoul said with indolent amusement. 'A fool isn't one of them.'

She'd had enough. Enough of this indomitable man, the party, and she wanted nothing more than to leave. Except her boss would undoubtedly frown on her early departure.

'Excuse me,' she voiced coolly. 'There are a few business associates I really should speak to.'

He let her go, watching as she eased her way across the room, pausing to chat momentarily before moving on. She possessed a natural grace, a fluidity of movement that reminded him of a dancer on stage.

'Lovely evening,' a pleasant feminine voice intruded, and he shifted his attention to the strikingly beautiful young blonde at his side, who, he acknowledged cynically, was aware of every feminine ploy and not averse to using each and every one of them.

Her conversation was scintillating with just the right degree of sexual promise in the full mouth, the touch of her hand on his arm.

Yet she didn't interest him, and all too frequently he found his attention straying to an attractive blue-eyed strawberry blonde who was as intent on fighting the sexual tension between them as he was in pursuing it.

Stephanie sipped the contents of her glass and fought the temptation to check her watch.

'All alone?'

Her heart sank a little as she summoned a polite smile.

'Samuel,' she acknowledged. As an advertising executive, Samuel Stone was almost without equal. As a man, he possessed one fatal flaw: he believed he was God's gift to women.

'You *have* moved in exalted circles tonight. The elder Lanier brother, and none other than Bruno Farelli himself paying you attention.' He moved close and ran an idle finger down the length of her arm. 'Nice going, darling. I wonder who you'll choose.'

'Neither.'

'Thus leaving the coast clear for me?'

Stephanie swept him a cool glance. 'When are you going to stop playing this wearisome game?'

His smile held a slightly cruel twist. 'You're the one I haven't caught, Stephanie.'

'You never will,' she stated dryly.

'Never is a long time, darling, and I'm remarkably persistent.'

'Two years, and you still haven't got the message.' She shot him an exasperated look. 'How many times do I need to spell it out?'

'You do disinterest well.'

This was becoming tiresome. 'It's for real, Samuel.'

'Why don't I believe you?'

'Because you have a serious ego problem.' She caught sight of two waiters setting up urns, cups and saucers. Thank heavens!

'Come out with me afterward. We'll go on to a nightclub, dance a little, get comfortable…'

'No.' She turned away from him only to have his hand take possession of hers. 'Don't do this, Samuel,' she warned in a deadly quiet voice.

'I believe the lady said no,' a faintly accented voice stated with dangerous silkiness.

Oh Lord, this was just what she needed. Two men at daggers drawn in a bid for her attention. She should have been flattered. Instead she felt vaguely sickened.

'I was hoping to change her mind,' Samuel indicated, releasing her hand.

Raoul's gaze was intent. 'I would say your luck just ran out.'

Samuel inclined his head in an elaborate bow. 'See you around, Stephanie.'

Not if I see you first, she vowed silently.

'You work with him?' Raoul queried when Samuel was out of earshot.

'Liaise,' Stephanie enlightened. 'Advertising and marketing go hand-in-hand.' She drew a deep breath and released it slowly. 'If you'll excuse me, I'll go get some coffee.'

'I'll join you.'

She gave him a sharp look, opened her mouth to decline his company, then closed it again.

'Emma has fully recovered?'

'Yes.' She was conscious of being unobtrusively led toward the table where coffee and tea were being dispensed. 'Yes, she has.'

'Two coffees. One black, the other white with one sugar,' Raoul instructed, then with a cup held in each hand he indicated the wide expanse of floor-to-ceiling glass. 'Let's go take a look at the view.'

Darkness had descended, and the many high-rise buildings appeared as brightly lit towers set against an inky sky. There were boats anchored in the vast marina, and the water resembled dark satin ribboned by the reflection of an ascending moon.

Stephanie stood in silence and sipped her coffee, increasingly aware of Raoul's close proximity as she focused on the immediately adjoining restaurant complex. Patrons enjoying their meal were partly visible, and there were couples, families, strolling along the boardwalk, pausing from time to time to admire some of the large cabin cruisers moored side by side.

It was a peaceful sight, with the sound of music providing a background to the chatter and laughter.

A powerful engine sprang to life from the marina, and minutes later a fully lit cruiser eased out from its berth and headed toward the main channel.

'This reminds me a little of the south of France,' Raoul revealed, indicating the marina. 'Have you traveled at all?'

'North America.' It seemed ages ago, a part of her past she no longer chose to dwell on.

'A holiday?'

'Yes.' A conducted tour in the company of the man she was to marry. Post Ben, pre-Emma.

'You visited New York?'

'I loved the beat of the city, the pulse of life. Seen as a tourist,' she ventured quietly. 'I imagine everyday reality causes it to lose some of the glamour.'

She finished the last of her coffee. 'I really must leave. Sarah has exams tomorrow, and I promised not to be late.'

'I'll walk you to your car.'

'There's no need. I parked in the Mirage shopping complex, and the area is well-lit.'

'Come, we'll find Bruno and you can tell him you've enjoyed a pleasant evening.'

'I can do that quite well on my own.'

He took her cup and placed it down onto a nearby side table along with his own.

'You don't listen, do you?' Stephanie vented with angry resignation as he accompanied her across the room.

Bruno was engaged in conversation with two men, and he looked up as Raoul drew close.

'You are leaving? So soon?'

'It's been a lovely evening,' Stephanie complimented with a warm smile. 'Thank you.'

'I will be in touch with Raoul about dinner. Toward the end of the week?'

'I don't think—'

'We'll confirm with you,' Raoul indicated smoothly.

Stephanie waited until they gained the main foyer before trusting herself to speak. 'Just what did you think you were doing back there?'

'Specifically?'

'Accepting a dinner invitation on my behalf!'

'My exact words conveyed we'd confirm.'

She shot him a baleful glare as they passed through the front entrance. *'We?'* Her voice rose a fraction. *'You* can make whatever plans you like!'

'I intend to. Be aware they'll also include you.'

'The hell they will!' They gained the pavement, and she turned to face him, anger emanating from every pore. 'I don't need a bodyguard, and I especially don't need you to assume a role in my life.' She undid the clasp of her evening purse and extracted her car keys. 'Good night!'

She'd parked the car at street level, and there was only a short distance to walk. She gained less than half a dozen paces when Raoul fell into step at her side.

'You are, without doubt, the most infuriating man I've ever had the misfortune to meet!' she vented furiously as she reached her car.

'In that case, I have nothing to lose.' In a swift synchronized movement he brought her close, slid one hand to cup her head as he captured her lips with his own.

For several long seconds she fought against succumbing to the melting sensation threatening to destroy all rational thought. Her hands lifted to pummel his shoulders, only to fall onto each forearm as she opened her mouth to him.

Oh God, she begged in silent plea as his tongue took an evocative exploratory sweep. Don't do this to me. Why, *why* were her emotions at such variance with the dictates of her brain? All it took was his touch, and she fell to pieces.

Raoul sensed the moment she gave in, and he deepened the kiss, taking her to new heights in emotional intensity.

Her response drove him to cup her bottom and lift her close against him. He wanted more, much more, and the temptation to invite her to his hotel suite was imperative. Except such an action would destroy any advantage he might already have gained.

Instead he eased the pressure, lightening the kiss until his lips brushed gently back and forth over her own, and he slid his hands to cradle her face as he slowly lifted his head.

Her eyes were wide, dilated, and filled with shimmering moisture. The sight of those unspilled tears caused his gut to tighten, and undid him more than any words she might have uttered.

He brushed his thumb over the lower curve of her lip, and felt its faint tremor. He wanted to draw her back into his arms, and simply hold her. Rarely had he glimpsed such naked vulnerability in a woman's eyes, and there was a part of him that seethed in silent anger against the man who had put it there.

He saw the effort it cost her to regain control, to gather her defenses together and step back from him.

His hands slid down her arms and settled on her wrists. 'Stephanie—'

'I have to go. Please.'

The last word held a slightly desperate edge, and he released her, took the keys from her nerveless fingers, unlocked the car door and saw her seated behind the wheel.

Stephanie fired the engine, then barely resisted the temptation to reverse at speed, then send the car tearing out onto the road.

It was only supreme control that stopped her, and she didn't cast Raoul so much as a glance as she eased into the flow of traffic.

She wasn't conscious of having held her breath until she released it in a long pent-up groan. *Why* had she allowed herself to fall into that kiss?

A choked laugh caught in her throat. Raoul Lanier hadn't really given her an option! Except she hadn't fought him, and she should have. For her own emotional sanity, not to mention her peace of mind.

She drove automatically, conscious of the traffic, the intersections, the computerized lights as she traversed the main highway toward Mermaid Beach.

Yet she retained a vivid image of how Raoul's mouth had possessed her own, the slide of his hands, and her body's damnable reaction.

She had sworn after Ben that she'd never allow another man to get close to her again. She'd trusted one, and had that trust broken. Just as she had loved, and discovered her interpretation of *love* and Ben's didn't match.

There was Emma, dear sweet innocent Emma. It was enough. She didn't want or need a man to complicate her life. And she especially didn't need Raoul Lanier, who, in a week or two, would board a plane and jet off to the other side of the world to take up where he left off with his life.

He probably had a mistress.

Now why did that cause her stomach to perform a painful somersault? She didn't *like* the man, she definitely disliked the way he affected her, and she had no intention of allowing a personal relationship to develop between them.

Stephanie reached the fringes of suburban Mermaid Beach, and minutes later she turned into her driveway, activated a modem and garaged the car.

Indoors, Sarah relayed all was well and gathered up her books, then Stephanie kept watch until the girl reached her home safely before locking up.

Emma slept peacefully, and Stephanie tucked in the blanket, moved the teddy bear, then quietly retreated to her own room.

CHAPTER FIVE

IT HADN'T been the best of mornings, Stephanie reflected as she checked her computer's electronic mail. No doubt compounded by the fact she hadn't slept well and was nursing a headache.

One message was headlined as Urgent, and she uttered a soft curse as she clicked it open. The date for the movie's photographic shoot needed to be rescheduled. Could she contact the Sheraton management, organize a suitable time to check the proposed layout, liaise with the photographer and confirm this afternoon?

She reached for her phone, only to have it beep, and she automatically lifted the receiver. 'Yes?'

'I have Raoul Lanier on hold,' Isabel intoned.

Stephanie's stomach immediately curled into a tight ball. 'Have him call back.'

'Okay. Any message?'

Not one you could repeat, she ruminated darkly. 'No,' she managed to say evenly. 'Can you get me Alex Stanford on the line? Try his cell phone.' The photographer was one of the best, and with luck he'd be able to spare half an hour to go over the proposed shots.

Thirty minutes later she'd tied it all together, and

ignoring her scheduled lunch break she slid into her car and drove to Main Beach and the Sheraton Hotel.

Alex was waiting in the lobby when she arrived, and together they descended the central staircase, walked out to the pool area, tossed around indoor and outdoor locations, the portrayed mood she wanted to convey, and fixed on a few possible time frames for the following week, subject to confirmation.

Stephanie extracted her diary, wrote in the dates and times, noted contact names at the film studio, advertising, wardrobe.

'Okay, that's it,' she assured, replacing the diary into her satchel. 'I'll ring when I've pinned it down. Thanks,' she added with a genuine smile as they reentered the lobby. 'I appreciate your help.' Her cell phone rang, and she wriggled her fingers at Alex as he departed for the lift, then she took the call.

Five minutes later she pushed the cell phone into her bag and made for the central stairs leading up to reception. Her stomach grumbled, reminding her she'd had to forego lunch, and she contemplated whether to cross the footbridge to the shopping complex for a coffee and sandwich, or whether she'd simply stop somewhere and pick up something to eat on the way back to the office.

She reached the top of the stairs and made her way through the foyer. Coffee and a sandwich in a café overlooking the Broadwater won out.

'Stephanie.'

It was an instantly recognizable male voice, the

drawling faintly accented tone causing all her fine body hairs to stand up in protective self-defense as she turned to face the man who had indirectly caused her a sleepless night.

Raoul Lanier. Looking every inch the powerful executive, attired in a dark business suit, crisp white shirt and dark silk tie. Expensive tailoring emphasized his breadth of shoulder, accentuated his height and added to an overall aura of sophistication.

She looked...fragile, Raoul decided as he subjected her to a studied appraisal. Her eyes were the deepest blue, and there were faint shadows apparent that indicated she hadn't enjoyed a peaceful night's sleep...any more than he had. Something that pleased him.

Stephanie saw that he wasn't alone. Bruno Farelli, an attractive blonde, and a young child were with him.

Her cool gaze was controlled, her slight smile a mere facsimile. 'Raoul, Bruno,' she acknowledged.

'A pleasure to see you again,' Bruno enthused, and indicated the woman at his side. 'Allow me to introduce my wife, Adriana, and our daughter, Lucia.'

The little girl stole her heart, she resembled a miniature angel, beautifully dressed with gorgeous blond curly hair and a winsome smile.

'Adriana.' Stephanie's features softened as she greeted the child. 'Hello, Lucia.'

'Bruno mentioned you,' Adriana offered warmly. 'We have just emerged from a long lunch.'

Stephanie responded an appropriate platitude. 'I hope you enjoy your stay here.'

'You must join us for dinner,' Adriana pressed with a smile. 'I believe you have a little girl of Lucia's age. It would be delightful for them to meet. Are you free tomorrow evening?'

Oh hell. How did she handle that? With grace, she decided reluctantly. Bruno Farelli was a very influential man, and the agency she worked for was handling his account. To refuse would not only be impolite, but a bad move, professionally. She could only hope Raoul Lanier wasn't included in the invitation.

'Thank you, I'd like that.'

'Shall we say six, at our apartment?'

Her cell phone rang, and she reached for it, ascertained the combination of digits displayed in the window, and offered an apologetic smile. 'I'm sorry, I'll have to take this. If you'll excuse me?' She focused her attention on Adriana. 'Six, tomorrow evening. I'll look forward to it.' She inclined her head briefly, then she turned and activated the call as she made her way toward the main entrance.

Definitely a latte and sandwich, she decided minutes later, and she ordered, then ate beneath a shade umbrella, opting to check Bruno's lingerie boutique window display whilst in the shopping complex.

It was almost three when she entered the office, and what remained of the afternoon was caught up with numerous phone calls together with the completion of a lengthy report.

Consequently it was well after five when she collected Emma from the day care center, and the headache that had bothered her most of the day developed sufficiently to warrant medication.

At eight, with Emma safely asleep, she took a leisurely shower, luxuriating in the relaxing jet of warm water as it soothed the kinks from her neck. Rose-scented soap left her skin silky smooth and exuding a delicate fragrance. Toweled dry she added matching dusting powder and pulled on a freshly laundered T-shirt.

Not exactly an ultrafeminine image, she mentally derided as she caught a glance of her mirrored reflection. Not that it mattered one little bit, for there was no man in her life to tease and tantalize with silk and lace.

Nor did she want one, she silently assured as she applied a thin film of night cream to her face, smoothed the excess onto her hands, then switched off the light and crept into bed.

So why did she lay awake haunted by one man's profile? And have her thoughts stray as she imagined how his skin would feel beneath her touch? Would his muscles flex as he sought control? And at what point would he lose it?

He had the look, the touch, she acknowledged, that promised unbridled primitive passion. The skill and intimate knowledge to drive a woman wild.

Thinking just *how* wild was an infinitely dangerous exercise, for it brought a vivid reminder of her relationship with Ben...a man who had taken his pleasure without consideration for her own. And she, through reticence and naiveté, had enjoyed the closeness and warmth, while longing for more.

Blind trust and immature love, she acknowledged with innate honesty. Had she been older, wiser, in the ways of men, she'd have seen the weakness, the selfishness for what it was. Instead she had made excuses for him and blamed herself for his shortcomings.

Fool. How long before she would have seen him for what he was? Her pregnancy had been an act of God...and a gastro bug, which destroyed the contraceptive pill's effectiveness at the most crucial part of her cycle.

Emma, dear sweet Emma. Ben's reaction had been so abhorrent, from that moment Emma had become *hers,* solely hers.

With a determination Stephanie barely recognized in herself, she'd left Sydney, family and friends, and relocated to the Gold Coast, carving a niche for herself at what she did best...marketing. She'd worked up until two weeks before Emma's birth, taken a month's maternity leave, then returned to the workforce.

Her mother visited twice a year, and took Emma back to Sydney for a few weeks, and Stephanie returned there for her annual holidays.

For almost four years she'd been happy and content with her life. Until now, when Raoul Lanier had appeared on the scene, disrupting her carefully chosen lifestyle, attacking her libido, and causing her to long for something that could only bring grief.

The only way out was not to see him again. A silent bubble of laughter rose and died in her throat. How did she do that, when he had involved himself in one of her work assignments? Everywhere she went, he seemed to be *there*. Legitimately, she had to concede.

She closed her eyes then opened them again to stare into the room's darkness.

A week or two, then he'd be gone. Surely she could survive that length of time?

The shrill peal of the phone jerked her instantly into a sitting position, and she reached for the bedside lamp with one hand and the extension receiver with the other.

Her voice was breathless, startled, apprehensive, and she inwardly cursed herself as she checked the time.

'Did I wake you?' Raoul's voice was deep, and vaguely husky.

She wasn't conscious of holding her breath, until it released in a rush. 'No.' She clutched the receiver, and mentally counted to three. 'No, you didn't. What do you want?'

'You neglected to return my call.'

'I wasn't aware it was necessary,' she said coolly. 'Besides, I understand my secretary asked you to call back.'

'I didn't have the opportunity until now.'

'It couldn't wait until tomorrow?'

'Michel requests you fax him an update on estimated marketing and advertising expenses. He wants to check them against the preliminary figures. Have you a pen and paper handy? I'll give you his e-mail address.'

'Just a minute.' She opened the pedestal drawer and extracted a pad and pen. 'Okay, what is it?' She wrote it down, then repeated it. 'I'll get on to it first thing in the morning.'

'There is just one more thing,' he drawled.

'And that is?'

'I'll collect you and Emma at five forty-five tomorrow evening.'

She closed her eyes and opened them again. Why, for one minute, had she thought he might not be included in Bruno's invitation? 'No. I'll drive to the hotel.'

'*Sacré bleu,* why must you be so independent?'

'You're already staying at the Sheraton,' she stated with cool logic. 'Why collect me?'

'You would prefer to drive home at night to an empty house with a young child in your care?'

This was too much. *He* was too much! 'I would *prefer* it if you weren't there at all tomorrow night,' she flung angrily.

'My presence unsettles you?' Raoul pursued with mocking amusement.

'You flatter yourself,' she said icily. 'If there's nothing else you need to discuss, I'd like to go back to bed. And in future,' she added for good measure, 'please keep business calls to business hours.'

He laughed, a deep-throated chuckle that incensed her to such a degree she hung up on him.

Insufferable man. She thumped her pillow, snapped off the light, then pulled up the covers and settled down to sleep.

Except sleep was never more distant, and she cursed him to hell and back as the dark hours crept slowly to midnight and beyond.

The insistent peal of the alarm clock brought her sharply awake, and she depressed the button before slipping wearily from the bed.

Feed and dress Emma, feed the cat, take out the trash, make coffee, eat, pack Emma's lunch and fill drink bottles ready for day care...

Stephanie went through the motions automatically, completed essential household chores, then she dressed for work, delivered Emma to the day care center and drove in to the office.

It proved to be a day where anything that could go wrong, did. She needed every organizational skill she possessed to arrange the smooth transition from delivery of stock to television promotion. A company drivers' strike provided a delay while she arranged alternate mode of transport. Wardrobe didn't supply the right size or the right color for the model promoting the product. Phone calls weren't returned, and she had to chase up advertising.

When she left the office at five all she wanted to do was collect Emma, go home, relax and unwind.

Instead she needed to bathe and dress her daughter, grab a quick shower, throw on some clothes, apply makeup...all in the space of twenty-five minutes.

There was a part of her that wanted to ring and cancel, except that would amount to a cop-out, and she was damned if she'd allow Raoul Lanier the satisfaction. She'd attend, and enjoy herself. For Emma's sake, and that of her hosts. The indomitable Frenchman could, she decided, go *jump* for all she cared.

It was nothing short of a miracle that she was ready on time. Elegant evening trousers with matching camisole in a deep ultraviolet highlighted her cream textured skin and emphasized her eyes. Emma wore a pale blue print dress with white shoes and socks. Her very best outfit, Stephanie mused, taking pleasure in her daughter's delightful anticipation of the evening ahead.

From a personal aspect, she hadn't had the opportunity to give it more than a passing thought. Now that they were on the verge of leaving, the prospect of spending yet another few hours in Raoul Lanier's company bothered her more than she wanted to admit.

'Okay, sweetheart,' she said gently as she collected her keys and evening purse. 'Let's go.'

They made it to the front door, only to have the bell peal as Stephanie reached to open it, and her heart raced into overdrive at the sight of Raoul Lanier standing on the porch.

'You shouldn't have come,' she said at once, doing her best to remain polite in Emma's presence.

He spared her a long hard glance. 'I said I would collect you.'

He was angry, she could tell from the set of his jaw, the slight thickening of his accent. It was becoming a battle of wills—*hers, his*—and for some reason, despite her determination, she felt she was treading shaky ground.

Raoul turned to greet Emma, who, an innocent traitor, appeared delighted not only to see him, but excited at the prospect of being driven in a different car.

A large late-model sedan, Stephanie saw at once. 'I'll need to get Emma's booster seat,' she indicated, and crossed to the garage. 'She's under the legal age to be able to travel without it.' *One of the reasons I would have preferred to use my own car,* she added silently, then caught Raoul's perceptive look, and knew he wasn't fooled in the slightest.

Three more minutes, and their cars would have passed in the street. He wanted to shake her. Independence in a woman was a fine thing, but this particular young woman was intent on carrying it too far.

Raoul drove with care, traversing the northbound highway with the ease of a man well used to handling both left- and right-hand drive.

Emma's excited childish chatter precluded the need to search for conversation, and Stephanie experienced a mixture of apprehension and trepidation as Raoul swept the car into the underground parking lot beneath the Palazzo Versace.

Save your nerves for a few hours' time when you leave, she admonished silently. Although with luck, Raoul would indulge in a few glasses of wine during dinner, and she could insist on taking a taxi home.

Two hours, three at the most, then she could leave, social obligation complete, and thereafter contact with Bruno Farelli would be restricted to office hours and confined to business matters.

Some hope, she realized with a sinking heart, as the evening progressed. *Luck* wasn't on her side, in any respect.

Emma and Lucia, with the natural instinct of children, bonded immediately. To the extent it seemed as if they'd known each other from the cradle.

Adriana's warmth and sparkling humor made it impossible to retain a polite distance. Both she and Bruno were friendly convivial hosts who went to great pains to ensure Stephanie felt at ease.

They would have succeeded handsomely if it hadn't been for Raoul's presence. For it was *he* who set her nerves on edge. He who caused her heart to beat faster as she forced herself to sample the various courses, sip a little wine, and converse with apparent ease.

Did any one of them realize just how tense she was beneath the relaxed facade? Could anyone detect the way her pulse thudded at the base of her throat? Or how her body tingled with electrifying awareness because of the man seated at her side?

The food was superb, she was certain of it, except her taste buds appeared to have gone on strike.

This was madness. A divine insanity that had no base in her reality.

How long before she could escape? There was dessert still to come, followed by coffee. Another hour?

'Which theme park would you recommend for Lucia's benefit?' Adriana queried. 'We are only on the Coast for such a short time.'

'Dreamworld is wonderful,' Stephanie answered automatically. 'And Seaworld. Each have various rides and attractions. I've taken Emma to both, and while she enjoyed Seaworld, Dreamworld was her favorite.'

'Bruno has Saturday free. We'd love you and Emma to join us. The girls get on well together, and it would be so nice for Lucia to have Emma's company.'

'Dreamworld,' Emma parroted with excitement. 'Please, Mommy.'

'*Si,*' Lucia echoed. 'Dreamworld.'

'English, Lucia,' Adriana admonished gently.

'Perhaps Stephanie already has plans for the weekend,' Raoul indicated, offering her a silent challenge to refuse.

'Saturday is fine,' Stephanie answered evenly in a determined effort to prove she wouldn't rise to his bait. 'Thank you. We'd be delighted to join you.'

Adriana looked pleased as she stood and gathered up the dinner plates. 'I'll get dessert. I hope you like tiramisu?'

'Love it,' Stephanie assured. 'Can I help with anything?'

'You're very kind, but everything is organized.'

Coffee followed the superb dessert, and it was almost nine when Stephanie indicated she must leave.

'It's been a lovely evening,' she said warmly, extending her thanks. 'I'll look forward to Saturday.' She meant it, for Adriana was delightful, and Emma would love sharing the adventures of Dreamworld with Lucia.

'Let me have your telephone number.' Adriana beckoned for her to cross to an escritoire, where she extracted pen and paper. 'I'll ring and arrange a time to meet.'

Stephanie withdrew her cell phone. 'I'll call a taxi.'

Adriana gave her a thoughtful glance, and opted to remain quiet.

A few minutes, the dispatcher relayed, as a taxi had just dropped someone off at the Sheraton.

Collecting Emma, bidding her hosts good-night, was achieved in minimum time.

'Cancel the taxi,' Raoul instructed with deadly quiet as they made their way toward the lift.

'No.'

His expression hardened, and his eyes resembled dark gray slate. 'Cancel, Stephanie,' he voiced quietly. 'Or I will.'

She shot him a cool glare, which changed to scandalized surprise as he calmly took the cell phone from her hand, pressed Redial, and canceled the taxi.

She badly wanted to tell him to go take a flying

leap, except such behavior would only startle Emma. It would have to wait, she decided vengefully, until they were alone.

Stephanie was supremely conscious of him as they rode the lift down to the car park, and it took every reserve of strength not to wrench Emma from his arms.

Who did he think he was, invading her life, taking charge, issuing orders? It was a wonder steam wasn't escaping from her ears as she banked down her anger.

Fortunately Emma's excitement resulted in practically nonstop chatter during the fifteen-minute drive to Mermaid Beach, which meant Stephanie was able to respond to her daughter and totally ignore the man behind the wheel of the car.

The instant Raoul pulled into her driveway she undid her seat belt, and no sooner had he brought the car to a halt that she slid from the passenger seat in a bid to extricate Emma as quickly as possible.

'There's no need for you to get out,' Stephanie said tightly as he copied her actions. 'I can manage.'

'I am sure you can,' he evinced silkily as he crossed to her side. 'Let me take Emma.'

She didn't want him in the house. 'No. I'm fine. Say good-night, darling,' she bade Emma seconds later, only to give a startled gasp as Raoul removed the keys from her fingers and pushed one into the lock of the front door.

Naturally he got it right the first time, and she

clenched her teeth in exasperation as he followed her indoors.

Stephanie threw him a look that should have felled him. 'I'd like you to leave. Now.'

'Put Emma to bed, Stephanie,' Raoul drawled in a deceptively silky voice. He smiled at the little girl nestled in her mother's arms. 'Good night, poppet. Sweet dreams.'

'Kiss good night,' Emma said with unblinking solemnity, and held out her arms.

Raoul leaned forward and brushed a soft childish cheek with his lips, then watched as Stephanie turned away and moved down the hallway.

Did he have any idea what that gesture did to her? Almost before her eyes man and child were forming an affection that had no place to go. It wasn't fair to Emma, she decided as she undressed her daughter and went through the routine of getting her ready for bed.

It took a while for her to settle, given the excitement of the evening and the prospect of a visit to Dreamworld. But halfway through the usual night-time story the long silky lashes began to droop as she drifted to sleep.

Stephanie waited a few minutes, then she adjusted the covers, turned down the light and gently closed the door as she left.

Raoul was in the lounge, one hand thrust into a trouser pocket, and he raked her slender form with compelling intensity as she crossed to stand behind a single chair.

'Don't presume to judge me by Emma's father.'

Her eyes flashed blue fire and her chin tilted as she threw him a venomous glare. 'You know nothing of Emma's father.'

'I know he holds no importance in your life.' He indicated the picture frames holding pride of place on the dropped table. 'There is no evidence of his existence.'

Anger flooded through her like an unstoppable tide, and the desire to shock caused a flow of words she had no intention of uttering.

'Ben is dead.'

If that stark announcement surprised him, he gave no evidence of it, and that infuriated her further.

'You want to know details?' she vented. 'We were childhood sweethearts who grew up together, fell in love and got engaged. Then I fell pregnant. A classic mistake caused by a low dosage pill and a gastric attack.' Her expression sobered, became shuttered as some of the pain returned.

'The man I thought I knew as well as I knew myself suggested I *take care of it* on the grounds a child would complicate our lives.' Her face paled at the memory of those ghastly arguments. 'I refused.' She felt her features tighten as scenes flashed through her mind. The anger, the stinging retribution. 'He opted out and took a flight to Canada, only to die a few months later in a skiing accident.'

She drew a deep calming breath, then released it, hating herself for the tirade, and hating him even more for goading her into it.

'You intend excluding all men from your life, because one man ran away from responsibility?'

She'd dealt with this four years ago. Dealt with the pain of rejection, the degree of guilt for Ben's death. She didn't want to revive the past, for she'd learned the hard way that it had no part in her future.

'I want you to leave.'

'Not yet.'

'Who do you think you are?' On impulse she picked up a nearby ornament and hurled it at him only to see him field and catch it.

The action horrified her, and she stared at him in stunned disbelief for several long seconds.

'Dammit! What do you want from me?' The query came out as a strangled whisper.

'The opportunity to prove I'm not Ben.' His voice was dangerously quiet, and she was unable to look away.

'To what end?' she demanded, sorely tried. 'You're on the Coast how long? A week, two at the most.' Her gaze pierced his. 'Then what? You move on, New York, Paris...wherever. I can qualify a pleasant sojourn, but what about Emma? How does she deal with someone who affords her affection, then leaves?'

'I want to be with you.'

His meaning was unmistakable. 'Are you suggesting we scratch an *itch?*'

Her scandalized expression amused him. 'When I take you to bed,' he vowed silkily, 'it won't be merely to *scratch an itch.*'

'No,' she denied heatedly. 'Because you won't get anywhere near my bed!'

Raoul regarded her silently for a few seconds. 'You are so sure about that?'

She wasn't sure about anything where he was concerned. Already he'd managed to get beneath her skin, and that in itself was dangerous.

'Go find some other woman to fill your needs. I'm not into experimentation.'

'Neither am I,' Raoul assured pitilessly. 'And if I merely wanted a woman to *fill my needs,* why would I choose to continually do battle with *you?*'

'Because I make a change, and therefore present a challenge?'

'Is that what you think?'

'Damn you,' Stephanie snarled, almost at the end of her tether. 'What else is there for me to think?'

'You could try to trust me.'

'I trusted a man once,' she flung heatedly. 'Someone I'd known all my life. Why should I trust *you,* someone I've known for only a week!'

'Because I give my word that you can.'

'Words are easy,' she said bitterly.

She wasn't aware of him moving, yet he was close, much too close, and there was nothing she could do to escape his descending head as he claimed her mouth in a kiss that took her by complete surprise.

She expected force...a fierce unprincipled onslaught that was nothing less than an invasion.

Instead his touch was tactile, an evocative exploration that was incredibly gentle. Bewitching, enticing, it mesmerized her with a magic all its own, hinting at hunger and passion withheld.

Heat coursed through her veins, arousing acute sensuality, and her body swayed into his, craving closer contact as her arms slid up his shoulders and clung.

Raoul deepened the kiss, slowly and with infinite care, eliciting a response that drove him to the brink.

This wasn't the time, or the place, and he gradually withdrew, lightly brushing her lips with his own until they sought and rested against her temple.

How long they stood like that she wasn't sure. Long seconds, maybe minutes. Then he shifted a hand and cupped her chin, forcing her to meet his gaze.

'You want to deny *this?*' He cradled her face, and felt a tremor race through her body. 'Reject what we might have together?' He smoothed a thumb over her lips. 'I want you. For all the right reasons. I need you to want to take the first step.'

He lowered his head and kissed her, lightly teasing her tongue with his own, then he withdrew.

'I'm going to walk out the door. You have the number of my cell phone. If you don't ring me before I reach the hotel, I won't attempt to see you again.' He ran his thumb lightly over her lower lip, then pressed the pad against the slightly swollen center. 'Okay?'

'I don't want this,' she said in a desperate whisper.

'Wrong,' he denied gently. 'You don't want to be hurt.'

'That, too,' she admitted wretchedly, and he smiled.

'One day at a time, *cherie,* hmm?'

She wasn't capable of uttering a word.

He placed his hands over her own and gently disentangled them from his shoulders.

Her eyes clung to his, wide, dilated, unblinking as he stepped back a pace. She saw his lips curve into a faint smile that held quizzical warmth, and something else.

Then he turned and left the room. She heard the faint *snick* as the front door closed and the lock engaged, and seconds later his car engine purred into life, only to fade with distance.

Stephanie didn't move, she simply stared into space as she tried to collect her thoughts.

If she rang him, her life would never be the same. Yet if she didn't…would she live to regret not having taken that chance?

Life was all about chance. You could choose whether to welcome it with both hands. Or you could choose extreme caution, question every possibility, and never realize a dream.

What did she have to lose?

A hollow laugh rose and formed a lump in her throat. Oh *hell.* She was damned if she did, and damned if she didn't.

Impulse stirred her to action, and she extracted Raoul's business card, then made the call.

He picked up on the third ring. 'What took you so long?'

'A fight with my subconscious,' she answered honestly.

'Merci.'

His voice sounded deep and impossibly husky, and did strange things to her equilibrium.

'Good night.' She cut the connection, then stood in reflective silence.

What had she done? She was mad, *insane.* To contemplate aligning herself with someone of Raoul Lanier's caliber was akin to riding a tiger. But what a ride, a tiny imp taunted mercilessly.

Too restless to sleep, she retrieved fresh linen and made up the bed in the spare room ready for her mother. She also dusted, and put out fresh towels.

Then she made a cup of tea and flicked through the channels on cable television in the hope of finding something engrossing to watch, only to switch it off and pick up a book.

CHAPTER SIX

A *DELIVERY* of roses, a dozen beautiful pale pink buds sheathed in cellophane arrived in reception midafternoon, and Stephanie ignored her secretary's curiosity as she extracted the card.

Dinner tonight. Seven. Raoul.

'Shall I fetch a vase?'

She looked up at the sound of Isabel's voice. 'Thanks.'

'Your three-thirty appointment is waiting in reception. Shall I show her in?'

'Give me a few minutes, I need to make a call first.'

Seconds later she punched in a series of digits, and tried to calm her shredding nerves as she waited for Raoul to pick up.

A kiss didn't mean anything, despite the fact it was very skillfully executed and pushed all the right buttons, she conceded rationally, only to stifle a groan. Who did she think she was kidding?

'Lanier.'

His voice was deep, businesslike, and she forced herself to respond in kind. 'Stephanie.' She turned away from the desk and looked at the scene beyond the plate-glass window. 'Thank you for the roses.'

She felt like a gauche teenager, which was ridiculous!

'My pleasure.'

The husky faintly accented voice seeped into her body and curled around her nerve endings. She lifted a shaky hand and pushed back a stray tendril of hair.

It was crazy to feel so distracted, and her fingers tightened on the receiver as she sought composure. 'I can't make it tonight. My mother is arriving from Sydney on the evening flight.'

'You need to collect her from the airport.' He sounded vaguely amused, almost as if he *knew* the struggle she was having in order to remain calm.

'Yes. I'm sorry.'

'I'll look forward to meeting her—'

'Raoul—'

'When I collect you and Emma tomorrow,' he continued. 'Adriana mentioned meeting in the hotel foyer at nine-thirty.'

'It will be easier if I drive to the hotel.'

'We've been down this path before,' Raoul drawled. 'Nine-fifteen, Stephanie.'

'I don't like domineering men,' she retorted, and heard his soft husky laughter. Her voice assumed a definitive coolness. 'I have a client waiting.'

'Tomorrow, Stephanie,' he reminded a bare second before she disconnected the call.

'Nanna's coming, Nanna's coming. Big airplane,' Emma chanted on the way home, during her bath, over dinner and all the way down to Coolangatta airport.

'*Nanna.*' Stephanie had to physically restrain her from running to the entry doors the instant Emma caught sight of her grandmother walking the concourse.

'Celeste.' Stephanie greeted her mother with an affectionate hug, and took her carry-on bag so Celeste could gather Emma into her arms.

There wasn't a chance to get a word in edgeways as Emma excitedly regaled every detail about day care, her friends, the beach, the pool. Nonstop childish chatter ruled as Stephanie collected Celeste's bag from the luggage carousel.

'How are you, darling?' Celeste inquired of her daughter when there was a temporary lull.

'Fine,' Stephanie answered warmly. 'The job is going well.' She shot Celeste a quick smile. 'As you can see, Emma is great.'

'Dreamworld,' Emma chorused from the rear seat. 'Tomorrow me and Mommy and Lucia, and Raoul—' she struggled getting the name out '—are going to Dreamworld. Can Nanna come, too?'

'We'll talk about it later, sweetheart,' Celeste conceded.

It took a while for Emma to settle after they arrived home, and it was almost nine when Stephanie entered the lounge.

'I made some tea, darling.' Celeste indicated the sofa. 'Now come and sit down.'

'How is Dad?'

Celeste smiled warmly. 'Philip is fine. Still working too hard, but he enjoys the legal process, and criminal law is his life.'

It was lovely to catch up on all the news. Family comprised several cousins, aunts and uncles, her grandparents, and it was almost eleven when Celeste caught sight of the time.

'I think we should go to bed. We have plenty of time over the weekend to chat.'

'Would you like to come to Dreamworld with us tomorrow?' Stephanie asked as she straightened cushions and switched off the lamp.

'You're going with friends, aren't you, darling? I might just relax at home, and prepare a roast for dinner.'

Ever the mother, Stephanie conceded affectionately. Roast dinners, baking tins filled, extra for the freezer. She placed an arm around Celeste's waist as they traversed the short hallway. 'I've already washed curtains and bedspreads,' she warned with a smile. 'So don't even *think* about any spring-cleaning, okay?'

'I like to do things for you. I don't get the chance very often.'

Stephanie switched on the light in the spare bedroom. 'Sleep well, Celeste. I'll see you in the morning.'

A bright sunny day, with the promise of high temperatures, Stephanie saw as she opened shutters and let the light in.

It was early, only seven, but Emma had already stirred, and she popped an educational video into the VCR. 'Sit quietly,' she said. 'I'll get you some juice, then we'll have breakfast.'

Celeste joined them, and at eight-thirty Stephanie dressed Emma, packed a holdall with sunscreen cream, snacks, juice, bottled water, the utilitarian first-aid necessities and the seemingly hundred and one things needed when taking a child out for the day.

Then she quickly changed into stonewashed jeans and a blue singlet top, added a blouse, then tended to her makeup.

Emma had positioned herself on a chair beside the window overlooking the front driveway, and Stephanie heard her excited voice calling, 'Raoul's here. Raoul's here, Mommy.'

'There's no such thing as a quiet arrival,' Stephanie said wryly as Celeste rose to her feet.

'Oh my,' Celeste murmured as Raoul entered the hallway.

Attired in casual dress jeans, a navy polo shirt and trainers—sunglasses pushed high—he resembled something out of the pages of a men's fashion magazine.

Stephanie performed introductions. 'My mother, Celeste Sommers. Raoul Lanier.'

'A pleasure,' Raoul inclined, and Stephanie could almost sense his effect on her mother.

'Raoul, Raoul.' Emma launched herself at him, and he caught and lifted her high against his chest.

'*Bon jour,* Emma,' he greeted solemnly.

'Dreamworld. Got a cap.' She put a hand over the cap pulled down over her hair. 'Can we go?' She turned to her grandmother. 'Bye, Nanna.'

'Have a nice day,' Celeste said warmly.

Raoul took Emma to the car while Stephanie set the booster seat, and within minutes Raoul reversed down the driveway and headed toward the highway.

They entered the theme park shortly after ten, and both Emma and Lucia chattered with delight as the adults indulged them in a variety of rides and other features suitable for the very young.

Stephanie was supremely conscious of Raoul at her side, the light momentary brush of his hand at her waist, her shoulder. His smile did strange things to her composure, and her whole body seemed like a finely tuned instrument awaiting his touch.

It was madness, a madness she couldn't afford. For four years she'd marshaled her emotions and vowed never to allow another man to get beneath her skin. Now, no matter how hard she tried to avoid it, Raoul had skillfully managed to penetrate her defenses.

Could he sense her ambivalence? Probably, she perceived wryly. He seemed to have developed the uncanny knack of reading her mind, anticipating her thoughts.

Together with Bruno, Adriana and Lucia, they watched the tigers, rode the paddle steamer and witnessed the little girls' awe at the enacted mock train robbery.

There were several stops for liquid refreshment as

the day wore on, and after an alfresco lunch both little girls began to tire.

'I'll take her,' Raoul indicated when Stephanie lifted Emma into her arms, and as she was about to protest Emma leaned toward him with arms outstretched.

What could she say? To refuse would seem churlish. Besides, Emma was only copying Lucia, who was happily settled in the curve of her father's arm.

It didn't take long for two little heads to droop against two male shoulders, and Stephanie tried to ignore the sight of her daughter nestled comfortably in Raoul's arms. It looked natural, much too natural, and there was a part of her that wanted to tear Emma away.

Don't get too close. It's unfair, she longed to hurl at him. But with Bruno and Adriana within hearing distance, there wasn't much she could do except appear relaxed and at ease with the situation as they wandered in and out of several tourist and souvenir shops.

Lucia stirred a short while later, and almost on cue Emma lifted her head, focused on her surroundings and pointed to where several cartoon costumed characters were mingling among the crowd.

'Kenny Koala,' Emma chanted with renewed energy, and there were photographs taken with each costumed character, then after time-out for refreshments, they slowly made their way toward the main gate.

'It's been a lovely day.' Adriana leaned forward

and caught hold of Stephanie's hand. 'Thank you for bringing Emma. Lucia has had a wonderful time.'

'We've hired a cruiser and crew to tour the waterways tomorrow,' Bruno relayed as they reached their respective cars. 'We would like to have you join us.'

Raoul inclined his head. 'Stephanie?'

She'd been on edge all day in his company. The thought of spending yet another day with him sent her stomach fluttering with nervous tension. 'It's very kind of you, but my mother is visiting from Sydney.'

'Bring her, too,' Adriana encouraged warmly. 'Please, it will be fun to spend another day together, our last on the Gold Coast, for we leave on Monday.'

Stephanie didn't have the heart to refuse. After all, she wouldn't be alone with Raoul. 'I'll check with Celeste and see if she has anything planned, then call you.'

There was a general exodus of people and cars from the theme park, consequently it took a while to gain clear passage onto the highway. Although once there, Raoul was able to pick up speed, and it was after five when he pulled into her driveway.

Extracting Emma, the booster seat, took essential minutes, and Stephanie could hardly refuse Raoul's help. It followed that he came into the house, and Celeste seemed bent on offering him a drink, inquiring about the day, which together with Emma's excited verbal contributions took some time.

He could, she decided with unwarranted cynicism,

have politely declined the drink and retreated within minutes. So why hadn't he?

Worse, he looked very much at ease and far too relaxed for her peace of mind as he conversed with Celeste. Cruising the waterways and an invitation to join them the next day was presented with superb verbal strategy, achieving his objective with a skill she could only admire.

'I'll be delighted.' Celeste beamed warmly. 'Perhaps you'd like to join us for dinner?'

No, Stephanie silently cried, don't do this. But it was too late.

'Raoul may have plans,' she interjected quickly, willing him to refuse.

'No plans,' he returned easily, meeting her gaze as he offered a faint musing smile. 'Thank you. Celeste.'

Fine, let Celeste entertain him. *She* had things to do. Bathing Emma was one of them, not to mention unpacking the holdall of drink bottles, fruit and a number of other comestibles essential to a day out with a young child.

'If you'll excuse me?' She extended her hand to Emma. 'Bathtime, sweetheart.'

Emma's cheerful questions and observations provided a welcome distraction, and afterward Stephanie took time to freshen up. Although she refused to change on the grounds that it would seem as if she'd done so strictly for Raoul's benefit.

'Raoul insisted on buying wine to go with dinner,' Celeste indicated as Stephanie entered the kitchen.

'He should be back soon.' She expertly turned the roast vegetables and slid the pan back into the oven. 'He seems nice, darling.'

Nice? He was many things, but nice? Determined, overwhelming. *Lethal.*

'No comment?' Celeste teased, and caught her daughter's wry glance.

At that moment Raoul returned, and Stephanie busied herself setting the table, then helped Celeste dish the meal.

Her mother was an excellent cook, and Stephanie fought hard to do justice to the food on her plate.

'Do you have family, Raoul?'

Here we go, Stephanie inwardly groaned. The maternal need for background details. She studiously avoided looking at him as she helped Emma with her vegetables.

'Two brothers, Michel and Sebastian. Michel is currently in Australia with his wife. Sebastian and Anneke recently married and are at present touring Europe.'

'Your parents live in France?'

'My mother died a few years ago, but my father resides in the family home and continues to take an active interest in business.'

'Do you live in a big house?' asked Emma, her expression solemn as she waited for his answer.

'Some of the time.'

'Do you have a dog?'

He gave Emma a warm smile. 'Yes, two of them. And two cats, some hens and ducks, geese and a parrot who tells everyone who comes near him to have a happy day.'

Emma's eyes became very round. 'A parrot talks?'

Raoul's eyes gleamed with latent humor. 'Yes,' he enlightened gently. 'He really does.'

'Is it very far away?'

'Raoul lives in Paris, darling. Many thousands of miles on the other side of the world,' Stephanie elaborated.

'Can we come visit?' Emma ventured, innocent of distance.

'I would like that.'

'Shall I serve dessert?' Stephanie queried as she rose to her feet and began stacking cutlery and plates.

A delicious lemon pie was an excellent complement, and she waived Celeste's offer to take care of the dishes.

'You cooked, I'll do the dishes,' she said firmly.

'I agree,' Raoul added as he stood and pushed in his chair. 'You go and sit down. I'll help Stephanie.'

He probably hadn't cleaned a dish in his life. 'Thanks,' she said sweetly. 'You rinse, I'll stack the dishwasher, then you can attack the pots and pans.'

He shot her a dark gleaming glance, almost as if he divined her thoughts, and set about proving her wrong with quick deft thorough movements she found hard to keep pace with. He scoured pots and pans with considerable skill, and when they were all done he wiped down the sink bench, then leaned one hip against the bench and watched her finish up.

'Why don't you go put Emma to bed, while I make coffee?'

It was worth it just to watch those beautiful dark blue eyes dilate and pink color her cheeks. As long as she was angry he didn't have anything to lose, he determined as he caught hold of her chin and possessed her mouth in a brief hungry kiss.

'How dare you?' she whispered furiously, and heard his quietly drawled response,

'Easily.'

She walked from the kitchen without offering a further word, and when she returned he was seated comfortably opposite Celeste, conversing as if he'd known her mother for years.

It was an acquired trait, an entrepreneurial strategy someone kindly disposed would term *charm*. Was it genuine? Celeste seemed to think so, and her mother was no fool when it came to judging character.

'If you'll excuse me, I must leave,' Raoul intimated and rose to his feet. He took hold of her mother's hand and lifted it to his lips. '*Merci*, Celeste, for the meal and your company.'

'I'll see you to the door.' A few minutes and he'd be gone, then she could relax.

He was close, much too close as she preceded him down the hallway, and before she had a chance to open the door he cradled her face and took possession of her mouth in a kiss that tugged at the very depths of her heart.

When he lifted his head she could only look at

him, her breathing as unsteady as her rapidly beating pulse.

'*Bonne nuit, mon ange,*' he bade gently. 'Until tomorrow.' He pressed the pad of his thumb to her lower lip. 'I'll be here at nine.' His mouth curved with sensuous warmth. 'Sleep well.'

He opened the door and moved lightly down the steps to his car, and Stephanie watched as he slid behind the wheel, then reversed down the driveway.

She closed the door, secured the locks, then reentered the lounge.

Celeste wisely didn't comment on the faint color tinging her daughter's cheeks. Instead she mentioned a new social club she'd joined in Sydney, discussed two recent movies and refrained from mentioning Raoul's name. At ten, she stifled a faint yawn, then indicated the need for an early night.

Stephanie followed her down the hallway, closing lights as she went, and in her own room she stripped off her clothes, then indulged in a leisurely shower before slipping into bed to lay staring at the darkened ceiling.

She must have slept, because when she woke sunlight was streaming through chinks in the wooden shutters at her window.

A tap at her door brought her sitting up in bed, and Celeste entered with a cup of coffee in her hand.

'Morning, darling. I thought I should wake you. It's after eight.'

Oh hell. 'Raoul will be here at nine.' She threw

aside the bedcovers and reached for her robe. 'Where's Emma?'

'Watching one of her videos. She's had breakfast, and I've packed the holdall with most of the things I think she'll need.'

Stephanie took a sip of the strong, sweet coffee and felt its reviving effect. 'Thanks, Celeste. I'll grab something to eat, then change.'

Stephanie chose fatigue-style beige shorts, a pale blue singlet top and slid her feet into trainers. Makeup was a thorough application of sunscreen cream, a light dusting of powder, and lipstick.

Raoul arrived at nine, looking ruggedly attractive attired in casual navy shorts and a white short-sleeved polo shirt. He was fit and tanned, with the muscular build of a man who enjoyed exercise and physical fitness.

It was easy to imagine him playing tennis, racquetball, or training in martial arts. He had the look, the physique, and displayed an aura of control.

It was a beautiful day, the sun warm, with just the slightest breeze stirring the palm fronds and tree leaves.

'Going on a boat,' Emma relayed during the drive to Marina Mirage.

A very large luxury boat, Stephanie saw as Bruno led them through the security gate and indicated the berth where the cruiser lay moored.

For the wealthy tourist, private charter was ideal. Captain and crew, plus catering staff ensured a very pleasant excursion without any of the attending hassle.

Celeste took delight in Lucia, and the little girl reciprocated twofold.

'You remind her of her beloved Nonna,' Adriana confided as they settled in the spacious midsection fitted and furnished as a luxurious lounge.

It was evident Raoul and Bruno shared the camaraderie of long friendship, and Stephanie felt her pulse race each time she met his gaze.

He stirred her emotions in a way no man had ever done before. And he knew. It was there in the faint gleam in his eyes, the sensual pull of his mouth as it curved to form a smile.

Throughout the day he made little attempt to touch her, and then it was merely a light brush of his hand on her arm. Emma was generous in her affection, trusting with the unaffected instinct of a child. As far as her daughter was concerned, he was Santa Claus and the Easter Bunny rolled into one.

And you, a persistent little gremlin taunted. What is he to you?

Someone, she conceded cynically, whom she need regard with caution. There was the fear of being hurt, of being let down. And having to pick up the pieces. She'd done it once, and she didn't want to do it again.

Don't think about it, she chastised silently. Enjoy the day for what it is—the company of charming people—and just *be.*

The captain cruised the coastal waterways, the

main Nerang river and the larger inland canals. So many beautiful homes lined the water frontage, many with large cabin cruisers moored at individual jetties. Landscaped gardens, huge stands of palm trees and swimming pools.

The captain gave a commentary on various landmarks, and relayed anecdotes about several different men who had made and lost fortunes during the spasmodic ''boom and bust'' cycles over the years.

After lunch the cruiser headed through the main channel to Sanctuary Cove, then retraced its path via Couran Cove, Stradbroke Island, passed Seaworld theme park, and slid into its berth at Marina Mirage shortly after six.

It had been an incredible day, and Stephanie said so, thanking Bruno and Adriana as they disembarked.

'Please, join us in our apartment for an hour or two.' Adriana issued the invitation with warm enthusiasm. 'I can make a salad, the men will cook steaks on the open grill.'

'But you're leaving tomorrow, you must need to pack—'

'Only a few things,' Adriana assured. 'It is easier to have a wardrobe in each of our apartments. Please, it would give us pleasure for you to visit for a while.'

'The girls are tired,' Stephanie indicated. 'It's been a long day for them.'

'I don't think an hour will make much difference,' Celeste offered as they cleared the security gate and entered the shopping complex.

Two against one, Stephanie reflected wryly. Make

that three, she mentally adjusted as she caught her daughter's expression. Held in the curve of Raoul's arm the little girl looked enchanting, her gold-blond hair so fair against the darker features of the man who carried her.

Seared steaks, fresh salads, eaten with a crusty baguette cut in thick slices, and washed down with a light wine, then followed by coffee made for a appetizing repast, and a fitting relaxed end to the day.

It was almost eight when Raoul drew the car to a halt outside the house, and he released a sleeping Emma from her booster seat, then carried her indoors.

'Third door on the left,' Stephanie instructed, leading the way down the hall. 'I'll change and put her to bed.'

Five minutes later she entered the lounge. 'Can I get you some tea, coffee? A cold drink?'

'Not for me, darling,' Celeste declined, and Raoul shook his head.

'Thanks, but no. I must get back to the hotel. I have some work to do before I catch the early morning flight down to Sydney.'

He was leaving? For how long? And why did she suddenly feel *empty?*

'I'll be back Wednesday evening, Thursday if I encounter any delay.'

He turned to Celeste and bade her good-night, and Stephanie saw him to the door.

'Thanks for a lovely day.'

His smile caused her toes to curl. 'I will phone from Sydney.'

She met his mouth without conscious thought, angling her head to fit his, in a kiss that was dazzling in its intensity, and all too brief.

CHAPTER SEVEN

STEPHANIE deliberately sought a hectic work schedule to ensure there was little time to focus much thought on Raoul. For eight hours each day she was mostly successful. Nights were the worst, for no matter how hard she tried, his image came far too readily to mind.

He even managed to invade her dreams, and more than once she woke in a state of restless anticipation only to discover the image in her mind was precisely that...an image.

He rang twice, relatively brief calls which were confined to inquiries about her day, and Stephanie was able to elicit only that he was deeply involved in delicate negotiations that could delay his return.

Flowers were delivered to her office on Tuesday, with the words ''Missing you, R'' on the card. Stephanie kept them at work where the air conditioning helped keep them fresh.

Deciding what to wear to the gala dinner on Saturday evening caused a thorough appraisal of her wardrobe, and she withdrew three suitable gowns, then discarded each one of them.

What she needed, she determined, was something really spectacular...not flamboyant, but quietly and expensively spectacular.

She found it at an exclusive boutique. A figure-hugging design in black with thin jeweled straps, and the saleslady's approval merely added to her own. The price tag was astronomical, but worth every cent, she assured as she arranged for the hemline to be altered.

So far, the marketing strategy for the film was on schedule, and she made a note to ring Alex Stanford. She really wanted a preview of the shots he'd taken.

Wednesday evening Stephanie arranged for Sarah to baby-sit while she and Celeste went to a movie, a charming tale with an all-star cast featuring English women living in Italy during World War II. Afterward they stopped for coffee in one of several boutique cafés lining a trendy street current in vogue at Broadbeach.

'I'm so pleased to see you enjoying a social life, darling,' Celeste said gently as they waited for their order.

'You mean Raoul,' Stephanie responded without preamble.

'Yes.'

She shook her head in silent negation, assuring, 'It isn't going to happen.'

'I think you should leave your options open.'

A teasing smile curved her lips. 'Celeste, are you suggesting I sleep with him?'

'I'm your mother, darling. Mothers don't encourage their daughters to—'

'Indulge in wild sex,' Stephanie completed, offering Celeste a wicked grin.

'You deserve to be with someone,' Celeste ventured quietly.

A waitress delivered their coffee, and Celeste discussed the movie they'd just seen, the quality of the acting...a subject that lasted for the time it took to savor the superb lattes, before driving the short distance home.

The next day Raoul rang to say he'd be back on the evening flight, and the anticipated pleasure of seeing him again was overwhelming. She'd tried to tell herself she hadn't missed him, but knew she lied.

Friday morning there was another delivery of flowers. Flower, she corrected, unsure how to view the single red rose in its cellophane cylinder. The accompanying card held no message, just the initial *R*.

Lunch was a sandwich eaten at her desk and washed down with bottled water as she ran a check on the photo stills that had arrived by courier from Alex Stanford. He'd noted his selection, and she agreed with him. The shots were good, very good.

The lead actress, Cait Lynden, looked great alongside the two professional models. The lead actor, Gregor Anders, had perfected the right angles to portray himself to the best possible advantage.

Michel Lanier should be well pleased. Especially, with the photo stills of Sandrine. There was something about her, some indefinable quality that commanded a second glance. Add unaffected appeal, exquisite bone structure, and you had a visual winner, Stephanie qualified.

The glossy fashion magazine was due to hit the newsstands next week, the interviews and photo segments would appear in two of the weekly women's magazines the same week. A comprehensive one-on-one interview with Cait Lynden and Gregor Anders was scheduled for the magazine section of the Sunday newspaper in three major states, and television interviews were due to air in two weeks' time.

Then there were the social pages. Cocktail party, the gala charity dinner, to which some of Brisbane and the Gold Coast's social elite were invited, together with photographers and journalists to note and record the event.

It was all part of a well-presented media package aimed to attract public interest, a teaser to encourage paying cinema customers, Stephanie accorded wryly.

It would be nice, she reflected ruminatively, if the movie broke even. Although Michel Lanier could well afford to take the loss.

Filming had finished, and next week the marketing team would attend a private screening and decide which segments should appear as trailers. Meetings, conferences, release dates. It was a comprehensive and exacting project.

Stephanie reached for the phone and made a series of calls, logged data into her computer and ran another check on the table seating for the charity gala dinner to be held in the Grand Ballroom at the Sheraton.

She needed to collect her new gown for the event,

and a call to the boutique ascertained the alterations were complete.

It was almost five-thirty when she parked the car at the Marina Mirage shopping complex. Ten minutes later she emerged from the boutique, an emblazoned carry-bag in hand.

With luck, if the traffic wasn't too heavy, she'd be able to collect Emma from the day care center and be home just after six. Celeste was preparing Emma's favorite meal, and they planned a quiet evening together.

Stephanie stepped onto the escalator and idly scanned the ground floor with its marbled tiles, an attractive water fountain and tables set out for casual alfresco dining.

She glimpsed a familiar male head, and recognized Raoul...in the company of a tall stunningly beautiful woman with dark hair pulled back into a sleek knot, classic features, exquisite makeup and a figure to die for.

Worse, one hand was curled round Raoul's forearm. They looked...*cozy,* Stephanie decided.

Did hearts stop? She was willing to swear hers did. And there was a sudden searing pain in the region of her stomach.

At that precise moment he lifted his head and saw her. For a shocking few seconds his expression assumed a still quality, and he removed the woman's hand from his arm, murmured a few words at her protest and moved toward the base of the escalator.

There was no way Stephanie could avoid him, and

although it took considerable effort she summoned a polite smile as she stepped off.

'Raoul,' she acknowledged with cool formality.

'*Mon ami,* are you not going to introduce us?'

French, Stephanie deduced, huskily feminine and infinitely feline.

'Of course,' Raoul inclined with unruffled ease. 'Ghislaine Chabert. Stephanie Sommers.'

Ghislaine stroked a hand down Raoul's forearm, gifted him a witching smile, then transferred her attention to Stephanie. Her eyes hardened and became cold. 'You are one of Raoul's business acquaintances?'

Oh my. A tigress. With sheathed claws and a mean disposition. 'Michel's,' Stephanie corrected succinctly.

'Stephanie is in marketing.'

Perfectly shaped eyebrows lifted fractionally. 'Ah,' Ghislaine inclined with condescension. 'Sandrine's little movie.'

This could only get worse, and she didn't intend hanging around to discover how much worse. 'If you'll excuse me?' She cast Raoul a measured glance, and inclined her head toward Ghislaine. 'I'm already late to collect my daughter.'

'I'll walk you to your car.'

'Please don't bother.' She stepped to one side and began walking to the set of central escalators that would take her down to the car park.

He said something to Ghislaine in French, brusque

words that were totally incomprehensible, then caught up with Stephanie in a few long strides.

She should have known he'd follow her. Without breaking step she continued toward the escalator, all too aware he was right behind her.

He snagged her arm as she stepped off the escalator and turned her to face him.

'Whatever you're bent on surmising—*don't,*' Raoul warned silkily.

'You haven't a clue what I'm thinking,' Stephanie declared distantly.

'Yes,' he reiterated. 'I do.'

'You read minds?' she flung icily, and glimpsed the cynicism in his smile.

'Yours is remarkably transparent.'

'There is no point to this conversation.'

'*Sacré bleu,*' he swore softly. 'You try the patience of a saint. Ghislaine,' he informed hardily, 'is the daughter of an old family friend, who arrived unannounced, and not by my invitation,' Raoul continued hardily, wanting to kiss her senseless until the doubt, the insecurity, disappeared.

'You don't need to explain,' she declared coolly.

Oh, yes, he did. With concise honesty, right now. 'Ghislaine has booked herself into the same hotel. She's not *with* me,' he said with deliberate emphasis. 'She never has been.'

She directed him a level look. 'Why are you telling me this?'

He wanted to smote his fist against something

hard. 'Because Ghislaine is a femme fatale who finds it amusing to play games.'

Stephanie took in a breath and released it as an exasperated sigh. 'I'd love to stop and chat, but I have to pick up Emma.'

'And you don't believe a word I've said.'

She retained his gaze fearlessly. 'You're free to do whatever you like with whomever you please.' She looked pointedly at his hand on her arm.

'You're making obstacles where there are none.'

'No,' she refuted as he released her. 'I'm making it easy.'

Dignity won out every time, she assured silently as she crossed through two rows to where she'd parked her car. Except dignity didn't do a thing for the way her nerves were shredding into numerous strands. Nor did it help ease the painful ache in her stomach.

She unlocked the door and slid in behind the wheel, then she fired the engine and sent the car up to ground level.

Perhaps it was as well she'd planned a quiet evening at home with Celeste and Emma. She needed time to think.

When Raoul rang at eight, she had Celeste tell him she was putting Emma to bed. She didn't return his call.

Her mother wisely maintained a silent counsel, for which Stephanie was grateful. Maternal advice, no matter how well-meaning, wasn't high on her list tonight.

Together they viewed a video, followed by a program on cable, before reaching a mutual agreement to retire.

There were too many images invading her mind to promote sleep, and Stephanie didn't even try. Instead she plumped an extra pillow against the bed head and picked up a book.

Two hours later she snapped off the bed lamp and stared into the darkness.

Tomorrow was going to be a long day, followed by an even longer night. There were press interviews and photographers scheduled to cover the film cast at Movieworld. She needed to take Celeste and Emma to the airport for the midday flight to Sydney. Then there was the gala dinner.

Would Ghislaine inveigle an invitation? It wouldn't be difficult to acquire one. The Grand Ballroom was large, the staff adept at setting up an extra table or two at the last moment, providing seating wasn't already at maximum. All Ghislaine needed to do was have a discreet word in the right ear and pay for the privilege.

Stephanie stifled a muffled curse and thumped her pillow.

The image of Ghislaine *clinging* to Raoul's arm was vivid in her mind. And how had the Frenchwoman known where Raoul was staying?

She vowed it didn't matter. But it did. It mattered a lot. Despite her efforts to prevent it, he'd managed to scale every protective wall she'd erected, and was close to invading her heart.

Raoul's warning returned to haunt her. Ghislaine liked to play games, huh? Well, let the games begin!

It was a wrench depositing Celeste and Emma at the airport, and Stephanie experienced a mixture of acute loss and emotional deprivation as she hugged Emma close in a final farewell as they passed through security. Watching the jet taxi down the runway, then ascend, was never a good idea. Maybe, when Emma grew older, she'd be able to discard the practice. But now, the little girl was so young, so vulnerable…yet so excited and happy to embark on an adventure.

Emma would have a wonderful time, Stephanie assured herself as she slid into the car and drove toward the car park exit.

It was *she* who needed to adjust to an empty house, the lack of childish chatter and laughter. The umbilical cord connecting mother to child, although cut at birth, was never really severed, she mused as she gained the northbound highway.

Stephanie stopped off at home, heated a slice of Celeste's quiche and ate it, checked her answering machine, then she collected a container of commercially bottled water from the refrigerator and returned to her car.

Dedication to the job was a fine thing, and she could easily have delegated an appearance at the Movieworld shoot. Except she considered it important to be present for any on-the-spot decisions. It was precisely that dedication to detail that had seen her rise through the marketing ranks.

Away from the comfort of air conditioning the heat was intense. As the afternoon wore on, dispositions became frayed, artistic temperament increased and the suggestion they move to another location brought voiced dissent from a few.

'It'll add another dimension,' Alex Stanford assured as he packed his camera and hefted the bag over one shoulder.

'Okay,' Stephanie indicated, trusting his judgment. 'See you there.'

She'd almost reached the car when her cell phone rang.

'Not returning my calls is becoming a habit of yours,' Raoul's voice drawled close to her ear.

Her pulse rate picked up and quickened to a faster beat. 'It's been quite a day.'

'I'll pick you up at seven.'

'Please don't,' she responded quickly, aware of the need to be at the hotel early.

'Stephanie.' His voice acquired a warning edge she chose to ignore.

'Once we're seated, I'm off the hook,' she relayed succinctly. 'Prior to that, I'll be working the job. You'll be superfluous.'

'What time do you have to be there?' His slightly accented voice sent a shiver feathering down her spine.

The sound of a car horn distorted audible clarity, and she put a hand over one ear. 'I have to go,' she indicated.

'Six-fifteen?'

She would have argued, endorsing her decision to meet him at the hotel, except she didn't have the time to conduct a verbal sparring match. 'Fine.'

The afternoon was fraught, and by five even the television camera crew were relieved to dismantle equipment and head for their vehicle.

Consequently it was five-thirty by the time Stephanie reached Mermaid Beach, and home. Forty-five minutes in which to shower, wash and dry her hair, apply makeup and dress didn't present an enviable time frame.

With speed and efficiency she managed it...just. The doorbell pealed as she was in the process of attaching ear studs, and she quickly slid her feet into stiletto-heeled pumps, spritzed perfume to a few pulse points, then she caught up her evening purse and headed for the front door.

The breath caught in her throat at the sight of him. It wasn't the dark evening suit, nor the snowy white pin-tucked shirt, but the man himself and the significant aura of power he exuded. There was a sense of strength, an innate quality that had little to do with his muscular frame or chiseled facial features.

'We really should leave,' Stephanie said coolly.

The gown did wonderful things for her, it was precisely the reason she'd seriously challenged the limit on her credit card. Her job called for what she termed ''a working wardrobe,'' yet the motivation for the purchase of this particular acquisition had been personal rather than professional.

'Beautiful,' Raoul accorded gently, and glimpsed pleasure appeared briefly before she masked it.

'Thank you,' she returned solemnly. He made her nervous, and she hoped it didn't show.

No other man had the power to arouse such a complexity of emotions. Why *this* man? she asked silently as they traveled the northbound highway toward Main Beach.

It was a question that increasingly haunted her with each passing day. *What are you going to do about it?* an elusive imp persisted. *Have an affair?* One week of heaven, followed by a lifetime of attempting to deal with it?

A silent bubble of hysterical laughter died in her throat. Never had she been so prey to such a range of ambivalent feelings, swinging like a pendulum from *go for it and to hell with the consequences* to *don't do this to yourself.*

'You're very quiet,' Raoul observed, shooting her a discerning glance as they neared their destination.

'Just a hectic day,' Stephanie revealed evenly. She was still angry with him, but mostly she was angry with Ghislaine.

'Fragile egos, interrupted schedules that went way over time?'

And that only accounted for the *day.* She offered him a rueful smile. 'How did you guess?'

Six-thirty For Seven on the invitations meant there were guests already mingling in the lounge area outside the hotel ballroom.

The prestigious yearly event in aid of charity ensured attendance by the social glitterati, and the very reason why Stephanie had seized the marketing opportunity to have key members of the cast attend. The publicity potential was too good to miss.

Four leading European fashion houses with boutiques in the upmarket Mirage shopping complex had compiled a fashion parade with models displaying the new season's releases.

However, it was the fragile egos that had her running a personal check of the table seatings. The charity organizers had arranged their own tables, but the few set aside for important guests and dignitaries required personal attention.

Stephanie located the tables up front, ran a check on place names, made one change, then returned to the lounge, caught sight of Alex Stanford and crossed to confer with him about the shots she wanted.

'Where are our exalted stars?' Alex queried. 'Bent on making an entrance?'

'Michel and Sandrine have just arrived,' she indicated. 'There they are talking to Michel's brother.' And Ghislaine.

Now why didn't that surprise her?

At that moment the main doors opened and the guests began entering the ballroom. Women wearing designer gowns and sufficient jewelry to warrant security measures, while the men observed the formal evening wear, black tie dress code.

Michel and Sandrine drew near, closely followed by Raoul and Ghislaine.

'You are joining us?'

Stephanie met Raoul's enigmatic gaze and held it. 'Soon. I need to have a word with the photographer.'

Ghislaine slipped an arm through Raoul's and cast Stephanie a brilliant smile. *Mine,* the gesture stated.

The Frenchwoman looked stunning, her gown a strapless, backless masterpiece that shrieked European couturier. A single strand diamond necklace looked expensive, and was matched with a bracelet and ear studs.

Stephanie greeted Michel and Sandrine, acknowledged Ghislaine, then she excused herself and went in search of Alex Stanford.

Five minutes later she entered the ballroom and began weaving her way toward their designated table. There was still no sign of Cait Lynden or Gregor Anders, she saw at a glance. However, Tony the film's director was seated at an adjacent table with the producer, two of the Warner Brothers Movieworld executives and their wives. And Ghislaine.

Whose influence had Ghislaine used to secure a seat at one of the main tables? Raoul? Possibly Michel? Stephanie assured herself she didn't want to know.

She slid into her seat just as the lights flickered indicating the opening speech was about to begin, and suddenly there was Cait Lynden and Gregor Anders, their progress to the head of the room spotlighted and captured by a clutch of professional photographers.

It was almost amusing, Stephanie alluded wryly,

if only one could manage to see the humour in the situation. Michel was under siege from the expressive attention of the lead actress, who, it appeared, was intent on displaying subtle designs on Sandrine's husband.

Whereas on the adjacent table, Ghislaine was doing her very best to garner Raoul's attention.

The charity chairwoman gave an introductory speech, followed by a word from the mayor, then the waiters emerged bearing trays containing the starters.

The food was attractively presented, but Stephanie merely forked a few morsels, and barely did justice to the main course.

'Some more water?'

Stephanie cast Raoul a polite glance. 'Thank you.'

His eyes darkened fractionally, and he restrained the desire to rattle her composure.

The announcement the fashion parade was about to begin precluded the need for silence, and Stephanie was grateful as the room lighting dimmed and spotlights highlighted the catwalk.

Beautiful clothes in several categories, although emphasis was placed on after-five and evening wear, specifically aimed, Stephanie conceded, for the society women in attendance. Expertly choreographed and commentated, the parade provided forty minutes of glitz and glamour.

There was a time lag before the serving of dessert and coffee. It was then the photographers sought to capture their shots, and she employed diplomacy when Cait Lynden instructed a photo be taken with

Michel, who had given prior instructions that any photo taken of him must also include his wife.

'Both Lanier brothers?' Alex Stanford suggested, motioning for Raoul to join Michel and Sandrine.

'Why not include the marketing manager?' Raoul countered smoothly as he stood to his feet. He held out a hand. 'Stephanie?'

'Alex has been instructed to involve me in a group shot with Tony, the producer and the Warner Brothers Movieworld executives.'

Raoul was too skilled in psychological manipulation to condone defeat. 'I imagine Alex is not limited to the number of film rolls he is able to use?'

Alex, sensing a display of wills and mildly amused by its possibilities, merely endorsed Raoul's suggestion by motioning her into position. 'Let's do it, Stephanie.'

To refuse would seem churlish, and she slid to her feet and stood where Alex positioned her, between Sandrine and Raoul with Michel at his wife's side.

Raoul slipped an arm along the back of her waist, and she stood completely still as all her senses kicked into vibrant life.

She was suddenly conscious of every breath she took, and consciously regulated each and every one of them in a bid to reduce the rapid beating of her heart. She could feel the thud of it reflected in the pulse at the base of her throat, her wrists, and the warmth it generated deep inside.

Even her skin seemed acutely sensitized, and she

was willing to swear heat whispered through every vein in her body.

Stephanie almost jumped as his fingers caressed the base of her spine, then moved to the back of her waist in a slow, soothing pattern. Was he aware of the effect he had on her? She hoped not.

'One more,' Alex called, and the flashbulb caused a second's blindness.

'Not so difficult, *oui?*' Raoul murmured musingly as they moved back to their table.

'Do you always get your own way?'

'Yes.'

Guests were moving between tables, socializing briefly with friends and acquaintances before the evening wound down to a conclusion.

Stephanie placed a hand over her glass as he lifted a bottle of wine. 'No, thanks.'

Raoul's smile held sensual warmth. 'The need for a clear head?'

'I rarely drink,' she said quietly, frozen into immobility as he lifted a hand to her cheek and trailed his fingers down to the edge of her mouth. Her eyes widened, their depths darkening as the pupils dilated, and she barely controlled an involuntary shiver as he traced the sensitive chord of her neck and rested briefly in the hollow there.

'Stephanie, I need you to be part of the executive group shot,' Alex Stanford intruded, and the mesmeric spell was broken.

Thankfully, she assured silently as she followed the photographer. It wasn't easy to slip away, for the film director and producer were in a gregarious mood, so too were the Warner Brothers' executives, and almost fifteen minutes passed before she was able to leave.

Sandrine was not in evidence, nor were the two dignitaries who comprised part of the table seating. Raoul and Michel were engrossed in conversation, and seated in an empty chair...*her* chair...was Ghislaine.

It would have been polite for the Frenchwoman to move, but Ghislaine obviously had no intention of observing conventional good manners.

Stephanie collected her glass, and crossed to another table where two of her associates were seated. If Ghislaine wanted to command Raoul's attention, she could have the figurative floor all to herself.

It didn't help that Samuel Stone occupied a chair next to the one empty seat at the table. Nor that he'd generously imbibed of the wine, and had moved on to spirits. Maybe if she ignored him, he wouldn't even notice her presence.

Fat chance, Stephanie accorded within seconds. She'd merely exchanged one awkward situation at one table for a worse situation of a different kind at another table.

'Darling Stephanie.' Samuel leaned close, much too close, and lifted his glass. 'I salute you.'

'Thank you.' She wasn't quite sure what he was saluting her for, but it seemed prudent to agree with him.

'You're good,' he continued. 'Very, very good,

darling.' He curved an arm over her shoulders. 'Why don't you come work for me?'

Wouldn't that be a move in the wrong direction, she derided silently.

Instinct caused her to glance toward Raoul. He looked completely at ease, his posture relaxed, his features portraying studied interest. Yet almost as if he could sense her attention his gaze shifted, and his gaze locked with hers.

She saw him say something to Michel and Sandrine, then he rose to his feet and moved toward her.

CHAPTER EIGHT

STEPHANIE indicated her intention to leave. 'If you'll excuse me?'

If Raoul thought she'd calmly return to their designated table and watch Ghislaine continue her *clinging vine* performance, he was sadly mistaken!

She'd only taken two steps when he drew level.

His eyes were dark. Too dark, she discerned.

'We've been invited, together with Michel and Sandrine, to party on at the hotel's nightclub. I understand the cast, studio marketing and advertising executives intend to transfer there.'

She looked at him carefully. 'And Ghislaine?'

Something moved in those dark depths, and a muscle tensed at the edge of his jaw. 'She's free to do as she pleases.'

'As I am,' Stephanie responded quietly. 'Now, if you'll excuse me, I need to freshen up.'

'Damn.' The curse fell from his lips with restrained anger. 'Why would I choose to spend time with her, when I prefer to be with you?'

'She's French, gorgeous, eminently suitable and she adores you,' she responded flippantly.

'And if I do not adore her?'

The mere thought of him adoring another woman made her feel slightly ill. Yet some irrepressible imp goaded her to offer, 'Consider the amalgamation of two family fortunes.'

'Go freshen up, Stephanie,' he drawled. 'Before I say something regrettable.'

Without a further word she turned and made her way toward one of the exit doors.

'Mind if I join you?'

Stephanie caught the faintly wry tone, glimpsed an edge of exasperation evident and offered Sandrine a wicked smile.

'On an escape mission?'

'You've got it in one.'

A queue in the powder room meant they were in for a short wait.

'Now that filming is over, I imagine you'll be returning to New York,' she began in an attempt at conversation.

'We're flying down to Sydney tomorrow for a few days before heading home on Tuesday…sans Cait Lynden,' she concluded quizzically.

A faint chuckle emerged from Stephanie's throat. 'Like that, huh?'

'Oh, yes.'

Even an unsuspecting bystander couldn't have misinterpreted the lead actress's marked play for Michel's attention. Although having witnessed the occasional exchanged look between Michel and his wife, she doubted Sandrine had anything to worry about.

'For what it's worth, Ghislaine has been on the scene for several years,' Sandrine offered gently.

'The Lanier men don't waste time going after what they want. If Raoul wanted Ghislaine, he would have had a ring on her finger by now.'

'It really doesn't interest me.'

'Doesn't it?'

Was Sandrine especially intuitive? Or was she merely attempting to elicit an indication of Stephanie's feelings?

Somehow the latter didn't ring true. She was spared a response as a stall became empty and the actress moved forward to occupy it.

Minutes later they took time for makeup repairs, then together they emerged to find Raoul and Michel examining the picturesque waterfall adjoining the lounge area. Cait, Gregor and Ghislaine stood close by.

'Into battle,' Sandrine murmured, and Stephanie successfully hid a faint smile. *Battle* could very well be the operative word if Cait Lynden continued to monopolize Michel's attention.

The hotel nightclub was situated on the next floor, and the exclusive club was alive with people. Funky music emitted from strategically placed speakers, and subdued lighting added to the overall ambience.

Stephanie hadn't frequented a nightclub since she broke up with Ben, and she was quite content to observe rather than participate.

Cait and Ghislaine made a good pair, she determined as she observed each young woman's attempt to encourage Raoul and Michel onto the dance floor.

'Do you want to escape the performance?'

There were any number of females present who would have drooled at the chance to dance with Gregor Anders. Stephanie wasn't one of them.

'Your bête noire has just entered the milieu,' Gregor intoned cynically. 'Do you really want to have to fend him off?'

A surreptitious glance confirmed Samuel Stone's presence, and if she had to choose between the two, Gregor got her vote.

'This really isn't my scene,' she assured as he drew her onto the crowded floor.

'So…treat you gently?'

Her faint laugh was genuine. 'No fancy flamboyant moves,' she warned.

'We could try for up close and personal.'

'Considering the beat of the music, that might not be wise.'

'Where's your sense of adventure?' He pulled her close, and expertly led her through a set of basic steps. 'Well, well,' he murmured close to her ear. 'An update in the manhunting stakes sees Cait cast aside by Michel, who has very wisely made it clear he prefers his wife. And there,' he revealed with theatrical timing. 'We have Raoul giving Ghislaine the flick.' He executed a sweeping turn. 'Now we see the elder Lanier brother beating a path toward us. *You,* my dear, appear to be his target.'

'You're mistaken.'

'Want me to play the shining knight?'

'And have those good looks marred?' she countered, and saw him wince.

'I agree. He's a formidable quarry, in more ways than one. Prepare yourself for takeover.'

Stephanie sensed Raoul's presence a few seconds before he drew level, and her whole circulatory system immediately went into overdrive.

She was willing to swear the blood traveled faster through her veins, and her pulse seemed to jump to an accelerated beat. Even her skin's surface prickled with awareness.

'Do you mind, Gregor?' The voice was a deep drawl that held an edge of steel.

Gregor didn't mind at all. He didn't even feign reluctance. So much for the shining knight offer!

'Be my guest.' The words scarcely left his lips than he faded away between the milling patrons.

The music changed from fast and funky to a soulful ballad, and Raoul drew her close against him.

She should object, and pull back a little, but although the mind dictated, her body chose not to obey. She fit perfectly, and there was a part of her that wanted to lean in and just drift.

For a few minutes she did just that, succumbing to an insidious sensuality that intensified with every passing second. Treacherous, primal, *raw*.

The music changed, and she told herself she was glad. Sexual passion in any form wasn't on her agenda. Especially with a man who lived on the other side of the world, and to whom she was merely a passing fancy. Someone to be his social partner and occupy his bed for a limited time.

Even the thought of engaging in sex with him

turned her bones to liquid. Instinct warned that this man would not take his pleasure without thought for hers, and just thinking how he could pleasure her was sufficient to set her pulse racing into overdrive.

Dangerous. Infinitely dangerous, she perceived, unwilling to admit even to herself that with each passing day her resistance was gradually ebbing away.

Was he aware of it? Probably, she conceded, for he was far too attuned to her psyche. Having someone anticipate her thoughts, her actions, made her feel uncomfortable. And guarded.

'We're leaving,' Michel indicated, then he turned toward his brother. 'I'll ring you early Monday morning.'

Raoul inclined his head, and Sandrine leaned forward to touch her cheek to Stephanie's, murmuring 'good luck' as she did so, then drawing away she offered Stephanie a warm smile. 'I hope we get to meet again.'

Words, sincerely meant, but expressing a desire for something that would probably not eventuate. Nevertheless, Stephanie returned the words in kind.

'Stephanie!'

Oh Lord, Samuel Stone, more than a little the worse for wear and on a mission, from his determined expression.

'Dance with me.'

'We were about to leave,' Raoul drawled. 'Perhaps another time?'

Not if she could avoid it. 'Sorry, Samuel.'

'C'mon, Stephanie.' He reached out and caught her arm in a viselike grip. 'Let's give it a whirl.'

'I think not, my friend.' Raoul's voice was deceptively quiet, like steel encased in silk.

Samuel's expression assumed alcohol-induced belligerence. 'Staked a claim, have you?'

Raoul didn't move an inch, but the air suddenly seemed charged with threatening promise. 'Yes,' he acceded with hard inflexibility.

For a heart-stopping few seconds Stephanie froze, unaware of the room, the people, the noise. There was only Raoul, and the indomitable power he portrayed.

Then Samuel released her arm and spread his hands in a conciliatory gesture. 'Your round, ice princess,' he conceded with deliberate mockery, and melted through the crowd.

'Trouble, darling?' Ghislaine arched delicately.

Lose one, gain one, Stephanie accorded silently. 'Nothing to be concerned about,' she said with an edge of mockery.

'Raoul is very good at defending a woman's honor.' Ghislaine cast him a sultry look. 'Aren't you, *mon ami?*'

'Good night,' Stephanie issued when Raoul didn't answer.

'Oh really, darling?' The pout had been practiced to perfection. 'You're leaving so soon? It's early.'

'For you, possibly,' Stephanie remarked steadily. 'But my day began at dawn this morning.'

'Why interrupt Raoul's enjoyment? I am sure you can take a taxi home.'

'No,' he said with chilling softness. 'That isn't an option.'

'Aren't you taking chivalry a little too far?' Ghislaine queried with a hint of disdain.

Raoul placed an arm along the back of Stephanie's waist. '*Bon nuit,* Ghislaine.'

His tone held indolence and the smoothness of silk.

'I'm impressed,' Stephanie declared as he propelled her toward the entrance. 'Do you do this often?'

'Do what, precisely?'

They exited the nightclub and made their way to the lift that would take them down to the car park.

'Defend one woman and destroy another, both at the same time.'

'You have a way with words,' he alluded cynically, and she cast him a dazzling smile.

'It's one of my talents,' she assured.

'I have to fly down to Sydney tomorrow,' Raoul informed as they rode the lift. 'I had a call this afternoon to say the deal has been finalized and the contract will be ready for my signature on Monday.'

Her heart plummeted. Finalizing the deal meant there was no reason for him to stay.

'Will you take a direct flight from Sydney to Paris?'

He cast her a sharp glance, saw the carefully composed features, and noted the visible pulse beat at the base of her throat. Not so composed, he conceded with satisfaction.

'I intend returning to the coast Monday evening.'

She wasn't aware she'd been holding her breath, and she released it slowly, evenly. 'I see.'

They reached the car, and Raoul freed the lock. 'Do you?'

Now, there was a question. How did she answer it without incriminating herself? Best not to even try, she bade silently as she slid into the passenger seat.

He fired the engine and eased the car toward the main exit, then gained the divided road that led to the main southbound highway.

'No answer?'

'There isn't one,' she said simply.

Brightly colored neon detailed shops and cafés as they passed through the heart of Surfers Paradise.

Motels lined both sides of the highway. It was a vibrant colorful city, geared for the tourist dollar, and offered a multitude of entertainment services.

The flow of traffic at this hour of the night was smooth, and it seemed only minutes before they drove through Broadbeach and entered the fringes of Mermaid Beach.

Raoul brought the car to a smooth halt in her driveway, and cut the lights and the engine.

She released her seat belt, then undid the door clasp and slid out, aware he was duplicating her actions.

'There's no need for you to come in.'

He crossed around and held his hand out for her keys. 'Yes, there is.'

At that precise moment she was prepared to agree with Ghislaine. There was a limit to chivalry.

'I'll be fine,' she assured as he unlocked the door and switched on the lights.

'Are you afraid of me, *cherie?*'

Confrontation was admirable, but right now she wasn't sure she cared for it. 'No,' she answered honestly.

It was herself she was afraid of. Afraid that if he kissed her, she might not be able to control her emotions. And if she relinquished that control, she knew precisely where it would lead.

To experience his lovemaking would be…incredible, she qualified. To take him to her bed, and wake to his touch… Dare she?

She looked at him, saw the strength evident, the heat carefully banked, and felt her body leap with answering warmth.

Stephanie made her way through to the lounge, aware he followed close behind. Her composure was rapidly falling into shreds, and she mentally chastised herself. Nerves were hell and damnation. Raoul was just a man, like any other.

A lot you know, she silently derided. It's four years since I was intimate with a man, and I feel gauche, awkward…dammit, *scared* in a way that has nothing to do with *fear.*

This could, he cautioned, disintegrate in a second. She was a complex mix that comprised integrity and honesty, with a well of passion a man could drown in if he wasn't careful. Yet there was also deep-seated pain and distrust.

'Go make some coffee,' he said quietly.

So he wasn't about to seduce her…at least, not right now. She should have felt relieved, but instead there was a sense of delaying the inevitable, and that in itself only worsened the state of her nerves.

Stephanie entered the kitchen, filled the carafe with water and set it into the coffeemaker, measured out and added ground coffee beans.

'I imagine Celeste has rung to confirm their safe arrival?'

He'd moved so quietly she hadn't heard a sound, and she spared him a quick glance as she extracted two cups and saucers from a cupboard.

'Yes. Everything's fine.' A few steps to the refrigerator to retrieve milk. 'Would you like something to eat?'

When she closed the refrigerator door he was there, and she felt her eyes widen as he took the milk container from her hand and set it on the bench.

'You. Just you.'

He didn't give her time to protest as he drew her close, and his mouth fastened on hers in a slow evocative tasting that became a feast of the senses.

Impossibly sensual, it dispensed all rational thought as she angled her head and indulged in an emotional ride that swept her high to a place where there was only the man, the moment…and desire.

Dear heaven, it was all she could do not to slip

her hands beneath his jacket and tear the garment free. Loosen the buttons on his shirt in her need to touch his skin. To feel the warmth, the pulsing life of muscle and sinew, to savor the taste of him. And have him taste her.

The kiss deepened into possession as his hand slid to her derriere and pulled her close against him. His arousal was a potent force, electrifying and primal as she instinctively reached for him.

She felt a tremor race through his body, and for an instant she gloried in the power, the supreme, albeit brief moment of having him at her mercy.

Then the control was all his as he took his mouth from her own and began trailing a tantalizing path down the edge of her neck, drifting to tease the hollows at the base of her throat, before slipping low to the soft swell of her breast.

A beaded shoestring strap slid off one shoulder, and a faint groan escaped from her lips as he bared one breast, then shaped it, stroking the creamy contour until she thought she'd go mad.

His lips sought the sensitive peak and tantalized it with his tongue, grazing it with his teeth as he held her on the knife edge between pleasure and pain.

When he took the distended peak into his mouth and suckled she arched up against him as sensation arrowed through her body.

It was almost more than she could bear, and she made no protest as Raoul slid an arm beneath her knees and lifted her high into his arms.

His mouth returned to claim hers, and she wound

her arms around his neck as she kissed him back, exulting in the sensation he was able to evoke.

It was relatively easy to discover which bedroom was hers. Feminine in soft peach and pale mint green, an antique bed, and numerous lacy pillows stacked against the headboard.

He shrugged off his jacket, discarded the bow tie and paused to brush light fingers down her cheek as she sought to free the buttons on his shirt.

In tandem they slid off shoes, then Raoul sought the zip fastening at the back of her gown and slid it free.

She was beautiful, slender curves, delicate bone structure and pale skin. Lacy bikini briefs were the only item of clothing protecting her from total nudity, and he shrugged off his shirt and dispensed with his trousers in two fluid movements.

Stephanie could only admire his physique. The well-honed muscular chest and shoulders, the taut waist and flat stomach.

The state of his arousal gave her a bad moment, and her insides involuntarily clenched at the thought of accommodating him.

He curled a hand round her nape and shaped her head as he took possession of her mouth, kissing her with such eroticism she almost cried at the sweet sorcery of his touch.

One tug was all it took to pull the covers from the bed, then he tumbled her down onto the sheeted mattress and knelt over her.

His eyes were dark and slumberous, and his

strength was a palpable entity as he buried his mouth against her neck.

Stephanie lifted her arms and linked them at his nape, only to have him gently disengage them and carefully place them above her head.

She felt a tremor race through her body as he traced a path to her breast, explored at leisure, then trailed down to the soft indentation at her waist.

A faint gasp escaped her lips as he moved lower, and she whimpered out loud at the path traced by the tip of his tongue.

Raoul took intimacy to a new level, evoking a response from her that was wild and wanton. Libidinous, she added, as sensation spiraled through her body, taking her higher than she'd ever been before.

Dear heaven. If this is what he could do with his mouth, how on earth would she survive when he took possession? Go up in flames? Self-destruct?

Both, Stephanie acknowledged a long time later as she lay cradled against him on the edge of sleep.

Every nerve ending had flared into impassioned life as he'd begun a slow invasion, stirring her emotions to fever pitch with long hungry kisses that dispensed with any inhibitions. She'd met and matched his rhythm in a wild pagan dance that surpassed her wildest imagination.

She'd thought he might vacate her bed, shower, then dress and leave.

Instead he curved her close in against him and

stroked her hair, pausing every now and then to brush light fingers across her cheek.

Her body ached, and she was willing to swear she could still *feel* him deep inside.

She wasn't conscious of drifting off to sleep, except she must have, for she came slowly awake at the soft tracing movement at her waist. Fingers slid over one hip and brushed against her thigh, and she shifted restlessly as he began an evocative pattern.

Stephanie leaned forward and nipped the skin close to one male nipple, and had the satisfaction of hearing his intake of breath.

'So you want to play, hmm?'

In one fluid movement he pulled her on top of him, and she arched back in a supple feline movement.

'You woke me,' she protested teasingly, loving the feel of his hands as they shaped her body, her breasts, and took a tantalizing path down to where she straddled him.

'Now I have your full attention?'

Oh, yes, he had that. She wriggled a little, and took pleasure in his husky groan, the heat of his arousal pressing against her.

With provocative intent, she moved a little, causing a sexual friction that was just as electrifying for him as it was for her.

In one swift movement he curved a hand around her nape and pulled her head down to his, taking possession of her mouth in a manner that left her weak-willed and malleable.

When he released her she rose with graceful fluidity, then carefully positioned herself and took him deep inside.

She had control, and she used it mercilessly as she rode him hard and fast, then eased to a slow erotic pace that had him growling low in his throat as he rolled her onto her back.

At some stage they both slept, and woke late to the sun streaming in through the curtains.

Together they rose from the bed and showered together...a long shower as Raoul pulled her high against him and she curved her legs over his hips in one final passionate coupling, then they dressed and breakfasted on strong coffee, eggs and toast.

It was after ten when Raoul caught her close and bestowed a lingering kiss. 'I have to leave,' he said gently. 'I'll call you from Sydney.' His smile held a warmth that made her stomach curl. 'Take care, *cherie.*'

Without a further word he slid in behind the wheel of the car, fired the engine, then reversed out onto the road.

Stephanie stood watching until the car was no longer in sight.

CHAPTER NINE

THE day stretched ahead, presenting a number of possibilities. However, the first priority was to put a call through to Celeste.

Stephanie crossed to the phone and punched in the required digits, then listened to Emma relay an excited account of the flight, the drive with her beloved 'Poppa,' playing with Jake the dog and a visit to the beach as soon as she woke from her afternoon nap.

'Sounds like fun,' Stephanie said lightly when Celeste came back on the line.

'It is,' her mother assured. 'And you, Stephanie? Did everything turn out well last night?'

Now there was a question she couldn't answer with total honesty! Revealing to your mother that you'd just experienced the best sex in your life, not once but several times in the past eight hours wasn't exactly a confidence she felt inclined to share.

'Really well,' she responded easily. 'We achieved the necessary publicity, there were no mishaps. It was very successful.'

'And Raoul?'

Oh my. 'He seemed to enjoy himself.' A masterpiece in understatement! 'He left this morning for Sydney. Business,' she elaborated.

'But he'll be back?'

'Yes.'

'Good.'

Don't, Stephanie urged silently. It can't go anywhere, because there's nowhere for it to go.

'I'll ring tomorrow evening,' she indicated, then added gently, 'Thanks, Mom. I know Emma will have a wonderful time.'

Housework beckoned, the washing and some ironing, and when it was all done she went down to the local supermarket and bought milk, bread and a few essentials.

Afterward she curled up in a comfortable chair and indulged in the luxury of reading several chapters of a seven-hundred-page historical saga. The rich texture of the writing kept her enthralled until the natural light began to fade, and she was about to switch on the lamp when the shrill insistent peal of the telephone had her reaching for the receiver.

The male voice was deep, husky and the slight accent identified it as belonging undeniably to Raoul. Just the sound of it sent primitive awareness radiating through her body.

'How are you?'

'Fine.'

His throaty chuckle did crazy things to her equilibrium. 'That's it? Fine?'

'What would you have me say?' she countered unsteadily, and wondered if he was aware just how he affected her.

'It can wait, *cherie.*'

There was a part of her that ached to see him again, yet there was also caution and a certain degree of despair. If only she had a casual attitude to sex without needing any meaningful emotional attachment, she could view the interlude for what it was... a brief affair with no strings.

'Michel and Sandrine are joining me for dinner tonight.'

Stephanie curled her fingers over the receiver. 'Enjoy,' she bade lightly. 'What time is your meeting tomorrow?'

'Early afternoon. I'll call you.'

'Okay.'

'Bonne nuit, cherie,' Raoul drawled. 'Sleep well.'

She didn't, of course. There were too many thoughts chasing through her brain for an easy rest, and she woke next morning with the distinct need for a few hours more sleep.

However, the day awaited, and her work schedule was bound to be hectic.

A shower, followed by cereal and fruit, then she changed into a pencil-slim black skirt, added a peach-colored camisole and pinstriped black jacket, tended to her makeup and caught up her keys before heading for the car.

Only to discover she had a flat tire. The curse she stifled was pithy, and adequately described her frustration. Changing tires was becoming a habit, she muttered beneath her breath as she shrugged off her jacket and tossed it onto the passenger seat.

She crossed to the rear of the car, popped the boot, removed the spare tire, the jack and set to work.

After it was done, she retrieved her keys and went back into the house to wash up.

An essential call into the local tire mart to drop off the damaged tire for repair took up valuable time, added to which traffic was heavy, taking at least three changes of lights to get through each intersection, and consequently she was late entering the office.

Coffee, hot, strong and sweet helped, and she went through her diary, made a number of notations, then logged on to her computer.

The interoffice phone rang and she reached for it.

'I have a Miss Chabert on the line,' Isabel revealed. 'She insists on speaking to you personally.'

Ghislaine? What on earth could she possibly want? 'Put her through.'

'Ghislaine,' Stephanie greeted with polite civility.

'Stephanie. We should do lunch.'

Oh, no, we shouldn't! 'I'm really busy right now,' she responded calmly.

'Meet me at the Terraces. One o'clock.'

The imperious demand grated, and she drew in a deep breath, then released it slowly. 'I can't—'

'Be there.'

This was a joke, a very bad joke. It was almost laughable, except instinct warned there was no humor in the situation at all. 'I can't think of a thing we have in common.'

'Raoul.'

'There's nothing to discuss,' she said quietly, and replaced the receiver. Jealousy, she perceived, was an ugly state of mind.

Lunch was a salad sandwich she sent out for, and ate at her desk. Washed down by bottled water, it sufficed as sustenance as she made necessary calls, checked paperwork and determined the film's scheduled release date. It was important to prompt public interest by running the trailers on television and follow-up media coverage in the trade magazines. She made a note to check with advertising.

At three she broke for coffee, qualifying she needed the caffeine to get her through the afternoon. The way things were going, she'd need to take work home.

It was after four when reception alerted a Ghislaine Chabert was at the desk. Stephanie muffled an unladylike curse. She didn't have time for this. Whatever bee Ghislaine had in her bonnet, this was neither the place nor the time to deal with it.

'You told her I'm busy?'

'Miss Chabert insists on seeing you.'

She quickly checked her diary, then made a split-second decision. 'All right. Show her in.' She stood and smoothed a hand over her hair. 'Ring me when my four-thirty appointment arrives.'

Lipstick was an essential repair, and she'd just recapped the tube when her secretary gave her door a peremptory tap prior to swinging it wide.

The Frenchwoman swept in on a cloud of perfume, expensive couture clothing, her face an exquisitely made-up mask.

Calm, composed, in control, Stephanie reminded herself of the affirmation as she indicated a chair.

'Ghislaine. Do sit down.' She crossed behind her desk and remained standing. With a cool, calculated action she cast her watch a deliberate glance. 'I can spare you five minutes.'

'I'd prefer to stand.'

They faced each other across the desk like two opposing enemies. Stephanie watchful and distinctly wary, while Ghislaine played the haute dame to the hilt.

'Leave Raoul alone. He is *mine*.'

Straight to the point, with as much subtlety as a sledgehammer. Stephanie deliberately arched one eyebrow. 'Really? The purpose of your visit is to warn me off?'

Ghislaine raked Stephanie's slender form with scorn. 'Why else do you think I am here?'

'Are you done?' she posed quietly, already regretting her decision to have Ghislaine enter her office.

'No, I am not nearly done,' the Frenchwoman responded bluntly. 'Raoul didn't come back to the hotel last night. Was he with you?'

'I don't think that qualifies an answer,' she said carefully, and saw Ghislaine's expression harden.

'You are just a diversion, someone new, different,' the other woman said scathingly. *'Temporary.'*

Stephanie felt the anger flare, and sought measured control. A catfight here, now, didn't form part of her agenda! 'I think you'd better leave.'

'Stay away from him.'

'What if he chooses not to stay away from me?'

'Our respective families want us to marry. I intend to see that it happens.'

She caught the vindictiveness, the irrational sense of purpose in those hard dark eyes, and experienced a chill of apprehension. 'Then I must wish you *good luck,*' she said evenly. 'And ask you to leave.'

Almost on cue the phone buzzed, and she picked up the receiver, listened, then replaced it onto the handset.

'My client is waiting.' She crossed to the door, and opened it. 'Goodbye, Ghislaine.'

'Don't underestimate me' was issued as a silky warning as the Frenchwoman exited the office.

Stephanie took a deep breath, very much in need of a minute or two to dispel her anger, then regain a measure of composure.

Ghislaine was a witch, possibly a dangerous witch with a problem. Sandrine's words came to mind, but it offered little reassurance.

Meantime, she had a job to do, and keeping a valued client waiting overlong in reception didn't form part of her plan.

It was after six when she arrived home, the owner of two new tires, for when she'd called in to collect the repaired spare, the young man shook his head.

'Couldn't fix it, ma'am. It'd been cut.' At her faintly puzzled expression, he elaborated, 'Slashed. With a knife, I'd say.'

How? More importantly, *who?* 'I guess I need a new tire.'

'Two, in the front, make 'em even.'

She didn't even blink. 'Can you do it now?'

'We're due to close soon.'

'Please. I really need my car.'

'Okay, for you I'll make an exception. Take a seat.'

Ten minutes later she wrote a check, then slid into the car and drove home.

Indoors, she changed into shorts and a singlet top, then crossed into the kitchen. She'd prepare a tossed salad and have it with some cold chicken, then follow it with fresh fruit.

After she'd shower, pull on a robe, and put in a few hours at the laptop. But first she'd call Celeste and catch up on Emma's day... A ferry ride and a visit to Taronga Park Zoo, she learned, and tomorrow they were going to ride on the monorail.

'You're spoiling her,' Stephanie protested, and heard her mother's chuckle.

'No, we're having fun.'

It was reassuring not to be missed, but she experienced a very real feeling of loss at not hearing her daughter's voice, the hugs, the kisses.

Work, she determined, as she set the laptop onto the dining-room table more than an hour later, would occupy her mind.

It did, and she became immersed in entering data, saving it on disk ready to print out at the office in the morning.

The doorbell ringing startled her, and she checked her watch, wondering who on earth would call in at nine in the evening without using the telephone to check it was okay.

The security door was locked, she had a safety chain on the door, as well as a peephole. There was no sense pretending she wasn't home, for the lights indicated otherwise.

The doorbell rang again, jerking her into motion, and she moved quickly to the front of the house.

One look was sufficient to determine it was Raoul who stood on her doorstep, and with nerveless fingers she dealt with the chain, the lock and undid the security door.

'Hi.' As a greeting it was inane, and Stephanie felt the warmth creep into her cheeks as he let his gaze roam over the short silk robe, her bare legs, before returning to settle on her expressive features.

'Were you in bed?'

He sounded indolently amused, and she ran a check on the tie of her robe, then pulled the edges more tightly together.

'No,' she said quickly. 'I was working.'

He was something else, his height and breadth of shoulder impressive. His exclusive brand of cologne teased her senses, and her eyes were mesmerized by the sensual curve of his mouth. He'd removed his jacket and held it hooked over one shoulder.

'Aren't you going to ask me in?' he queried gently, and she stood aside at once.

'Of course.'

Raoul stepped down the hallway and she followed him. 'Would you like some coffee?'

He came to a halt in the lounge and turned to face her. 'Not unless you're making some for yourself. Otherwise a cold drink will do fine.'

She went to the refrigerator and fetched a can of cola, pulled the tab, then extracted a glass and handed both to him.

'Did you eat on the plane?' Of course he'd eaten on the plane, she derided silently. It was after nine, for heaven's sake!

He poured the dark sparkling liquid, then took a long swallow. 'Yes.'

'How was your meeting?' She was aware of the need to make polite conversation, and equally aware he found it amusing.

'Successful.' He placed the empty can down onto the bench, and subjected her to a slow, warm appraisal.

'The contract is signed, the deal completed.'

'Then there's nothing to keep you here.'

The glass followed the empty can, and he leaned one hip against the edge of the bench. 'Yes,' he denied indolently. 'There is.'

Something twisted inside her stomach.

His gaze didn't waver, and she felt as if she was teetering close to a precipice.

'*You,*' Raoul stated solemnly.

That was certainly direct. But in what context? Given Ghislaine's venomous revelation, there was only one possibility.

'As a temporary diversion?' she posed, and saw his gaze narrow fractionally.

'A diversion from what?'

'Ghislaine, and your forthcoming marriage.'

He didn't move, but it seemed his long muscular frame uncoiled and became a formidable force.

Stephanie caught a glimpse of the persona he undoubtedly presented in the business arena. There was a dangerous stillness apparent, a waiting, watchful quality that revealed nothing and gave no hint of his reaction.

'Ghislaine possesses a fanciful imagination,' he drawled. 'Fostered by overindulgent parents in a desire to link Chabert to Lanier.' Facial muscles shifted and reassembled over chiseled bone structure. 'A business merger is out of the question, and there are no marriage plans.'

'Ghislaine appears to think differently.'

'And you believed her?' His voice was quiet, deadly.

Her eyes sparked blue fire, and the anger she'd managed to hold at bay for the past few hours rose to the surface. 'She was very convincing.'

'Yes,' he acknowledged cynically. 'I imagine she was.'

'There's no purpose to this,' Stephanie refuted, sorely tried.

'I disagree.'

Her chin tilted. '*Why?* The result remains the same.'

'You're so sure about that?'

I'm not sure about anything, damn you! But even with the most generous heart, I can't see it happening any other way. A proposal and happy-ever-after belong in fairy stories.

'Raoul,' Stephanie commanded unsteadily. 'Go home. Please.' She wanted him out of here, now, before she did something totally stupid. As it was, her eyes ached with repressed emotion. 'I really do have a few hours work ahead of me.'

He looked at her, saw the tiredness, the emotional strain evident, and subdued the anger he wanted to direct against Ghislaine for having caused Stephanie grief.

Without a word he caught hold of her shoulders and pulled her into his arms, curving a hand beneath her nape as he slid the other down to splay over the slight curve of her bottom.

She twisted against him in an attempt to break free, then fought against dissolving into him as his lips sought the vulnerable hollow at the edge of her neck.

'Don't.' The word emerged as a despairing groan. She didn't want this. She couldn't afford the sweet slide into emotional ecstasy, and she doubted her ability to survive the exquisite passion without fragmenting into a hundred shimmering pieces.

How long they stood together she had no idea. There was the sensation of it being right, as if some ephemeral force was at work. And dear heaven, it was so *good* to lean against him, accept his strength, his assurance.

Like this, she didn't care how long it lasted. It was enough he was here, and they had the night. So what if there were too few nights left? The truth was she didn't want to deny herself the ultimate pleasure of shared intimacy with him. Was that so bad?

Slowly, gently, he disentangled her arms and stood back a pace. Then he caught her chin between thumb and forefinger, lifted it, and tried not to drown in those dark sapphire depths.

'Go do whatever it is you have to do to finish on the computer,' Raoul bade easily. 'I'll get the coffee.'

Stephanie opened her mouth to protest, only to close it again. Her lashes swept wide as he tucked a stray lock of hair behind her ear, then he trailed his fingers down the curve of her cheek and let them rest against the edge of her mouth. He leaned down and dropped a soft kiss on the tip of her nose, then he pushed her gently in the direction of the table, and the computer.

It took her almost two hours, and there was a sense of satisfaction in pressing the Save key and transferring the data onto disk.

She'd been conscious of Raoul sprawled comfortably at ease on the large sofa in the adjoining open plan lounge. He had the television on low, and he looked totally relaxed. Every now and then she'd been conscious of him sparing her a watchful glance, and experienced the answering tremor as her body leaped in response.

With automatic movements she closed down the program, then disconnected the power inlet.

She didn't hear Raoul move, and a slight gasp escaped her lips as she felt his hands close over her shoulders.

His fingers began a deep soothing massage of her shoulders and neck muscles, gradually easing out the kinks until she sighed and let her head roll forward in a gesture of total acceptance.

It felt so good, so very good, it was all she could do not to express her pleasure in a purr of gratitude. When he began on her scalp she closed her eyes and surrendered to the magic.

There was little sense of the passage of time, and she made a token protest as his hands slid to her shoulders, then caught hold of her waist.

In one fluid movement he lifted her into his arms and carried her down the hall to the bedroom.

'Raoul—'

'Don't think,' he said huskily as he swept aside the covers and tumbled down onto the bed with her. His lips caressed the edge of her mouth. 'Just feel.'

He discarded his clothes with ease, shrugging out of his shirt, discarding trousers, shoes and socks, briefs, then he gathered her close and began a long, slow loving that had her begging for release.

It was flagrant, evocative, as his mouth took a tortuously slow path over every inch of her body. Caressing, tasting, in a supplication that drove her wild. The blood sang in her veins as sensation spiraled to impossible heights, and he caught her as she fell, only to wreak havoc as he sent her soaring again and again.

Skillful fingers knew where to touch, to stroke, as

he paid sensual homage to every pleasure spot, each heightened nerve ending. Just as she thought she'd experienced it all, he followed the same path in a tasting feast that made her cry out in all-consuming ecstasy.

Her whole body was one pulsating ache, and her response was unrestrained as she captured his head and dragged his mouth to her own.

He took her then, melding his body to hers in one powerful thrust, stayed there, then began a tantalizing withdrawal, before plunging deeper in a slow primal rhythm that built in pace until there was only the raw passion of two lovers in perfect accord.

Afterward they slept, held close in each other's arms in a tangle of sheets as the moon disappeared and the night became shrouded in darkness.

At some stage Stephanie stirred, felt the soothing slide of fingers down her back, and settled comfortably against warm skin and muscle, subsiding easily into relaxed somnolence.

The shrill sound of the alarm was an impossible intrusion, and Stephanie automatically reached out to close it, only to come in contact with a hard, muscular forearm intent on the same task.

'Six-thirty,' a slightly accented male voice drawled with a degree of amusement. 'Time to rise and shine.'

'Shower's mine,' she voiced drowsily, then yelped in shocked surprise as his hand slid down to create renewed havoc, bringing her to orgasm with such tactile skill it stole her breath. 'I think I should get up.'

Raoul's mouth nuzzled the soft hollow at the base of her neck. 'Only think?'

'Affirmative action is essential,' she said weakly, and slid out from beneath his grasp. 'Otherwise I'll be late.'

He rolled onto his back and linked his arms behind his head. Then he smiled, and Stephanie felt the powerful tug of desire.

She couldn't imagine anything she'd rather do than sink down onto the bed and give in to the hunger, the sheer sensual pleasure of his touch. To gift him a similar pleasure.

What would it be like to wake every morning like this after a night of exquisite lovemaking, only to do it all over again?

Sex. She closed her eyes, then opened them again. Very good sex. It wasn't—*couldn't*—be anything more. Could it?

Oh God. What she felt wasn't love. *Was it?* Realization washed through her body, quickly followed by apprehension. *No,* she screamed a silent denial. This wasn't happening.

Raoul observed the play of emotions chase across her expressive features, saw the shocked surprise evident in her eyes before her lashes swept down in a protective veil, and caught the faint tremor as she lifted a shaky hand to tuck back her hair.

His gaze narrowed fractionally as she caught up her robe and made for the en suite.

Minutes later she stepped into the shower stall, turned on the water and picked up the bottle of shampoo. Only to have it taken out of her hand within seconds of wetting her hair.

'You can't—'

'Yes, I can,' Raoul drawled as he poured thick liquid into one cupped palm, then he massaged it over her scalp.

When he was done, he picked up the soap and began smoothing it over her body. It became a teasing, evocative action that brought a groan to her lips.

At this rate, she'd need to forego breakfast. But oh dear Lord, it would be worth it just to savor his touch, to gift him a similar supplication.

'Raoul.' His name silvered from her lips, and anything else she might have said remained locked in her throat as his mouth closed over hers in a kiss that became a possession all of its own.

Nothing else mattered as he slid her arms up to link at his neck, and when he lifted her close she simply held on, exulting in the shape and feel of him, his strength, his earthy taste and raw sexuality.

She could almost believe he was bent on assaulting her senses…in an attempt to achieve what? she wondered idly as she snagged a towel and removed some of the excess moisture from her hair.

Soft color stained her cheeks at the thought of her craven response, and how easily he was able to achieve it. In his arms she became a wanton, eager to sample every sexual delight he cared to introduce.

Toweled dry, she went through the personal routine, collected fresh underwear, then hurriedly selected an elegant trouser suit, applied makeup, brushed her hair and slid her feet into high-heeled pumps.

Stephanie didn't even bother running a check on the time. It hardly mattered what the clock said, when it was obvious she was going to be late.

She caught up her bag, crossed to the laptop and retrieved the disk, then moved toward the front door.

He was right behind her, his holdall in one hand, his personal laptop in the other. He'd shaved, and in place of the suit he wore tailored trousers and a dark polo shirt.

Stephanie crossed to the garage, used the remote to open the automatic doors, then swore beneath her breath when she saw her car had a flat tire. Something she wouldn't have noticed had she not crossed around to the front passenger side to shift a garden rake, which seemed to have slid forward and lay resting against the bodywork of her car.

'Problems?'

Stephanie gestured toward the front wheel. 'This is the second time I've had a flat tire in two days,' she vented angrily. 'If this one is slashed, too, I'm going to report it to the police.'

'Slashed?' Raoul queried with deceptive quiet, and she inclined her head.

'That's what the guy at the tire mart said. He fitted two new tires for me last night.' She pushed a hand through her hair, and stifled an inward sigh. 'I'll get the spare.'

'Leave it,' he instructed. 'I'll drive you.'

'Dammit, I *need* my car.'

'And collect you from work. Give me the remote module, a spare key to the car and I'll take care of it.'

She opened her mouth to argue, then simply closed it again as he brushed the knuckles of one hand lightly along her jaw.

'No contest, *ma cher.*'

It was easier to do as he said, and as he negotiated traffic she retrieved her cell phone and called reception, alerting her imminent arrival.

Stephanie reached for the door clasp the moment Raoul swept to a halt outside the entrance to her office building, and she uttered a hurried 'thanks' as she slid from the car.

CHAPTER TEN

As MORNINGS went, Stephanie's was a doozy, and losing an hour merely made a bad situation worse. Everything that could go wrong, did. Worse, her secretary had called in sick, and her temporary replacement didn't have a clue.

Coffee, hot sweet and strong helped some, and she prioritized paperwork, telephone calls, and didn't stop until one, when she deemed it sensible to take a lunch break. Otherwise she'd never make it through the afternoon.

There was a café close by, one of a few which catered for staff working in the many tall office blocks in this part of Southport, and Stephanie covered the short distance, choosing a table outdoors.

Numerous spreading tree branches provided shade, and there were bright striped awnings and umbrellas to protect patrons from the heat of the summer's sun.

The food was superb, the service swift, and within a very short space of time she was presented with a chicken and salad focaccia sandwich and a cappuccino.

It was a beautiful day, and from where she sat she could see the park, the sparkling waters of the main channel, and beyond it the architectural white sails of the Marina Mirage shopping complex soared against the background of blue sky. Next to it stood the condominium complex of the beautifully designed Palazzo Versace.

A view, she conceded with warmth, to die for. The café was well patronized, but not sufficiently so to warrant anyone requesting to share her table, and she took time to enjoy the food, the ambience. Entitled, she assured, by virtue of working late at home last night.

Thinking about what had happened *after* she'd closed down the computer last night set every nerve-end tingling alive. Dangerous, she mused, definitely dangerous to focus overlong on the passion Raoul had aroused...and her answering hunger.

Tonight's cocktail party for the marketing executives was a ''must attend'' function. Although she need only stay an hour, two at the most, and she'd be able to leave.

Stephanie finished her sandwich, drained the last of her cappuccino, then paid her bill at the counter and walked out into the sunshine.

She hadn't covered more than a few steps when a feminine slightly accented voice said her name.

No, please tell me it isn't Ghislaine, she prayed silently, only to turn and discover her prayers unanswered. What on earth was the Frenchwoman doing in this part of town?

'I took the wrong exit from the shopping center,' Ghislaine offered in explanation. 'I was looking for a taxi rank.'

'Way wrong,' Stephanie agreed. 'You can either

retrace your steps to the center and get directions for the right exit, or,' she suggested, wondering why she should be so helpful, 'I can ring the taxi company and have them send a car here.'

'Oh, *here* would be wonderful.'

It took only minutes to organize, and she replaced the cell phone into her bag. 'You'll have to excuse me. I need to get back to the office.'

'Before you go,' Ghislaine began with pseudo sweetness. 'I want to thank you.'

'For what?'

'Discrediting me with Raoul.'

Stephanie's stomach executed a painful somersault at the thought Ghislaine had probably deliberately set up watch on the off chance she'd frequent her usual lunch venue today.

'You managed to do that all by yourself,' Stephanie responded carefully.

'Raoul rang me this morning, suggesting we meet for coffee at the Terraces.' Her eyes glittered with ill-concealed anger. 'I looked forward to a tête-è-tête. Surely my visit to your office was private?'

Stephanie could almost visualize Ghislaine sharpening her metaphorical claws.

'Or do you always run to your men and tell tales?'

Grr. She was inclined to unsheathe her own! However a scene on a public street simply wasn't on her agenda. Silence, in some instances, was more effective than mere words.

'Who are you? A nonentity with no noble breeding, no social standing, *nothing!*' Ghislaine stated with scathing insolence.

'Whereas you are eminently qualified in each criterion?'

'*Yes,* damn you!'

Stephanie felt her blood heat. 'Sadly, blue blood and lineage don't necessarily guarantee desire.'

'*Bitch.*' She took a step forward and swung the palm of her hand, narrowly missing her target as Stephanie twisted her head to one side.

'Perhaps I should remind you that verbal defamation can warrant legal prosecution, and physical abuse will land you in court.'

'Raoul belongs to *me.*'

There was no way she was going to stand here and take any more of Ghislaine's verbal vitriol. Without a word she stepped forward and began walking.

'Don't you *dare* turn your back on me. I haven't finished with you!'

She didn't pause, or even bother to look back. A mistake, she learned seconds later, as something heavy careened into her back and almost sent her sprawling to the pavement.

A shoulder bag, she saw as she straightened, and swung with Ghislaine's weight behind it. 'That amounted to deliberate assault.'

Ghislaine's attractive features were brittle with fury. 'Where are your witnesses?' She gave an expressive shrug. 'As far as I'm concerned, you tripped. Pity you didn't fall.'

This had gone quite far enough! 'You want to go

the distance, Ghislaine? Raoul won't be impressed to learn you paid someone to slash my tires. Not once, but twice.' Her eyebrows rose. 'You didn't think I'd find out?'

'I don't know what you're talking about.'

Stephanie drew breath, and aimed for the kill. 'No? What did you think your scare tactics would do, Ghislaine? Send me running in the opposite direction?' She shook her head. 'I don't frighten that easily.'

'He just wants you for sex!'

'If that's true,' she opined carefully. 'Why me, when you're so willing to service him?'

Ghislaine looked as if she was going to throw the mother of all hissy fits, for her face paled, then tinged pink. Her eyes assumed a glassy look, her mouth thinned, and if it was possible for steam to emit from a human's ears...

'If you weren't on the scene—'

'It would be some other woman,' Stephanie offered. 'Accept it for the truth, and move on.'

'As you will?'

A horn blast close by alerted the taxi's arrival, and Ghislaine stepped across the grass verge and slid into the rear seat. Seconds later the taxi accelerated down the road.

Within minutes Stephanie walked through the entrance foyer and took the lift to her floor. Outwardly she appeared composed. No small achievement, when inside she was a mess of conflicting emotions, uppermost of which was the need to hit out in re-strained anger at Ghislaine's obsessive behavior.

'You have two urgent calls to return, three faxes are on your desk and your three o'clock appointment has rescheduled thirty minutes early.'

It was back to work with a vengeance, and she continued at a punishing pace until five. The worst of it had been dealt with, and what hadn't could wait until tomorrow, she decided wearily as she shut down the computer, collected her bag and exited the office.

Raoul was waiting for her in the downstairs foyer, and her heart skipped a beat at the sight of him. His dark suit was perfectly tailored, his grooming exemplary. He really was something else, she conceded as she drew close. She'd miss him like hell when he left.

'Hi.'

Her greeting was bright, too bright, Raoul decided as he took in her pale features, the air of fragility apparent.

'Tough day?' he queried lightly, and saw her faint grimace.

'An understatement.'

With a swiftness that surprised her he captured her mouth with his own and kissed her. Thoroughly.

She could only gaze at him in startled surprise when he lifted his head, and he smiled, watching her eyes darken and dilate. 'You looked as if you needed it.'

She did, but not for the reason he imagined.

Traffic was heavy, and it took twenty minutes to reach Mermaid Beach.

'I'll go shower and change,' Stephanie intimated as they entered the house. 'Help yourself to a drink.'

He let her go, and crossed into the kitchen, selected something nonalcoholic from the refrigerator, then entered the lounge.

The bank of framed photographs caught his attention, and he picked up one of Stephanie holding Emma as a young baby.

He traced her outline with his finger, his lips curving slightly at her celluloid smile, the brave tilt of her head. Strong, courageous, she possessed integrity, passion, and a sense of self he found admirable.

Emma's father had been a fool, he accorded silently. In more ways than one.

Raoul replaced the frame and crossed to the window, then stood looking out over the grass to the neat bordered garden running the length of the fence separating the house next door. Flowers bloomed in carefully tended clumps, and there were shrubs, a few palm trees indicative of the tropical Queensland climate.

Stephanie found him there as she entered the lounge, and he turned, taking in her slender frame, the light red-gold hair styled in a neat bob, the delicate facial bone structure.

'Stunning,' he complimented, noting the way the electric-blue silk emphasized her cream-textured skin and highlighted her eyes.

'Shall we leave?'

Raoul caught up his keys and followed her out to the car. 'You'll need to give me directions.'

'It's not far.'

The private home was owned by a wealthy client who was known for his generosity and his penchant for entertaining. Located in a one-way street running parallel to the foreshore, the extensive three-level mansion was one of many very exclusive homes overlooking the ocean.

There were perhaps thirty invited guests sipping champagne and indulging in bite-size canapés.

'The purpose of this soiree is business?' Raoul inclined as more guests drifted into the large lounge.

'Definitely. Charles is one of the firm's most influential clients.' Stephanie wrinkled her nose at him. 'Who likes to lead into the festive season with the first of the pre-Christmas cocktail parties.' A faintly wicked smile tugged the edge of her lips. 'Yes, I know. It's only the first week in November.'

During the ensuing hour they mixed and mingled, together and separately as Raoul was drawn into conversation while a guest snagged Stephanie's attention.

She was good at her job, he perceived. Her interest was genuine, and she had a head for dates and figures that earned her respect from her peers.

His gaze lingered as she laughed spontaneously at someone's joke, then moved easily into conversation.

At that precise moment she lifted her head and looked at him, aware instinctively that he'd been watching her, and she smiled, offering him a slightly raised eyebrow in silent query.

Was it possible for two people to communicate without words? Did he sense that she wanted him so badly she could almost feel his touch?

Stephanie felt the heat rise deep inside, sensed the prickle of awareness scud across the surface of her skin, as she endeavored to contain her wayward thoughts.

With a sense of fascination she watched as he murmured a few words to the man he was with, then he made his way toward her.

'Having fun?' she lightly teased as he drew close, and almost melted beneath the warmth of his smile.

'By any definition,' Raoul drawled, and lifting a hand he trailed the pads of his fingers across her cheek.

Her eyes flared, and she was willing to swear her lower lip shook a little in involuntary reaction. She felt her body sway fractionally toward his, almost as if it had a mind of its own.

'Hungry?' He let his hand trace the length of her arm to her wrist and threaded his fingers through hers. 'For food?' she countered with a wicked smile, and felt the faint pressure as his fingers curled around her own.

'That, too.'

'I know of an intimate restaurant not far from here that serves the most divine Italian food.' She waited a beat. 'We could take some home and have a feast.'

'You don't want candlelight, Chianti and Andrea Bocelli singing sweet ballads on the CD player?'

She felt a bubble of laughter rise in her throat. 'Well,' she conceded, offering him a deliciously seductive smile. 'If you insist on an authentic ambience.'

They left a short while later, and it took only minutes to reach the small restaurant situated in a long block of shops fronting the southbound highway.

Owned and operated by an extended Italian family, they were greeted at the door by a courtly uncle, served wine by the eldest son, a daughter served the food, while both parents and the uncle's wife reigned in the kitchen.

The aroma of fresh herbs and spices mingled with wine and a host of tantalizing sauces, and there was music...

'Pavarotti,' Raoul drawled as Stephanie opted for a table, 'Making me wait, hmm?' he murmured with a teasing smile as he followed her to a spare table on the far side of the room.

'It's called anticipation.'

'I'll get my revenge later.'

Her eyes gleamed with wicked humor as they each took a seat. 'I'm trembling.'

'As well you should.'

Raoul ordered a mild red Lambrusco, and they settled on a starter each and followed it with another, rather than a main, choosing a clear soup, followed by spinach and feta ravioli served with mushrooms.

'Perfecto,' Raoul declared when they finished the dish and ordered coffee.

It was after eleven when Raoul paid the bill and they left. The night was warm, and the sky held a myriad of stars, heralding another fine day tomorrow.

How many more days did she have left? Two, three? Don't think about it, a small voice cautioned. They had the night, and it was enough. It *had* to be enough.

Yet how could it be, she agonized hours later as she lay spent beside him. A long, slow loving so incredibly tender she'd almost wept as he brought her to orgasm, then just as she thought it was over he took her soaring to impossible heights and beyond.

Afterward she had pleasured him, embracing every muscle, annointing every inch of skin in a flagrant trail that left him groaning with a need so intense it was almost beyond control.

What followed was nothing less than a pagan coupling, primitive and unrestrained as they were driven by an intoxicating frenzy that was wild, erotic and totally shameless.

Slowly, with infinite care, Stephanie slid out from beneath the covers, caught up her robe and moved silently down to the lounge.

Moonlight slipped through the partly open shutters, and she adjusted them slightly to ensure a clear view of the yard. Everything was still, and the moon cast long shadows from the few trees and shrubs.

In the distance a dog barked, then quietened, and

she stood gazing out into the opalescent night, silent and lost in introspective thought.

It was there Raoul found her, after stirring and finding an empty space beside him, and he'd moved quickly, silently, through the house until he reached the lounge and saw her slender form outlined beside the window.

Something tugged at his heart. She stood so still, so obviously lost in thought. How long had she been there?

Her arms were crossed at her midriff, and she looked so alone, almost forlorn.

'Unable to sleep, *cherie?*' he queried quietly as he moved to stand behind her. He slid his hands around her waist and drew her back to rest against him.

Stephanie felt his lips caress the delicate pulse beat at the edge of her neck, and let herself sink into him.

'It's a beautiful night,' she said huskily, and felt a sensation arrow through her body as he nuzzled an earlobe.

'Oui.' His fingers splayed down over her stomach and slid between the opening of her robe. 'I have to fly back to Paris at the end of the week.'

Her heart lurched, then stopped beating for a few seconds. Pain seeped through every pore in her body, and she could almost swear she forgot to breathe.

The moment she'd been dreading had finally arrived. Why, in her wildest dreams, had she hoped that it wouldn't?

What could she say? *Don't go?*

'I want you with me.'

Paris? *Paris*. It wasn't possible. How could she even consider it? What about Emma? Celeste was wonderful, but she couldn't expect her mother... Besides, there was her job. 'We live different lives on opposite sides of the world.' She was breaking up inside. 'But we don't—'

'Have a future?' His hands slid to her shoulders and he turned her around to face him. 'Yes, we do.'

Pride was responsible for the way her chin lifted, and her gaze was steady. 'As sometime lovers who spend a week or two together whenever the timing is right?'

'No. I have something different in mind.'

'I'm not *mistress* material,' she assured sadly.

His teeth showed white as his mouth curved to form a musing smile. 'I'm relieved to hear it.'

'I have a child, a career,' she stated.

'This career, *here*, is too important for you to give up?' Raoul queried.

'I have responsibilities, financial commitments.'

'If the financial commitments were removed?'

'What are you suggesting?'

'Marry me.'

Shock deprived her of the ability to speak, and when she found her voice, the words emerged as little more than a whisper. 'What did you say?'

'Marry me,' Raoul repeated gently.

'You're not serious?'

'I can assure you I have never been more serious in my life.'

'But—'

'If a career is so important to you, I can arrange a position in marketing, or any field you choose.'

She didn't doubt it. 'Raoul—'

'I have an apartment in Auteuil, and a home in the Chinon wine region of the Loire Valley. Emma will delight in spending weekends and holidays there.'

'You're going too fast,' she protested.

'No,' he denied quietly. 'I want you with me, as my wife, wherever I happen to be in the world. Emma is a part of you that is everything to me. Perhaps in a few years there will be a sister or brother for her to love and care for. But for now, we share whatever the future holds...together.'

Stephanie felt the prick of tears, and fought hard to control them.

'I have important meetings in Paris next week. Four days, *mon amour,* then I'll be back and we will arrange our wedding. Your parents will return to Paris with us for Christmas.'

Christmas was only weeks away. 'It's too soon...we can't—'

'We can. Easily.' Money, sufficient amounts of it, had a power of its own.

'You love me.'

It was a statement, not a query. She could only wonder at her own transparency, and how long he'd known.

He cradled her face in his hands, glimpsed the fleeting emotions, and appraised each and every one of them. 'I took one look at you that first day on the film set,' he revealed softly. 'And knew my life would never be the same again.'

Any minute soon she'd wake and discover this was nothing more than wishful thinking on the part of her subconscious mind.

'Be with me, stay with me. Eternity. *Je t'aime, mon coeur.*'

Her bones turned to liquid, and she wound her arms around his neck and pulled his mouth down to hers, initiating a kiss that reached to the very depths of her soul.

'I fought against becoming emotionally involved with you every step of the way,' Stephanie revealed in a voice just above a whisper. 'I tried so hard to convince myself you were a complication I couldn't afford. But everywhere I turned, there you were. I couldn't seem to escape you.'

His lips were creating an evocative path at her temple, and she could almost feel his smile.

'You noticed.'

'You didn't play fair. You charmed my daughter, not to mention my mother.'

'They were my strongest allies.'

'It was almost as if you had a hidden agenda.'

'Assignment,' Raoul corrected, and nuzzled her soft curve at the edge of her neck. 'Father to Emma. And husband...*yours.*'

It took her a moment to catch her breath, then a slow sweet smile curved her lips. 'Reverse the order,' she teased unmercifully. 'And I might think about it.'

'Might you, indeed?' Raoul growled huskily. He swept an arm beneath her knees and lifted her against his chest.

A bubble of laughter escaped her lips. 'What is this, persuasion?'

'Sweet torture,' Raoul assured huskily. 'Until you say *yes.*'

It didn't take long. Not very long at all.

CHAPTER ELEVEN

THEY were married by a Celebrant in a civil ceremony held in a restored nondenominational church
set in beautiful gardens by the river. Stephanie's father gave her away, Celeste was matron of honor,
and Emma the flower girl.

The bride wore a short cream dress overlayed with
scalloped lace, while the groom was resplendent in
a perfectly tailored black suit.

Afterward they ate fine food and drank Cristal
champagne.

Two days later Raoul, Stephanie and Emma, together with Celeste and Philip flew to Paris where
they held another ceremony, a reaffirmation of their
vows, for the benefit of Raoul's family.

Sandrine and Michel attended, as did Anneke and
Sebastian. Henri stood proudly as head of the family,
and Madeleine, the elderly matriarch, gave her bless-
ing and thanked Stephanie for introducing a great-
grandchild into the family. Premature, perhaps, for
the legal adoption that would change Emma's surname from Sommers to Lanier would not be official
for a while.

Two Lanier wives hid a secretive smile, and remained silent. It was too soon to share the news that

next Christmas, God willing, there would be two babes for Madeleine to fuss over.

Raoul noted Stephanie's faintly wistful expression and linked her fingers with his own.

'Happy?'

She turned her head toward him, and her radiant smile took his breath away.

'Yes,' she said simply, amazed that he needed to ask, when every night she responded to his lovemaking with such a wealth of unbridled passion. 'How would you feel about—'

'*Oui.*'

'I didn't finish.'

He lifted her hand to his lips and brushed a lingering openmouthed kiss to the pulsing veins at her wrist. '*Mon coeur,* you don't need to.'

Her eyes sparkled with wicked humor. 'You read minds?'

'Yours, *mon amour,* is particularly transparent.'

'That's something I'm going to have to work on,' she said with mocking amusement, and heard his soft husky laughter.

'You are the other half of me, part of my soul. I look at you, and know your mind, your heart, as well as I know my own.'

'*Tu es ma vie. Je t'adore.*'

His mouth brushed her temple. '*Merci, mon ange,*' he said gently, and felt her fingers tighten around his own.

Life, he acknowledged, didn't get any better than this.

MILLS & BOON®

Helen Bianchin v Regency Collection!

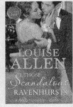

MILLS & BOON®

Let us take you back in time with our Medieval Brides...

The Novice Bride – Carol Townend

The Dumont Bride – Terri Brisbin

The Lord's Forced Bride – Anne Herries

The Warrior's Princess Bride – Meriel Fuller

The Overlord's Bride – Margaret Moore

Templar Knight, Forbidden Bride – Lynna Banning

Order yours at
www.millsandboon.co.uk/medievalbrides

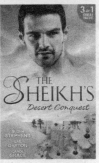